W9-BUI-984

The Elm at the Edge of the Earth

A NOVEL BY

W · W · NORTON & COMPANY · NEW YORK · LONDON

ROBERT D. HALE

Printed in the United States of America.

The text of this book is composed in Garamond #3,
with display type set in Athenaeum.
Composition and manufacturing by Maple-Vail Book Manufacturing Group.
Book design by Antonina Krass.

First Edition

Library of Congress Cataloging-in-Publication Data
Hale, Robert D.
The elm at the edge of the earth : a story / by Robert D. Hale.
p. cm.
I. Title.
PS3558.A35715E46 1990
813'.54—dc20 89–26450

ISBN 0-393-02861-5

W.W. Norton & Company, Inc., 500 Fifth Avenue, New York, N.Y. 10110
W.W. Norton & Company, Ltd., 37 Great Russell Street, London WC1B 3NU

1 2 3 4 5 6 7 8 9 0

"Yes, I have tricks in my pocket, I have things up my sleeve. But I am the opposite of a stage magician. He gives you illusion that has the appearance of truth. I give you truth in the pleasant disguise of illusion."

—Tennessee Williams, *The Glass Menagerie*

PROLOGUE: THE COUNTY HOME

Rich dark brown trimmed white clapboard dwellings connected by arcades so old people and society cast-offs who were inmates, as well as staff who took care of them, wouldn't have to brave the outside during long harsh winters housed the unique community. Clustered close by were service outbuildings: laundry, bakery, dairy, cold storage icehouse, carpenter shop, and others. Beyond, down a gentle slope, was an enormous barn for a herd of dairy cows and draft horses. Riding horses were stabled in another building. Poultry houses, pigpens, and a beef cattle shed were only the largest of the main barn's many satellites.

This isolated collection of structures sat on a rise in the midst of a thousand-acre farm of fields and forests, ponds, and pastures, all so expertly managed that the institution was basically self-sufficient. What food could not be produced on the place was paid for by selling crop surplus. Valleys falling off on three sides gave the County Home a prominence that was visible for miles. On the fourth side, the south, hills rose again, starting slowly with the night pasture then abruptly soaring up to an escarpment that became the horizon, in the middle of which stood a single centuries-old elm.

The County Home was residence for approximately one hundred and sixty people, depending upon whether or not the recently departed were replaced by new arrivals. Some residents spent most of their lives there. Mary Delancy, for instance. Nobody knew where she was born, but she was only a few hours old when a farm worker found her wrapped in a fur robe on top of a bran bin in the granary. She didn't look like a human baby, with eye slits around on the sides of her head and only gaping holes where a nose and ears should be. Her arms and hands were perfect, but she had stumps for feet. Other than that she proved to be healthy. Her name was taken from a book the Keeper's wife happened to be reading at the time. Mary spent her entire life, just short of seventy years, at the Home. She was sixty-four the year of the hot summer.

Roy Cross was fifty-two. He came to the County Home when he was twelve, placed there by his father, an important banker in the middle part of the state who was embarrassed by a son whose lips were too large for a head that was too big for a body that was rapidly approaching seven feet in height. Cross Senior set up a trust fund that would pay Roy's expenses with some left over for spending money, and ignoring his wife's pleas sent their only child away forever, insisting publicly that he never had a son. Mrs. Cross came for regular visits as long as she lived, fostering Roy's inborn love of music with a series of phonographs and shelves of classical records, and encouraging his self-education with what grew to be a sizable library of fine books.

Rose Scheider as a young woman in her early thirties was sentenced to an open-ended term of punishment, confinement in a barred room in the women's building of the County Home for the murder of her husband. She had been confined for twenty years that summer.

Not all long-time residents were inmates. The Keeper and his wife, Mr. and Mrs. Fleming, supervised the County Home for four decades. When he had a stroke that left him paralyzed and speechless, he was nursed until he died in the bedroom he had occupied as the man in charge. But that happened long after the story we are about to tell.

Several married couples worked at the Home, among them the head cook who supervised food preparation for the entire community, and her husband who was responsible for the well-being of male inmates. He always referred to them as patients. Her name was Maude. His was Will.

Maude had a sister, younger by eighteen years, who was victim of a serious illness that required long periods of hospitalization. During those periods her son was brought to the County Home to be cared for by his aunt and uncle. The boy was neither an inmate nor a member of the staff. He was the only child at the Home. That hot summer he was not quite nine years old.

The Elm at the Edge of the Earth

CHAPTER ONE

ib overalls clung to my body, glued by sweat. I could feel flecks of peeling blue paint from the steps on which I lay sticking to the undersides of my arms. Creases in my neck and the crooks of my elbows itched. I would get a rash if this heat continued many more days.

I thought of the pump-house pond, its deep black water icy cold even on one-hundred-degree days. If you are careful you can sit on rocks above the dam and stick your feet in, which is a great way to cool off. The pump house was about a quarter of a mile from the County Home buildings, in the hardwood forest just before the pine groves. Water from the pond was pumped through pipes almost a mile long into a large storage tank on top of the hill over on the other side of Center Road, next to the cemetery. Pond water was used for everything except drinking. Drinking water came from wells. You probably wouldn't die if you drank the pond water, but it didn't taste very good. I had tried it. Aunt Maude would have a fit if she knew, but she didn't know. She didn't know a lot of things I did.

Mary Delancy was sitting above me, sprawled over several steps. Mary's appearance scared a lot of people, big people as well as children, but I wasn't afraid. I suppose that's because I'd known her since I was a baby, and it never occurred to me until I overheard a stranger's comment one day that maybe Mary should look some way other than the way she looked. She was always nice to me, but we didn't become buddies until I was eight, shortly before the terrible hot spell. It was when I broke the Keeper's sugar bowl. What a day that was.

I was having breakfast at a kitchen table and decided I'd try sugar instead of salt on my melon, as I'd seen somebody else do the morning before, so I went into the pantry to get a bowl of sugar. I could have taken any one of a dozen, but I spotted Mr. Fleming's. It was a large white bowl with a domed cover that had an acorn for a handle. Maybe it was the acorn, I don't know, but whatever it was, that bowl is the one I had to use. I got it down from the shelf without any problem and was headed back across the kitchen when Aunt Maude noticed what I was carrying. She let out a shriek that so startled me I let go of the bowl and it smashed to the floor exploding into a million pieces with sugar splashing all over the place.

It wasn't the gritty sugar that made her roar, though she hated spilled anything in her spotless kitchen. It was the precious bowl I'd broken. It seems, I was told later, that bowl had been in Mr. Fleming's family for generations, or belonged to his mother or something like that. Anyway, he thought a lot of it, and I never should have touched it.

I was used to Aunt Maude's shouting. She did a lot of that, but I realized the look in her eye went beyond the usual when I glanced up from the mess, so I lit out without thinking where I was going. I wheeled around, racing back through the pantry and across the Keeper's dining room, slamming the door behind me when I got to the staff men's washroom, running from there through the male inmates' dining room and the lower kitchen, swerving into the arcade leading to the women's building. I could hear Aunt Maude's bellows getting closer. Up the steps into the women's sitting room I panted, but where to go from there? The stairs to the second floor were too obvious so I dashed around them and into the west ward.

There was Mary Delancy sitting all by herself, rocking and humming. She stopped when I rushed in.

"I gotta hide. If Aunt Maude catches me, I'm dead," I hissed with my lips touching the side of her head.

"In here," Mary hissed back, reaching out to shove me into a clothes cupboard where I was muffled by hanging nightgowns, Mary's and those of the other women who slept in that ward. Through the closed door, over the noise of my heart pounding in my ears, I could hear Aunt Maude's voice.

"Mary, have you seen David?" She was winded, I could tell.

"Who? I can't hear you, Maude." Mary probably put the black tin trumpet into her earhole. She was truly deaf as well as almost blind.

"Never mind." I heard Aunt Maude pounding away.

Of course I did have to face the music eventually. Aunt Maude cut a switch from a pear tree, her favorite tree for whippings, and laced the backs of my legs with it. She cried harder than I did, during and afterward, and then she put an herb salve on the welts.

From that day on, Mary and I were buddies. She told me I could hide in her clothes cupboard any time I wanted. We couldn't do much together because walking was so difficult for her, and she didn't know much about anything except the

County Home because she'd never been any place else so she had little to talk about except local gossip, but she was interested in whatever I was doing, so I'd go over to see her and we'd carry on crazy conversations that made us both laugh. I was able to understand her better than most people, even though her mouth was misshaped and she didn't have all the inside parts. Her rasping croak was no more like an ordinary voice than her face was ordinary. She sprayed a lot of spit when she spoke but I didn't mind.

Anyway, that terrible hot day when the peeling paint from the sunroom steps was sticking to my undersides, Mary and I were sprawled out wishing it would cool off, wishing there was something we could do to be less miserable.

"If the temperature don't drop soon, I'm going to," Mary spluttered.

"Me too," I groaned. Looking out over the vegetable garden I could see heat rising in waves from the orchard beyond as black and white heifers moved restlessly from apple tree to apple tree trying to find a shadier spot, their tales swishing to keep flies away. "It's the humidity," I announced. Grown-ups had used that phrase constantly the past few days.

"Whatever it is, I wish it would go away." Mary fanned herself vigorously with a woven palm frond fan on which was printed in red letters, "Jesus loves YOU." The preacher who came from time to time to save the souls of what he called "resident sinners" had passed out the fans Sunday a week before. I noticed he only gave fans to those who put money in his velvet-lined mission basket. I regretted I didn't have one as I watched Mary stir a waft of air in front of her face, but hadn't put the dime Aunt Maude had given me in the collection because I wanted to spend it later at Harry Woolf's store.

"I wish you could walk better, Mary. We'd go down to the pump-house pond and stick our feet in the water."

"Couldn't make it, not on my stubs," Mary sprayed. "You go if you want. I'll just sit here and melt into a puddle of grease." She snorted a laugh at her own joke.

"Aunt Maude would kill me if I went near that pond alone," I said. I couldn't help grinning. "I have already, but she doesn't know it."

Mary cackled. She was much closer to Aunt Maude's age than mine, but she always thought it funny when I got away with something.

"If you can't make it to the pond, let's at least go to the pump and get a cold drink of water." I jumped up and grabbed Mary's wrists.

"It's too far," she said, pulling back.

"Not that far. C'mon, I'll help you." I gave her a heave. She was both heavy and helpless. We almost fell down the steps giggling before I managed to haul her upright.

I loved the pump, a tall, skinny, black cast-iron contraption standing in the angle of the ell-shaped back porch that skirted both the upper and lower kitchens. Shiny beads of clear water formed on the cold iron on hot days. A tin-lined wooden trough far below the spout carried excess water off the porch into a drain set in the slate sidewalk, so that if you raised and lowered the long pump handle as fast as you could, a torrent gushed out that turned into a miniature falls at the end of the trough. One of my favorite pastimes was to play with the pump, listening to the creaky noises it made and watching the water flow. I couldn't do it very often because the pump was just outside Aunt Maude's pantry window and she'd yell at me that I was wasting perfectly good drinking water.

On a post next to the pump hung a tin dipper which anybody could use. All you had to do when you got through drinking was slosh water around inside to rinse it out, then hang the dipper back on its nail. Nights when I was in bed I could hear from my window above the porch whoever came for a drink. It was a wonderful series of sounds, first the creaking of the pump handle, then the rush of water and silence while whoever it was drank, and then another creak of the handle for the slosh water, and finally a splat when the rinse water hit the driveway where it was thrown. If there were not other night sounds like peepers, I could even hear the clink of the dipper being put back on the nail. I pictured everything as it was happening and always wondered who it was at the pump, wanting to call out to them.

When I was little I couldn't reach the tin dipper, but as I grew taller I discovered that if I stood tiptoes on the rim of the trough, I could stretch up and give the dipper a knock so it would fall off the nail into my hand. Water from that well drunk from that dipper was better than any water any place else ever.

Instead of going around the outside of the buildings on the slate sidewalk, I suppose we thought it would be cooler to go the inside route. The sun room as we entered it wasn't cooler, or course. Sun had been beating through those bamboo-shaded windows since dawn, turning the long narrow room into an oven. Heat from the sun made that room very popular during cold months when women argued over which chair in the row of rockers was theirs, but nobody in her right mind would sit in the sun room facing east in the summer.

Once we stepped inside the main part of the women's building, we instantly felt a difference. High ceilings, bare polished floors, and cross ventilation must have had something to do with it. There were lots of doors off the hallway leading from the sun room to the sitting room. A couple of storerooms were always kept locked which I thought was a big deal until I followed Julia into one of them and saw it was only filled with sheets and towels and toilet paper and medicines, things like that. Farther along the wall on the right were doors to the east ward and the west ward and in between a big bathroom with five blue-veined marble sinks, five toilet stalls, and a single bathtub. Across from these doors was a wide staircase leading to the second floor, matching a duplicate staircase at the far end of the sitting room.

Tucked in under the east staircase was a door with bars on it. It was a regular door, except where there must have once been a glass window there were now iron bars. Rose Scheider lived in that room. Rose had killed her husband with a butcher knife. Of all my friends at the County Home, and really they were all my friends, Rose was my best friend.

I had to walk as slow as I could so as not to get too far ahead of Mary stumping along behind me. If she got discouraged she would never make it to the pump. When I got to Rose's door, I pressed my face to the bars. "Hi, Rose. Mary and I are going to the pump for a drink of cold water. You want me to bring you one?"

"No, thank you."

I could see Rose lying flat on the bed. She had pulled the green window shade down to the sill of her single window so the room was dark.

Getting across the big women's sitting room took time. Mary's felt-slippered feet slid on the shiny oak floor, so that every five steps forward she'd slip back two or three. The sitting room was empty in the heat of the day. Usually half a dozen or so women would be there, reading, chatting, playing a game at one of the tables, or just staring into space. Windows were filled with plants, some of whose fragrance combined with the odor of disinfectant to create a very pleasing smell. There was a jungle of rocking chairs and love seats with low hassocks in front of them, and in the corner an ornate pump organ with a square stool you could make go up and down by spinning the needlepoint-covered seat around.

Off the women's sitting room, at the foot of the west staircase, was the women's dining room. Casters for condiments were spaced every few feet on the long white cloth-covered table that stood in the center of the room. On the wall across from the windows was a pair of high sideboards used for storage, with a large buffet for serving in between. Not all women inmates could sit at the dining-room table at the same time, but that didn't matter because many of them were bedridden or preferred trays in their rooms, especially if they lived on the second floor.

I dawdled along, sometimes leaning against a chair, or when we got to the arcade steps sitting down as Mary never stopped moving, gasping for breath, and spraying spit. It was a major project for her to get down the arcade steps, but she kept at it. The lower kitchen was silent and empty when we got there. Mrs. Davies and her helpers, staff and inmate, must have been taking naps. The bank of gigantic black coal ranges continued to radiate heat from noon dinner. They wouldn't be fired up again until breakfast. Summer suppers were usually not only light but cold, sliced meats and salad, fruit, things like that.

When we finally, what seemed like hours later, came out onto the back porch, Mrs. Sawyer and her daughter Alma were sitting gazing across the lawn up to the southern hills in the distance, Mrs. Sawyer on the porch floor, her feet dangling off the edge, cotton stockings rolled into doughnuts around her ankles. Alma, a twisted arthritic lump, was, as always, in her wheelchair. I liked Mrs. Sawyer. Uncle Will said she resembled Pansy Yokum in the funny papers and she did sort of. Her face was thin, with high cheekbones and a long nose that hooked down as if it might someday touch her chin which pointed upward.

Mrs. Sawyer was always laughing. I don't know how she could be so lighthearted because she was much smaller than her crippled daughter, yet she had to constantly lift Alma in and out of that wheelchair. The Sawyers came to the County Home when Mrs. Sawyer's other daughter decided her mother was too frail to care for Alma at home. Not that it made much difference. It seemed to me she took all the care of Alma at the County Home, except of course for Julia Gammon, who was in charge of the women, and who took care of Mrs. Sawyer too.

Maybe it was the food. Maybe Mrs. Sawyer couldn't cook anymore. Mrs. Davies was a wonderful cook and she cooked in the lower kitchen for the inmates. Everybody always said if you want good food go to the County Home. I loved Mrs. Davies's cooking almost as much as Aunt Maude's, who cooked in the Keeper's upper kitchen. If fact there were times when the inmates were eating something I especially liked that I persuaded Aunt Maude to let me eat down below. Things like Mrs. Davies's hash browns. I watched her lots of times so I know exactly how she did it. She took peeled baked potatoes and cut them into very small square pieces which she put in large shallow pans, dropping plenty of dabs of butter in between the layers and sprinkling each with salt and pepper. When the pan was almost full, she covered the potatoes with heavy cream and rebaked them until they were a crusty bubbling brown on top. Delicious. I never ate much of anything else when I was allowed to have several helpings of hash browns.

Mrs. Sawyer was flapping her apron to fan herself as I came along behind her. "Hi," I said. "We're going to have a cold drink of water. Would you like one, too?"

"That would be very nice, David, thank you." She smiled and her mouth sank back. I watched closely in case her nose and chin touched this time, but they didn't. Alma, who never said much, nodded that she would like a drink.

As I was reaching for the tin dipper, Mary lurched past the Sawyers. Not wanting to be left out of any conversation, and wanting always to include everyone she could see, she croaked, "It will cool you off."

"What did she say?" Mrs. Sawyer frowned at me.

"It will cool you off."

"I can never understand her." Mrs. Sawyer shook her head sadly. "I don't know how you can, David."

I shrugged and raised the pump handle. On the downward thrust cold water flowed into the tin dipper I was holding under the spout. When the dipper was full I carried it over to Mrs. Sawyer, who drank about half the water, then gave the rest to Alma. "It is refreshing," she said as her daughter drank. "There's nothing better than cold water straight from the well."

When they finished I took the dipper back to the pump and filled it for Mary, who guzzled it empty without a pause, splashes spilling onto the front of her checkered dress. Then I had a drink for myself while Mary demanded more. I filled the dipper again and waited while she drank, this time more slowly. I thought she'd never finish and I wanted another.

Mary paused for several deep breaths and then in a grand gesture raised the dipper and poured what was left of the water over the thin silver thatch on top of her head. It ran down her face and off her chin stubble onto her bosom, which was getting soaked. "That feels good," she snorted. "More, David." She held the dipper under the spout so I could fill it again, then raising it high, and after a cringe, emptied its contents over her head. This time some of the cold water went down her back, making her squeal. The Sawyers were watching with their mouths part way open.

About the sixth time I refilled the dipper for Mary's pouring performance, I suggested it would be easier if she just put her head under the spout so I could pump the water directly onto it. "Besides," I added, "if your head is lower than your neck, water won't run down your back."

Mary didn't argue, but it was difficult for her to get to her knees. I had to hang onto her so she wouldn't topple off the porch as I guided her hands to the sides of the trough. While we were getting into position, Mrs. Sawyer rose to her feet to see better, turning Alma's wheelchair around so she wouldn't miss a thing either.

"Ready?" I yelled at Mary.

"Ready." Her muffled response was eager.

"I never." Mrs. Sawyer laughed, making her stomach that was shaped like a basketball bob up and down.

Turning the whole thing into a game, I jumped around and yelped Indian war hoots as I raised the pump handle and brought it down, raised it and yanked it down again so the water came like a river and Mary shrieked. Letting themselves go, the Sawyers hung onto their sides and began to snort. We were making a din to rouse Rip Van Winkle which would have been okay, but who we roused was Aunt Maude from her afternoon nap upstairs in the rooms she, Uncle Will, and I shared with two other staff members.

Every day after all the noon dinner work was done, Aunt Maude went upstairs, removed her white Red Cross rubber-soled shoes and her apron, as well as the big tortoise-shell hairpins that secured the bun at the back of her head, and otherwise completely dressed, she lay down on her bed, drew a light blanket up to protect her from drafts, and dozed for an hour and a half. She had been working since five o'clock in the morning so she deserved a rest.

I was supposed to take a nap too, and sometimes I did. Aunt Maude didn't care, she said, if I slept or not so long as I rested quietly. I expect she knew that lots of times I sneaked out when I heard her snoring in the bedroom across the living room from mine. When she heard the ruckus we were making at the pump, she obviously knew I wasn't napping. I'll bet she muttered as she got up so fast she was dizzy, "That boy will be the death of me yet."

Mary and I were having such a good time I didn't hear Aunt Maude's thundering approach, or I would have prepared to defend myself from attack. It was a matter of seconds after she clamped onto my right ear, pinching it in a vise grip between her thumb and a knuckle, before pain and the message reached my brain. I yelped as I dropped the pump handle and reached up to relieve my ear, but then remembered that nothing ever unhinged her clamp until Aunt Maude had accomplished what she wanted to accomplish. I could hardly relax, but I did stop struggling and pleading for mercy, hoping total surrender would soften whatever was to follow, for as sure as it was August, there'd be sobs of outrage at the ingratitude of a child who purposely did things to hurt her.

Over the years such scenes had been a regular part of my life. Actually, I'd come to dread the crushing expressions of love that followed more than the angry shouts. I could think about something else when she was scolding me, sometimes even when she was pinching and twisting my ear, knowing it would all be over in a few minutes, but when she pressed me to her breasts and held me there for tearful eternities of joy, I wondered if I'd smother. I experimented in survival techniques. I'd take quick extra deep gulps of air before the love press began, and then let it out as slowly as possible during the clutch. Sometimes there was no way to release the air because my nose and mouth were buried in her corseted bosom and I could not budge in any direction. If she was extra emotional and kept up the pressure, and kept it up, I was sure I'd explode. To keep from panic I'd count slowly, one and two and three, to see how many seconds before I'd black out. Those experiences convinced me I knew how it felt to drown.

The Sawyers went stone silent when Aunt Maude appeared. While not guilty of anything other than watching and laughing, they paled at her anger. When the noises of the pump and gushing water were no more, I became aware that Mary was making animal hurt sounds rather than cries of pleasure. Aunt Maude heard them, too. She released my ear which made the pain worse as the blood rushed back, and bent to help Mary up from her crouched position. Mary looked like a dumped basket of laundry. Aunt Maude used the hem of her own starched housedress to dry Mary's face.

"David, run up to Uncle Will's closet and get his heavy flannel bathrobe. Quick now before Mary catches her death." Pulling Mary's shaking body against her own, Aunt Maude said in a tone that combined alarm and comfort, "Poor woman is drenched to the skin."

Aunt Maude was always bossy but she was also fantastic in emergencies, even if she had to create an emergency where none had existed before. "Everything is going to be all right, dear"—she rocked the sobbing, drooling Mary in her arms. "We'll dry you off and get you into bed, then I'm going to make you something hot to drink. Would you prefer tea or cocoa?"

I preferred cocoa, but she didn't asked me.

Mary collapsed into Aunt Maude's embrace, responding to loving touch. She didn't act as if she heard anything that was said to her. Suddenly it came to me that ice-cold water had poured directly into Mary's ears, or the holes where her ears should be. Remembering how it felt when I got water in my ears while trying to swim, I understood that what had started as great fun had probably turned into misery for Mary. She was confused, as she tried with Aunt Maude's help to get to her feet. "I hurt, Maude," she blubbered.

"I'm sure you do, dear." Aunt Maude kissed the top of Mary's head; what little hair she had was plastered to her skull. "Don't stand there gawping, David," Aunt Maude snapped her eyes at me. "Go get that bathrobe and be quick about it."

The realization that I might have hurt Mary shook me. Having Aunt Maude mad was nothing new, I could handle that, but the thought that I had harmed Mary, even if I hadn't meant to, upset me so I wanted to cry. I ran as fast as I could upstairs and rushed back, with the heavy braided cords of Uncle Will's bathrobe whipping around my ankles. Together, Aunt Maude and I wrapped the robe around Mary, then half carried her back to the women's building. As soon as we got to her ward, I was sent to fetch Julia Gammon. When Julia arrived, Aunt Maude told me to go to my room and stay there. She said she'd deal with me later. As I left, I heard Julia say she thought Dr. Davis should be called.

I didn't get cocoa, nor tea, I was locked in my room. Not that locking my door meant much, I could always go out the bedroom window and across the porch roof, but I didn't. And I was told there would be no supper for me. The punishment session with Aunt Maude could have been worse. After she'd done everything for Mary that she could, she lectured me on how I had to be aware of Mary's frailness, and be careful because I could really hurt her. I certainly hadn't meant to hurt her. Pumping cold water on her head on a hot day seemed harmless, a good thing really if it cooled her off. I prayed, while Aunt Maude was still delivering her lecture, that Mary would not get the new monia Aunt Maude kept talking about. I hoped Aunt Maude was overplaying this the way she did everything else. Outbursts were part of every incident in Aunt Maude's life, the more major the incident, the more impressive the outburst, and for Aunt Maude nothing was ever minor.

Aunt Maude never had any children of her own, though she told everybody a jillion times that I was born right into her heart, whatever that meant. She was always trying to persuade Mother and Dad to let her and Uncle Will adopt me. Sometimes I wished they would agree, other times I was glad they wouldn't. Aunt Maude could be rough to live with.

She worked very hard, getting up at five o'clock to have breakfast ready when the men came in from milking. Staff breakfasts at the County Home meant meat and potatoes, eggs, fruit and cereal, breads and doughnuts and cookies, and from time to time pancakes or waffles, always lots of food, and all of it made from scratch by Aunt Maude and her helpers. She also supervised the dairy where Roy Cross made butter and cheeses, the bakery where Mr. Beveridge made all the breads, the lower kitchen in the charge of Mrs. Davies, plus the cold meat lockers and larders and other storerooms. No wonder it gave her high blood pressure.

She was dark complected, with beautiful brown eyes that

were large and far apart, bordered by long black lashes. When trouble was brewing, the corners of her mouth turned down and she'd glare at me as if one good bite would split me in two. I'd look up into the face of that anger and find myself thinking, What pretty eyes she has.

She yelled at Uncle Will more than she yelled at me or anybody else. She always had, I guess. That they really loved each other was apparent to everybody, however. If he happened to swallow the wrong way she'd go hysterical, screaming at him, "Will, Will, are you all right?" You knew if he died, she'd die too, right on the spot.

Uncle Will was fair, with thinning reddish-brown hair, tall and skinny with a nose that jutted out between deepset blue eyes then arched down. I heard his nose called both Roman and Greek, but I thought it looked exactly like Dick Tracy's nose, only better. He blew it a lot. I think he had sinus problems.

Going to bed without supper wasn't terrible punishment because I knew Uncle Will would bring me something to eat later, and he did, just as it was getting dark outside, a bowl of fresh peach shortcake with Aunt Maude's light as a feather butter-drenched baking powder biscuits and gobs of whipped cream on top. I ate it kneeling by my windowsill looking out over the backyard. Several people came to the pump for a drink of water while I was eating. I wondered if they all knew about my latest crime.

It hadn't cooled off much. The moon was a hazy patch seen through branches of the elm tree in the middle of the yard. Cicadas were clicking and crickets singing. Soon tree frogs would join the chorus. From my window I could see part of the women's building, Rose's window for instance, but I couldn't see the other side where Mary was. I could picture her tucked in even though she hated the heat.

"Please God, don't let Mary get serious sick," I whispered. God was real to me, as close and reassuring as the sound of the pump, but I knew He couldn't be absolutely relied on. I tried not to ask Him for things He might think silly, so I couldn't blame Him afterward if I didn't get them. On the other hand sometimes I implored Him, and was disappointed. Rose kept reminding me that the key phrase in the Lord's Prayer was "Thy will be done" and His will might not always coincide with my wishes. I didn't think He'd take it out on Mary, however, for something stupid I did.

I climbed into my white iron bed with hollow brass knobs on top of each of the four posts and was surprised at how cool the sheets felt. I fell asleep looking around the high-ceilinged room with its cream-colored walls and varnished oak moldings, then toward the single window that overlooked the porch roof and the back lawn.

It was tree frogs chittering louder than usual in the hot stillness, and a full moon's brightness after the haze cleared, that woke me in the middle of the night. I hadn't been sleeping all that well anyway. I got out of bed and stretched, thought about going to the bathroom, then decided I didn't need to make that long trip down the hall. More for something to do than anything else, I went over to the window and looked out. There was a gray-blue figure in the moonlight. Her arms hung loose at her sides, but her head was tilted back and her chin thrust up high like that picture of the praying Indian on a horse. I knew it was Rose. Her hair was undone down her back. She wasn't wearing a bathrobe, only her nightgown. She just stood there, staring, not moving. I guessed she was looking at the elm tree silhouetted on the ridge up south.

We talked about that elm a lot. It was the first thing you noticed if you looked beyond the barns and pastures, up toward the horizon. The lane going from the cow barn to the pasture went downhill to the gate, but then the pastures sloped uphill. Past the pastures and a stretch of sumac that bordered the County Home property the land rose like a cliff into a ridge you could see for miles. And in the middle of the ridge, on its highest point, stood the biggest elm tree in that part of the state. Uncle Will said it was a landmark. Everybody knew the elm tree but it seemed to have special meaning for Rose.

She said it stood at the edge of the earth. "Beyond that tree is the abyss."

"You're wrong, Rose," I said, but she paid no attention.

"That wild free tree against the sky whips in gales, yet never bends, riding the ridge like a mighty many-masted ship," she would say, staring at the tree through her barred window. Once she added in an eerie kind of voice, "It stands guard at gates to the end of everything."

"Rose, there's no abyss up there, if by abyss you mean a deep hole. It isn't the end of everything. The tree is behind Ott Alwardt's barn, and if you go over the ridge past the Alwardt farm you come to Middlebury." I tried to convince her.

In the moonlight she was standing under another elm, growing in the middle of the backyard, its branches reaching out in all directions touching eaves of the Keeper's building, the women's building, the laundry, and even the meat locker. Rose said she knew the backyard elm by its every leaf and twig. "This is a friendly tree that protects us with its canopy. But it's kin to that untamed tree on the edge of the earth, the one that beckons."

Once she told me, "My life is bound by two elms, the known here outside my window, and the unknown I can see up there but not touch, that wild majestic tree that fascinates and frightens." Then she went strange, and trancelike. "If I could get to that elm at the edge, I'd be free. I know I'd be free." She whispered so low I had to strain to hear her.

I never understood what she was driving at when she talked that way. I knew what the words meant, but putting them together as she did confused me. That she had her facts wrong I tried to tell her again and again, but when she made any sign that she'd even heard me, she'd just smile a sad smile and reach through the bars to take my face in both her hands, saying, "There is always possibility, David, never deny possibility. Many things we know nothing about are, and some of the things we think we know well aren't at all." That stopped me. I didn't argue anymore.

All that talk over and over about the elm at the edge is why I knew she was looking at it in the moonlight. I wanted to yell out to her that I'd be right down to join her, but if I did yell I'd wake everybody up, and that would cause a riot, as if I wasn't in enough trouble already. I was supposed to be sound asleep, and Rose wasn't supposed to be out of her room alone ever, though I'd seen her or the shadow of her on the lawn in the middle of the night a couple of times before.

I could have crawled out onto the porch roof and then crept along quietly until I came to Roy's sitting-room window, and so gone down that way, surprising her, but she looked as if maybe she didn't want anybody, not even me, to be with her. It gave me a lonesome feeling thinking Rose might not want me, but as long as I didn't push it and actually go down there I'd never know one way or the other, so I decided to just watch from the window.

She stood there like that praying Indian for what seemed hours. I think I fell asleep a couple of times with my chin on the windowsill. When my knees began to hurt I decided I might as well go back to bed, but before I could do anything about it, I noticed Rose was turning ever so slowly to look up at my window. I didn't move a muscle. I didn't know if she could see me, and if she could what I should do about being caught spying on her, so I didn't do anything.

She stared and stared as if she was peering straight into my brain, then turned and walked slowly toward the women's building, disappearing into the darkness. I watched her go, wondering if I was the only one who had seen her.

CHAPTER TWO

he next time I woke up it was bright sunshine and already hot. I'm sure Aunt Maude called me a dozen times, but I hadn't heard a thing. My first thought was about Mary. I was sorry I hadn't sneaked over to her room during the night to make sure she was okay. I could have easily enough without anybody seeing me, but how would I know whether she was okay or not once I got there? Unless she was breathing funny, which she did all the time, I'd have no way of guessing if she was fine or about to die.

I made the mistake of going down to breakfast barefoot, which was one more thing to draw Aunt Maude's attention to me. "Back upstairs, young man, and put shoes on. Sneakers or moccasins, your choice, but one or the other." I should have known better. Usually I wore shoes to breakfast and then stashed them someplace outside.

As I started for the stairs she stopped me. "We had lamb chops, sausages, and cottage fries for breakfast. Do you want that, there's plenty, or would you prefer an egg?"

"I'd like an egg, please," I replied.

Staff breakfast was served at six o'clock sharp, dinner was served exactly at noon to both staff and inmates, and supper was at six on the dot for staff. Inmates ate breakfast an hour later and supper an hour earlier, which is why the only meal of the day Mrs. Davies ate at the Keeper's table was supper. That's when she caught up on all the news.

Farm hands got up at four o'clock each morning to milk a herd of black and white Holstein-Friesian cows, which meant it was before daylight no matter the season. I seldom got up that early, though sometimes in the summer I'd do it if I happened to wake up because the men let me go down and open the gate at the end of the lane so the cows could get from their night pasture to the milking barn. Just walking alone down that lane in the dark was scary and thrilling. Everything remotely visible took on weird shapes. Buildings hovered and trees reached out to grab me. I could hear the cows stomping and breathing hard, but couldn't see the critters until I was right up to them, nostril-steaming monsters held back only by a gate. Holsteins are among the biggest of all cows, and though they won't hurt you on purpose, if they step on your foot or knock you down by mistake you're a goner. They aren't too smart I guess because whenever one went in the wrong stanchion—and each of them had an assigned and numbered stanchion—Uncle Deane or one of the other men would push her out and mutter, "Stupid bitch."

It took an act of fierce determination to unbolt the gate, because the cows didn't just wander through, they thundered, their full udders swinging, swishing tails that sometimes flicked me in the face, and that stung. The gate was weighted to swing open easily, so if I did it just right I could hop on after I'd undone the bolt and ride the gate back to its stop post.

Then when the cows had all gone through, I'd secure the gate so it wouldn't close by itself, and follow the beasts up to the barn, trying not to step in fresh cow flops. Once when I did, Uncle Deane made fun of me in a singsong chinee voice, "He who stares at stars steps in shit."

Even if I didn't get out of bed to go to the cow barn, sometimes I got up just to have breakfast with the staff. When I did I ate almost as much as everybody else even though I hadn't done anything to build a hunger. I think it was the atmosphere in the dining room. With the breakfast table full, there was lots of laughing and joking as everybody ate heaped-up plates of food and drank pitchers of freshly squeezed orange juice and cup after cup of wonderful-smelling coffee which Aunt Maude boiled in a big granite pot with eggs smashed in it, shells and all.

Aunt Maude was the favorite for all the men to tease, probably because she always reacted to what they said. One of them would say, "Something is wrong with this spoon bread. I guess I'll have another helping with that hot maple syrup to see if I can figure out what it is."

If Aunt Maude snapped back that there was nothing wrong with her spoon bread, somebody else would join in the teasing. Those times when she didn't rise to their bait they'd say such icky sweet things about her cooking that she'd blush.

There was as strict an order about where everybody sat in the Keeper's dining room as there was where each cow belonged in the milking barn. Men occupied the east side of the long table facing women staff members sitting opposite. The Keeper and his wife, referred to by staff and inmates alike as Pa and Ma Fleming, had armchairs in the middle of each side. Everybody else had straight chairs. If a person missed a meal, his or her chair was left vacant. Nobody ever sat in anybody else's seat. Seating was by what Uncle Will called "seniority," which was why Aunt Maude sat right next to Ma Fleming. The man on the staff with the most years, Uncle Will, sat to Pa Fleming's left, and then the other men followed to Uncle Will's left. When company came, extra places were squeezed in next to the Flemings.

My chair was at the very end of the table toward the kitchen, which was an improvement over the years I had to sit in a high chair next to Aunt Maude.

Each morning she started calling me at a quarter to six if I was not already up and in the barn. If I didn't respond, which mostly I didn't, at six-thirty she'd begin "Are you going to lay abed all day?" More times than not I'd make it down between seven and seven-thirty, which was too late for staff breakfast and too early for the Flemings who had their breakfast at eight o'clock. If I did lallygag until eight, Aunt Maude made me eat at the big table with Pa and Ma Fleming, just the three of us. Those Keeper's breakfasts were consumed in near silence. The Flemings sat in their armchairs ten up from me reading the morning papers, and only occasionally mumbling something I couldn't make out.

Pa Fleming was a large man, broad-shouldered and tall but not fat. Red suspenders kept his pants up. His hair was glistening white, as was his clipped mustache, and he wore round steel-rimmed glasses. Ma was short and plump and walked with a rolling gait on bowed legs. Usually she wore an apron over a rather spiffy housedress, though I never saw her do any housework. A hairnet was intended to keep stray hairs from flying, but couldn't keep her wig straight. The wig's part was usually askew, either too high or too low on the left side of her head. Her round glasses had no rims at all.

Ma Fleming had the same breakfast every morning: broiled

grapefruit with a spoonful of current jelly in the middle, bran toast with comb honey, and China tea. Pa Fleming ate whatever the staff had been served earlier. She was so deaf she made little attempt to carry on a conversation with me, perched way down there miles away from her. Instead, she'd smile from time to time, bob her head, and say in a hollow, non-hearing voice, "That's nice." I never knew what was nice, but having been taught to be polite, I'd smile and nod back.

One morning Pa Fleming, without looking up from his paper, asked me, "What are your plans for the day, David?"

I knew he wasn't listening, so I said, "I think I'll saddle the bull and ride him over to Middlebury."

Both Pa and Ma said in unison, "That's nice."

Most mornings, however, I ate breakfast by myself in the Keeper's—actually Aunt Maude's—kitchen, sitting on a stool pulled up to one of the butcher block work tables across from the coal range. I preferred that because after I'd been given what I was supposed to eat, nobody paid any attention to me. I didn't have to carry on conversation if I didn't want to, and I could poke around in the ice chests and the pantry picking at whatever I found there, especially after Aunt Maude left for her daily conference with Mrs. Davies in the lower kitchen. I loved the spicy sausages Aunt Maude made, for instance, and took seconds or thirds if I could manage without being yelled at.

Then too I could listen to Aunt Maude and her kitchen helpers, Aureta and Eunice, gossip. They didn't think I understood their codes for things I was "too young to hear," but I knew very well what they meant when they said some girl was "that way." I didn't know how she got that way, but that she was going to have a baby was no mystery.

Best of all about those kitchen breakfasts was Roy Cross,

who read his morning paper in a chair in the corner just about the time I was eating. He'd read the funnies to me, or sometimes massage my neck and shoulders if I asked him to. Or we talked about whatever we wanted to talk about. If I just wanted to think, he'd not say a word. Roy spoiled me and I knew it, but he seemed to like doing what he thought I wanted.

The first time I came to stay at the County Home with Aunt Maude and Uncle Will, I was a baby. I don't remember it, of course, but they say Roy could hold me high in the air in the palm of one hand. Having him near gave me a greater sense of being safe than anything else when I was little. I've heard that those who watched him wipe away my tears or hold a "now blow your nose" handkerchief thought it some kind of miracle that his huge hands could be so gentle. One Christmas I was given a set of bisque soldiers which I dropped as I was carrying them upstairs to my room. Out came Roy's handkerchief so I could blow into it, then he carefully picked up every piece and flake and over the next weeks and months glued those soldiers back together again so they were good as new.

Roy's job was to do whatever heavy work Aunt Maude and her "girls" weren't supposed to tackle, lugging scuttles of coal for the cooking range, or hauling out the ashes and keeping the stove polished glistening black. He was also the one who did the actual work in the dairy. While Aunt Maude supervised and salted the butter and put seasonings in the cheeses, it was Roy who took the raw cream or milk and processed it by churning or cooking and cooling, washing and whatever else was necessary to turn it into crocks of rich yellow butter and pots of savory cheeses supplying both upper and lower kitchens.

Each evening he listened to his records for several hours in the little square living room above the pump, off one of the staff corridors that Pa Fleming insisted be his, though some of the staff who lived on that corridor complained about the "noise." Roy left the door open hoping somebody would join him, eager to share what he enjoyed so much, but nobody ever did, except me. It wasn't because the staff felt funny about socializing with an inmate. They just couldn't appreciate Roy's music.

Rose listened, sitting by her barred window whenever the weather was warm enough so she could have the window open. Sometimes even when it was chilly, she'd wrap herself in a shawl and sit there. Of course Roy had to have his window open too, or she couldn't have heard anything, but they worked that out between them. When he was leaving the dairy he'd cross the driveway to her window, and say, "I'm going to be playing *Butterfly* tonight," or, "What are you in the mood for, Rose?" and they'd discuss the evening program. I thought it was too bad Rose couldn't just come up into the little square living room with Roy and me. She sure could have heard it better sitting next to the Victrola. When I said that to her once, she told me she liked hearing it floating through the air, coming in to her on a breeze from outside.

Roy was sitting there in his corner of the kitchen when I stomped back up the stairs to put something on my feet. I was glad Aunt Maude hadn't checked my underwear because I wasn't wearing any. That always gave her a fit. She said it was "disgusting" to run around without underwear. Maybe so, but it was also cooler.

I knew while I was doing what she told me to do she would be taking out the little iron skillet and dropping a generous plop of butter into it before putting it on the back of the coal stove. When she decided the skillet's temperature was just right, the butter simmering but not sizzling, she'd carefully drop two eggs in, making sure not to break the yolks. As the whites set, she'd gently flip each egg, and then when both were upside down, she'd use the spatula to press lightly until she could see yolks bleeding underneath, blending into the salty butter to cook until firm.

I loved eggs cooked that way and Aunt Maude knew it. After we'd had a dustup she'd make something special for me, such as those eggs. I guess it was her way of saying she was sorry she had to punish me, even though I deserved it.

When I got back to the butcher block table, there were my eggs just the way I liked them, with a quarter of ripe musk melon I had smelled from the top of the stairs, and a tall frosty glass of orange juice. She put two slices of homemade rye toast on my plate, gave me a quick kiss on top of my head, and said, "I'm off to see Mrs. Davies. You eat everything now." When I left my food on my plate Aunt Maude said it looked like the Cherry Valley massacre. I promised her I'd finish every morsel.

"If he doesn't, I will," Roy said softly so only I could hear. He did sometimes help me out when my eyes were hungrier than my stomach.

Aureta was at the sink at the far end of the kitchen, washing up, her scrawny neck sticking out of a too large starched white collar. Her dress hung on her as if she had a skeleton rack for a body. Where her fanny should be there was a sunken place in the back of her dress.

"How is Mary?" I asked Roy between bites.

"Dr. Davis is on the way," he replied from behind his paper. "Julia thinks she has pneumonia."

"Jeepers," I gulped. That's what I had been worrying about ever since Aunt Maude first said the words. I knew people died of "new monia." It happened all the time at the County Home.

It didn't seem to matter what else was wrong with them, when they died, new monia was usually the cause.

Roy put down his paper and began to rub my shoulders. "She's going to be all right." His words didn't reassure me. "I'm going to start the churns now. You come along in a little while and I'll let you lick the dash."

"Yep." I got off the stool to carry my dishes to the sink where Aureta was waiting when I heard, "Oogit, ooogit." It was the horn on Charley Smith's old Dodge jitney. "Oogit, ooogit," it sounded again as I hurried to let Charley know I'd heard him. I was flustered as to whether I should run to the screen door with my dishes and yell, or take them to the sink first and then run back to the door.

"Be careful, David," Aureta cried as she watched me skitter about. "Remember what happened when you dropped the Keeper's sugar bowl."

"How could I forget the crime of the century?" I asked, hastening to hand her the dirty dishes as I did a sharp reverse to rush out the door and off the porch.

I jumped on the jitney's loose running board. "What's up, Charley? All that honking is going to rile people." The jitney made enough noise just running without Charley's honking adding to the calamity. Of the old truck's three remaining fenders one was about to fall off from a constant clattering wiggle caused by the engine's asthmatic idle. Thick coats of mud and dust and years of grime covered the cab and accumulated junk in the back that was there only because it was too heavy to blow away. There were several pieces of rusty iron, part of a soapstone sink, half a sack of cracked corn that was spilling out rat- or mouse-made holes in the burlap, and a wooden crate that a framed picture for the Keeper came in and which Charley thought was too good to throw away. Aunt Maude called Charley's jitney a moving dump.

Charley was no treat himself, black greasy matted locks spilling around a grinning unshaved face shaded by the remains of a genuine Stetson. He bragged that his teeth, such as they were, were his own, few in number, twisted, broken, and stained from an ever present chaw of cut plug, which had also permanently browned the cracks and crevices of both corners of his mouth.

"I know," Charley said about the oogits, "but Maude don't like me comin' to the kitchen door. She says I stink of the pigpen." He spat a splotch of tobacco juice out the driver's window.

"You do," I agreed, "but I don't mind."

"That's mighty Christian of you," Charley grunted, letting go with a major spit between the gaps in his front teeth. Charley was in charge of pigs and chickens on the farm, but they weren't to blame for his aroma. "I'm goin' down to the Center. Ya wanna ride along?"

The Center meant Harry Woolf's store. "You bet I do, wait a minute while I go get my money." I kicked off my moccasins, tossing them through the window of the jitney. As I raced off to get my cash, I could see that one had landed on the seat while the other fell through a hole in the floorboards, landing with a thump on the driveway below.

"God-damned kid," Charley cursed as he reached through his window to open the door from the outside, there being no handle that worked from the inside on either side. I watched him walk around the front of the unbraked jitney as it rolled downgrade against him. "Whoa," he shouted as if he was talking to a horse, "Whoa, God damn it." He lifted his foot and gave the old Dodge a kick on its shaky bumper. It must have reached a cog in a gear just then because it stopped. "Son of a bitch." Charley gave it another kick, then noticed me watching. "Go get yer money. Ya think I'm goin' to wait all day? God-damned kid."

I ran upstairs and popped off the top half of one of the hollow brass balls on my bed. In that knob I had six pennies, a nickel, and the dime I had not put in the mission basket on Sunday. Removing the dime, I firmly replaced the brass half-sphere. Two of the other knobs also held treasures. A dried bright blue seed I found in the woods was in one, along with a perfectly preserved June bug corpse. In another was a miniature book with the Twenty-Third Psalm that Roy had given me and an English coin Aunt Latzy said was very old. No matter how hard I pried I couldn't get the fourth brass knob off, so as far as I knew it was empty. A prime hiding place going to waste.

Charley was crawling out from under the jitney when I jumped off the porch. My bare feet splatting on the sidewalk startled him. "What are you doing, Charley? Is something broke," I asked, playing dumb.

"Nothin', I'm not doin' nothing'," Charley barked. "I got bored waitin' for ya, so decided to crawl under. Here's yer shoe, God damn it." He threw it at me and stumped around to the driver's side, giving the front bumper an angry warning kick on the way. "Get in, we ain't got all day for Christ's sake."

We spewed gravel as we lurched around the corner of the Keeper's building and out onto the Center Road, not because Charley was a race car driver, but because being mad had discombobulated his never smooth footwork on the clutch and accelerator. Then, too, the old Dodge wasn't what Uncle Deane called "fine-tuned." I loved watching the road whiz under us through the hole in the floorboards. Riding in Charley Smith's jitney was much more fun than riding in Uncle Will's new '34 Ford.

"Whadja have to go and drown Mary for?" Charley's voice gurgled a mouthful of tobacco juice.

"I didn't drown her."

"Well, ya tried to, holdin' her head 'neath the pump for sweet Christ's sake."

"I did not hold her head under the pump. She put her head under and I pumped. That's all there was to it." My vision was blurring as my eyes misted over.

"Dumb kid." Charley concluded the conversation by hacking up a mouthful and spitting out the window.

Harry Woolf's store stocked everything needed by man, woman, or beast, from black leather dress-up ladies' pocketbooks to bag balm, barrels of brown sugar, and boxes of player-piano rolls. Walking in the door you were overpowered by a million scents, each one better than all the others, mixed up together in a combination I could recall no matter where I was. Sweet black molasses and coffee beans, oiled harness, rubber boots, kerosene and spices, dried herbs, chocolate, the newness of heavy woolen jackets and the old dust of forever.

Mr. Woolf looked like pictures of Moses, with a mass of white, wavy hair Aunt Jessie called angel hair, and it did look like that stuff you put on Christmas trees. He sounded like Moses too, each word producing an echo. "Good morning, David. How is your Aunt Maude today?" he asked in his Ten Commandments voice.

"She's fine, Mr. Woolf." I walked toward a glass showcase with a curved top. "I'd like to buy some penny candy please." The showcase contained Whitman's Sampler boxes on the bottom shelf, an assortment of candy bars, Baby Ruths, and others on the middle shelf, and a wide variety of penny candy on the top shelf. I went for the top shelf because I knew I got a lot more for my money up there, most of the penny candy being several pieces for a cent. Harry Woolf was waiting, brown paper bag in hand. "I'll have six Tootsie rolls, four raspberry twists, two licorice twists, and two jawbreakers. Does that come to seven cents?"

"Seven cents exactly," the heavens resounded.

"Good. Here's a dime." I handed my mission basket money to Mr. Woolf. "And, I'd like to buy Charley three cents worth of cut plug, please."

"I'll take Red Chief," Charley barked from over my shoulder where he'd been waiting as if he knew I was going to treat.

"Thank the lad." Mr. Woolf glared down from the mountain.

"Thanks, Davey," Charley muttered.

"You're welcome, Charley."

I left him and Harry Woolf to conduct whatever business had brought us to the store while I wandered. I pressed my face into a stack of dollar straw hats and breathed deep. They smelled as sweet as fresh-cut clover. I stopped at a glove display. Mr. Woolf had a large supply of gloves, both winter and summer, for work and for best. I picked up a pair made from deerskin and touched them to my cheek, closing my eyes to concentrate on their softness. I quietly climbed four steps up onto the ladder that was attached to a track in the ceiling and pushed myself along the dry goods shelves. I'd learned long before that Mr. Woolf didn't object if I went slow and careful. He could skim along the wall like a boat on the water after only a single push, but I never managed anything more than a short, jerky ride. I only pretended to look at the bolts of cloth, it was the ride on the ladder I wanted, but I spotted a printed cotton with an overall pattern of tiny blue flowers from which Aunt Maude had just made a batch of new aprons trimmed with dark blue rickrack. I could see why she'd chosen that particular bolt, it was prettier than all the others.

"Let's go, kid." Charley led the way out of the store carrying a much larger brown paper bag than the one I clutched.

"Can I ride in the back?" I asked.

"No."

"Why not?"

"You know why not. Don't be pesky. If anybody saw ya in the back of the jitney while it's in motion, Maude would skin me alive."

"Who's to see me?"

"Anybody. Get in here." Charley opened his door and crawled into the cab.

"Pleeeeeze, Charleeee," I dragged each word out for a slow count of five.

"If anything happens God damn it . . ."

"Nothing will happen." I pulled myself onto the tailgate and crawled over the debris to the back of the cab where Charley had welded an iron crossbar for a place to tie pigs. It was perfect for hanging on.

"Sit down God damn it."

I scrunched. Charley put the jitney in gear and made a grinding U-turn to head back to the County Home. When the bucking circle was completed I stood up and undid the clasps of my bib overalls so they could drop down around my waist. As we picked up speed, air rushed over my skin making me tingle.

"Faster, Charley, make it go faster." Through the cab's rear window I could see Charley's foot plunge the gas pedal to the floor. There was no change at all for a minute, then the thumping engine belched and the jitney leapt forward like a greyhound seeing rabbits for the first time. My hair flew into a frenzy then laid straight back, the wind cementing it to my scalp. I was covered with goosebumps from being both scared and excited. "Faster, Charley," I shouted again.

"She won't go any faster for sweet Christ's sake," Charley shouted back. "She's about to throw a rod now."

Eddies of dust rolled in our wake, billowing along both sides of the road as the wind whistled in my ears. My overalls fell down around my ankles. I was starkers but didn't dare let go of the iron bar to pull up my pants. It didn't matter, we were going so fast I'd be just a blur if anybody tried to look at me. Besides, it felt great, the wind wrapping around all of me.

It was a short drive, from the Center back to the County Home, over too soon. I wished Charley would whiz right on past, roaring up the hill and over toward Middlebury. When we were in sight of the County Home buildings, Charley slowed down and turned onto the East Road. "I'll go in the back way," he shouted. "Soon's I stop you jump off'n nobody'll see ya was ridin' in the back."

"Okay. Thanks, Charley, that was great." I managed to pull up my overalls while hanging on with one hand, but couldn't reclasp the bib until we really slowed down to turn into the driveway. I grabbed my bag of candy as we crunched to a stop and crawled over the old sink and the picture crate, then without looking jumped off the tailgate, almost into the arms of Uncle Will. He was standing there by the driveway talking to Burt Culbertson. His face when he saw me was a mask of sorrow.

"Charley," he said, putting his hands out to keep me from

toppling over. "You know David isn't allowed to ride in the back of that truck." His voice, quiet but urgent, had a tone of regret rather than reprimand.

"I know, Will," Charley whined, "but the boy wanted to bad, and I drove so slow, he could'a beat me if he'd been walkin'. Ain't that so, Davey?"

I was frozen in place, not blinking to agree or disagree. Uncle Will could see dust still hadn't settled along the Center Road if he cared to look. Lies are guaranteed to bring down the instant wrath of God I'd been told by everybody who claimed to know, yet Charley told whoppers all the time, like now, and nothing happened. I waited, expecting lightning to come out of the hot hazy sky and strike Charley dead. Maybe Charley had an arrangement with God, or maybe God didn't bother with Charley because Charley never took a bath. If cleanliness is next to Godliness, and I heard that one at least twice a day, then perhaps Charley was so far from the throne of the Almighty, God never heard any of his "God damns" or his "for sweet Christ's sakes" or his lies, not even when Charley was shouting instead of whining.

"Slow or not, Charley," Uncle Will continued sounding as if he was apologizing, "don't let David ride back there again."

"You won't tell Maude?"

Uncle Will shook his head sadly, as if he knew nothing had been settled. Obviously he had no more control over Charley Smith than God had.

"Thanks, Will." Charley let fly a mouthful of tobacco juice out his window, aiming it clear across the driveway, a victory spit. The jitney backfired, then lunged forward before screeching to a halt again. My moccasins flew out Charley's window. His "God damn kid" was plain to hear as he rattled away.

I smiled a don't hate me smile at Uncle Will, who smiled back and roughed up my hair. Uncle Will never could get cross with me.

While it was almost as hot as yesterday outdoors, the heat hadn't yet penetrated inside. The women's building felt cool. By the time I reached Rose's door I was no longer nervous from being caught riding in the back of Charley's jitney. I pressed my face to the bars.

"Rose, are you in there?"

"No."

"Yes you are. I can see you rocking by the window."

"Where did you think I'd be?"

"I don't know. Rose, I brought you some licorice twists, two of them. Here." I pushed them through the bars.

Rose got up from her rocker and came toward the door, her slippers making a ssh-ssh-ssh sound on the polished floor. "Thank you, David." She took the limp black twists, twining them around and between her fingers. "They match my mood."

"Why are you in a black mood? Don't answer until I get settled." I dropped my bag of candy on the floor and hurried around the corner of the sitting room to get the swivel stool from the organ. Its needlepoint cover was fading and losing its stuffing, but sitting on the stool which I could twist up as high as I needed was much better than standing outside Rose's door hour after hour while we had our long talks. When I was perched, I said, "Okay, now tell me."

"Tell you what?" During my flurry of activity Rose had brought the straight chair that stood beside her bed and placed it against the door on the inside. She was sitting there biting into a licorice twist.

"Why are you in a black mood?" If she was eating hers, then I'd eat a piece of my candy. A raspberry twist would do just fine.

"I've forgotten." She chewed slowly the way a cow works its cud. She was looking at the wall, or at nothing actually. At least it didn't appear she was seeing anything.

"Couldn't have been a very black mood then. When you have the real uglies, you don't forget why." Raspberry twists taste as good as they smell. I knew my lips were getting red from the juices. I hoped I didn't have it on the end of my nose too as I sniffed and took another bite.

"Don't remind me."

We chewed our twists in silence for a few minutes. "I saw you standing out in the moonlight in your nightgown last night," I said.

"You must have been dreaming."

"No, I wasn't, Rose. I saw you. I was going to crawl out the window and join you, but you looked as if you wanted to be alone."

"I did."

"See, I told you I wasn't dreaming. You really were there. Were you looking at the elm tree on the ridge?"

"I was dreaming."

"Here we go again," I sighed, not wanting to plow through that old business of who was and who wasn't dreaming, what was and what wasn't though it appeared as if it was.

"Seems to me you've reason for an ugly yourself, instead of sitting there chewing raspberry twist chirping like a cricket." Rose skipped over things she didn't want to continue talking about. "Mary's pretty sick, I hear."

"Has she got it?"

"Got what?"

"New monia?"

"Dr. Davis says next thing to it. He left just a few minutes ago." Rose dabbed her lips with an embroidered white handkerchief, and checked the time on a small gold watch that hung from a rose-shaped brooch pinned to the front of her dress.

"Zowie," I cried. "Next thing to it isn't it."

"Hush, David," she commanded. "You know better than to shout in here. People might be resting."

"Sorry, Rose." I used my finger to free a piece of soft raspberry twist that had become wedged between my upper lip and my gum. "Can I see her, do you think?"

"How do I know? From the sounds over in that corner of the building I think Julia or somebody is with her most of the time. What's one more?"

"I can't talk to her if Julia is there."

"What do you want to say, other than you're sorry?" Rose's black eyebrows arched in a question as her chin pulled down in disapproval. Her long sallow face sought an answer. I didn't have one. I was so glad Mary didn't have new monia that was all I could think about.

"Rose, I didn't do anything wrong, honest. Mary wanted me to pump that water to cool her off."

"Did she want you to pump it into her ear so it filled her head and lungs?"

"No, but I didn't think about that. If she had regular ears it wouldn't have run into her head that way."

"Now we're getting somewhere." She shook her long finger at me. "It's because you didn't think that you're in trouble. If you had thought about the water and Mary having only holes for ears, then you'd have known it might hurt her." Up went her eyebrows again. She nodded, smiling wisely, as if at last she'd solved the riddle.

"Jeez. I can't think of everything, Rose. When I broke that God-damned sugar bowl everybody had such a fit about, Aunt Maude yelled at me to think what I was doing. How am I supposed to always be thinking?" The more I said, the more excited I became, so I didn't notice the look on Rose's face until it was too late.

"David!" Her angry voice stopped me. "You've been with Charley Smith again. If I couldn't smell him, which I can, I could tell by your language." She got up from her chair and strode, not ssh-ssh-sshed, to the sink where she turned on the water, held her finger under the tap, then rubbed it on a cake of Ivory soap until she raised a lather. I knew what she was planning to do. With finger pointing straight out in front of her, she returned to the door, put her hand through the bars, and ordered, "Open your mouth, David."

"Rose," I groaned.

"Your mouth!"

I squeezed my eyes shut but opened my mouth and leaned forward. She thrust her soapy finger in and moved it around, coating my mouth with 99 and $^{44}/_{100}$s percent pure. It made me gag. I couldn't help it.

"I'm going to be sick," I moaned.

"No, you're not. You are going to stop repeating Charley Smith's filth." She wiped her finger on the embroidered white handkerchief.

I swiped the back of my hand across my mouth, but the taste wouldn't go away. Ivory soap, no matter how pure, tastes poisonous in combination with raspberry twist. I had to spit. My first thought was to run to the pump where I could rinse out my mouth, but the pump was right outside Aunt Maude's pantry window, and if she saw me hacking and spitting and carrying on, she'd want to know what was wrong, and if I told her, well I couldn't tell her, so I'd have to lie or be in trouble all over again. The whole thing was making me so mad I wanted to scream as all those thoughts flew through my head, "See, God damn it, thinking before I do something keeps me from doing anything at all!" I could die while I was standing there gagging trying to figure things out.

In desperation I ran to the women's bathroom between the two first-floor wards. There was no time to knock, besides it was a bathroom for lots of people to use at the same time. I barged through the door and to one of the sinks where I spit out as much as I could. I cleared my throat and hacked, then looked in the mirror expecting to see my mouth foaming but it wasn't, so I bent over again and put my lips directly on the faucet, taking big fast gulps to rinse away the taste of the soap.

I heard somebody speaking to me, but in the crunch of a crisis I paid no attention. When I was through spitting, I turned around. Adeline Bullock was standing in the bathtub, rubbing a white towel through her globe of shining black hair. Her wet skin was the color of coffee without cream.

"Were you talking to me, Adeline?"

"I wuz only askin' you, boy, why is you in here? This happens to be a lady's latrine in case yore little pea brain forgot." Adeline talked that way, using words like "latrine" and "little pea brain." She gave her hair a shake, showering water all over the place, then went back to towelling in a slow, lazy motion.

"You ain't s'posed to be crashin' in here when a lady is takin' her bath." She wrapped the towel into a turban and stepped out of the tub, dripping puddles of water onto the linoleum floor.

"I had to spit, Adeline. I said a swear and Rose washed out my mouth with soap."

Before Adeline could ask for details, and Adeline loved details, Julia Gammon walked in, rustling her starched white uniform and shaking her head so her nurse's cap wobbled. She noticed Adeline's puddles.

"Adeline Bullock, I couldn't count the times I've told you to bathe in the upstairs bathroom. Your room is on the second floor, you use the second-floor bathroom. It's as simple as that. This one is for the women on this floor. Now dry yourself, mop up those puddles, then go to your room and get dressed. I'm sick of you traipsing around naked."

"Julia, is Mary going to be all right?" I didn't mean to butt in, but Julia would know.

"I hope so. She's feeling poorly now, thanks to you, but Dr. Davis thinks she'll be . . ." Then I guess she registered where we all were because she began to sputter, "David, what in the world are you? Why are you in here when Adeline is? Adeline cover yourself, and you, young man . . ."

I could tell words were failing her.

"I came in to spit."

She grabbed my overall straps, and half lifting me off the floor, shoved me out the bathroom door back into the sitting room.

" 'Scuse me," Adeline said with exaggerated politeness as she pushed past Julia and me, with the towel turban around her head and rivulets of water running down her sleek back end.

"Adeline, cover yourself," Julia shrieked.

Adeline made no response, except to give her bare butt a shake as she disappeared around the staircase.

Rose laughed out loud, covering her mouth with her hand,

when I told her about Adeline and Julia and me in the bathroom. She said she'd heard Julia shouting but didn't know what it was all about.

I couldn't remember when I'd last heard Rose laugh. She didn't laugh much anyway, but recently she hardly laughed at all. It did wonderful things to her face which couldn't be called pretty. Aunt Maude said Rose was a handsome woman. There's a difference. She had olive skin, inherited, she said, from her Amaral ancestors, of whom she was very proud. Her gray-black hair was parted in the middle and drawn back into a twist. Her mouth was hard, but her eyes were soft.

Rose made all her own clothes. That's what she did before she killed Scheider, her husband, made clothes for people. I guess the money she earned is what supported her and Scheider. Now she only made things for herself, out of what she called "goods" you couldn't get at Harry Woolf's store. About once a year she'd have a conference with Pa Fleming, and he'd order a whole bunch of stuff for her, which she paid for out of an account she said was secret. She didn't have a sewing machine, so it took her a long time to make a dress. Most of the time when we'd be having conversation through the bars, Rose was working on whatever she was making. She spent hours covering little round buttons with the same goods the dress was made from, self-covered buttons she called them.

She liked lots of buttons, and most of her dresses had a row of them down the front, from the high collar under her chin to the bottom down near her ankles. She said when Scheider was alive she put buttons on the back, but when she didn't have anybody to help her with them anymore she redesigned the pattern. Aunt Jessie, who prided herself on how well she dressed, said Rose Scheider was the best-dressed woman in the whole county. That made Rose smile.

Over the years she told me the story of Scheider. He was German and Irish. They met when he was rebuilding a chimney on the house next door to where she lived with her parents. She said her parents thought no man was good enough for their only child, so they never let her walk out with anybody, which is why she was still unmarried when she reached thirty. That part must have bothered her because she talked about it very seriously. Anyway, when the younger Irish bricklayer began making eyes at her, Rose thought it was fine but her parents had a fit, her father especially.

I'm sure Rose didn't tell me everything, because suddenly in the story she and Scheider decided to get married. She knew better than to ask permission, so they ran away, thinking her mother and father would forgive her once it was all done, and, Rose added, once they realized what a fine person Brian Scheider was. When she told me that part she went strange and silent. I had to keep asking her to go on.

"Then what happened, Rose?" Sometimes she'd continue and sometimes she wouldn't, mumbling that we'd had enough "ancient history" for one day.

One time when she was talking about the train they were on the night they got married, she murmured almost to herself, "Out of those work clothes he was pink, freckles all over and pink." She smiled at that. She'd already told me Scheider had red hair.

I'd known for a long time that Scheider drank a lot, because once when I asked Aunt Maude why Rose killed her husband, Aunt Maude just said, "He was a drunkard," as if that was reason enough. It took years for Rose to go into any details with me. She didn't mind in the beginning when he came home slightly drunk, she told me. "A bit of booze loosened his tongue, and relaxed him," which was fine, but it got worse and worse until he was drinking more than he was working, and went mean when she tried to sober him up. He began to beat her. I would have thought being hit hurt the most, but she told me what hurt her worst of all was when he began calling her "the old Dago."

"I had taken his pounding and cleaned up his vomit. I nursed the bruises he brought home from fighting, but I couldn't take his taunting. He knew I was older when he married me. He knew I was Italian, a proud Neapolitan, not something to be spat on." Rose straightened her back and lifted her head high when she came to that part. "Neither of us realized in the beginning I was the more intelligent," she said. "Or maybe it was the booze drowned his wit." Then she'd be silent for a while, thinking I suppose, remembering, because other times she'd told me how funny Scheider was in the beginning, and very affectionate.

"One night," she told me, "there was nothing left." She smiled a twisted smile. "I can still see the surprise on his face when he felt the first bite of the blade. He couldn't believe what was happening because I didn't say anything. I didn't shout or cry, I just stood over him raising the knife and striking again and again. I didn't count the times."

She stopped there. No matter how much I begged her to go on, she'd shake her head. She'd get up from her chair and go stare out the window, ignoring me as if I'd gone away. Then one day when we weren't talking about anything, just sitting there, Rose covering her buttons and me leaning my back against her door, swinging my legs off the stool, she said, "Do you think I might now be adjudged fit to be free in society?"

"I don't know what you mean, Rose."

"When I told them I'd killed Scheider but wouldn't say another word, I never told them as much as I've told you, they found me guilty. The judge decided I was no threat to any other human being but had to be punished, so he sentenced me to be confined in a locked and barred room 'until such time as she shall be adjudged fit to be free in society.' That was twenty years ago last Thursday. The judge is dead. Who is to adjudge me fit or unfit? Nobody said when 'such time' is."

"But your door isn't locked, Rose."

"It's supposed to be."

"But it isn't, so maybe they judge you fit."

"The door isn't locked because they know I have no place to go. It's a game we play. Everybody knows the door isn't locked, but we all pretend it is. You and I know it isn't because we occasionally sneak down to the garden for a bite or two of raw vegetables, and sometimes we don't get caught. Only God knows how many people watch me when I wander out at night for a breath of air in the moonlight. The door is barred yes, David, but locked no, not in many years. Nothing is what it appears to be. It never was after I ran away and married Scheider."

The smile she smiled when she said that to me was very different from the smile she smiled when I told her about Adeline and Julia and me.

When we'd settled down again after laughing about Adeline, Rose suggested, "David, you should do something nice for Mary."

"Such as." A red-hot jawbreaker was overpowering the taste of Ivory soap.

"A pretty bouquet on her bed stand."

"She can't smell flowers, Rose. She can't smell anything, and she can't see much either. It's all a blur, she tells me."

"I imagine strong vibrant colors would make an impact on her."

"Like red, you mean?"

"Yes, red, or, well I can't think of another color, but red would do, I'm sure. There must be some lovely red annuals in the garden now."

"If you say so." I put my bag of candy down on the floor beneath the organ stool next to my mocs, and headed dutifully into the heat.

The cutting garden was a broad strip of flowers along the northern edge of the vegetable garden which covered the entire slope between the back entrance driveway and the orchard at the foot of the hill. It was a garden to behold. Every kind of vegetable grew there in long straight rows kept cultivated and weed free by a small army of gardeners, inmates mostly, who puffed with pride whenever anybody mentioned how magnificent the garden looked. It supplied fresh vegetables for months, from early peas in the spring to parsnips that were best dug after frost. Rituals had grown around exactly when was the best time to harvest just about everything, asparagus for instance. Aunt Maude insisted the steamers be going on the stove before the asparagus was cut so that it was only minutes from the garden to the hot serving platter. Mrs. Davies was convinced it was better cut before the dew was off it first thing in the morning, then placed in buckets of ice water until cooked. They both agreed that the water had to be boiling as sweetcorn was being picked so that from stalk to plate was not more than half an hour. Aunt Maude and Mrs. Davies were fussy cooks with a passion for freshness.

A grape arbor ran down the middle of the vegetable garden, with benches on both sides of the covered path which was wide enough to drive a team of horses and a wagon through. Those benches were popular snoozing places all year round, except in the coldest weather, or when it was pouring rain. Aunt Maude and her crew made gallons of grape jelly and dozens of pies from grapes picked in the arbor.

There was a cross path leading from the middle of the arbor over to the flowers bordering the vegetable garden on the East Road side. I didn't always stick to paths. It was faster to cut across the rows of vegetables, and it did no harm if I was careful not to step on anything. Besides, I liked the feel of warm crumbly earth under my bare feet. The dirt in the vegetable garden was special because it had so much manure and compost worked into it. When it was damp, you'd swear it was velvet you were walking on.

Anybody who wanted to could have a section of the flower garden. Quite a few inmates planted rows of zinnias or marigolds or cosmos, all kinds of things from seed they either sent away for or bought at Harry Woolf's store. Some of the staff had parts of rows too. Aunt Maude loved gladiolas. She read catalogues all winter, and then sent off for something that especially appealed to her.

At first I didn't see a thing in the garden that I thought would get through to Mary. Everything was pink or pale blue, yellow or some other dim color. Then I spotted in Aunt Maude's rows of gladiolas six or seven tall spikes of brilliant red. Why hadn't I noticed them the first thing? They stood out like blood on snow. Mary could see those all right. If I'd had my wits about me, if I had been thinking what I was doing, I would have known they were there because evenings after supper when I didn't ride down to the home place with Uncle Will to feed his horses, I'd help Aunt Maude carry buckets of manure tea from the vat next to the arbor over to where her gladiolas grew. She said it was manure tea that made the stalks reach four feet and sometimes plus. When all the other flowers wilted in August's heat, Aunt Maude's glads stood straight. She took a lot of joshing about manure tea.

Those red gladiolas were exactly what I needed for Mary. Her almost blind eyes couldn't miss them. The next problem was how to pick them. I could never break them off without pulling up the bulbs and I didn't want to do that. I needed a knife to cut through the stalks. Going to either of the kitchens was out because this was just before dinnertime, all the knives would be in use. Then I remembered the knife Rose kept on top of her wardrobe, hidden under a cut-velvet bag. She and I had used the knife lots of times when we sneaked down to the vegetable garden to sample cucumbers or tomatoes.

"Rose, Rose," I cried, rushing back down the hall toward her room. "I've found the perfect flowers for Mary. They are the best red you've ever seen, but I need a knife to cut them. Can I borrow yours?"

"Sssssh," her hushing hiss was fearsome. "What knife? Go away." She withdrew to the darkest corner of her room, standing so deep in the shadows her grayness made it difficult for me to see her.

"You know," I persisted, "your knife, Rose, the one on top of your wardrobe, the one we use when we sneak down to the vegetable garden." I decided she'd gone daft if she couldn't remember that for pete's sake.

"No one knows about that knife," she whispered in a hoarse voice.

"Rose, you know and I know, as you're always saying. It's like the locked door that's unlocked, so can I borrow it please? I'll bring it right back, I promise."

Rose muttered something in Italian that sounded like an angry oath, but she emerged from the corner and reached up to the hidden knife. "You are going to bring us all down with your thoughtlessness," she complained, gingerly passing the knife through the bars, wooden handle first.

"I am thinking, Rose. I'm doing just what you told me to do, thinking what I'm doing while I'm doing it. I could have gone to the kitchen for a knife, but I thought they'd be needing all their knives to get dinner on."

"Don't continue. I believe you." Rose sighed deeply.

While I had seen the knife many times, I had never touched it before that minute. Rose would never let me. It was mean-looking, and heavy. I turned it slowly, examining the thick blackened steel blade with its bright sharp edge. Then lights went on. Could it be? I had to know.

"Rose, is this the knife you used to kill Scheider?"

"Of course not." Her voice was tired. She reached through the bars again, this time to pat my cheek. "Go cut Mary's flowers but don't cut yourself, and don't let anybody see you with that knife." She gave me a gentle push. Her anger had disappeared and the strange way she looked. She was herself again.

Rose talked a lot about self-discipline. I guess getting herself under control after being cross with me is what she meant. She said she needed discipline to keep from going mad. She was by herself most of the time. All of her meals were brought to her room on a tray so she ate alone. I was the only one who ever stopped by her door to talk. The inmates said she was a snob. They said Rose thought she was better than they were. When I told her that's what they were saying, she agreed, "I am." Members of the staff were good to her, but they didn't provide company. Julia or somebody else had to be with her when she went across the sitting room to the bathroom, but whoever went with her didn't talk to her except to comment on the weather, which Rose cared nothing about.

Which doesn't mean Rose was cut off from what was going on at the County Home. Because her room was right in the corner of the main sitting room in the women's building, she could hear every word anybody said in that room without whoever it was realizing. That's how she knew what Dr. Davis had said about Mary. Then, too, I kept her informed as best I could about other things. She said I was better than a local newspaper.

She never talked about being lonely, except sometimes she'd say quietly how much she missed her mother and father. Her parents did not forgive her after she married Scheider, refusing to see her after she ran off with him. I asked her if they came to her trial. She just shook her head. Pa Fleming came to tell her when each of them died. She said she felt closer to them now that they were gone than when they were still alive. Once she said, "I sometimes think they are sitting up there on the ridge under that guardian elm tree, waiting for me." When I told her I didn't think they were, she said she knew better, she was just talking. "You are my confidant and confessor, David. I tell you things I've never told anybody, things I'd never tell a priest."

"I tell you things too, Rose," I said, which was the truth.

"We trust each other," Rose said. "You drink in everything I say to you without judging me. I think I could tell you anything, David, and you'd not feel any different toward me."

"I wouldn't, Rose," I said, wondering what she might tell me.

There wasn't a soul around when I returned to the garden with Rose's knife, not even on the arbor benches. I took a sniff of the gladiolas before I made my first cut. There was no fragrance, but it didn't matter because Mary couldn't smell anything anyway. I bent over and sliced through the thick stalk. Rose's knife was so sharp it was a breeze. "Timber," I cried as the bright red flower crashed to the ground. It was more of a problem knowing what to do with the gladiolas once I'd cut them off. Each one was so tall and heavy I couldn't hold it while I was cutting the next one, so I laid them carefully on the ground between the rows.

When I finished, and what a sight they were piled up like a stack of blazing logs, I gathered them in my arms, but realized I could not carry flowers and knife too, nor could I put the knife in my pocket because it would slice right through and probably take off a toe when it fell down my leg. Frustrated, I laid the flowers down again and ran to return Rose's knife. "It worked just fine," I cried. "Cut 'em off easy as nothing." I handed the knife to her through the bars.

"Why don't you ring the chapel bell, David, and make a public announcement when everybody comes running?" Her voice had an unpleasant edge.

"What?"

"Never mind." She took the knife and hid it in the folds of her dress. "Do you have something to put the flowers in? You can't just lay them across Mary's bed, you know. They'll need water."

"Yipes. I never thought of that."

"If those gladiolas are as tall and heavy as I think they are, it will have to be something substantial or else they'll tip over."

"How about that big pottery pitcher Mrs. Davies sometimes uses for cider?" I asked. "It's on a sideboard in the women's dining room."

"How would I know about any such pitcher?" she grumped.

"But if it's a heavy one, give it a try. Better get your pitcher ready before you bring in the flowers, hadn't you? I mean, wouldn't that be easier?"

"I suppose so. Jeez, Rose, this is turning into an all-day event." I didn't have the cussed flowers out of the garden yet, and already I was exhausted.

She gave me a warning look as if I'd said a swear again. "Don't complain to me, David. You pumped the water in Mary's ear."

I ground my teeth and trudged off to the women's dining room. There was the pitcher sitting right where it always sat unless Mrs. Davies was using it for cider. Blind Theresa was going from place to place, feeling to make sure everybody had a full setting. She was born blind, but did a lot of things to help, as well as playing the pump organ for hymn singing, not very well but loud.

"Hi, Theresa," I said, going past her to get the pitcher off the sideboard.

"Hello, David. How are you today?"

"Fine, thank you, and you?"

"Very well."

As I was lugging the pitcher toward the door I got a whiff of roast beef from the kitchen arcade. "Dinner smells good," I said.

"It sure does, and I'm hungry, but then I'm always hungry." She laughed a girlish laugh. I don't know how old Theresa was, but she was far from being a girl, yet because of that laugh and her being short and thin everybody always referred to her as a girl rather than a woman, and she was always called Blind Theresa, the same as Blind Dan was always called Blind Dan. But nobody ever called Alma Sawyer Crippled Alma, or Arthritic Alma. I don't know why.

The pitcher was much heavier than I thought it would be. There was no way I could fill it with water and then carry it, so I took it into Mary's room first and put it on her nightstand empty. She was snorting and fapping away but didn't look too bad to me, not much different from the way she always looked.

"Are you asleep, Mary?" I whispered. I guess she was because she didn't answer.

No one else was in the room. Her three roommates must have been taking strolls before lunch because they weren't in the sitting room either.

I had to make a lot of trips with Mary's drinking water carafe between the sink in the corner of her room and the nightstand before I had the damn pitcher filled. Then I began the trips to the garden to bring in the gladiolas. By the time I was ready to put them in the pitcher, the only thing I wanted to do was crawl up on one of the beds and take a nap. But I wasn't anywhere near through yet because the top of the pitcher was so high I couldn't reach it when I grabbed a gladiola stalk with both hands to put it in, which meant I had to pull over a chair, pick up a stalk, climb up on the chair, stick the stalk in the pitcher, get down, pick up another stalk, climb back upon the chair, and on and on. It was the dumbest piece of work I'd ever had to do.

Sweat was soaking my overalls again, which made me mad because I'd felt fairly cool after the ride in Charley's jitney. Worse, when I put the sixth stalk into the pitcher, water overflowed through the spout. I'd filled the pitcher too full. Just when I thought the end was in sight I have another damn crisis. It wasn't a big overflow, not one that anybody'd notice, I decided, so I went through the process for the seventh and last time, and as I stuck in that final gladiola water rushed over the top of the pitcher, flooding Mary's nightstand, running from there onto the edge of her bed.

"Good God Almighty!" I swore a Charley Smith oath under my breath, one I used only in last-straw emergencies. I grabbed the linen towel off the bar on Mary's nightstand and mopped up the best I could. There was nothing I could do about the large wet place on Mary's bed, not that she seemed to notice. I'd better get out of there. If Julia caught me making a mess, she'd tell Aunt Maude and I'd get yelled at.

I hung the towel back on its rod, put the chair back where it belonged, patted the snoring bulge, whispered, "Hope you like the flowers, Mary. I'm sorry I made you sick," and scooted out of the ward and across the sitting room to Rose's door, where I had to eat two Tootsie rolls and suck on another jawbreaker to regain my strength.

The rest of the day was uneventful. I actually took a nap in the afternoon as I was supposed to, which made Aunt Maude look at me as if I were sick or something.

There was corn on the cob for supper that night, my absolutely favorite food at the moment. I was on my third butter-slathered ear, biting alternate clumps of kernels out of every other row which gives the cob a checkerboard effect, when I noticed Uncle Will watching me. He winked, but if Aunt Maude caught me playing with my food as she called it I'd be in trouble, so I began to clean up the checkerboard and listen once again to table conversation.

"What are we entering in the County Fair this year?" Pa Fleming asked, using a steak knife to slice kernels off a cob onto his plate. You can always tell who has false teeth, or no teeth at all, if they have to shave the kernels off the cob.

"We're going to enter Chub in the yearling class," Hank was the first to reply. Hank was in charge of horses on the farm, and very proud of them. Chub was a Belgian colt, strawberry color with a blond mane and tail. "Begin to stir up some interest in him for the future."

I knew what he meant. He meant interest in Chub as a stud. Everybody else knew what he meant too I suppose, but you couldn't talk about studs or stallions or bulls at the table. Even though it was a farm, the business of breeding was not considered polite conversation. The way men talked in the barn and at the table was two totally different languages.

"We've got some early Golden Sweet apples I think look good enough to show," Warren added, "and maybe some of that new strain of carrots. The beets are extra nice this year too." Warren supervised the orchards and vegetable garden.

"How about you, Maude?" Pa Fleming gave his clipped white mustache a swipe with a napkin. "An angel food cake again this year?" Bright blue eyes sparked from behind his glasses.

"No." Aunt Maude looked almost shy when she answered, though I couldn't imagine her being shy about anything. Her angel food cakes had won blue ribbons for centuries, what was there to be shy about?

"She's decided to give somebody else a chance this year." Uncle Will radiated love at her from across the table.

"I'm going to enter some of my gladiolas for the first time." Aunt Maude recaptured the conversation. "I have never had better luck with them than I've had this season. Those bulbs I sent out to Michigan for were well worth the price."

"Nothing is worth what you paid for those bulbs, Maude," Uncle Deane teased, but for a change he didn't get a rise out of his older sister.

"Well, these were worth it, especially the Tahiti Sunset. I

don't know how many of you have noticed them, but you should go down and take a look. They are the most overpowering red and perfectly shaped on stalks at least four, almost five feet tall." She was demonstrating with her hands how tall the stalks were.

I put my ravaged ear of corn down on my plate. There was loud agreement at the table that those red gladiolas were the most beautiful any of them had ever seen.

"I have seven stalks," Aunt Maude continued, "that I'm going to cut at the very last minute, then plunge in buckets of ice water and rush down to Floral Hall. If I don't win a first prize I'll die of disappointment."

Hattie Berkemeyer had won the cut flower competition year after year for her bronze dahlias, but nobody at the table doubted that Maude's glads would end Hattie's streak of blue ribbons.

I heard what was being said, but it sounded as if they were all down a well, or as if I was. I, or they, were far far away. Every kernel of corn I'd eaten began to churn in my stomach, threatening to erupt like a volcano. "What have I done?" I groaned to myself. Afraid I might have said it aloud, I clapped both hands over my mouth. My eyes were bulging. My stomach was grumbling like a threshing machine. My ears rang, my toes tingled, my temperature was rising.

"David, are you all right?" Aunt Maude had noticed. "You look as if you're about to be sick."

I shook my head sideways no in answer to the question, and nodded up and down, agreeing I was about to be sick.

"Well, for pity's sake, don't sit there, leave the table." She pushed her chair back, then pulled me away from the cloth. Everything was moving in slow motion. Voices at the table sounded the way Roy's Victrola sounded when it needed winding. "Come along now."

With her leading me we retreated through the pantry. "Do you want to go into the bathroom?" she asked, half supporting me as we went up the stairs. "Or will you feel better if you just lie down?" One arm was around me while her other hand felt my brow. "You are very hot."

I nodded, the motion of my head making me feel more seasick. After she had sponged me off with tepid water and helped me into fresh pajamas, Aunt Maude tucked me in bed. I hated being tucked in, but said nothing, assuring her I would be okay.

"You lie quietly, sweetheart, and I'll be up shortly." She brushed the hair back from my forehead, then brought a chair over next to the bed and took a chamber pot out of the washstand, placing it on the chair. "If you feel sick, throw up in the thunder mug. Don't try to get to the bathroom. Ring your bell if you need me."

I had a silver button bell exactly like the one next to Ma Fleming's place at meals. Neither of us ever used them. Aunt Maude gave me another kiss, murmuring as she bent over me, "I don't like to have my darling boy sick."

When I heard her white rubber-soled shoes going down the stairs, my tears started. They ran down each side of my face onto my pillow. No matter how much faith I had in God, He wasn't about to put those red gladiolas back on their stalks in the garden. If I thought there was a chance, I'd get out of bed and down on my knees. Just in case, that's exactly what I did.

"Please, God, I know I've asked you to do some dumb things, and most of the time you don't, but this time—because it isn't for me, it's for Aunt Maude—is there any way we could go back and undo what I've done? If you want me to, I'll march into that dining room right this minute, in my pajamas, and tell everybody I cut the gladiolas, those Tahiti whatevers. I'm willing to take the blame because I did it even though I didn't know I was doing anything wrong."

There was no response. The prayer wasn't going anywhere. I got up and back into bed.

What could I do? How was I supposed to know those particular flowers were special? Aunt Maude was always giving people bouquets. She never said anything about entering gladiolas in the County Fair. I had watched her watering them every night, but she watered all her flowers every night, not just those reds. She'd not said a word to me about not picking them, and she was always telling me what not to do.

"God," I whispered, "why is it that everything I do is wrong? Is there something serious the matter with me?"

Again, God didn't reply.

Sometimes I asked God things and then with my eyes closed opened a Bible and stuck my finger on a page. Somebody told me God would answer through whatever verse my finger pointed to. The results were generally murky. Besides, there was no verse in the Bible to cover the crisis of the moment. I decided to skip that routine.

The problem wasn't that I feared being skinned alive when Aunt Maude found out. I'd been skinned so many times I was immune to it. It was that I truly hated to hurt her. I wouldn't keep her from winning that prize for anything. The thought crossed my mind that if I could get over to Hattie Berkemeyer's I might pick all her dahlias, but how would I get over there, and if I did get over there what difference would it make? Aunt Maude still wouldn't have her Tahiti Sunsets to enter, and she had said it was the reds that would win for her. She also said she was going to cut them at the very last minute and then plunge them in ice water before rushing off to the fairgrounds. If she hadn't said that I might lie, Charley Smith did it all the time, and say I'd cut them early to save her the effort.

In the struggle to think of some solution I must have exhausted myself, because I dozed off even though it was still light outside. I didn't hear another thing until I was awakened by sobs coming from Aunt Maude's bedroom. "There, there, Maudie, you'll make yourself sick if you carry on this way," Uncle Will was saying.

"But, Will, who would be so mean? Who would do a thing like that, steal my Tahiti Sunsets as if they were weeds along the road. They never touched one of the others, and everybody knew those reds were my entry for the Fair."

"Nobody knew until dinnertime tonight, when you told them," Uncle Will was trying to soothe her.

"They all teased me about how much I'd spent on bulbs from Michigan," Aunt Maude wasn't listening. "Nobody expected I'd raise anything as nice as I did." Her sobs grew louder and more wrenching. She was unaware of my barefoot approach, until I was standing right in front of her, tears streaming down my face. "Oh, my darling brown-eyed boy." She reached up and drew me next to where she was sitting on the bed. "Don't be frightened. Aunt Maude is going to be all right."

She sniffed and looked up at Uncle Will. "He hates to see me cry. There, there." She wrapped her arms around my body, which by that time was shaking with breath-holding sobs. "It isn't that bad, sweetheart. It could be so much worse. Something might have happened to you."

Her concern for me, her loving attempts to comfort me made me feel more horrid than I had felt before. I wanted to shout my sin aloud, throw myself out the window, plunge Rose's knife into my chest—anything to rid myself of guilt.

She straightened me up and put me far enough away from her so she could wipe my eyes with her handkerchief. "If anything should happen to you, I'd die. It was only a few flowers I lost, that's all. What are a few flowers, hmmm?" She began to smile, her beautiful eyes even brighter than usual because of the tears in them. "We'll just hope that whoever took them is enjoying them as much as I did." That made her mouth pucker and the tears start again, but she was brave.

"Now you go back to bed, David. I'm sorry I disturbed you. Give us a kiss. That's a good boy. I'll be in shortly to tuck you in." She gave my rump a parting pat.

How could she not know I did it? I decided it would be best, everything considered and thought about, if she never found out—now that she seemed to be over the worst of it.

Later that night, after I'd been tucked in again and kissed goodnight, not once but twice, and after I was sure everybody else in the suite was asleep because I could hear their snores, I crept out of bed and crawled through my bedroom window onto the porch roof, moving very slowly so as to make no noise on the tin. I crossed to Roy's living-room window and went in, hurrying from there down the stairs to the men's washroom, through the men's dining room, the lower kitchen, and the arcade into the women's building.

I was lucky. Nobody heard me. In Mary's room I lifted a chair and carried it to the bedstand. I carefully removed each of the seven gladiola stalks from the pitcher, then fled, not bothering to put the chair back where I found it, nor return the heavy pitcher to the women's dining room. Tiptoeing as best I could with a heavy load I retraced my steps through the arcade and lower kitchen, then went out the door onto the porch, and from there down the hatchway into the furnace room. It was black as a pocket, without even a sliver of light from Charley Smith's hideaway which was in the corner around behind the furnaces. I knew the territory well, so I managed in the blackness to open one of the furnace doors, and then with a mighty heave threw the flowers deep inside. The furnace door made a clunk sound when I closed it, but I couldn't help that.

It didn't occur to me that I was leaving a trail of black footprints until I looked back across the silver tin roof when I crawled in my bedroom window. "God damn," I muttered. There was nothing I could do about it, except hope for rain. I did have sense enough to wipe my feet off before getting into bed. Aunt Maude would certainly suspect something if the sheets were covered with coal dust. She'd tell me they'd never come clean in the laundry, and that would be the least of her grief.

Just when I was about to drop off to sleep, hoping I'd put the whole matter behind me, a terrible thought came into my mind. Lots of people must have seen the red gladiolas on Mary's table. They probably wondered how they got there, then when they heard the story about Aunt Maude's Tahiti Sunsets, they'd wonder what happened to them, put two and two together and come up with me. Surely Julia Gammon would have noticed. She noticed everything having to do with her patients. But Julia wasn't at the supper table tonight when Aunt Maude told us about her plans. Maybe, if I was lucky, Julia would never ever hear about the tragedy, and would only be confused by the pitcher of water and the chair not where it belonged.

"God," I prayed. "I've cleaned up most of this mess by myself. Would you please take care of the loose ends? Thank you."

CHAPTER THREE

deline Bullock didn't like clothes. She wouldn't wear any at all at any time if she could get away with it, but she didn't have her way. Julia and others constantly badgered her about covering herself. Her mother had long since given up, shaking her wizened gray head as she rocked by her window on the second floor, muttering about Adeline's assorted "foolishments." While she was grumbling, Mrs. Bullock also had something to say about Johnny, her son, who joined his mother and sister at the County Home every winter, but the rest of the year was off working at whatever he could find to do. "They's times he don't shed enough light to see by." She smiled then and scrunched up both eyes at me. "But he mainly keeps out of trouble. He be comin' to see me soon."

"Not 'til it's cold, Mama," Adeline said, pulling at the edge of her skirt, trying to find a loose thread she could pull to start unraveling.

"Leave that dress be," Mrs. Bullock cried. "You gonna put me in my grave sooner'n I'm ready."

"You been sayin' that, Mama, since I was smaller than David, yet you go on rockin' in that chair year after year."

"You want me to die, Adeline?" Mrs. Bullock opened her eyes wide and stared at her daughter.

"Not 'til you ready, Mama, jus don't go on about me puttin' you in the ground all the time. You must be least ninety now, so I guess I haven't been all that threatenin' to your health." Adeline flipped her skirt back down around her ankles.

"Oh, I'se more'n ninety by a lot."

"How old are you, Mrs. Bullock?" I was purposely staying out of Aunt Maude's sight as much as possible. She seemed to have gotten over the disappearance of her Tahiti Sunsets, but she was not in a good mood. I also didn't want to hang around the first floor of the women's building too much, even though I had things to tell Rose, because Julia was in and out of Mary's room and she might ask me questions I didn't want to answer. So I spent some time talking to Adeline and Mrs. Bullock. I was running out of things to say.

"Hard to say, child." She scrunched up her eyes as if she was trying to remember. "I was a slave baby when President Abraham Lincoln freed my people. That was a long time ago." She closed her eyes and rocked, humming a lullaby.

After a few minutes she stopped rocking and opened her eyes. "How old you gonna be, Adeline?" she asked.

Adeline shrugged. I guess Mrs. Bullock wasn't expecting an answer because she barely paused before continuing. "The Lord gave me Johnny and then Adeline after I was already a grandma. They's uncle and aunt 'fore they was born." She chuckled at that, the laugh deepening her cocoa-colored wrinkles.

She rocked and hummed again, then opened her eyes to look straight down at me sitting on the floor leaning against Adeline's bed. "I'se old enough to be surprised when I wake up in the mornin', and thankful each night when I goes to bed for the generous Jesus who give me one more day." Mrs. Bullock smiled and went back to rocking and humming.

"You want to go for a walk, Adeline? We could go down to the pump-house pond and stick our feet in the water." I realized after I said it Mrs. Bullock might object, but she didn't pay any attention.

"Might's well do that as sit here and stifle," Adeline yawned.

We went and had been sitting on an overhanging branch with our feet dangling for about an hour, sticking our toes in the water, then pulling them out, bored with what we were doing and not coming up with much conversation, when Adeline turned around the other way and jumped off the branch.

"C'mon, boy, I'se 'bout to teach you a fertility dance." She started walking away into the pine grove.

"What's a fertility dance?" I asked, jumping down to follow her.

"You's too young to know."

"Why are you teaching it to me, then?"

"I didn't say you's too young to know how, jes too young to know why."

Adeline and I had been friends for years but she said things to make me mad lots of times, like always telling me I was too young.

The ground in the pine grove was covered with years of sweet-smelling needles that were spongy when you walked on them. Spotted around were patches of green vines with red and white berries. Some inmates collected the vines late in the fall and made wreaths, combining them with other greens and cones and things. Mr. Fleming took the wreaths to a flower shop in town that sold them so the inmates would have pocket money.

We stopped when we got to an opening where the sun streamed in.

"Take off your clothes," Adeline ordered, pulling her dress over her head. She didn't have anything on underneath and her skin glistened. Today it was the same shade as the walnut stain Roy was using on a stool he'd repaired. I wished my skin was as beautiful as Adeline's instead of mealy bug color.

I undid my bib overalls and stepped out of them. "My underpants too?" Just in case Aunt Maude checked me out at breakfast, I'd put them on that morning. Thinking of everything to keep from getting into trouble could be boring.

"You can't dance a fertility dance in underpants, stupid."

That's the sort of thing she said that made me mad, but I didn't blow up, just dropped my underpants and kicked them onto my overalls.

Adeline planted her feet flat and far apart, bobbing her head to tell me to do the same. "Now follow me," she said, "I'll go slow 'til you know what to do." She stretched her arms out as far as they'd reach to the left. "Stretch, boy." I stretched. Then she clapped her hands twice, and I clapped my hands twice, though it wasn't easy stretching and clapping at the same time.

"C'mon, chile, not baby pattycakes. Clap those hands."

I put my hands back down at my sides, and stomped my feet next to each other. "Adeline, I'm not going to do this silly dance one more minute if you call me a baby. I am not a baby."

She grinned, then grabbed me and pulled me to her for a bear hug. "Course you's no baby. You think I be teachin' babies fertility dances?"

I shook my head but was still mad.

"Now," she pushed me away. "Git those feet where they belong, and stretch way out to the left, and clap."

I clapped as loud as I could. She rewarded me with a big smile. Then I followed her as she stretched her arms way out to the right and clapped twice, then both arms as far as possible in back and that time clapped three times.

"That's hard to do, Adeline," I complained.

"Nothing's easy, boy. It's two to the left, two to the right, and three to the back. C'mon now, and listen to the beat. It ain't gonna work ef it don't have beat."

"Adeline, are you making this up?"

"Close your mouth and do as I tell you."

We stretched and clapped and stretched and clapped over and over until I must have been doing something right because Adeline said I had the beat. She gave me another hug.

"That's the easy part. Now we does the feet." She really was patient with me as we stomped our right feet twice while stretching our arms and clapping to the left, then reversed and stomped left feet and stretched to the right. We stomped in place when we reached backwards and clapped. After I'd done it right a couple of times, she speeded us up, and I began to giggle. She gave me a cross look and said in a disgusted tone, "I hope you's up to learnin' what comes next."

"You do think I'm dumb, don't you?" She was making me mad again. "You keep saying I'm too young or too stupid or something. I don't know why you bother with me at all." I was trying to remember everything she told me to do, and I thought I was doing it pretty well for the first try.

"Stop poutin'," was all she said before telling me she would drum so we could keep time. "We begin on the third boom. Ready?"

"Ready," I said, but I wasn't. I was set on the mark but I didn't go, when she said "Boom" the third time, and she started clapping left and stomping right. What stopped me was the sound of Adeline's voice, which was ordinarily little and high-pitched. I'd never heard it as low or loud as when she boom, boom, boomed.

"Wake up, stupid," she shouted giving me a poke in the ribs, beginning again, "Boom, boom, boom."

On the third boom I almost fell over in my hurry to clap and stomp as she'd taught me, but I didn't and we kept going. By the time we'd done it half a dozen times I was stomping so hard the ground echoed under my feet. I liked that. Even when Adeline changed the time between booms, so it wasn't always boom boom boom, but sometimes boom boom, boom boom, and sometimes boom boom, boom boom boom, and other ways like that, I didn't get mixed up.

"Hallelujah, now we is gettin' somewhere," she shouted with a grin, moving us on to the next part, which was whirling around three times after doing the back clap and triple stomp in place. The first time I tried it I lost my balance and did fall down which made me laugh so hard I couldn't get up.

Adeline stood over me looking down as if I'd committed a crime. "I don't s'pose a white child can learn this dance. Maybe we best give up."

"Not now, Adeline, it's just getting fun."

We did the new part okay, and then she added hip jerks from side to side for front and back clapping and as hard as we could hip jerks forward and backward for an over the head clapping routine, all the while boom, boom, booming. I was glad that Roy had a long time ago taught me to rub my stomach and pat my head at the same time, or I'd never have been

able to do all the crazy things Adeline said were part of a fertility dance.

"Boom, boom boom, boom, boom boom boom," Adeline's voice throbbed low. "You runnin' sweat yet?" she yelled without letting up her stomping and thrusts and twirls. Sweat was pouring down her body.

"I get soaked, but I don't run sweat," I puffed, not missing a boom.

"You will," she said, speeding up the dance.

"How long before I pour sweat like you?" I shouted, pounding my feet to the ground.

"You ain't gonna make it today, boy. How old is you now?"

"Eight and a half, almost nine."

"Tha's what I thought. You ain't old enough to have a grown-up runnin' sweat yet."

That stopped me cold. "Damn it, Adeline, there you go, telling me I'm not old enough again. You keep this up and we won't be friends anymore, ever." I stood stock still with my hands on my slippery hips. They felt pretty sweaty to me.

"Don't get vexed, chile, you plenty old enough to be Adeline's friend," she shouted, grinning broadly as she kept on dancing.

"Can we stop now?" I asked. "I'm tired and hot." It wasn't just that. As I watched Adeline dancing all by herself I was sure I'd never be able to do it as fast as she was going, nor look the way she did. Even when I was doing it right and having fun, I felt kind of stupid, but Adeline was like some perfect thing out of a picture book, twisting and turning in the sunlight.

"Ha," she cackled. "Now I knows you is too young if you is tired. Fertility dancin' don't end with tired."

"That's it. That's it," I shrieked, swinging out and giving her flying butt a smack so hard it made my hand sting.

Adeline stopped and looked at me as if she didn't know who I was or why I was there. I wondered if she was going to give me a smack back, but instead she dropped down on her knees and wrapped her arms around me, crooning, "Don't mind Adeline, sweet baby. I gets carried away by the drums." She rocked me against her damp breasts that weren't standing out straight now as they had been when she was dancing, but hung on her front like a pair of balloons that had lost their air.

"You'se my best friend, Davy Boy, my only friend to tell the truth. Adeline wouldn't do nothin' to hurt you." She held me at arm's length looking straight into my eyes. "You know that, don't you?"

"You're my friend too, Adeline," I said, "but not my only friend."

She cackled and pulled me back against her which felt good because I was beginning to be cold. "I know that, child. You is everybody's friend."

We stayed like that for a while, clinging together and rocking on the bed of pine needles. Adeline sang one of her mother's songs, so quiet and gentle I almost fell asleep, and I think she did too because her cheek was resting heavy on my head, but then we heard the noon dinner bell and we bolted, getting into our clothes as fast as we could. It was a snap for Adeline because all she had to do was drop a dress over her head.

"Lord love us," Adeline snickered. "We is in big trouble again. Where we bin when they ask?"

"Looking for berries," I puffed pulling up my bib straps.

"It's too late for berries," Adeline snorted. "I'd hate to count on you for lies."

"Charley Smith would think of something better. He's a great liar," I groaned. "Come on, Adeline, run."

We raced through the woods and to our separate dining rooms. When I got to mine, Aunt Maude twisted my ear and made me go into the washroom to scrub my face and hands. Then I had to go upstairs and put something on my feet before I could come to the table. I was afraid everything would be gone by the time I got there, but it wasn't.

Even though Aunt Maude would not enter anything in the County Fair, no matter how much everybody begged her to do one more angel food cake, there was never any question about whether or not we'd go to it. You'd have to be dead not to go to the County Fair, the biggest event of the year. Because Laura and Jap Dailey were celebrating their fortieth wedding anniversary toward the end of Fair week and Aunt Maude and Uncle Will planned to take a couple of days to spend with them, we decided to go to the Fair on Tuesday. I would have gone on Monday too if I'd had a chance, but that wasn't how it worked. Pa Fleming and several members of the staff who had cars took loads of inmates in on Monday, but Aunt Maude said I couldn't go without her. Monday night when Roy told me about the exhibits and the sideshows and best of all the food, I hardly slept a wink waiting for the next morning.

We left right after breakfast. The temperature had dropped some, which was a blessing, Aunt Maude said. She announced she wouldn't go near Floral Hall, but planned to spend the entire day in Grange Hall selling chances on a quilt the Baptist Ladies Aid Society had made to raise money. Uncle Will would spend most of his time on the fairgrounds looking over the animals on exhibit and the horses that were there to be raced.

He regretted there wasn't a horse show at the County Fair anymore, because the horses he raised at the home farm were Thoroughbred hunters and jumpers, not racers. Uncle Edwin had a couple of racehorses, however, so everybody in the family would be hanging on the rail or in the grandstand when they raced.

Grandpa and Grandma would be there, too. Gramps went to the Fair every day it was open, Monday through Saturday. He had retired from farming, so didn't exhibit any longer, but he sometimes judged, and he said it took him at least a week to talk to all his old friends. Grandma's legs bothered her, so she didn't walk around very much, preferring to sit in one of the Grange booths where she could be of some use and still see people she wanted to see. I sometimes thought the chief purpose of the Fair was talk; "visiting," they called it.

There was such a line at the front gate waiting to get in that Uncle Will drove us around back to park. I could hear music from the merry-go-round and smell all kinds of good food smells. I thought we'd never get onto the grounds. As soon as we did, Aunt Maude and I headed straight for Grange Hall where we were to meet Grandma. I could smell pine trees before we got inside. Every grange in the county had an exhibit, and they all used pine trees as a backdrop, no matter what the exhibit was supposed to be. Grandma was halfway down in a hospitality booth where they gave out lemonade and cookies to grangers on duty in their exhibit booths. She was surrounded by tables, at each of which sat a woman selling chances on something. Charley Smith said buying those chances was the same as gambling, but he never said that in front of Aunt Maude who was death on gambling—she didn't even approve of rummy—but she was always selling chances on something to raise money for a good purpose.

Grandma had on her light brown leghorn hat, its high crown decorated with dark brown velvet flowers. She smiled a big smile when she saw us coming, her eyes that were a lot like Aunt Maude's sparkling behind her round, butterscotch-rimmed glasses. "How's my big boy?" she asked as she hugged me.

"Fine."

"Your grandfather has been here looking for you half a dozen times. He said you are to meet him in the poultry barn the minute you arrive." Grandma had the softest face. It was covered with thousands of tiny wrinkles that felt like warm goose down when you rubbed your cheek against hers.

"Can I go now?" I asked Aunt Maude.

"May I?" Aunt Maude corrected.

"May I?"

"Are you sure Pa is in the poultry barn?" She asked Grandma, bending over to kiss her.

"Tuesday is poultry barn day. He'll be there."

I raced off to find Gramps, trying not to be tempted along the way by the most amazing things. People who had invented things came to the Fair to show them off, so you saw things there nobody had ever seen before, or so they all said, though I remembered the woman who made roses out of radishes from the year before. Uncle Will had given me a dollar, so I did make one detour to the Vernor's ginger-ale booth for a fast glass of the best ginger ale ever, straight from a barrel. The men in the booth wore pointed green elf hats. I could have drunk a second glass, but I had to save money for waffles and other things.

In the middle of the poultry barn was a big snow fence enclosure around a pond, with dozens of ducks and geese in it, each bird with a tag on its foot that some of them pecked at trying to get off. All around the sides of the barn were cages that went up higher than my head and in these cages were chickens of all kinds, hundreds of chickens. They must have been excited to be at the Fair because roosters crowed constantly.

I was standing looking at the biggest Buff Orpington rooster I'd ever seen when somebody put his hands over my ears, shaking my head from side to side. I knew it was Gramps. He always did that. He called it "boxing" my ears. Before he took them away so I could turn around, he gave me a loud smacking kiss on top of my head. I could feel his walrus mustache brushing against my hair. When he let go I swung around and hugged him as tight as I could around his middle, pressing my face into the leather vest he wore, feeling the watch chain that draped across his stomach.

"Well, if it isn't my brown-eyed boy!" he said, trying to act surprised. "Where did you come from? I never expected to find you here."

"Gramps," I said, knowing he was only fooling.

"What do you think of that Orpington rooster, David? Isn't he a beaut? Belongs to Gus Heidenreich. Won a first and deserved it."

"You ever have Orpingtons, Gramps?" I asked.

"Oh yes," Gramps nodded. "I guess I've tried all the breeds at one time or another. I always like best the breed I have at the moment, but at the same time it would be nice to have something else."

"You like the Favorels you've got now?"

"Favorels are a very pretty bird, and they've been good to me, but I'm thinking maybe I'll buy some Wyandotte pullets I saw yesterday. Don't tell our grandma. She doesn't suspect yet." He laughed and I laughed too. We both understood that while Grandma didn't know what kind of new chickens he was buying, she knew he was buying something.

It took a terrible long time to move around the poultry barn because every couple of feet Gramps stopped to talk to somebody. I got restless and wished he'd speed it up. He was talking to Leander Gay when I urged him to hurry.

"Leander, you know my grandson David? Rea's boy." Gramps tapped my shoulder to let me know I should shake hands with Mr. Gay.

"Of course I know David," he drawled, "though I might not have recognized him. He's growing into a young man so fast." Leander Gay was skinny and appeared about a mile high to me. He wasn't anywhere near as tall as Roy, but Roy was big all over so you didn't notice. At least I didn't.

"What do you think of those ducklings, David?" Mr. Gay pointed to a little low fenced-in place at the end of a bank of cages.

"Ducklings at this time of year, Leander?" Gramps asked, moving alongside me to peer in. I was down on my knees reaching in to pat one of the scurrying bits of fluff.

"Well, now, I'll tell ya." Leander began a long explanation about how this ignorant Muscovy couldn't tell one season from another so one day a week ago came waddling out of the bushes followed by fourteen ducklings.

"They're awful cute," I said. They didn't seem to be afraid at all, not only letting me touch them but rushing up to my hand to see if I was something good to eat. They nibbled at my fingers but didn't hurt. Mother duck paid no attention at all, just kept on preening her glistening feathers. I wondered if Aunt Maude would let me have one, and if she would, which one I'd choose. It would be a hard choice because all of them were so friendly. Maybe I could buy one, I thought, with what I had left of my dollar.

"What are you going to do with these ducks, Mr. Gay?" I asked.

"Haven't quite made up my mind," he said, rubbing his chin and lifting his straw hat off to scratch his head.

"Would you consider selling one?" I asked so quietly I wasn't sure anybody heard.

"No I wouldn't," he said, so he had heard. "It wouldn't be right to sell one. The poor little critter would die of loneliness. No, I'd not sell one, two maybe or three or the batch, but not one."

"Oh," I said.

"On the other hand I'm not sure I want to sell them. I'm not really in the duck business. I only keep ducks to make me laugh now and again, Mrs. Gay likes to make cakes from duck eggs. No, I don't think I'd sell them."

"Oh," I said again.

"But then I might give them away—not one, probably not two, but three minimum. Yes, I think that's what I'd do, give them away in threes if somebody didn't want the whole kit and caboodle." He lifted his straw hat off and on again so he could give his head another scratch.

I stood up and looked at Gramps, thinking as hard as I could, hoping the message was getting through to him so I wouldn't have to say anything aloud. He looked back at me and rubbed his chin the way Leander Gay had a minute ago. Both of them wore clean, go-to-the-fair bib overalls and dark blue denim shirts.

"What do you think?" I said.

"I think your Aunt Maude would have a fit."

I knew he was right. I knew Aunt Maude wouldn't let me have them, not because she was mean, but "Where will you keep them?" she'd ask. When I tried to catch a kitten in the barn and got badly scratched for my efforts, she told me when she was painting my hands with iodine that it just wasn't possible to have pets at the County Home. It didn't matter that Aunt Latzy had her white rat and Chet Foster his little sheepdog.

"Well, now, that's not all that unusual, is it?" Leander Gay was asking.

"What?" Gramps looked at him.

"For Maude to have a fit. However, I've known her since she was smaller than David here, and I can't remember she ever did anybody any damage." He reached down and picked up one of the ducklings, which settled into his palm as if it were a nest.

"From what I hear, Tine," Mr. Gay went on, "Maude really dotes on this boy. If he wants three of these ducks and promises to take care of them so's nothing bad will happen, I bet you she'd let him take them home. What do you think?"

"I'm not going home, Mr. Gay," I interrupted. "At least not today. Aunt Maude and Uncle Will are going away for a couple of days, so I'll be staying with Aunt Jessie."

"That does make a difference. If your Aunt Jessie saw these baby ducks she'd take the whole mess." Mr. Gay's laugh was a loud barking guffaw.

"I tell you what, Leander," Gramps said, "you're probably right about Maude, but because David isn't going back to the County Home tonight, why don't you let me speak to her and to Jessie to see what we can work out? It's mighty generous of you to offer these ducklings to David."

"Oh Gramps, thank you." I bounced up and down beside him.

Leander Gay said he thought that a splendid idea, and promised me, even though I didn't ask, he wouldn't give any of them away until I had a chance to come back and pick out the three I wanted.

"Do you think she'd let me have all of them?" I asked Gramps.

"Don't push your luck, boy. I think three is a nice number to have." Gramps shook Mr. Gay's hand, and prodded me to do the same, then suggested it was time we high-tailed it off to Grange Hall to meet Grandma and Aunt Maude and Uncle Will for a picnic lunch. "We'll ask her when her mouth is full," Gramps said with a wink, "then before she can say no she'll have a second or two to think it over. Maude never talks with food in her mouth, and she always comes through in the end."

And that's exactly what we did, and she did. Gramps, being a saint, said he'd take the ducklings home with him, and then we could pick them up after Aunt Maude and Uncle Will got back from Laura and Jap Dailey's. That way we wouldn't have to involve Aunt Jessie and Uncle Wallace. Then, too, we'd have to figure out a place to keep them at the County Home.

When he and I went back to the poultry barn after our picnic, there was Leander Gay, as good as his word. I told him Aunt Maude had said yes after almost choking on a piece of cold chicken, and he said he wasn't surprised for a minute. Picking out three wasn't any easier than I thought it would be, but after lots of picking up and putting down I made my choices. Leander had a ball of blue yard in his grain box, from which he cut three pieces, tying one to a leg of each of the three ducklings I'd chosen. That way there couldn't be any mixup with others that people might want.

I thanked him again. Gramps told him he'd be back mid-afternoon with a box to take them home. Then he and I went off to see what we could see. We went on a couple of rides, the not too scary ones like bumper cars and the Ferris wheel, and walked through the sideshow section where they had the largest ox in the world, the fat lady who was there every year, a man with no head, only wires coming out of his neck, and other interesting things. Mostly we ate. Gramps liked Vernor's ginger ale as much as I did, so we'd have a waffle at the waffle stand, then go over and drink a glass of Vernor's. Then we'd try a sausage at the sausage stand, and have to have another glass of Vernor's to wash it down. Neither of us liked the cotton candy, and we agreed our candy apples were an iffy thing—if you could bite through the red candy on the outside, the apple was so sour you couldn't enjoy it.

After we'd done Floral Hall—and Hattie Berkemeyer's bronze dahlias were there with a big blue ribbon stuck in front of them—we decided to have one more waffle and call it quits. I was willing. I should have stopped before that last waffle because the skin over my stomach was stretched to the breaking point, but I managed to get it down and wasn't too concerned about the powdered sugar that covered my front. Gramps said he wouldn't need any supper. I said I wouldn't either. I just hoped I wouldn't be sick.

"Maybe Jessie will bring you to the Fair tomorrow," Gramps said. "Your Uncle Edwin has two horses racing in the afternoon. Be too bad if you missed that."

"I'll ask her," I said, wishing there was someplace I could lie down.

Everybody kissed everybody else when we parted. Gramps and Grandma were waiting for Uncle Edwin to take them home. Gramps had the box of ducklings on the grass next to their picnic basket. Nobody dented Uncle Will's new Ford, but Aunt Maude kept squealing at him as we drove out of the parking lot that he was going to hit first this car and then that one. I knew I'd feel better if I threw up.

CHAPTER FOUR

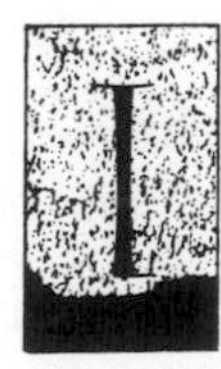

I didn't throw up, though I felt as if I was going to all the way from the fairgrounds to Aunt Jessie's. It was no help having Uncle Will notice so many interesting things along the way that he looked at whatever interested him rather than watching the road, so we kept edging over to the side which made Aunt Maude squeal, "Will, we're headed for the ditch." I was never so glad to get any place as I was when we drove into Aunt Jessie's yard. Because Aunt Maude and Uncle Will were already on their days off, they could stay for supper. I said I didn't want any supper which made Aunt Maude realize I was sick, and if I was really sick she said they would cancel their trip to Laura and Jap Dailey's.

"He's not sick, he just ate too much at the Fair. Isn't that right, David?" Aunt Jessie asked, running her hand across my hot forehead.

"I think that's it," I replied.

"Would you like some Pepto-Bismol?" Aunt Maude also felt my forehead.

"No!" The thought of Pepto-Bismol made me feel even more like throwing up.

"I'll fix him some bicarbonate of soda. That will do the trick." Aunt Jessie went to the kitchen. She was a great believer in bicarbonate of soda for almost everything. And it did work. I still didn't want any supper, but after a prolonged session of loud burping I no longer thought my guts were going to explode. It was worth having to say "Excuse me" each time.

While everybody else was eating supper I laid on the living-room floor listening to Mr. Keen, Tracer of Lost Persons, on the radio. Uncle Wallace called him Mr. Trace, Keener than Most Persons, which made it hard to take the program too seriously, but I listened anyway. Uncle Wallace made a joke out of everything. He had red cheeks and a pointed nose and chin. Aunt Jessie said they were the only thin parts of him. She was always trying to put him on a diet to lose weight, but Uncle Wallace said he gained an ounce every time he inhaled.

After about a dozen or so hugs and being told to "be good," Aunt Maude and Uncle Will left. Then Aunt Jessie and I took a walk along the Center Road. It was as dark as pitch except for dim lights showing through neighbors' windows, which meant you could see every single star sparkling blue billions of miles away. Aunt Jessie pointed out the constellations, the same as Gramps did every time he and I were out together on a dark night. I couldn't see what they saw; oh I saw the stars, but I couldn't make those stars look like bears or hunters or anything else, except a big dipper and a little dipper. They were easy.

The air was filled with hundreds of lightning bugs, blinking on and off as they floated around aimlessly. "What do they eat?" I asked Aunt Jessie. "Somebody must know, but I don't," she replied. "We'll see if we can find out."

We walked as far as Harry Woolf's store, which didn't show any light at all so the Woolfs must have gone to bed. On the way back we heard a horse coming toward us. It wasn't in any hurry. Clop, clop, clop, clop, it walked along slow and easy, getting nearer to us. We couldn't see the horse or the rider, so they probably couldn't see us either.

"Let's see how close we can get before they sense we're here," Aunt Jessie whispered.

"What if they run over us?" I whispered back.

"I hope we're not stupid enough to just stand here and let that happen," Aunt Jessie snickered.

I swear I was beginning to feel the horse's hot breath on my face and I know I could have reached out and touched him before Aunt Jessie said, "Hal, is that you?"

"Aunt Jessie?" somebody asked directly above me.

Then I definitely could feel the heat of the horse. I reached my hand out carefully, and there it was. The horse must have thought I was a fly or some other bug because he wiggled his skin the way horses do when they're tickled.

"I thought it sounded like you coming home," Aunt Jessie was saying. "Have you been visiting Doris?"

"Yep." Hal sounded as if he might be blushing.

"David is with me. We're out for a walk before we turn in." Aunt Jessie put her arm around my shoulders.

"Hi, David," Hal said.

"Hi, Hal. Can you see anything?"

"Nope, nothing but the stars, but it doesn't matter because Wonder knows the way home."

"Can Wonder see in the dark?" I asked.

"I guess so. I just leave it up to him and he always gets me home."

"We've got to be getting home too," Aunt Jessie said. "Tell your mother I have a couple of jars of currant jelly for her."

"I will," Hal said. "Goodnight David."

"Goodnight Hal."

Hal and Wonder clopped on up the road in the dark.

I liked visiting Aunt Jessie and Uncle Wallace. They didn't fret over me near as much as Aunt Maude did, letting me sleep upstairs all by myself while they slept in a downstairs bedroom, for instance. When I was little, Aunt Jessie would crawl in bed with me until I was asleep, and I didn't mind it at the time. She told great stories, laughing, if they were funny, louder than I did. Sometimes the funniest part was hearing her laugh. She was also good at scary stories.

It was strange at first lying there in bed all by myself, not hearing back porch pump sounds when somebody went for water, and Aunt Jessie's house didn't have the antiseptic smell of the County Home, which I missed, but she did have tree peepers, so I concentrated on them to fall asleep. It occurred to me as I drowsed off that I should come up with names for my three ducks, but I was too tired to think. I knew Gramps would take good care of them for me until I could take care of them myself. I wondered if they missed their mother. If they did, they'd get used to it. I had.

Next morning Aunt Jessie called me earlier than usual, saying she'd decided we should go to the Fair, for part of the day at least. She said she was using the excuse that Uncle Edwin would not like it if we missed his horses racing. When my stomach was feeling so strange the night before I didn't care about ever going to the Fair again, but by morning I couldn't wait.

Aunt Jessie didn't have running water, so I had to go across the backyard to an outhouse to pee. When I came back I pumped water into a basin in the kitchen sink, which Aunt Jessie then warmed up with hot water from the teakettle so I could wash. It embarrassed me to wash all over while she was moving around the kitchen getting breakfast, but she didn't seem to notice. I had to use drinking water from the bucket in the pantry to brush my teeth because that was well water. The water from the kitchen pump was rainwater stored in a cistern. Rainwater is so soft soap slips out of your hand onto the floor if you're not careful. I dropped it a couple of times and had to chase it across the kitchen, which Aunt Jessie thought was very funny.

Aunt Jessie and Aunt Maude were only a couple of years apart but were very different in every way except their coloring, both having dark hair and eyes. Aunt Maude never came out of her bedroom without her hair perfectly combed into a neat, pinned-down bun, unless of course I'd caused a crisis, and she was always completely dressed in a starched housedress and immaculate apron before she went downstairs. Aunt Jessie scrambled eggs at the stove with her hair flying loose in spite of a rubber band at the back, wearing an old bathrobe that belonged to Uncle Wallace. Yet when we got into the car to go to the Fair, she looked like a million dollars.

I remember one time Aunt Maude and I dropped in on Aunt Jessie while Uncle Will went to do an errand. When we arrived, Aunt Jessie was darning underwear that Aunt Maude said looked "disreputable."

"If you didn't spend so much money on your hats, you'd be able to afford new underwear," Aunt Maude sniffed.

"Maude, nobody sees my underwear," Aunt Jessie smiled, trying to close an enormous gap with needle and thread, "whereas my hats are the subject of considerable comment."

She was wearing a hat as we drove to the Fair, a wide-brimmed navy blue straw. She called it a boater. It was decorated with spectacular bunches of red silk poppies, and as she had told Aunt Maude that darning day, crowd of people complimented her on its beauty as we strolled around the fairgrounds, "whereas" nobody knew whether or not her underwear had holes.

"Let's do everything we want to do today," she said, "without getting sick if possible."

I squeezed her hand as we headed straight for the waffle stand. Fortunately she liked waffles too, so we each had one before she did anything else.

We spent a lot of time in Floral Hall looking at all the exhibits of vegetables as well as flowers. Mrs. Berkemeyer was standing near her display of bronze dahlias, dipping her head and lowering her eyes every time somebody paid her a compliment. I was sorry about what I'd done, ruining things for Aunt Maude, but also glad Hattie Berkemeyer was enjoying one more year of victory. When Aunt Jessie told Hattie she'd come close to overwhelming competition in the shape of Tahiti Sunset gladiolas, Mrs. Berkemeyer said she'd heard about Maude's terrible tragedy.

"Is there any clue yet as to who did it?" she asked, looking genuinely concerned.

"We'll probably never find out," Aunt Jessie shook her head, making the poppies bounce, "but whoever did it deserves to suffer the way my poor sister did."

I excused myself and went to the cinderblock toilet house, where I stood in a long row of men and boys peeing in a trough that had water running through it. I wondered if I fell in that trough and drowned, everybody who was so upset about the gladiolas would be satisfied.

Uncle Edwin's horses won both their races, which was pretty thrilling. We'd been to the stables while they were groomed and hitched to sulkies. One of the horses was a vicious biter. I almost lost part of my head when I made the mistake of walking around in front of him. Nobody seemed to notice in the rush to get them ready.

Aunt Jessie and Grandma sat in the grandstand out of the sun, but Gramps and I watched the races sitting on the rail. Gramps liked to be as close as possible to the action. For years he had raced his own horses, and was as good a judge of horseflesh as he was of poultry. We talked about the ducks. He told me they were fine, but would be better when they were with me.

When it came time to go home I was lingering by the sausage stand while Aunt Jessie had one more visit with one of her friends. I think it was too many sausages mixed with all that ginger ale and waffles and other stuff that made me sick the day before, but the sizzling links of all sizes surrounded by steaming peppers and onions smelled so good I forgot and wanted to stand there sniffing as long as I could.

"Now, I must run or Wallace will be home before me and wanting his supper," I heard Aunt Jessie say as she exchanged pecks with her friend and rushed over to where I was standing.

"Do you think I could have a sausage before we go?" I asked. "I'm sure it won't spoil my supper."

"I have a better idea," Aunt Jessie said, her face lighting up. "Why don't we buy sausages for our supper? I had planned to reheat things, but sausages would be a special treat."

I thought it was a super suggestion. We examined the assortment of sausages carefully before making a single decision. It was hard to choose between Polish sausages and Hungarian, Italian, German, and other kinds too.

"Which are the Italian?" I asked. The sausage man pointed

to three different sausages, explaining that they were sweet, hot, and hotter. "I wish Rose was here. I bet she hasn't had an Italian sausage in years," I said quietly.

"We'll take her one. Which do you think she'd like?"

"Could we really?" I couldn't believe Aunt Jessie would go to all that trouble.

"Why not?"

We couldn't make up our minds which ones we wanted, so we took an assortment for ourselves and Uncle Wallace, and then chose an especially good-looking large sweet Italian link for Rose. The sausage man wrapped it separately, and piled fried onions and peppers around it, "for a blanket," he said. Then he put a grilled roll in a paper of its own so it would not get soggy.

Aunt Jessie always got into the spirit of whatever was happening, and getting Rose's sausage to her quickly became a challenge. She drove as fast as she dared the minute we left the fairgrounds, passing cars after we'd warned them with a loud blast of the horn, raising almost as much dust as Charley Smith flying along the Center Road. Wind coming in open windows forced the wide brim of her hat to stand straight up in front like a baseball catcher's visor. I laughed to see it that way, and she laughed at me laughing, so we must have been quite a sight when we roared right past her house with Uncle Wallace standing out front wondering why we didn't stop. Aunt Jessie gave him a honk, and we both waved.

Rose was thrown by what we'd done. When Aunt Jessie and I rushed up to her door and said we had a sweet Italian sausage with peppers and onions for her, she looked at us as if we were crazy, but then she must have gotten a whiff of it because her face lit up and a big smile cracked the corners of her mouth. I passed the two packages through the bars as she laughed out loud, saying things like, "Oh my, I don't know how to handle this," and, "I haven't inhaled such a fragrance in years."

The sausage man's careful wrapping had worked, so the Italian wasn't too cool when Rose put it in the roll which hadn't gotten a bit soggy. She smacked her lips over the onions and peppers, saying between bites, "This is the best food I've ever tasted."

We knew she didn't exactly mean it, but she probably thought so at the moment. I brought the organ stool over for Aunt Jessie to sit on while Rose munched away. I didn't mind standing. It was like having a party. Rose said she loved Aunt Jessie's hat, so Aunt Jessie took it off and insisted Rose try it on. First we were going to press it through the bars, but then Aunt Jessie said she'd paid much too much for the hat to risk crushing it, so she opened the door a crack and passed the hat in to Rose, who took it after wiping her fingers and mouth on one of her embroidered handkerchiefs, then went to try on the big hat in front of her mirror.

"Oh Rose, it's magnificent on you," Aunt Jessie exclaimed. "Tilt it a bit over your right eye. That's the way. What do you think, David?"

"I think she should never take it off."

"Well, she has to eventually because I want to wear it too, but you keep it tonight, Rose, I won't need it until the end of the week. I'll come back for it."

"Oh no, Jessie, you mustn't do that," Rose objected, carefully removing the hat and coming to pass it back around the door.

"I insist, Rose. That hat suits you to a tee. You wear it until you go to bed, then all day tomorrow. Don't even take it off when you go to the bathroom. It'll do you good. How long has it been since you wore a blue straw boater with bright red poppies on the brim?" Aunt Jessie could make anybody happy.

"I never did have a boater quite like this one," Rose said, "though I had a blue sailor hat when I was first married. It had long grosgrain ribbons that hung down my back." She replaced Aunt Jessie's hat on her head, tilting it this time even more than before.

It was unusual for Rose to sound cheerful talking about when she was married. I guess Scheider must have liked the blue sailor hat.

"That settles it." Aunt Jessie got up from the organ stool. "Now, David, we must get Uncle Wallace's supper to him, or he'll be sending the sheriff after me."

I put the organ stool back while Rose and Aunt Jessie touched each other's cheeks through the bars, then Rose gave me a pat on the head and we raced back down the Center Road as fast as Aunt Jessie's car would go.

CHAPTER FIVE

he next day I was playing in a dirt pile with Benny Watson who lived a couple of houses down the road from Aunt Jessie and Uncle Wallace. Benny had his toy trucks and cars and I had mine, and we were building stupid roads and bridges to run them on. I was bored, but there wasn't much of anything else to do. Benny was older than I and bigger, but he didn't have too many ideas about how to pass the time. It would never occur to Benny to go exploring down in the gully in the woods, or just go talk to Mamie Dodge, an old maid who lived in a spooky house next door with dozens of cats. They said all those cats slept in the same bed, between the sheets, with Mamie.

Late afternoon a car pulled up in front of Benny's house and his father got out. Mr. Watson worked the same place Uncle Wallace did, and they rode back and forth with a third man who lived farther up south. "Better come home soon for supper," Uncle Wallace called out the car window as it pulled away. "I will," I called back.

"Want to watch me milk the goats first?" Benny asked.

"Sure," I said. Watching goats get milked is not the biggest event of the year, but I didn't want to hurt his feelings.

We left our trucks and cars in the dirt pile and went to the goat shed, which was falling down, but so was everything else at the Watsons', including the house they lived in. "Aren't you going to wash your hands first?" I asked.

"What for? They ain't dirty," Benny snorted, snatching a bucket off a peg in the sagging beam, while he yelled to the goats who were browsing loose around the yard.

I didn't care because I wasn't going to drink the milk anyway, but at the County Home the men scrubbed themselves clean with brushes and soap before milking and all the pails were sterilized in scalding water. Who knew what bugs had made a temporary home of that goat bucket Benny grabbed off the beam? Obviously, he wasn't going to wash it either.

The goats crowded around not needing any coaxing, chewing their cuds and climbing up onto the milking platform one after the other as Benny pulled on their fat teats until he had drained each udder. A bunch of scrawny cats congregated too, sitting in a semicircle watching Benny milk. Benny squirted milk in their mouths, and sometimes all over them which he thought was a riot. The cats didn't seem to mind; used to it, I guess.

"Bend over here and I'll squirt milk in your mouth," Benny said in an if-you-dare tone of voice.

"Not if you're going to squirt it all over me," I said, drawing back a bit.

"A little goat milk never hurt anybody," he sneered.

"I'm not afraid of goat milk. In fact I like it, I just don't want to take a bath in it."

"I won't squirt you," he promised.

I came closer and leaned forward. Benny took aim and squirted a stream of milk right in my mouth. It surprised me so much I almost choked. Then I started to laugh, and that did make me choke. When I was through gasping for air, I leaned forward again. "I wasn't expecting it that time, try again."

"What makes you think I won't drown you with milk this time?" Benny had that dare tone again.

"Because you promised."

"Promises don't mean shit," he snorted, "but I promise anyway." He took aim. I had my mouth wide open, but the milk didn't go in my mouth. It hit me right between the eyes, running down both sides of my nose.

"Cut that out," I yelped, backing away, but Benny kept squirting me with milk, dowsing my hair, my front, my feet. I stepped on a cat because I didn't see it in back of me, which made it yowl, and that startled the goats who scattered, bashing into and almost knocking down Mr. Watson who was just coming into the shed.

"What the hell's goin' on here?" He had a bottle of beer in his hand.

"Nothin', Paw, only milkin' the goats," Benny went from mean to scared in the flash of a second.

"What's the matter with you, twerp?" Mr. Watson was peering in my direction from under messy eyebrows that were mostly brown but had long white hairs sticking out of them.

"Me?"

"I ain't talking to the goats." He laughed at his own joke, which I didn't think was funny. I guess my not laughing made him mad because after he took a swig of beer from his bottle, he got a queer look on his face and then said in a high hoity-toity voice. "Me? Me?" I think he was trying to imitate me, but I knew that's not the way I sounded when I talked, not even when I was nervous and Mr. Watson made me nervous.

"Your family makes me sick. Think you're better'n anybody else, puttin' on airs."

I didn't say a word, nor did Benny, who was paying close attention to the goat he was milking.

"I saw you and your fat Aunt Jessie at the Fair yesterday. 'Course you didn't see me. You wuz walkin' around with your noses in the air, not lookin' at nobody."

"I really didn't see you, Mr. Watson," I said.

"Don't sass me," he growled. "Your Aunt Jessie," he let out a loud belch, "she thinks she's some kind of astacrat."

"What's an astacrat, Mr. Watson?" I asked before I thought, hoping he wouldn't take it for sass. I wasn't being smart, I'd never heard the word before.

"An astacrat," he explained in that hoity-toity voice again, "is somebody who goes around with her nose and her ass in the air." He belched again and guffawed, then said real ugly, not hoity-toity at all, "I'm surprised the old bitch don't fall over on her face from the tonnage of those big tits."

That sent Benny into a physical fit of giggling so he slopped the almost full bucket of goat milk, and that made his father so mad Mr. Watson hit Benny on the side of his head as hard as he could, knocking him off the three-legged stool onto the ground. Benny started to cry, then he too got mad and threw the milk bucket at his father. What milk was left in the bucket splashed out all over Mr. Watson. Mr. Watson roared like a bull and lunged for Benny.

I decided I'd better disappear before they took after me. Benny must have tackled his father's knees, or maybe Mr. Watson misjudged where Benny was and fell over him, because they both crashed to the ground bellowing and rolling around in the dirt. The goats leaped out of the way, then turned to watch. Cats went up posts or raced out of the shed. I didn't bother to pick up my truck and cars, which I didn't care much about anyway, as I ran for home, that is, for Aunt Jessie's house.

Naturally Aunt Jessie asked me why I was such a sticky mess when I came into the kitchen, so I told her about Benny squirting me with the milk. She allowed as how a little milk wouldn't kill me, so I told her that Benny himself might be dead by this time. That made her curious, so then I had to explain to her that when I left the goat shed Mr. Watson was beating Benny to a pulp, or about to, if Benny didn't do his father serious damage first. She wanted to know what made Mr. Watson angry, so I had to tell her about Benny spilling the milk because he was laughing fit to bust at what Mr. Watson said.

Uncle Wallace stood there grinning as I told the story. "I've never known Ed Watson to be very good at jokes," he said. "What was it made Benny bust a gusset?"

"It wasn't astacrat, though Benny did laugh a little at that," I began.

"What's an astacrat?" Aunt Jessie asked.

"I didn't know either, but Mr. Watson says it's somebody who goes around with her nose and her—" I paused, not knowing what to say. "Ass" was not a word used in the house.

"Go on," Aunt Jessie urged, her face expectant.

"With her nose and her ass in the air." I could see Aunt Jessie and Uncle Wallace were somewhat amused, but they also appeared worried, Uncle Wallace especially.

"It wasn't astacrat or nose and ass in the air that got Benny giggling so he spilled the milk," I repeated my earlier point.

"It wasn't?" Aunt Jessie asked. She obviously expected me to tell the rest of the story.

I shook my head, and took a long breath. "What broke Billy up is when Mr. Watson said he, Mr. Watson, is surprised you"—I thought it better not to repeat "bitch"—"don't fall over on your face from the"—I paused again and stared at her for a second or two before taking another deep breath—"from the tonnage of those big," my voice was failing me, "tits of yours." I ended in a hoarse whisper.

Aunt Jessie covered her mouth with both hands. Her eyes were wide open and round. She didn't look as if she was going to twist my ear or anything like that. For a minute she just stared, then she started blinking while her shoulders shook up and down the way they did when she laughed.

Uncle Wallace wasn't laughing, but he was definitely shaking. His face had gone so red I thought blood would spurt out the little veins on the end of his thin nose. He stood there growing bigger as his elbows bent outward and his chest expanded. He took several very loud deep breaths, then headed for the door.

"Wallace. Wallace," Aunt Jessie called out to him, but he slammed the screen and stomped down the porch steps. "Wallace, you come back here," she cried, following him into the yard. He paid no attention, not even turning to look back as he disappeared around Mamie Dodge's house. "Oh dear," was all Aunt Jessie said when she came into the kitchen again.

I took off my milk-soaked overalls and washed as fast as I could to get out of the way, then went upstairs to put on clean clothes. When I came back into the kitchen, Uncle Wallace was just opening the screen door. He still looked determined, though not as red as when he left, not as if he was going to explode or anything. He was still shaking a little.

"What happened, Wallace?" Aunt Jessie asked, once again covering her mouth, but with only one hand this time. I could tell she was trying not to laugh.

"I went over there, and just as David said, Watson was pounding up Benny in the goat shed. They didn't hear me come in, until I shouted, 'Watson, stand up like a man.' The two of them stopped fighting. Benny crawled over in a corner, but Watson got to his feet and walked over to me. Before he could say anything, I hit him as hard as I could, with my fist, right square in the middle of his face. I think I broke his nose. He fell over backwards and I came home."

"Oh Wallace," Aunt Jessie said. She put her arms around him, the wooden spoon she'd been stirring chicken hash with hanging down his back. "My knight. My protector." Then she began to laugh, only a little at first, but soon so hard she was squealing.

"I don't think it's funny," Uncle Wallace said, his face getting red again, then after a minute he started snickering too. "You should have seen the look of him, Jessie. He had no idea why I was there. Probably still hasn't."

"I wonder if he'll be waiting for his ride tomorrow morning when you and Al drive up?" Aunt Jessie wiped her eyes and went back to stirring the hash.

Uncle Wallace grinned. "If he is, I may jump out of the car and hit him again, for good measure." He put his fists in the air and did a little dance like boxers do. "I've never hit anybody with a fist before. Maybe if I get good at it I can take on Joe Louis and make us a lot of money." He danced around again, throwing punches.

"Joe Louis would make mincemeat of you," Aunt Jessie laughed. "I think you'd better retire while you're still the neighborhood champion."

Then they both turned and looked at me. I was standing there, the worried one now, which must have seemed especially funny to them because they started laughing all over again louder than ever as they pulled me into a threeway clinch. In the space of half an hour I'd been in danger of losing my life in the Watsons' goat shed, had said swears over and over in the kitchen, and gotten Mr. Watson's nose broken, yet there they were hugging and kissing me, and roaring as if it was all the biggest joke ever. I wished I could see what was so funny.

CHAPTER SIX

hen I told Rose about Uncle Wallace bashing Mr. Watson in the nose, having decided by that time it must have been a pretty funny sight, I thought she too would laugh, but I could tell as I was describing the details she wasn't amused. Her warning left eyebrow was going up and the corners of her mouth were going down.

"You created trouble between your uncle and the man he rides to work with every day," Rose scolded.

"I wasn't creating trouble, Rose. I just answered Aunt Jessie's questions."

"You are having such a good time telling me all about it, I'm sure you couldn't wait to get back to your Aunt Jessie's to tattle what that dreadful man said."

"I did not tattle, Rose. Jeez, I wish I hadn't told you anything. You're in an awful grump today."

"I wasn't until a few minutes ago. You must learn, David, there are times when it is better to remain silent. You don't always have to repeat everything you hear." She smoothed the front of her dress, fingering the row of buttons. "Especially when you know in advance it is going to cause trouble."

"Rose, just the other day you said you and I can tell each other everything and it will be all right—no matter what it is. Yet, I come and tell you some of the things that happened to me while I was away and you give me what for." I kicked her door so hard I hurt my big toe.

"David, you and I telling each other things, no matter what, is all right as I said it was, but telling people what other people say about them is different. I don't know how to make you understand. When I figure it out I'll give you a better explanation." Rose brushed a wisp of hair off her forehead and pulled it back behind her ear.

We sat in silence for a while, just sat there, not looking at each other or anything. I decided to try something different. I hadn't had a chance to tell Rose about the dance Adeline taught me because going to the Fair got in the way.

"You ever danced a fertility dance, Rose?"

"A what dance?"

"Fertility."

"Do you know what you're talking about?"

"I think so. It's not all that easy, but if you figure it out before you begin and don't let your mind wander it's kind of fun."

"You dance fertility dances?" Both of Rose's eyebrows were raised.

"I've only danced it once so far, but Adeline says I'll get better the more times I do it."

"Is fertility dancing to become part of your daily schedule?"

"Only until cold weather probably." I could tell I had taken

Rose's mind off what had made her cross before. From the way she was looking at me I knew she was really interested in what I was saying. "You have to take off all your clothes."

Her jaw dropped and her eyes opened wide.

"We couldn't do it in here, Rose. You'd break your feet pounding them bare on the hard floor. I don't know if you have to do it in a pine grove, but it works pretty well there because the ground is soft, you know, with the pine needles underneath and all."

"Of what does this fertility dancing consist exactly?" The wisp of hair was loose again. This time Rose wet her finger on her tongue and drew it over the hairs before putting them once more behind her ear.

"I beg your pardon?"

"What do you do after you've taken off all your clothes?"

"Mostly stomp and clap with some whirling thrown in. Then of course you have to jerk your hips around from side to side and backward and forward." I jumped off the stool and gave her a short hip jerk demonstration.

"Fascinating. And how do you conclude this fertility dance?" she asked.

"Conclude?"

"Finish. Is there a suitably colorful ending? What happens after you've clapped and stomped and done whatever it is you've just done?" She appeared to be searching for words.

"I slapped Adeline's butt because she made me mad, then she hummed one of her mother's songs and we almost fell asleep but the dinner bell rang."

Rose stared at me, then shook her head. "I won't ask for further details, having only moments ago urged you not to utter every bit of news you know,but I must admit this dance picture isn't yet clear."

"I don't wonder, Rose. It's one of the hardest things I've ever had to learn. You see, you stomp and clap and turn and shake your butt all at the same time but in different combinations. It's very confusing, which is why you can't let your mind wander."

She put her hand through the bars and placed it gently across my mouth. "You don't need to go on, David. While I may not understand everything you have said, I trust you."

"Trust me? To do what?"

"When are you going to get your ducks?" she asked, obviously changing the subject. "I hear Roy is building a coop for you in the corner of the potato barn."

"Yes. Pa Fleming said I could keep them there. As soon as Roy is finished Uncle Will is going to drive me over to Gramps' so I can pick them up."

"Have you chosen names for them yet?"

"Not yet. Charley Smith said he'd name them Ike, Mike, and Mustard, but then he said that's a dirty joke he 'dassn't' tell me."

"I'm sure it is. How surprising he didn't tell you the joke dirty word by dirty word."

"I asked him a couple of times, but he refused."

"He's turning saintly in his senility."

"It isn't that, Rose. He said Aunt Maude would really do him in if he told me."

We were interrupted by a commotion. When I turned around, there was Mary sagging and swaying but clumping across the sitting room hanging onto Blind Theresa's arm. If Charley Smith had been there he would certainly have something to say about the blind leading the blind. Mary was not in her bathrobe but fully dressed, except for her stockings. First time I'd seen her in anything but a nightgown in days.

"Hi, Mary. You must be feeling lots better if Julia let you out of your room." I walked over and gave her a hug. She snorted and gave me a wet kiss on my forehead.

"She can only stay for a few minutes," Theresa said. "I'm supposed to make her walk a little farther each day so she'll get her strength back."

"I get pooped," Mary croaked, spraying spit halfway across the sitting room. It was good to have her back. She sank down in a chair and began rocking back and forth, the rockers making a rrump, rrump sound as she and the rocker moved crossways of the floorboards. "Anybody here other than us?" She stopped rocking to peer around the room through her milky blue slits.

"Just us," I said.

"Good, then nobody can holler at us. 'Rese, play something on the organ so we can sing."

"What would you like me to play?" Theresa asked, going to sit on a stool that wasn't there.

"Wait a minute," I warned, dashing over to Rose's door for the stool.

"Oh please," Rose groaned, holding her head as she backed away from the door.

"Please what, Rose?" I asked.

"Please nothing," she replied.

" 'Rock of Ages,' " Mary told Theresa, unaware of my rush to get the stool under Theresa before she fell to the floor. "But wait 'till I get my breath back."

"Oh God," I heard Rose say from behind her bars.

When Mary said she was ready, Theresa pumped the bellows of the organ with her feet and began to sing, "Rock of ages, cleft for me. . . ." Mary and I joined in, singing as loud as we could. Once when I was small and didn't know any better I told Mary she wasn't a very good singer. She said I should listen to myself. It didn't matter anymore what we sounded like because we weren't singing for anybody but ourselves. I knew Rose was probably lying on her bed with her hands over her ears.

We sang every note, not on pitch it was obvious even to me, but at the top of our lungs. Somebody from upstairs yelled down, "Cut out that caterwauling!" We paid no attention. We were celebrating having Mary out among us again.

When we finished the last chorus of the last verse, we argued about which hymn to sing next. I kept asking Theresa to play "In the Garden" which is fun to do, but Mary said that one was too slow and hard for her because of the low parts. Before we could agree on a selection, Julia came along and told Mary she'd had enough exercise for now and had to go lie down. Mary and I hugged again, and off she shuffled, leaning on Blind Theresa.

"How did you like our singing, Rose?" I was teasing as I peered through at her lying on her bed just as I thought.

"I didn't."

"Is it because you're Catholic and that hymn is Baptist or something?"

"Not really."

"David, there's a surprise for you outside," Uncle Will called to me from the arcade steps.

The surprise was Grandma and Gramps, who had come over in their buggy to bring me my ducks. Gramps was a first-rate mechanic, Uncle Deane said, but he preferred driving horses to cars. Prince, a chestnut Hackney / Thoroughbred cross, was Gramps' favorite.

"We thought it was a nice day for a ride, so here we are," Gramps said, pulling me to him after he'd boxed my ears.

Grandma had already gone into the kitchen with Aunt Maude. Prince munched oats in a nose bag, not bothered at all when I rubbed his face.

"Can I take Prince for a drive?" I asked.

"After dinner," Gramps said. "He's come a long way this morning for an old codger. We'll let him rest a while."

I'd forgotten all about the ducks until one of them quacked. They were in a box in the back of the buggy, the same box Gramps used to take them home from the Fair. Now they filled it.

"They've doubled in size," I gasped.

"The way they eat, they'll be full grown in no time."

"Then we can eat 'em," Charley Smith said over my shoulder. I hadn't even heard him come up behind me. "Muscovies make damn good eatin'."

"Not these Muscovies," I shot back.

"We'll have to leave them in the box until I get their cage finished," Roy said. He and Mr. Beveridge had come out of the dairy to see what was going on.

"Do you have much more to do?" Uncle Will asked. "I can help you this afternoon."

After dinner, while Roy and Uncle Will were nailing the last of the chicken wire onto the uprights, Gramps rubbed Prince with a soft cloth, then put his harness back on and hitched him to the buggy. "Is there anybody you want to take for a ride?" he asked. "I'd prefer you not go off by yourself."

"I'd like to take Rose but she can't leave her room, and Mary isn't able to go out yet, and Roy's busy doing the coop." I thought of Aunt Latzy but that was impossible. "How about Adeline?" I said. Why hadn't I thought of Adeline first thing?

"Will she keep her clothes on?" Gramps blinked his eyes.

"If I tell her to," I answered, running off to get her.

"Who's gonna drive this here horse?" Adeline fluffed her hair as she followed me slowly down the stairs from her room.

"I am."

She stopped. "How much time you spent drivin' horses?"

"Adeline, this isn't just any horse. This is Prince. I've played with him like he was a toy. He's known me forever. If I hiccupped he'd bring me a glass of water."

Her lower lip jutted out pink as she stood pondering. "It'd be worth hiccups jes to see that."

Gramps handed me the reins and stepped back. "Don't trot him, David, because he's still got to get your grandmother and me home. Remember he's old."

I assured Gramps on all counts and we started out after a delay because Prince wouldn't move until Gramps said quietly, "It's okay, Prince."

"So much for a glass of water," Adeline sniffed.

We drove out onto the Center Road, then turned west on the East Road. There weren't any hills in that direction to tire Prince. Gravel crunched under the buggy wheels as Prince's feet made soft steady clomping sounds. Birds chittered in the trees and ever present late summer cicadas sang in the distance. I loved the slowness of a horse and buggy. You could really look at everything and hear what there was to hear. To make it more perfect Prince lifted his tail and dropped warm steaming balls of manure on the road. I closed my eyes and took a deep whiff.

"Doesn't that smell great, Adeline?"

She turned to look at me, fanning her hand in front of her face, her forehead a washboard of worry wrinkles. "You is truly weird, boy."

"Adeline," I raised my voice to convince her. "I mean it. Horse manure smells wonderful, especially when it's fresh, though dried horse manure smells pretty good too. Take your hand away from your face and breathe in." I did as I told her to do. She didn't. "Cow manure stinks and pig makes me sick to my stomach, but horse manure. . . ."

"How you do run off that mouth of yours. Is this why you axed me out for an airin', to discuss the goods and the bads of different kinds of shit?" She sat back and folded her arms. "I think we better make a 'pointment with Dr. Davis for you, and soon. You is sick."

"Jeez," I puffed. "What's the big deal? Horse manure smells good, ask anybody. You're the one who has a problem if you can't appreciate that." I was getting mad.

"How far you plannin' to take me?" she interrupted.

"Up to the crossroad and back. We can turn around at the corner."

"Long's we're out, might be nice to trot down to Harry Woolf's store."

"We're going in the wrong direction. Besides, I didn't bring any money."

"Who said we wuz gonna buy anything? We could snoop around for a while. There's smells at Harry Woolf's store more to my likin' than horse shit."

"Sorry, Adeline, it's too far to go all the way back and then down the Center Road. Prince has to get Gramps and Grandma home."

"I never gets to go places." She slumped down in the buggy seat and began yanking at the hem of her skirt.

"Adeline, I promised my grandfather you would not take your clothes off, so don't start unraveling." My voice was firm. I meant it. What was supposed to be fun was turning into a disaster.

She stopped yanking, sat up straight, and looked at me

fiercely, her eyes wide and white. "Well, ain't we the one, givin' orders. Halt this contraption, boy, our ride is at an end."

"Adeline," I whined, sorry I'd made her mad.

"Stop, horse," she demanded, but Prince kept his steady clomping pace. Adeline turned in the seat to warn me, "Ef you don't bring this here thing to a standstill I'll mos' likely be killed when I jump out."

I pulled back gently on the reins and said, "Whoa." Prince stopped and Adeline jumped out, dancing up and down until her bare feet got used to the hot stones in the road.

"You go on 'bout your business, boy, pay me no mind." Her head high, she walked east, back toward the County Home.

"Adeline, wait," I pleaded. She didn't pause. I jumped out of the buggy after wrapping the reins around the whip holder the way Gramps had shown me, then went to Prince's head and taking hold of his bridle led him in a wide circle. The road was so narrow the front wheels scraped along the body of the buggy making Prince prance skittishly, but he was easy to calm down. When we were headed in the opposite direction, I got back in, and as I took up the reins Prince began to move.

When we came alongside Adeline, who was strutting like a banty rooster, I held Prince back. "Please get in, Adeline. I'm sorry I made you cross,"

"You," she stressed, "didn't make me anything. I jes prefers not to ride out with those who give orders and talk shit."

"The only order I gave you, Adeline, wasn't really an order. It was a request. I should have said please. We'd both be in trouble if you had half your dress unraveled when we get home." It was hard to keep Prince walking slow enough so we didn't go past Adeline. He knew we were headed for the barn and that excited him.

"What I do or do not do with my ravels ain't nobody's business but mine and Julia's." She waved her long thin fingers in front of her face. "Is it possible you could make less dust with that beast?"

It wasn't easy, but I persuaded her she wouldn't mind the dust if she was riding above it in the buggy, nor would the stones hurt her bare feet. When she got in she said something about the blessings of total silence, so not a word was spoken from that spot to the barn.

"How was your ride?" Gramps asked as we drove up, helping Adeline down from the buggy.

"The ride was fine," she sniffed as she smiled up at him, flashing her teeth and fanning the air with her hand, "but the talk was smelly."

"You weren't gone long." Gramps was using the soft cloth to wipe Prince's face.

"That's Adeline's fault," I said, jumping down. "She wanted to come back."

"Adeline's fault?" Gramps asked. "David, a gentleman never blames the lady."

"But Gramps," I began.

"Thank you for what was s'posed to be a lovely outin'," Adeline extended her hand toward Gramps, who took it gently and smiled at her. She smiled back, then fluffing her hair and humming, she turned and walked up toward the women's building.

I wanted to kill her. We could have had a great time if she hadn't gotten all persnickety when I told her to stop tearing up her clothes. Now she and Gramps were acting as if I'd done something wrong. He tried to explain to me after she was gone that it isn't polite to blame somebody else, especially when she was my guest. That it was her fault didn't seem to matter to him. Politeness is more confusing than fertility dancing, I decided. Nothing he said made me feel better. In fact it was making me so mad I almost bawled.

Worst of all, everybody made fun of me for looking so sour and they kidded me, asking me if I and my "best girl" had enjoyed our buggy ride. I was even angry at Gramps by the time he and Grandma pulled out of the driveway, and that made it harder than anything else to keep from crying. I didn't want to be angry at Gramps.

As much as I wanted those ducks when I saw them at the Fair, and though I appreciated everything everybody did for me, Roy building the cage in the potato barn and all, once they were there and I had to take care of them every day, I decided they weren't much fun. They never paid any attention to me after they found out I wasn't good to eat, and that's all they did was eat. It didn't matter how many times a day I filled their food dish, it was empty in seconds. And the water was a real chore. I had to lug a big bucket from way over in the far corner back across the length of the potato barn to the duck cage, slopping much of it out onto my legs and feet which didn't feel good. Those damn ducks went crazy when they smelled fresh water. They'd be all over the place no matter where I tried to step, so I spilled more trying to get it poured into their basin. That made the dirt floor a mire when it was mixed with tons of their droppings. The whole thing was a mess.

I did have fun once, even though it led to a pear switching, the day I took the biggest duck up to show Aunt Latzy. Aunt Latzy's real name was Elizabeth Victoria Acheson. To everybody else she was Lizzy Acheson, but for some reason when I was little I started calling her Latzy, Aunt Latzy, and it stuck.

She came from England and must have had a lot of money judging by the packages of goodies she ordered from Harrods in London. How she ended up in the United States I don't know, but her life was pretty good I guess until she was old and bedridden and needed somebody to take care of her, which is why she came to the County Home. She shared a sunny corner room on the second floor with an old grouch named Mrs. Ripley, who spent most of her time in bed too, or on it, though there was nothing wrong with her except what Julia called "terminal meanness." Mrs. Ripley may have stayed in bed because it was too much effort to move her three hundred pounds around. Aunt Latzy didn't pay much attention to Ripley, acting as if she didn't hear the fat old grouch complaining all the time.

While Aunt Latzy was beautiful to look at, all soft pink and white, she had a cleft palate and a hairlip. Add that to her English accent and sometimes she was almost as hard to understand as Mary Delancy. I listened carefully so I never had much trouble. Her hair was a snowy white puff like dandelion gone to seed. On top of it she perched a flat round piece of eyelet, that's what she called it, eyelet, with a baby pink ribbon around the edge that matched the pink ribbon trimming her white eyelet bedjacket.

Special talcum powder from London dusted her face and arms and made her smell like a marshmallow. On both hands she wore heavy gold rings with elaborate carved settings for rubies and garnets. She told me diamonds were common and emeralds "elemental," whatever that meant. Whenever I asked her, she'd let me take her rings over to the window where I'd hold them up to the light, turning them in the sun to see the deep red colors flash.

There were two more pink and white parts of Aunt Latzy's

life—pink and white peppermints and Harold. On her bedstand were two glass jars, one filled with white peppermints, the other with pink. Like the talcum powder, she had them sent to her from Harrods. Anybody who went anywhere near her room, they could be just passing by her door going down the hall, was invited in to have a peppermint or two. I ate mountains of them.

Harold was a fat white pet rat with pink eyes, ears, feet, and tail. Actually, his fur was beginning to turn yellow and that bothered Aunt Latzy, so she bathed him every day in the same imported lemon solution she used on her own hair, but it didn't help. Every year Harold's coat got more and more yellow. Harold had a cage on Latzy's bedstand, but he was almost never in it. Most of the time he was in Aunt Latzy's bed. You could tell where he was because the bed covers rose and fell as he waddled around underneath. Sometimes he sat and cleaned himself on the pillow next to Aunt Latzy's puff of white hair, and that made you really notice how yellow he was getting. He always sat there on the pillow when Latzy ate, begging bits of food from her tray. She'd hold up a piece of something for him and he'd take it in his front pink paws, turning it every which way before putting it in his mouth. He looked as if he was making sure it was something he wanted before he ate it. I guess she only gave him things he liked, or maybe he liked everything because I never saw him spit out anything.

"Someday I'm going to catch that filthy rat and flush him down the toilet," Mrs. Ripley warned at least once a day, but Aunt Latzy only laughed her bell-like laugh and pursed her scarred lips at Harold who would wiggle his whiskers in response. Julia said she'd given up years ago trying to keep Harold in his cage. "Besides," she said, "he has to be the cleanest rat ever. He never makes a mess in Lizzy's bed." My duck did.

"David, I'd so love to see your precious ducklings," Aunt Latzy sighed one day, popping a pink peppermint into her pink mouth. "I truly don't mind being confined to this bed, but there are times when I regret what I'm missing out of doors. Adeline tells me your ducks are quite cunning."

"Adeline said that?" I could hardly believe it. Adeline only made snide remarks whenever she looked at my ducks in their cage. I always came to their defense even after I began to agree with her that they weren't the most exciting pets in the world.

"I don't suppose you could bring one of them up to show me?" Aunt Latzy asked with a please on her face. She reached for Harold who was peeping out from under the white blanket cover. "I'm sure Harold would like to see one too, wouldn't you, Harold?" Harold sniffed at Aunt Latzy's nose, which is where her voice came from.

"You bring any ducks in here and I'll call the sheriff, not that he'd come," Mrs. Ripley snarled from her bed where she was eavesdropping. She was lying there with all her clothes on looking like a mountain range. She hadn't even taken her shoes off after coming back up from breakfast. I could only think Julia would call the sheriff on her if the old witch got her bedspread dirty.

"Of course I can bring one up. I'll be right back." I too popped a peppermint, then went to get a duck. While I was partly doing it to please Aunt Latzy, I was mainly doing it because Ripley had made a fuss. Anything I could do to upset her I'd do in a minute no matter how much work it was.

Naturally the damn fool ducks thought I was bringing them something to eat so they were all over me the second I stepped into their cage. But then when I tried to pick one up, he was slippery as soap in rainwater. The more I tried, the more scared they all became and the madder I got. Finally I managed to grab one and though I felt like strangling him I merely stuffed him inside the bib of my overalls so he couldn't get away. I hated his wet webbed feet pressing against my bare skin. Then he decided I was dinner and began furiously pecking at my chest. Because he couldn't do it very hard the way I was holding him he tickled more than hurt.

I got him up to Aunt Latzy's room without any problem, but as I came through the door Mrs. Ripley began shouting for Julia. "Help," she screamed, "heeelp, come quick. Filth, disease. Help!"

"Do be still," Aunt Latzy cried, and that made Ripley shout louder, but when nobody came she must have given up because after a long loud groan she laid there staring at us.

"Here, David, let me see the little darling." Aunt Latzy held out her white sweet-smelling arms.

I pulled the duck from under my overalls and handed him to her. I don't know if it was her powder or what but that duck acted as if Aunt Latzy was his mother. He didn't quack at all, just settled down nice and peaceful in her hands, preening his ruffled feathers.

"David, he's adorable," she cooed, making kissing noises toward the duck. "What is his name?"

"I think this one is Mustard."

"Mustard?"

"Yes. Their names are Ike, Mike, and Mustard."

"Peculiar names for beautiful ducks."

"Charley Smith named them."

"That explains it, but why did you agree? I'd name this one Andromeda." She held the duck up to her pink lips and actually kissed him on his clacking bill.

Harold came down from the top of Latzy's pillow where he'd been watching with much whisker twitching. Mustard, or Andromeda, whichever, didn't take to Harold, who I guess he hadn't seen before, and began quacking hysterically.

That set Ripley off. "Julia," she yelled. "Anybody, somebody, come this instant and rid us of filth and disease!"

"Oh dear, I do think Harold is a bit jealous," Aunt Latzy laughed, putting the duck down on the bed so she could pick up Harold and give him a kiss. Instead of realizing that he was safe because Harold was in Aunt Latzy's grasp, the stupid duck began running up and down the bed quacking his head off.

"Julia, Juuuulia." Ripley was carrying on as bad as the duck. I wanted to tell her to shut up, but that would not be polite and I had been lectured a lot lately about politeness.

"Perhaps you'd better take Andromeda back to her brother and sister," Aunt Latzy suggested, attempting to calm Harold who was becoming more and more agitated as his bead eyes watched that dumb duck racing around the bed he called home.

I agreed. If I stayed in that room one minute longer I was going over to bop old Ripley. I wanted to bad. But when I tried to catch the duck, he wouldn't be caught. Worst of all he began to poop, squirting as he raced up and down and across quacking as if he expected to be killed. He was reading my mind.

"Oh dear," Aunt Latzy said quietly the first time the duck let go with a greenish-brown splot. Then when he ran back through his own mess and began leaving web marks all over the white bedspread, she repeated it louder, "Oh dear, oh dear."

I don't know if what she said scared the duck worse or not. Probably not because Aunt Latzy was being fairly calm. It must have been old Ripley who was screeching, really screeching now, sitting up on the edge of her bed. Anyway, that duck all but exploded, spattering in every direction.

Harold jumped out of Aunt Latzy's grasp and retreated behind her head high on the pillow, peeking out from the safety of Latzy's dandelion puff. Old Ripley shouted, "Oh my God, oh my God," over and over. Aunt Latzy pulled a sachet from between her bosoms and held it under her nose. I popped a pink peppermint in my mouth for want of something better to do as I watched that idiot duck tearing around. All this time Aunt Latzy is saying, "Oh dear, oh dear, oh dear," but I noticed the sound was changing from worried to a kind of choking laughter. That sent Ripley truly hysterical, crying and yelling that she was in a room with maniacs, things like that.

Julia usually ignored Mrs. Ripley. She had to or Ripley's demands would have killed her. But she could hardly ignore the commotion that was going on. She came into the room with an annoyed look on her face. "What is it, Mrs. Ripley?" she asked, having to shout to be heard above Ripley's screams. Then Julia must have taken a breath, because she turned to look in our direction and her face went kind of the color of what the duck had done all over Aunt Latzy's bed.

There was a sizable scene which I won't go into. Aunt Maude cut fresh pear switches and I got the longest version of her "why do you do these things to hurt me" speech. You would think after that everybody would be convinced the ducks were a mistake, but no, they all lined up against me saying I asked for the ducks and now I had to take care of them, and taking care of them meant seeing to their welfare in the potato barn where they belonged, not carting them up into the women's building.

"You wanted them, David, they are your responsibility," Rose said.

Charley Smith put in his two cents worth. "You gotta keep the shitty critters at least 'till they got enough meat on 'em to make a decent meal."

"Little boys' eyes is often bigger'n they stomachs," Adeline offered, which made about as much sense as most of the other things she was spouting at the time. I don't know what was happening to Adeline, she seemed determined to make me cranky and she was succeeding. Ever since the buggy ride when I told her to stop unraveling she acted different toward me.

School opening came as a relief.

CHAPTER SEVEN

ecause I was going into fourth grade it was decided I should really go to school this time. Always before when I'd been at the County Home during months when I would have been in school, Aunt Maude and Roy and Mrs. Fleming taught me lessons I might be missing, but nobody knew how long my mother would be in the hospital at the end of that hot summer, so I was enrolled in the schoolhouse just down the road.

Mrs. Barrie taught eight grades to eleven students in one room. She said she was genuinely pleased to have me there, and I guess she was because she smiled at me whenever I looked at her, and was never cross the way Miss Colman, my teacher in town, had been. Mrs. Barrie was prettier, too. She had wavy brown hair, finger-waved somebody told me, and rimless glasses that made her eyes sparkle. Her dresses were always prints, flowers mostly, and except in the hottest weather she wore a bright-colored cardigan over her shoulders. I thought Mr. Barrie was a lucky man to have her for a wife.

I had to take some tests so Mrs. Barrie could tell what I knew and was good at, or not so good at. Afterward, she said I was ahead of my grade in reading and comprehension, but shaky in arithmetic. She also didn't think much of my penmanship, but instead of cracking me on the knuckles, she suggested I watch the girl sitting next to me to observe and learn what she called neat and legible writing. The girl's name was Marjorie. Marjorie's face turned bright red when Mrs. Barrie praised her penmanship.

The first day began badly. I arrived at school with a new pencil box Aunt Maude bought for me in town. It had a snap top that folded back so you could see the pencils and pen in their slots, with special compartments for the pen's nib, a ruler, a compass, and an eraser. Underneath was a drawer that pulled out, for papers and things. The pencil box was green, with clowns printed on it.

"You got your lunch in that contraption?" one of the older boys asked me.

"No," I shook my head, thinking he must be pretty dumb if he didn't know what a pencil box was, but when I looked around, I realized nobody else had a pencil box. I was the only one, which is why everybody was gawping at it, and at me.

"What do you do with it?" the big kid asked.

I had a feeling whatever I said was going to be a mistake. "I carry my pencils in it."

"Teacher gives us pencils and pens."

"I didn't know that."

"You a city kid?" He knew what I was and who. They all knew, the same as I knew their names and what farms they came from, what kind of cows they had, what crops they raised, and whether their family had had a good year or bad. What there was to know along the Center Road, everybody knew. I seldom talked at meals at the County Home but I did a lot of listening, and I heard talk about farm business not only up and down the road but in other parts of the county. When I didn't answer fast enough, he sneered, "I guess city schools don't give you pencils. D'ja bring your own books and paper too?" They all laughed, except one older girl.

"Leave him alone, Roger." She had long red finger curls that touched the wide white collar of her yellow dress. Bending down so her face was on the same level with mine, she said, "Don't let Roger bother you. If he does, you come to me. I think you're cute."

I thought I'd be sick. I wanted to reach out and push her face away from mine. What was she stooping over like that for? She wasn't all that much taller.

"You just do that, kid," Roger sneered. "Anybody bothers you, run to Louise. Maybe she'll let you feel one of her hot tits." All the boys roared, covering their mouths, but not before I noticed they all had bad teeth. The girls went red and looked at Louise.

Louise straightened up and without changing expression hauled off and hit Roger with such a wallop her hand left an imprint on his freckled cheek. "If you want to feel something hot, David, put your hand on Roger's face."

I wouldn't have touched Roger if they paid me. If I made a move in his direction he'd probably throw me over the trees into the gully. But at least nobody was looking at me any longer. Everybody was looking any place except at me or at Roger or at Louise. Mrs. Barrie came to the door and called us in from the school yard just about that time. I think everybody was as glad for the interruption as I was. Everybody that is except Louise, who sauntered along, swinging her arms so her hands kept catching her yellow dress flipping the skirt from side to side. It was obvious Roger didn't make her nervous for a minute.

My second major mistake of the day had to do with lunch. Mrs. Barrie announced that we'd eat before the usual time, so we'd have time to play games in the yard before early dismissal. All the other kids took brown paper bags or dinner buckets out of their desks and set to eating sandwiches. Mrs. Barrie came along with a milk jug she'd been keeping cool in a small root cellar next to the back door.

"David, didn't you bring lunch?" she asked when she saw me just sitting there with my hands folded on my desk.

"Roy's bringing it," I replied. Uncle Will told Aunt Maude I should take sandwiches, but she insisted I was not going without a hot lunch. She said she'd fix something special for me each day and send Roy over to the school with it at lunchtime so it would still be warm.

"I should have told your Aunt Maude we'd be eating earlier than usual today," Mrs. Barrie said. "Go get a cup and I'll give you some milk to hold you until he arrives."

"Thank you," I said, embarrassed because I had to get up and go to the water pail and bring back a tin cup, and naturally everybody watched every step I took. It was a million miles each way. Louise smiled at me in a sicky sweet way which didn't help. I sensed that her getting too cozy with me wouldn't increase my chances of survival with the older boys, Roger especially.

I sat there sipping on my milk, staring straight ahead at the blackboard when I heard tapping at the window. I looked over and saw Roy nodding to me, his face just above the high windowsill.

"Hey, David, your monster is here," Roger sneered. The other boys giggled.

It wasn't what he said that upset me, because I wasn't sure what he meant by monster, but by the way he sneered I knew he was making fun of Roy. I didn't think before I did what I did, nor did I think much while I was doing it, nor I guess did Roger think I would do anything at all because when I plowed into him after half climbing half jumping over a couple of desks to get to where he sat, he had his mouth open to take a bite out of a fried-egg sandwich. My fist and the sandwich got to his mouth at the same time. What a mess, egg and bread, catsup and blood all mushed together. Roger was surprised by the attack and so was I. He looked at me, his freckled face gone white which made his hair look even more orange. I glared at him and at the mush.

Mrs. Barrie was there before we know it, pulling me away. The other kids hadn't stirred from their seats, watching with their mouths open so if you wanted to you could see whatever it was each of them had been eating. Louise's sandwich was grape jelly. Roy was making distress frowns watching the whole thing through the window.

"David, we do not fight in this school," Mrs. Barrie shook me. "Roger, get up and go to the pump, wash that mess off your face, and don't be making unkind remarks about other people."

"No, ma'am," Roger and I said in unison, which caused everybody else to laugh, and that made me titter because we must have sounded silly, and besides I was nervous. Then, believe it or not, old Roger began to giggle a stupid giggle.

"David," Mrs. Barrie calmed us down with a look, "go to the door and get your lunch and please ask Roy to simply come in the front door from now on. He doesn't need to knock." Mrs. Barrie straightened her red and white dress which got twisted around while she was separating Roger and me.

Aunt Maude had sent enough food for a family picnic, a Thermos of hot mushroom soup, four pieces of fried chicken—dark meat—a little casserole of macaroni and cheese, buttered salt rising bread, a big piece of warm apple pie with a large chunk of Cheddar cheese. Mrs. Barrie kept telling everybody to sit down, but nobody seemed to hear her as they crowded around while I unpacked the basket on my desk. The aroma was fantastic, chicken, salt rising bread, apple pie, and cheese all mingling together. I knew the kids thought I was some kind of jerk from what had gone on since I arrived with the pencil box, and then not having a regular bag of sandwiches like a normal person, but their eyes said they considered my Roy-delivered hot lunch pretty spectacular.

"Anybody want anything?" I offered. "I'm not really hungry and there's plenty." I wasn't trying to be kind or even polite. I just felt stupid piling into all that food while they sat there watching me with peanut butter or jam on their face. As if all of them were ruled by a single brain, everybody looked toward Mrs. Barrie.

"You have to eat something, David, but you are certainly generous to share what appears to be an excess of good things." She seemed pretty impressed with what was all but falling off the top of my desk.

Roger came back from the pump in time to hear this and didn't bother to go back to his seat, but stood looking down on me and my goodies. Since I'd ruined his lunch, I let him be first to choose whatever he wanted. Naturally he took the biggest piece of chicken, a thigh, which was no surprise to anybody. Mrs. Barrie made him share it, taking a knife she'd been using on her apple to cut the chicken thigh into three pieces. Then it was a free-for-all. Each kid took part of something, and when it came to the pie, the piece was big enough so we all had a small bite, thanks again to Mrs. Barrie's knife.

"Your Aunt Maude is sure one great cook," Roger said, not grumpy or anything. "Maybe I'll marry her when I get old enough."

"She's already married," I said, but I knew what he meant.

From that day on lunchtime was a party. When I went home and told Aunt Maude what happened, not about hitting Roger, but about sharing everything she'd made, she fretted that I must be starved from not getting enough to eat. I wasn't of course, but to make sure, next time she filled the basket with even more food. It got so everybody waited for Roy as impatiently as I did. He didn't come to the window but rapped lightly at the door and then walked right in. I noticed nobody thought he was a monster after they got to know him. Mrs. Barrie had him set the basket down on a long table we used for geography and drawing, which gave us more room to spread out the food. The kids told their mothers what was happening and one day Louise came with a big bowl of rice pudding her mother had sent for everybody to share. She even sent bowls and a quart of heavy cream to pour over the pudding. Then other mothers sent things to put out on the table. Nobody else sent hot things, but that's because nobody else had Roy to do the lunchtime delivery.

Eventually most of the kids stopped bringing sandwiches, arriving at school instead with a pan of baked beans or a loaf cake or something like that. Even Mrs. Barrie who usually only ate an apple and cheese nibbled away at what she called "the buffet." She had trouble holding lunch hour to thirty minutes, so sometimes added an extra ten, taking away five minutes from both morning and afternoon recess. Nobody complained.

Roy never told Aunt Maude about me punching Roger, but he did tell Charley Smith and Charley was so excited by it he slapped me on the back and almost knocked me down. "There's hope for ya yet, kid," he grabbed my shoulder and gave it a bone-breaking squeeze. "I was afraid ya were goin' ta grow up a pansy er something. If that brute gives ya any more trouble, bloody his nose again."

"It sounds to me as if you've settled into school very nicely," Rose said one Saturday morning several weeks later. When I had told her about everything that happened that first day, the day after it happened, she shook her head then and said something about beginnings not being easy. "Have you made any friends?"

"Not really. Best time is lunch but then we're all eating. The rest of the time I'm reading or studying or listening to Mrs. Barrie. Sometimes I listen to her when she's teaching the other grades because it's more interesting than what I'm supposed to be studying. If she notices, she tells me to concentrate on my own work."

"What about recess times? Who do you play with during recess?" Rose had a way of always knowing the nub of a problem.

"I hate recess," I answered quietly.

"Why, for goodness sake? Isn't that when you play games?"

"I'm no good at games, Rose. Oh, I'm okay at tag because I can run pretty fast, but I never can catch the damn—the darn—ball when we play baseball, so nobody wants me on their team. Same thing with horseshoes. They never go where they're supposed to go, no matter how careful I throw."

"Not being good at sports is a handicap for boys, I'm sure." She made a sound with her lips and shook her head. "And I suspect you read better than anybody else in the school." Rose wasn't asking, she said it as if she knew.

"That's what Mrs. Barrie says. I wish she wouldn't."

"And you already know more history," she continued.

"Not more than Louise. She knows a lot of history and geography. But she's in seventh grade."

"Is there any other boy who is interested in reading?"

"I don't think so. Most of them stumble along when they read aloud. It's as if they're dumb or something, and I know they aren't. Fortunately I'm pretty bad at arithmetic."

Rose sighed. "You have already learned, David, there are times when it's easier to be less smart than those around you."

"Especially if you're no good at baseball," I said.

"Well, if you can't be better at ball, try not to parade the fact you're better at books. Isn't it a shame we have to hide our lights to survive?" I didn't answer because I didn't know what to say. After a minute's silence, she went on, "If I'd not been so quick to let him know how smart I was, maybe he wouldn't have become discouraged." She said it almost to herself.

"Scheider, you mean?"

"I mean Scheider. Men don't like their women to be too bright, at least not brighter than they are."

"And big boys don't like littler boys to be too smart either," I agreed. "The thing is, Rose, I don't like playing ball, so it doesn't bother me that I'm not any good at it. What bothers me is that my not caring makes so much difference to the other kids. They laugh at me when I don't catch the ball, but when I shrug, so what?, they act as if I'm from another planet."

Rose reached through and put her hand on my head, rubbing it around in a distracted circle. At first it felt good, but then it began to raise static and that hurt. I reached up and took her hand away.

"Sorry," she said.

"That's all right," I said.

CHAPTER EIGHT

deline watched me feed the ducks one afternoon when I got home from school. I think she was trying to make up to me or something because she'd been hanging around a lot the last few days. When she asked me how I was getting along in school I told her about being the last one to be picked for either side when we played baseball, and she told me not to fret, that I could probably teach those disagreeable kids a thing or two.

"Should I teach them the fertility dance?"

"What makes you 'speck you know it enough to teach somebody else?"

"Adeline, it isn't that difficult. We've done it how many times, three or four? I just have to remember when to bump and when to shake."

She cackled like a crazed egg-bound hen. "They's only the beginnings, boy. You got lots of refinin' to do 'fore you get it together. You may never. I ain't convinced white boys hear the drums."

"I hear them, Adeline, just as plain as you do, even if they aren't in my blood." I threw the grain scoop back in the barrel that held the duck food and slammed the lid.

She laughed a high-pitched squeal. "You go teachin' those wormy li'l farm gals a fertility dance, and there'll be blood right enough—yours no matter what color 'tis—all over the schoolhouse yard when they daddys catch you." She threw back her head and slapped a palm of each hand against her cheeks, going hysterical at the picture she was conjuring. "To say nothin' 'bout your Aunt Maude scouring your mouth with more'n Fels Naptha. Bon Ami mos' likely." She was about to fall over.

I couldn't help grinning, watching her crack up that way. "There's nothing wrong with a fertility dance. You said so." I did a couple of hip jerks to demonstrate.

That set her off again. When she regained control she gave me a couple of hip jerks back, but then she went all serious and looked me firm in the eye. "Babycakes, you gotta learn what's right for us, for the likes of you and me, ain't necessarily right for ordinary folks."

A couple of days later I had to pee bad during recess while the whole school was out playing in the yard. I didn't want to be seen going into the boys' outhouse because I'd be teased. None of the older boys would be caught dead using the privy. They went in the bushes and peed on the ground.

When I thought nobody was looking, I made a dash around the schoolhouse and across the back, past the girls' outhouse and then beyond the boys'. I barely made it without wetting my pants, but was happily letting go in a jungle of burdocks higher than my head when I heard someone coming up behind me. We'd been playing hide-and-seek, so it could be somebody looking for a safe place to hide, but then I sensed there was more than one person. I turned my head to check, and saw the three biggest guys in school looking down at me over the top of the burdocks. I froze. Their faces told me something was going to happen.

"Let's see your dink, kid," Roger gave me a crooked smile that wasn't exactly mean but still threatened. He'd not been too ugly to me since he began eating most of my lunch every day.

I turned around. Their chests and shoulders and stupid faces appeared to be growing out of the top of the purple and green burdocks.

"Don't be scared," Roger said. "We're not gonna hurt you, just size you up." The other two guys laughed loudly at this, then quickly glanced around to see if they'd been heard.

My penis was shrinking, disappearing back into my fly without me touching it, though I had my hands over the undone buttons of my overalls. I just wanted to get out of there, but there wasn't any place to go. Roger grunted and bobbed his head as if he wasn't going to bother repeating his command because I knew what it was and I'd better respond. I took my hands away from my front and stood there feeling stupid.

"I can't see anything," Roger said, "pull it out, if you've got anything to pull." The other guys fell apart over that remark.

I pulled it out as far as it would go. The three of them stared down at my thing, then glanced at each other and snickered. As scared as I was, I was getting sick of being the butt of these jerks' joke.

"Not bad for a kid," Roger smirked. "You wanna see mine?" Without waiting for an answer he stepped around the burdocks into the open space where I was standing, unbuttoned his pants, and flipped it out.

"Wow," I said, without thinking whether or not I was allowed to speak because I was truly impressed. "That's some dink, Roger."

"It's a schlong," Roger grunted, giving it a couple of shakes to show how long it was before stuffing it back in. "When it gets to be as big as mine, you don't call it a dink anymore, you call it a schlong."

The other two guys nodded a solemn agreement. Roger smiled down at me, in a decidedly more friendly way, I suppose because he'd won a contest, and put his arm around my shoulders. We walked out of the burdock patch together, which made me feel as if I'd been let into a secret club.

An early October day pleasant enough because it was like summer, warm and golden bright and lazy, became even better with this acceptance by the older guys. After school we all shouted "See ya" to each other as they headed down the Center Road and I headed up toward the County Home. Instead of taking off my sneakers as I did most days so I could walk home barefoot, I kept them on and skipped. I tried to whistle as I skipped, but that was too much. Whistling wasn't all that easy for me when I was standing still.

Adeline was waiting for me at the corner of the East Road. I waved as soon as I saw her, but she didn't wave back, just stood there motionless. Adeline never did anything you expected her to do.

"I thought we'd soak up a l'il sun in the pump-house meadow," she said as I skipped up to her. "You wanna?" Adeline loved to soak up sun, summer or winter.

We were lying there in the meadow with our clothes off, rolled up and stuffed under our heads like pillows, listening to insects buzzing, birds chittering and singing, and water pouring over the dam, each of us chewing on the soft ends of stalks of grass. The stalks weren't as juicy as they had been in summer, but they still tasted good. Adeline had her eyes closed but I knew she wasn't yet asleep.

"I saw my first schlong today," I said, raising my right leg to rest the calf on my left knee.

"What's a schlong?" Adeline asked, about to drowse off.

"Roger Hawley's dink, except when it gets to be as big as Roger's you don't call it a dink anymore, you call it a schlong. Actually," I said, thinking about it, "I never called mine a dink either, but that's what Roger called it, mine, not his."

Adeline sat bolt upright staring down at me, the stalk of grass dangling from her lip. She flared her nostrils the way a horse does and opened her eyes so wide I could see acres of red-veined white around the black pupils.

"Ef you is talkin' 'bout what I think you is talkin' 'bout, this here conversation is at a halt." She stared at me while I tried to figure out what had upset her. I remained silent as I went back over everything I'd said. I sure didn't want a repeat of the buggy-ride disaster. That took weeks to get over. While I was thinking, she started up again. "You is lucky boy I don't trot you off to the upper kitchen where your Aunt Maude would whup you ef I told her 'bout—what's that word you said?"

"Schlong?"

She blinked a couple of times, shaking her head. "I don't 'member hearin' it afore. Must be somethin' that nasty boy made up." She made grunting sounds. "You stay 'way from him. He's not for you to be messin' round with." She lay down again.

"We didn't mess around, Adeline, we just compared sizes of"—I didn't know what to call them because they had different names—"schlongs? dinks?"

"That does it, thaaat does it," she said, leaping to her feet and bending over to pick up her dress in one movement. Dropping the dress over her head, so for her she was fully clothed again, she continued, "I'm not 'bout to sit here and listen to you run off that filthy mouth one more minute."

"Adeline, God damn it," I cried. Her nonsense had caused a crisis, and it was in crisis I couldn't help but use swears. "What did I say that was filthy?"

She looked down at me with one eye shut tight and one eye open as far as it would go. " 'Effen you don't know, l'il smart-ass, Adeline's not 'bout to lightin' you."

She started to march away, her bare feet pounding the ground, then slowed to an easy shuffle. Without turning around she said with her head in the air, "I don't s'pose you can be blamed for igrunce. After all you is only a l'il chile." Whipping about with a big smile she chortled, "C'mon, we'll dance in the pines for a bit so's to forget." Up went her dress over her head. Waving it like a banner, she ran naked across the pump-house meadow and into the forest, headed for the pine grove, her breasts flapping from side to side and her buttocks jumping up and down.

Without knowing what all the fuss had been about, I got up and followed her, dragging my overalls behind me.

CHAPTER NINE

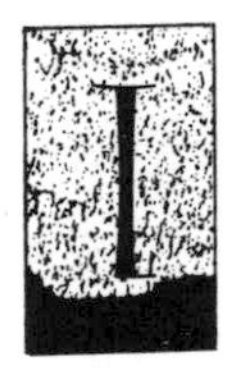

It got to be fun dancing with Adeline again. We did it about every other afternoon when I got home from school. Sometimes it was so cold we both started out with goosebumps, but they went away as we warmed up dancing. Now that I knew what I was doing she didn't holler at me so much, which meant we both had a better time. I couldn't believe it when, after we'd done an especially wild bunch of turns and stomps one afternoon, she yelled out between bumps, "Jes maybe there's a bit of black blood flowin' in the veins of that white chile." I was so proud it threw me off the beat. Before picking up again I tried to give Adeline a hug, but she pushed me away so I wouldn't ruin her rhythm, shouting, "Don't go gettin' mushy."

A couple of days after that, on a Sunday afternoon, we were sitting in her room listening to Mrs. Bullock croon lullabies. Adeline was sitting cross-legged on the bed pulling at her skirt, but not daring to actually unravel in front of her mother. I was on the floor and Mrs. Bullock was in her chair, rocking slowly back and forth with her eyes closed, singing old songs she said she'd known all her life. Her long cocoa-colored hands were folded in her lap, the skin on them so thin you could see curling blue veins underneath. From time to time she'd raise her right hand and move it around in the air as if she was conducting a choir.

Occasionally she'd say, "This here one is from my grandpappy's side. Lawd knows where it came from 'fore that." Or, "From my mam's family," or whatever. Sometimes she laughed after she finished singing, without bothering to tell Adeline and me what was making her laugh.

It was so peaceful lying there on the floor listening I had almost fallen asleep when Mrs. Bullock gave me a nudge with her slippered foot, "My son Johnny is coming soon for a grand visit. Ain't that nice?"

"Is he coming for the winter?" I asked because that's what Johnny did, came to the County Home every winter, then went off again in the spring to work at whatever he could do wherever he could find somebody to pay him to do it.

"I hope so," Mrs. Bullock said. "I miss him when he's gone so long."

"I don't," Adeline yawned a loud yawn. Mrs. Bullock didn't pay any attention to her. "I think I'll take me a short nap now. Mama, you wanna lie down?"

"That's a good idea, Adeline. Sunday naps is special, different from other days' naps." She leaned forward, waiting for Adeline to help her up out of the rocking chair. "You take a nap too, David. They's plenty room on these two beds." She smiled down at me. "I'll sing you 'nother lullaby ef you want."

"No thanks, Mrs. Bullock. I think I'll go see what's cooking around." I bent over and kissed her on the head while she gave me a pat on the arm.

Everybody was taking naps. Aunt Latzy was sound asleep and old bitch Ripley was snoring. Downstairs I peeked into Rose's room and said "Hi" kind of quiet, but she didn't answer, so I guess she was asleep too. I didn't need to go into Mary's room because I could hear all of them in the west ward zonking from way out in the sitting room.

Roy wasn't in his sitting room. Mr. Beveridge wasn't in the bakery. Aunt Maude was taking a nap and Uncle Will had gone horseback riding. I could have gone with him, but I didn't feel like it.

I went down in the furnace room looking for Charley, but his office door was locked with the padlock, so obviously he wasn't in there. As long as I was so close I decided I'd sneak along the tunnel and see if Scarzi was in his alcove working on a basket. The furnace room was underneath the lower kitchen, and two tunnels led from it, one to the men's building, the other to the women's building. The tunnel to the women's building was short and wide and brightly lighted. On either side of that one, and at the end, were coal bins as big as caves.

The other tunnel, to the men's building, was narrow, very long, and dark in spite of dim, far-apart overhead bulbs. That tunnel also curved so you couldn't see from one end to the other. Steam pipes ran along the ceiling and one wall. In the opposite wall there was a series of alcoves, about five or six feet wide and as deep, with arched ceilings. Most of the alcoves were used to store stuff people forgot a hundred years ago, but in one alcove, about two thirds of the way through the tunnel from the furnace-room end, under a single bulb hanging down on its cord, an old inmate named Scarzi sat much of the time making baskets.

Of all the people at the County Home he was the only one who truly terrified me. I wasn't afraid of Mary ever, nor Foster and Brumstead, the two old men who hung out in the carpenter shop and snarled, "What do you want?" whenever I entered their domain, though Foster and Brumstead did make me nervous. I was supposed to be afraid of Blind Dan because he was mean, that's what everybody said, "Stay away from Blind Dan, he's a mean one," but he was never mean to me, so I was not afraid of him.

But old Scarzi scared me. Maybe it's because he never said anything, just went rigid and glared no matter where he saw me. If he was eating and I walked through the men's dining room, he'd stop dead, hold his fork halfway to his mouth, and follow me with his deepset eyes until I was out of sight, or at least until I couldn't see him any longer. He had black eyebrows and a gray mustache, both bushy, and he wore a black foreign-looking cap with a leather visor, except when he was eating. Mrs. Davies wouldn't let any of the men sit at table with a hat on.

Everybody else at the County Home seemed willing to talk or listen, most of the time, of if they didn't feel too friendly at the moment, they'd say, "Not now, David," and I'd disappear, but Scarzi didn't say a word to me, in Italian or in English, ever. He'd just stop whatever he was doing and watch me. He gave me the chills.

When I was little I avoided him. If I saw him sitting in the grape arbor, I wouldn't go near the garden. Or if I thought he was making baskets in his alcove in the tunnel, I wouldn't go down in the furnace room or to the potato room next to the furnace room where Marion Evyns and his helpers boiled and peeled hot potatoes every morning.

As I grew older, I got bolder if not braver. I invented a let's see how far I dare go game. I'd tiptoe along the tunnel's stone floor not making a sound, until I could see the light in Scarzi's alcove. Then I'd force myself to creep nearer and nearer, going as close as I dared before turning around and beating it back out the other way. It took a lot of tries before I pushed myself close enough to actually see him sitting there weaving a basket from ash splints soaking in a tub of water beside his stool. Wicked-looking knives and other tools lay on the floor at his feet.

Slowly, after many more trips to the edge, I worked up enough courage to go those few steps farther, so not only could I see him but he could see me. The first time I did it he looked up startled and froze, not moving his hands, his mustache, eyebrows, or anything, just stared at me out of those fierce deep eyes. I knew I was a goner. I wanted to scream but couldn't, nor could I turn and run. My legs had turned to lead. There the two of us were, he on his stool and me on tiptoe, both staring, neither saying anything. It seemed we were that way for hours, but I don't suppose it was more than a minute or two, when he took the knife he had in his hand and pointed it in my direction, then made swift flicking slashing motions in the air.

That uprooted me. I got out of there so fast I raised dust, and I didn't go back again for a long time. I had nightmares about being down in that tunnel with him slashing his knife at me, then making a lunge and chasing me under the dim bulbs past all those other alcoves in which I was sure there were more basket makers with long arms and sharp knives waiting to grab me and slice me up. But every time I dreamt about it for some reason I woke up just when Scarzi was about to catch me, so that I got to know I was dreaming while I was having that nightmare and could stop it whenever I wanted to, and that became another dare game, dreaming the dream but putting off waking up until the last possible second before he grabbed me to cut off my head.

Eventually I worked up my courage to try the real thing again, determined not to run until he actually got up off his stool and made a move toward me. The first attempt was a repeat of what happened before, except I was expecting the worst so was ready to get out of there, and did, in spite of promising myself I wouldn't. The second time he didn't do the knife-waving thing at all, just stared and stared and stared, until I backed away. I was sure if I turned around he'd grab me from behind and slit my throat. After that, sometimes he'd glare and sometimes he'd look as if he was going to lunge, and sometimes he pretended he didn't see me at all. That added to the excitement, not knowing what he would or wouldn't do.

The final wrinkle in the dare game was when I decided to keep going right on past him, pressing myself as close as I could to the pipes running along the wall opposite his alcove, which put me definitely within his grasp. If he stretched his arm out from where he sat on his stool, he could easily grab me. My trial run of that was one of the most exciting adventures I'd had. I approached as always on tiptoe, realizing by that time he probably heard me coming no matter how quiet I was. He didn't bother to look up, though he did stop weaving. When he stopped weaving I stopped moving. When he didn't do anything after a minute, I took another step and another until I was directly across from him. I could have reached out and touched him and my arm was much shorter than his. My heart pounded in my chest. I was hot all over. I paused for just a half second, then took another step and had taken one more when his head snapped around and he glared at me over his shoulder. As if sprung from a trap I lit out for the far end of the tunnel and the basement of the men's building.

I made it, but then wasn't sure what to do next. There was nothing at the end of the tunnel except a cellar filled with stacks of broken furniture that somebody might repair someday. I could either turn around and go back through the tunnel past Scarzi, or go up the stairs into the big reading room on the men's first floor. That was perfectly safe but not very thrilling. The reading room stank of centuries of stale smoke and old spittoons. And no matter how friendly most of the men were who sat there all day napping or with their noses in books, they tended to growl when I interrupted whatever it was they were doing. However, the stairs to the reading room was the choice I made the first few times I did the pass-through routine because I was sure Scarzi expected me to come back and would really lunge and stick that knife in me.

When I finally decided to do the return trip, the funny thing is I think I scared him. At least he jumped. His back was to me as I crept along the tunnel. I guess he thought I'd gone up the other stairs as usual, so relaxed and went back to weaving his ash splints in and out. As I was creeping by, he must have caught sight of me out of the corner of his eye because he whirled around on his stool so fast his foot slammed against the tub, splashing water all over the place including onto his pants which made him roar. I didn't wait to see what happened next, but ran as fast as I could into the furnace room and up the stairs onto the sidewalk.

Once I felt I was safe I sat down on the edge of the porch and gasping for breath, laughed to split my sides. Being scared does that to you sometimes.

Anyway, on that Sunday afternoon when everybody in the

whole world was taking a nap, I decided I'd sneak a peek at old Scarzi. He wasn't there! I could hardly believe my eyes. The bulb hanging on its cord in his alcove was lighted, but there was no sign of Scarzi. For a minute I had a chill, thinking he was waiting for me in the dark around the curve, but I'll never know if he was or wasn't because I didn't care about playing the game just then, so turned around and went outside again.

Sundays were the worst days of the week because you couldn't get anybody to do anything. Everybody had to keep the Sabbath, or they used some other excuse. Just when I was about to give up and go lie down, which is what I was supposed to be doing anyway, I remembered Charley Smith told me he thought his pet calico cat had gone off to have a litter of kittens because he hadn't seen her in a couple of days. His calico was about the only cat on the place you could get anywhere near, and by near I mean she wouldn't spit and run away if she saw you coming, but you couldn't pat her or anything like that, not even Charley, and he fed her.

All the other cats at the County Home were as wild as lions and as friendly. Feral, Uncle Deane called them. But they were around to kill rats and mice, and bats and squirrels and other vermin, not to be pets. If you got too close to any of them they'd hiss and arch their back before spurting off out of sight. That was true of the kittens as well. I found lots of kittens in the hay mow, sometimes when I was looking and sometimes when I wasn't, and even if they didn't' have their eyes open, they'd spit and claw if I got too close.

Uncle Deane said the reason mother cats had their kittens in the farthest corners of the hay mow was to hide them away from the tom cats. He said toms would kill kittens if they found them. I don't know why. Maybe the calico's kittens would be different. She wasn't exactly friendly, but she did let Charley feed her and she didn't hiss at me if I didn't' try to touch her.

The hay mow over the cow barn, the granary, and the horse barn was a mammoth place, so high you couldn't see the roof struts unless the light was just right and miles long and almost as wide. It smelled fantastic, especially when the hay was fresh. Jumping off a crossbeam into the hay was fun if you were careful not to jump near any of the chutes where hay dropped down to the animals below. If you went down one of those chutes you'd land like a boulder on the cement floor, and if you didn't get killed, you'd probably break your back or your neck. It was more fun jumping when there was somebody to jump with, but nobody but Uncle Deane ever seemed much interested in the idea, so I mostly jumped all by myself when the hay was new and I couldn't resist. Then it was like diving into a bed of sweet perfume.

I entered through the horse barn, walking the middle crack-line in the concrete floor as if it were a tightrope, pretending if I stepped off on either side one of the horses would kick me way across the barn and then another horse would kick me back, and a third horse would kick me across again, back and forth as if I were a ball, until there'd be a final kick that would kill me, probably by Chub. Not that any of the horses had ever kicked me, nor raised a hoof at me, not even when I walked up next to them in their stalls.

The horses were all munching hay, making steady deep chewing and rumbling noises that didn't stop when they turned around to watch me as I tightroped past. Because it was there, I lifted the lid on the bran bin when I went through the granary and took a handful of bran to chew. I knew it would make me thirsty and swell up into a hard ball in my stomach, but it tasted good going down.

To kill time I inspected the oiled and polished harnesses on their racks in the tack room, reading the names of each horse on a shiny brass plaque above that horse's collar and bridle—Daisy, Clover, Reggie, Chad, Vic, Sampson, Chub, and so on. Most of the teams were Percherons, matched dapple grays or shiny bays with jet black manes and tails, but Vic and Sampson were Clydesdales with feet half the size of my whole body, and Chad and Chub were Belgians. Daisy and Clover were my favorites. They were dapples, so gentle I could climb up on either of their wide backs and lie down.

I went up the tack-room stairs to the mow and climbed one of the ladders so I could walk around on top of the hay to look for the calico's kittens. I wasn't expecting much because I knew she wouldn't let me touch them if she was anywhere near, so all I hoped to do was look at them and be able to tell Charley he was right. I didn't call out to her or anything, thinking it was best not to get her dander up before I happened onto wherever she'd hidden the litter.

It was always eerie looking in that dim light for kittens in the hay because you might not see a thing and suddenly there they'd be, under your feet hissing and spitting, carrying on like little leopards. I heard something, way over in a far corner. It didn't sound like kittens. I couldn't figure what it did sound like, but then I heard a voice murmur and that petrified me because as far as I knew I was in the mow all by myself.

I must have made a small sound of my own, because next thing I heard was somebody go "Shhh." And then, up out of the hay a head appeared. It was Steve, one of the farmers. He didn't have a shirt on, at least his shoulders were bare. With a broad grin he said, "David, surprise, surprise, what are you doing here?"

"I'm looking for kittens," I replied.

"Hmmm, well," he looked down, then back up at me again, "there aren't any kittens over here. I'm taking a nap. You'd better go back outside and play."

I said I would. As I was leaving, about the time I reached the ladder to climb down I heard a woman titter, and I realized if Steve was taking a nap he wasn't sleeping alone.

Out of curiosity, for a few days after that I tried to get the women who worked in the laundry and the women who helped Aunt Maude and Julia to titter so I would know who had been in the loft with Steve. I told jokes I thought were a howl, but most of the time the women groaned more than laughed, so I gave up. Why should I care anyway? Besides, I tried taking a nap in the hay mow once when I didn't have a shirt on and it was terrible. Hay looks soft but it isn't soft pricking into your bare back.

CHAPTER TEN

oger was making me mad. If just the two of us were together, he could be a buddy at school, but when the other guys appeared he turned mean, making me the butt of all his scrimy jokes. Worst of all, while he called me Davy or "D" when we were alone, in front of the guys he called me Dinky Dink. This never failed to make everybody jump around laughing. Then they'd start singing, "Dinky Dink, Dinky Dink, how's your dinky dink, Dinky Dink?" If the girls heard it, they blushed a little, but then they giggled too, and that made me want to punch each of them, one after the other, as hard as I could.

I couldn't tell Mrs. Barrie about it because that would be tattling, and I didn't tell Rose because after the way Adeline carried on when I first said the dink word to her I was afraid Rose would give me the Ivory soap treatment, but I had to tell somebody or bust, so it was back again to Adeline. She was the only one. At least she couldn't do any more than have another fit, and I'd grown used to her fits she'd had so many since summer. Besides, if things didn't change with Roger, I was prepared for a fit of my own.

When she actually listened to my story—Adeline was better at talking than listening—and she didn't appear even close to a fit, I couldn't have been more surprised. She raised her eyebrows as far up as they'd go and kept them there for a while, rolling her eyes around and around and wetting her lips several times, which meant she was thinking. When she'd done all that and I couldn't stand it a minute longer, I said, "Well?"

"Well what?"

"What should I do?"

"Stay away from him. He's evil. I tole you that long ago."

"I can't stay away from him, Adeline, we go to school together. There are only eleven of us. I'm the smallest and he's the biggest. It isn't as if I could hide out somewhere." The thought of hiding, or having to hide, made me even angrier. "I wouldn't hide if I could. I wish he'd get sick and die or at least not be able to come to school as long as I'm there."

"You is the soul a mercy," Adeline said, rolling her eyes around and around again, ending with them looking up. If she'd been a regular pray-er I'd think she was asking the Lord to forgive me. "Let me ponder it. I'll think a something."

"I didn't actually mean I wish he'd die," I said. "He's not bad when we're alone. Trouble is we're almost never alone. The other guys follow him around as if he was Moses headed for the Promised Land."

"He don't soun' like no Moses to me. He still eatin' your vittles every day?"

I nodded and shrugged. Who cared? Aunt Maude packed much more than I could possibly eat, so I didn't care about Roger scarfing up my food.

"We could put rat poison on somethin'." Adeline closed her

eyes so if anybody was watching she couldn't see them. She told me that never failed to work, people not being able to see you if you couldn't see them. I guess she wasn't sure if they could hear you, however, because she grinned a silly grin, looked heavenward in case God was eavesdropping, and said, "I's jes kiddin'."

"Adeline, I think you're headed over the edge. What's all this eye rolling you're doing?"

"You don' like the way I look, boy, don' look at me."

We were in the sitting room with a window wide open to let in cool air. They'd turned the heat on in the building and it was stifling. Julia warned us to close the window before Rose came out of the bathroom after taking a bath and washing her hair, but Rose assured Julia the fresh air felt good as she disappeared into what Adeline called the "ladies' latrine," so we left the window as it was.

Adeline was unraveling the sweater Julia had forced her to put on that morning, Julia being convinced everybody was going to catch cold the minute the temperature went below seventy. I was lying on the floor watching yarn pull away from the sleeve and pile up on the floor, thinking about Johnny, Adeline's brother, who would be turning up any day now, remembering what he'd told me about seeing ghosts.

"Adeline, have you ever seen a ghost?"

"Never." She gave the yarn a vigorous yank.

"Do you believe in ghosts?"

"I don' believe in nothin' I cain't see." After another yank to release wool caught on something, it pulled free and she went back to unraveling in earnest.

"You believe in God and Jesus, Adeline, and you've never seen them."

"Sometimes I do, 'n sometimes I don'. Depends. . . ." She glanced heavenward, but apparently didn't want another remark from me about eye rolling because she quickly looked back at the sleeve she was undoing.

I gasped at her saying she didn't believe, which made her stop unraveling and reach out to give my knee a shake. "Don' carry on so, idjut. When I thinks about it, I believes. Who knows what I believes when I's not thinkin'?" I didn't have a notion what she meant, but wouldn't admit it because then she'd say I was "too young" to understand.

"Johnny believes in ghosts. He calls them 'hants.' He's seen them, he says." I rolled over on my side.

"Johnny says lots of things."

"But he's seen them, Adeline, actually seen them—down the East Road, for instance, hovering around the old Cupeck place."

"Why don' you hesh and ball that yarn I'm pilin' up. Julia be comin' out a that latrine any minute, and maybe she won't be so vexed if I'm neat with my ravels."

"I don't know how." I didn't want to be bored balling yarn.

"What you don' know would fill an ocean," she grumbled, then laughed and threw her head back, opening her mouth so wide her pink tongue showed flat. "You may be the dumbest chile in history." She picked up a pile of yarn, poking at it until she found an end, which she handed to me, tossing the pile back on the floor. "You 'speck I can ravel and roll at the same time?"

It was no use. She always won. I pulled over a footstool with my toe and got up off the floor to sit on it. Holding the end she'd given me, I played really dumb. "Okay, how do I start?"

"Sweet baby," she crooned, bending over to give me a quick

kiss before showing me how to wrap yarn around a couple of fingers until I had the beginning of a ball. "I'll rest me from raveling a while, so's you can catch up."

"You're a saint, Adeline," I said sarcastically. She shook her head and shrugged, as if to say, it's nothin'. "There's no way I can catch up with you and you know it." Nor was there any way she could resist unraveling for a single second if she had something she could pull apart. I guess she thought I wouldn't notice if she started on the side of the sweater I couldn't see because very soon she had another pile of yarn building up on the floor over there.

When most of the sweater was either gone or going fast we decided to rest for a minute. Adeline's breasts showed through gaps. She hated underwear most of all clothes, and nobody could make her wear it, no matter how or what they threatened. I think she would have gone to the stake before she put on underwear. She got up and strolled over to look out the window, dragging still connected yarn behind her. "We should wander down to the pump house," she sighed. "It's near warm enough to stick our feet in."

"The pump-house pond is never warm," I yawned, rolling off the stool onto the floor again," but it sounds good. I'm game if you are." The pressed-tin ceiling of the sitting room had just been painted a bright cream color, so lying on your back on the floor you could see the pattern in the squares without squinting even a little bit.

The sound of Adeline's voice made me sit up straight. It had gone from slow and lazy as she talked about going down to the pond to a fierce growl deep in her throat. "What you lookin' at, old man?"

From outside the window Charley Smith's voice came back,

"You oughten be standin' there with nothin' on, showin' yerself to whoever's passin' by."

"Charley," I yelped, jumping up to join Adeline at the window. "When did you get back? When I got home from school they said you'd gone to town. I'd have gone with you if you waited."

Charley's jaw gaped open. "David, what are you doin' with that woman? You come out 'a there this minute, ya hear?"

"What woman you callin' 'that woman,' old man?" Adeline snarled. I looked up at her. Jeepers, grown-ups are dumb sometimes. It's perfectly plain Charley means Adeline when he says "that woman." He's all but pointing straight at her.

"I know who he's calling," I offered, but Adeline clapped her hand over my mouth before I could explain.

"You keep out'a this, boy."

"I'm referrin' to you, you loose darkie, runnin' round nekid all the time." Charley spit a stream of tobacco juice splat on the ground.

"Hear me, you old bag of farts, you move 'way 'fore I fly through this window and tear those squinty eyes from out your ugly face."

"Adeline," I yowled, "You say I have a rotten mouth. Listen to the swears you use, 'bag of farts'!" I covered my own mouth before she had a chance to do it, and so Charley wouldn't see me laughing at what Adeline had called him. I felt guilty, seeming to take sides against him, but Adeline was being awful funny.

"You come out here nekid, and this ole man'll show you more'n a pair of eyes, darky." Charley snorted as if he'd told the best joke of the day, letting fly with another spat of juice.

I thought Adeline was ahead of Charley in the joke department with what she'd said, but then Adeline began laughing so hard at what he'd said about eyes she must have gotten a catch in her side, because she grabbed at it with both hands. I didn't think Charley's line was anywhere near that good.

Charley grinned up at her. "Laugh, woman, but I ain't dead yet."

Adeline stopped laughing but still smiled broadly as she bent over so her breasts swung out through the holes in what was left of her sweater. "Tha's what you think, pig man. You bin dead longer 'n I bin alive." With that she reached up and pulled the green window shade all the way down to the sill.

I could hear Charley really swearing outside, demanding that I get away from "that woman," but I stayed where I was, shrugging my shoulders, not knowing what else to do, hoping Charley would go away and forget he saw me, and Adeline would go upstairs to her room and not expect me to agree with the nasty things she'd said about Charley. I thought I might be saved when Rose came out of the bathroom in her bathrobe with her hair hanging loose down her back. Julia walked along on the other side of her and fortunately didn't look toward us so she didn't see the mess we'd been making of Adeline's sweater.

Rose saw even though she hadn't looked either. Rose had eyes in the back of her head as well as in front. She saw everything, even around corners. "Whatever is going on over there had better stop now," she said, shushing along in her slippers.

"Yes'm," Adeline said in her ordinary little voice, sticking her tongue out, and bending over to pick up the balls of wool, as well as the loose yarn that had been dragged between the chair and the window and back again. "Meet you shortly down by the pond."

"I guess I'll be there," I answered, not knowing where to go.

"David, give me five minutes to get into my clothes, then come and brush my hair," Rose called from her room. I often brushed her hair, with her sitting down on a chair and me standing by the door reaching through the bars.

"I was going to the pond to stick my feet in," I replied. Adeline would be angry if I feeped out.

"It's too cold to go anywhere near that pond," Julia clucked coming out of Rose's room, her arms full of laundry. "Shouldn't you be doing something up in your own room, David?"

"I can't think of anything," I said, politely so Julia wouldn't get mad. She was always asking me if I didn't have something to do somewhere else.

"The pond," Adeline hissed from over the stair bannister. "We is goin' to the pond."

I nodded yes.

"Brushing my hair is much better for you at the moment than going off into the woods." Rose's voice drifted out across the sitting room. She not only had all-seeing eyes, she had the ears of a bat when it came to hearing.

Julia departed with Rose's linen, shaking her head and muttering about me being under foot every minute of the night and day. I looked up at Adeline whose eyes were boring holes in me from the stairs, then glanced toward Rose's room and wondered if maybe I could escape everybody and go off somewhere by myself. As if she could read my thoughts, Rose said quietly, "I'm ready, David."

"Wait for me and I'll go with you," I whispered up to Adeline, but she gave me that haughty "oh no you won't" look of hers and stomped up the stairs out of sight.

The next morning after breakfast when I had brushed my teeth and recombed my hair and been checked out by Aunt Maude who warned me to be careful on the road and during recess so as not to get hurt, and said goodbye to Ma Fleming who was fussing around in the kitchen driving Aunt Maude crazy, and tossed Roy a salute when he said he'd be along at noon with my lunch basket, I jumped off the back porch under the railing, even though Aunt Maude yelled at me through the window to "use the steps," and skipped down the walk and around the corner of the building, where I stopped to take off my sneakers before heading barefoot down the Center Road for school.

When I got to the East Road corner and the historical marker that said on this spot a bunch of Indians met to establish tribal boundries a hundred years ago, there was Adeline, waiting for me. I flinched because I thought she wanted to give me a hard time all over again for not going down to the pond yesterday the way we planned. Instead of looking mad or pouting or anything, she was smiling, broadly smiling.

"I is goin' to school with you." She stepped out away from the marker.

"Adeline, you can't go to school with me."

"I guess I can walk into that school yard same as anybody else effen I wants. Who's to stop me?"

"You can walk to school with me, I guess, but you can't go inside. Mrs. Barrie doesn't allow visitors."

"Who said anythin' 'bout goin' inside, Hateful?"

We started walking along side by side with me wondering what this was all about. Adeline hated to get up in the morning almost as much as she hated wearing clothes. I couldn't imagine her rousting out of bed just to walk to school with me. It didn't make sense.

"I got a way to stop that boy from messin' wi' you," she said.

I stopped. "Roger, you mean?" She grinned as wide a grin as she could grin and nodded. "Adeline, what are you planning? I'm not walking one foot farther until you tell me."

"You'll see," she sang in a little high voice, taking hold of my arm. "C'mon, don' be scared. Adeline gonna take care a you."

Oh God, I thought, how can I stop whatever it is she has in mind? It was bad enough at school me being different in so many ways from the other kids, without Adeline making me out to be stranger still. Having her appear with me would convince them I was hopeless. It wasn't her appearing with me, but her appearance that suddenly became the crisis in my mind. They made fun of Roy until they got to know him, but he hadn't heard them. I never told him they called him a monster. Adeline wouldn't be outside looking in through a window. She'd be standing there barefoot with only a skimpy dress hanging on her. If they said nasty things about her she'd hear them and she'd be hurt. I didn't want that.

"You should have worn shoes," I said.

"Look who's talkin' 'bout shoes," she pointed to my bare feet. " 'Sides, you knows I hates shoes."

"I don't suppose you put on any underwear this morning?" I knew better than to ask, but I was struggling to stop whatever was about to happen from happening.

Adeline shrieked a short ear-piercing laugh. "I gonna ask Dr. Davis to check you out nex' time he comes. Your mind is goin' fast." Her feet didn't pause slapping the road's hard-packed earth.

Maybe today was some kind of holiday I'd forgotten so nobody would be at the school, not even Mrs. Barrie, when we got there. Maybe everybody had come down with mumps in an epidemic that hadn't yet reached as far south as the County

Home. Maybe the schoolhouse had burned down in the night and everybody at the County Home had slept right through the excitement. That hadn't happened; I could see the chimney and the roof coming into sight above tall brown weeds along the edge of the road. Maybe I should knock Adeline out and push her in the ditch, then wake her up after school and help her home again. Maybe.

The first person I saw as we approached the school yard was Roger, and naturally he was playing a game of three-cornered catch with the other guys, which meant he'd dinky dink me, and telling Adeline about that is what brought about her visit to the school. Why hadn't I remembered Rose's warning not to repeat everything I knew?

"Well, if it isn't my friend Dinky Dink," Roger said right on cue, "and who's this with him, his nursey?" He tossed the baseball up in the air and caught it, then tossed it up again while he was talking to me. His buddies, grinning as they always did at his wit, joined him so that Adeline and I faced a barrier across the entrance to the yard.

"Roger, this is Adeline Bullock."

"Pleased to meet you, I'm sure," Adeline said in a party voice, smiling her prettiest smile as she put her hand out toward him.

Roger ignored her hand and curled his orange fuzz-covered upper lip. He was looking at Adeline in a way that made me want to hit him with a baseball bat, nudging the guys on each side of him, so they looked her up and down too and tried curling their fuzzless lips.

Adeline couldn't have not seen what they were doing, but she kept on smiling. I hadn't realized how tall she was, or maybe it was just that she was standing straight for a change. Her head was high, the way she carried it when she had a towel turban on after a bath, and her shoulders were back so that her bosoms stuck out in front of her instead of flopping flat against her chest.

"What you been callin' David is dirty." Her voice was different than any of her other voices, not high-pitched or whiney or a throaty growl the way it was when she snarled at Charley. It wasn't hoity-toity either, but almost.

Roger raised his eyebrows as if he didn't know what she was talking about and looked first to his buddy on the left then to his buddy on the right. Both of them shook their heads and raised bewildered eyebrows too. If Roger had flapped his arms and tried to fly over the schoolhouse just then, I know those other two jerks would have automatically started flapping.

"Calling David?" The way Roger said my name you could tell it tasted funny in his mouth.

"I hear you been makin' fun o' his peanut." Adeline was still smiling sweetly.

I wanted to die, but not before I killed her, with a rock, a club, my bare hands. I wanted to really push her in the ditch and jump up and down on her so she wouldn't be able to get up and walk home, ever. My peanut! for sweet Jesus Christ's sake, as Charley Smith would have bellowed. My life was over. Why wasn't I lying unconscious on the ground? I didn't dare look at Roger.

Without waiting for Roger to make any cracks about my for God's sake peanut, Adeline continued, "You speck a l'il boy oughta be as big down there as an older bully like you?"

I thought Roger was going to say something mean, but he didn't. He seemed fascinated by Adeline. At least he was staring at her with a snotty, totally stupid expression on his face.

Adeline forged ahead. "You is not bright, Bully Boy. You needs some learnin'."

Roger snorted, "And who's gonna learn me?"

"You know anythin' 'bout voodoo, Bully Boy?" Adeline's eyebrows were up as far as they could go and her eyeballs looked as if they were on the verge of popping out of her head onto the ground where they would roll around Roger's feet.

"What's voodoo?" Roger poked the kid nearest him so all three of the dumbass jokers laughed.

"Voodoo," Adeline began, looking more magnificent than I'd ever seen her, which was strange because only a second before she looked like a disgusting bug I wanted to squash, "voodoo is what I does to make things happen."

Now this was a shock. I'd never know Adeline to *do* anything other than unravel and dance and lie down in the sun. What did she mean voodoo is what she "does" to make things happen? She never mentioned voodoo to me.

Then I noticed she was pulling a cloth thing out of the pocket of her dress. It was a sort of doll made from scraps that I think came from somebody's cut-up old union suit. The doll was stuffed but not very well, its arms and legs were all wopsy and its head fell over sideways. If Adeline had made it, and she seemed to be taking credit for it, she had sewn on red wool for hair and buttons for eyes, nose, and mouth. "I made this doll," she said, confirming my suspicion. "What'd ya think of it?" She moved it around so I could see it better, and then I did see it. It! The doll had a penis or a dink or a schlong, stuffed much better than all the rest of the parts because that part stuck straight out from its limp body. "Mmmm?" she asked again, this time pointing it up toward Roger's face.

Roger guffawed and got so red-faced his orange fuzz disappeared. The other guys snickered too. I didn't snicker. I was embarrassed. Adeline had had a fit about these guys, Roger especially, being dirty and evil-minded and all that stuff, so I was supposed to stay away from them, yet here she is showing off as proud as can be a dirty doll she's made. I looked around to make sure Mrs. Barrie wasn't watching. I don't know where the rest of the students were, inside probably washing blackboards or something.

"It's you, Bully Boy." Adeline's voice was playing tricks again, going down the scale this time. She took a step forward, pushing the doll closer to Roger's face. Roger was blushing even more if that's possible. His buddies snickered nervously, not wanting Roger to suddenly get mad at them and he was acting real strange.

"With this here doll, I can do whatever I wants to do to you," she was looking straight at Roger, almost at eye level now, "jes by doin' it to the doll." Roger's eyes went from connecting with Adeline's eyes down to the doll, then back again.

"Ain't that easy, Bully Boy? You ain't even got to be 'round. You can be in your bed sleepin' for all I care, but," she waved the doll so its head and legs and arms flopped but its thing only bobbed, "whatsoever I does to this here doll, you gonna feel—wherever you is."

Roger had stopped blushing and smirking and maybe breathing. He didn't look scared, just seriously attentive. I bet Mrs. Barrie if she was watching wished he listened that way in class when she was trying to teach him something.

"Don' fret yourself over much, Bully Boy, I's jes here today to give you somethin' to think 'bout." Adeline's face was smiling but her voice wasn't. Her voice made me break out in goosebumps and she wasn't even looking at me, she was looking at Roger. "I'se not 'bout to do what I can do jes yet, 'cause I gonna give you a chance. I'se jes here learnin' you, you see?"

"You crazy nigger woman." After not saying anything for

so long, Roger's voice surprised all of us, except Adeline, who looked as if she was in complete control and had expected it.

"That does it, snotface." From the same pocket where the doll had been Adeline brought out a pair of scissors and, mumbling words I couldn't make out, raised the doll up at arm's length, then with a screech flashed it down to Roger's eye level, only inches from his nose, and with another blood-curdling yell, snipped off the tip of the doll's penis. Ravels from her blue sweater trickled out.

Roger doubled over in a scream of agony, clutching his privates and bouncing. "What have you done, nigger bitch?"

Adeline was all smiles, all sweetness again, standing tall and full-chested. With a wide-eyed, "who-me I haven't done anything wrong, ma'am," expression, she said in her party voice, "I done you a favor, Bully Boy. I jes stopped your root from growin. I could'a cut it all off, but I din't. What you got down there now is all you ever gonna have. How old is you, Bully Boy?"

Still bent over clutching his crotch, his face squeezed into a tight mask of horror, Roger croaked, "Fourteen."

Adeline shook her head sadly. "Too bad. White boys, bein' late starters, usually grows down there 'til they in their thirties or forties, I ben told. You not gonna be much of a bull when the rest of you is all growed up, Bully Boy." Roger was staring at her as if she was the voice of God. She gave him a pretty smile. "But tha's better'n no root at all, ain't it?"

The smile remained but the voice threatened again. "Which is what you have ahead o you ef you vex David again, 'bout anything. You hear me, Bully Boy?" She jutted her jaw about an inch away form Roger's quivering chin.

"I hear."

"Good. I'se gonna keep this here Bully Boy voodoo doll by

me, jes in case you slips up." She put the doll back in her pocket, gave the scissors a couple of snip, snips in the air, then put them away and beamed at the three guys. "I likes to make the 'quaintance a David's friends. Maybe I'll walk over 'n see you 'gain from time to time. Bye now."

"Goodbye," they said in unison, staring for a second before scattering like frightened mice around back of the schoolhouse, headed I was sure for the burdock patch where they could examine Roger's schlong.

"Guess I be goin' back to bed now," Adeline said as she stretched and yawned. "I ain't usually up and 'bout at this hour."

I wished I was going back to the County Home with her. No telling what Roger and the others would do to me after she was gone.

"Adeline," I had to ask, "what is voodoo?"

"Lord knows, chile. I hear'd 'bout it once't, cain't 'member where. I'se mighty pleased Bully Boy believes in it. I didn't think white folks do."

Whatever it was I prayed Roger wouldn't kill me for what had happened. I was curious and wished I was around there with the other guys in the burdock patch checking out his parts.

CHAPTER ELEVEN

ticky sweet steam rose from open vats of quince and apple juices being boiled into jelly. Aunt Maude, Mrs. Davies, and their crews were in the midst of canning. No more afternoon naps for anybody until the pickling and preserving was done. In the potato room beneath the kitchen Marion and his peelers worked through bushels of apples and quinces, then sent pails filled with them on the dumbwaiter up to the cooks. While Aunt Maude and Mrs. Davies put together the ingredients, Eunice, Aureta, and the others sterilized glass jars in boiling water, then filled them with thickening amber liquid. When they cooled, paraffin was poured on top, and Blind Theresa capped them with tin lids. Lastly Mrs. Sawyer dampened labels Aunt Maude and Mrs. Davies had written out in advance and put one on each jar so later when somebody was sent to the larder for apple cinnamon jelly, she'd know which was which.

The larder shelves were already stocked with hundreds of jars of icicle, sweet, sour, dill, chip, and other kinds of pickles, plus pickled beets, stringbeans and crabapples, a dozen kinds of berry jam—strawberry, raspberry, elderberry, blackberry, gooseberry—as well as rows and rows of canned peas, carrots, corn, peaches, pears, plums, and lots more. When you turned the lights on in that larder thousands of glass jars shone like a treasure of bright-colored jewels.

After a while, the women said I was getting in everybody's way, so I left and wandered over to talk to Rose.

"Can you smell the jelly, Rose?" I asked. She was lying down on her bed.

"I wish I was smelling veal Parmigiana."

"What's veal parma john?"

"It's a dish my mother made better than anybody else."

"I bet Mrs. Davies could make it for you."

"She wouldn't know how."

"She could look in a recipe book."

"No recipe book would have what I remember."

"Well, then you could tell her how to do it."

"No I couldn't."

"I could, if you're worried about bothering her. She's forever making things she knows I like. You tell me how to do it and I'll tell her."

"It's too complicated."

I sighed. "I think, Rose, you're in one of your moods."

She raised her head from the pillow and looked at me across the room, then let her head drop down again. "I think you're right."

"Would you like me to disappear?"

"That's not necessary."

I didn't know whether to go or stay. Rose had been acting funny recently, not at all as talkative as she usually was, and sometimes when I talked I had the feeling she wasn't listening.

When I told her about Adeline and the voodoo, she just looked at me as if I was crazy or something. As a matter of fact she said, "And I'm supposed to be the crazy one." But she never discussed it. I thought she'd have a lot to say about the whole thing, probably give me hell first of all for saying words which Adeline thought were dirty, then for tattling on Roger so that Adeline did the voodoo doll trick to stop Roger's schlong from growing.

I waited to see what Roger was going to do after Adeline cut off the tip of the doll's thing before I made a peep to Rose. When he kept his distance from me for a few days except at lunchtime, and then gradually began to be buddy-buddy again, calling me Davy or D, I decided it was going to be all right, and told Rose the story as much out of relief that I wasn't going to be killed and to celebrate as to keep her informed. It was a big letdown when she only said, "And I'm supposed to be the crazy one." While I didn't want my mouth washed out, a raised eyebrow or a grumble or two would have made her seem more interested.

"Are you bored of me, Rose?" I'd heard Aunt Maude ask Uncle Will something like that when he was trying to listen to Lum and Abner instead of listening to what she was saying.

Rose raised her head from the pillow again and looked at me for a minute, then sat up, sliding off the bed into her slippers. "No, David, I'm not bored with you. I'm bored with myself."

"Would you like me to brush your hair?"

"That would be nice, it needs it." She got her brush from the bureau and came back with a chair. When she had removed the pins from her bun, she turned around and sat down sideways. I reached through the bars to brush straight strokes from the top of her head to the tips of her hair down around her waist. As I pressed on the brush, pulling it back across the top of her head, she raised up arching her neck the way a cat does when it likes being patted and wants you to pat it some more.

"Am I doing it right?"

"Just right."

We didn't say anything for quite a while as I brushed and Rose arched, turning her body occasionally so I could reach both sides of her head. She finally broke the silence when she asked, "What are your thoughts on Heaven and Hell, David?"

"I don't know," I said. I didn't. I'd thought about both Heaven and Hell a lot, but I couldn't say what I had decided about them, and I knew that's what Rose was asking for; this is the way it is with thoughts.

"Surely you must know what you believe? What do you think Hell is?"

"It's a place you go when you die if you've been bad. At least that's what they say, but Aunt Maude always says when somebody dies that they've gone to be with Jesus in Heaven, no matter how bad she always said that person was before he died."

"That's because she believes they've been saved."

"The only way you can be saved is to say you're sorry and mean it and ask God to forgive you and accept Jesus Christ as your personal Savior, and I don't think some of the people I'm talking about believed in God, so it isn't likely they told him they're sorry."

"Maybe they changed their minds at the last minute and didn't tell anybody."

"Could be, I suppose, but I don't think so."

"Do you believe in God?" She arched and stretched her neck.

"Of course, don't you?"

She didn't reply at first, but then repeated what I had said, "Of course."

I kept brushing. "Rose, do you think Scheider is in Heaven with Jesus? You said he was pretty bad sometimes. Do you think he said he was sorry when you were killing him?"

She pulled away and turned to look at me in a cold stare, then softened her expression and sat back so I could continue brushing. "Who knows where he is? Wherever it is, I'd prefer not going there." She shook her body the way a horse shivers in its skin.

"Not even if he's in Heaven?"

"I doubt Scheider got past the Pearly Gates." She rose from the chair. "Thank you, David, that felt good. Is my hair shining?"

I could tell she was changing the subject. "It glistens."

Rose frowned. "Glistens? Where did you pick up that word?"

"I heard it on the radio and I asked Mrs. Barrie what it means, so I know it means the way your hair looks now."

She smiled at that, and went to the mirror to finish fixing her hair. While she was twisting it into a knot and pinning it on her neck I hummed a couple of choruses of "Blue Tail Fly." I couldn't get that song out of my mind since Uncle Ezra and his Hoosier Hotshots had played it on the radio a couple of nights before.

"Have you ever seen a ghost, Rose?"

"Only the ones that walk around here because they won't give up and lie down." The hairpin in her mouth made her lisp.

"Honest, Rose? You've seen ghosts walking around here? Where exactly?" Wow, I'm wondering all the time about ghosts and wishing I could see one and Rose is seeing them every day.

She turned to stare at me as if I was stupid, and took the hairpin out of her mouth. "David, I was referring to several of the near-dead inmates of this institution."

"Like who?"

"Like nobody I'm going to mention."

"You think I'll tell, don't you? I don't repeat everything I know anymore. I keep a lot of secrets to myself. Who do you think is a ghost, Rose?" I had the feeling I would wet my pants if I didn't go to the bathroom right away, but I couldn't leave until Rose answered my question.

She came back to the door. "David, I'm not talking about anybody. I was making a poor joke. What is all this nonsense about ghosts? First you're into voodoo and now it's ghosts."

So she had listened when I was telling her about Adeline and Roger! "Johnny Bullock talks about them a lot when he's here, and . . ."

"Is he back? I haven't seen him."

"No, he's due any day, Mrs. Bullock says, but when he was here last year he told me lots of ghost stories, about how they sound and how they look. I'd love to see one."

"Don't hold your breath."

"I haven't held my breath since I was a baby. I used to hold it every time I cried hard, Aunt Maude tells me."

Rose smiled and shook her head as if I was hopeless, putting her hand through to touch me. "I forget you are still a little boy." Before I could tell her I wasn't, she went on. "When I talk to you as if you were a grown-up, why don't you just say to me, 'Rose, I'm only a child,' and if I ask you something ridiculous, you add, 'there's no way I'd know the answer to that question.' "

"What do you mean, 'only a child'? You say it as if there's something wrong with me. 'Only a child,' " I spit out the

words. "The main reason I like you so much, Rose, is because you never talk to me as if I was 'only a child.' Everybody else treats me like a little kid."

The more you cry the less you pee, Aunt Jessie had said to Aunt Maude once when she was boohooing, and I felt now more as if I was going to cry than wet my pants. Adeline was always telling me I was too young and making me mad, but Rose never had done that before. Why was she doing it now? And why did Rose saying it make me want to cry instead of making me mad?

"David, David, there is absolutely nothing wrong with you." She tried to hold my face in her hands but I pulled away so she couldn't reach me through the bars. She withdrew her arms. "I'm sorry. I don't think of you as any age at all. You are my friend, David, and I miss you when you aren't around, but there are times when I expect too much of you." Then she stopped. "Anything I say now will only make matters worse, I'm afraid. Please don't be angry with me. I feel as if I'm about to fly off the wall these days and I certainly will if you are cross with me, or if I think I have hurt your feelings. Will you forgive me, David, if I said something stupid?"

She closed her eyes. I'd never seen Rose cry. It occurred to me that she might. No matter how sad she looked when she talked about Scheider or being locked up until somebody decided she was fit to be free, she never really cried. She opened her eyes again and they were wet, but just as it looked as if tears might roll out onto her cheeks, she blinked a couple of times and that was that.

I'd tried blinking them back lots of times, but I guess I didn't blink fast enough or something because I never succeeded in stopping them from pouring out. Clearing my throat

first, I said, "I have to go to the bathroom now and since Julia has such a fit when I use the ladies latrine I'd better go someplace else, but I'll be back and I'd really like to talk with you about ghosts."

"We'll talk about anything you want, David." She sounded and looked very depressed.

I can't remember why I didn't get back that afternoon but I didn't. In fact I didn't get to bring up the ghost subject with Rose again, even though I saw her every day, until after Johnny Bullock had arrived for the winter and one Saturday he and I went looking for bittersweet along the East Road and at the edge of the woods.

One of the things Johnny did to earn money was gather bittersweet that he tied into bunches and took to town where he could sell it, either Pa Fleming or Charley Smith driving him in. He also dug ginseng roots to sell, and wild horseradish which Mrs. Davies let him grind up in her pantry and put in bottles he'd rescued from somewhere and scrubbed clean. He had regular customers as well as people on the street who bought what he found in the woods. Most of the money he earned that way he spent on nice things for his mother and Adeline, things like sweet-smelling soap and perfume and talcum powder and pretty handkerchiefs. A long time back he saved up enough to buy his mother a plaid wool bathrobe with a gold cord. During the winter she wore it over her dress, and told everybody over and over and over again that her son Johnny had purchased it for her. She said she wanted to be buried in it.

That Saturday when I saw Johnny getting his things together to go picking bittersweet, I asked him if I could go with him, and he asked Aunt Maude if it was okay. "We be gone mos' the day," he told her.

"Then you'll need sandwiches. I'll make up something, Johnny, if you give me a few minutes. Meanwhile, David, you go upstairs and put on your warm sweater," Aunt Maude said.

I carried the bag of sandwiches and Thermos of milk and Johnny carried his knives and sacks and twine. We had just started down the East Road, not more than a few feet, when Charley Smith roared up beside us in the jitney.

"Where're you two pirates off to?" he wanted to know.

Johnny looked at Charley out of the corner of his eye but didn't stop walking.

"We're going to gather bittersweet," I answered, hoping Charley wouldn't want to go with us because I was dying to hear more about ghosts and I didn't think Johnny would talk if Charley was there.

"Ya wanna ride? I know where there's a shitload of the stuff," Charley offered.

"No, thank you all the same," Johnny said, bobbing his head.

"Then walk 'n see if I care. I'll not tell ya where it is." Tobacco juice flew out the window just missing Johnny.

"I knows where it's at, no need you tellin' us," Johnny said in a loud but not forceful voice.

"Stubborn dumbass darkie," Charley barked. "I thought you had better sense'n ta waste time." He threw the jitney into gear and jerked off down the road, covering Johnny and me with dust.

I went into a fit of coughing and spitting and brushing at my face as best I could with my arms full of food. Johnny just shook his head and muttered something that sounded like "sum bitch."

"You don't like Charley much, do you, Johnny?" I asked,

when I felt I wouldn't get it filled with grit if I opened my mouth.

"Not a case a me likin' or not likin'," Johnny replied.

"Adeline hates him. She shrieks and screams at him."

"Adeline ain't got the brains God give a peahen."

"She says Charley's a lech, whatever that means."

"Oh he's tha' right enuff, 'n more too," Johnny chortled. "He allus makin' me out a fool, but I ain't a fool all the time."

Johnny didn't look like a fool, but then I wasn't sure what a fool should look like, and Aunt Maude told me the Bible said I shouldn't call anybody a fool ever so probably I'd never know who was and who wasn't. "What does Charley do?" I asked.

Johnny chortled deeply again and shook his head from side to side. "Oh, one time I'se helpin' him out down ta the pig barn, 'n he sent me ta the powa' house to borry a bucket a steam."

"Did you get it?" I asked.

Johnny stopped dead in his tracks and looked down at me with his eyes wide for a minute before busting out again. "You'd a gone too, Davy Boy!" He dropped his bag of knives and twine in the road and holding his sides turned in circles cheering and laughing. When he calmed down a bit, he put his hand on my shoulder and bent to pick up his sack. "Lord a mercy, ole Johnny ain't the onliest fool around."

He was right. Once I was snooping around in the laundry storeroom and Charley saw me and said if I was so curious about what was in there I should take the plug out of one of the big metal drums and take a deep whiff. Because I love to smell things I did as he asked, and ended up flat on my back on the storeroom floor gasping for breath. While I thought I was dying he stood there grinning because I'd been dumb enough to inhale naptha. I never did again.

When he bent over to gather up his things, the sun caught the gold tooth in the front of Johnny's mouth, making it sparkle. He was given that gold tooth by the dentist in town whose yard he took care of every summer. Johnny not only brushed his teeth regularly, but polished the gold tooth with a special soft cloth he carried in his pocket and never used for anything else.

"Do you think Charley wants to make you look foolish, or is he just having fun?" I asked as we moved on down the road.

"Who knows what a white man's up to?" Johnny shook his head. "Mos' times I gets 'long jes fine, but then they's times I don' know effen white folks 'bout to take a fit 'n do me harm. Charley's allus on the edge of fittin'. Sometimes I speck he's evil and sometimes I speck he ain't. So I plays it safe 'n easy 'n tries not to set him off."

At the foot of the East Road hill, on the left-hand side as you headed east, stood the old Cupeck place, an abandoned house with a front porch that was falling down and no glass in any of the windows. The kitchen chimney had blown over, its bricks scattered across the shingled roof that had holes in it big enough for a grown man to crawl through. Another chimney leaned as if it too would go if anybody breathed on it, but that chimney had been leaning ever since I could remember so I guess it wasn't about to fall any minute soon. The yard around the house was a jungle and the old driveway had disappeared under a stand of chicory weed and grapevine gone wild. The grapevine covered everything around, including a couple of broken-down old pear trees.

I had fought my way through the underbrush one time when

I was exploring and got as far as the kitchen door. I couldn't push the door open far enough to squeeze inside because the floor had buckled up underneath. The old cellar hatchway cover was rotted away, so I could have sneaked in through the cellar, but I wasn't brave enough to go down there in the dark all by myself. A piece of curtain blew in and out an upstairs window and a glass windchime like the kind you buy at Woolworths kept tinkling in the breeze, making the whole place kind of eerie. I wasn't afraid, just nervous.

It was the windchime I heard the Saturday I was out with Johnny that gave me an excuse to ask him if he'd explore the inside of the house with me, but before I got out more than, "Johnny, let's go over to the Cupeck house," he jumped the ditch on the right side of the road and said he was going to climb the fence and walk through the orchard for a ways. He was on top of the fence when I said, "Why, Johnny? It's no shortcut, and besides, I want to go look inside the Cupeck house."

"The Cupeck house is why I'se goin' the orchard route," Johnny answered, plopping down on the other side of the fence.

"I don't understand."

"No need ta understand. You go howsoever way you wants to go, 'n I meets ya down the road a piece."

Nothing I said changed his mind. He just kept plodding along the fence in the orchard carrying his sacks and stuff. As I passed the Cupeck house I tried walking on tiptoe so I could see more, but I couldn't get up high enough to do much good. The only way was to battle the jungle again sometime soon, and go in through a window. I was sure the house would be full of neat things, not real treasure of course but things it would be fun to have, and because nobody had lived there for years it would probably be all right for me to take whatever I wanted, not that I'd asked Aunt Maude about it, or anybody else.

The way we worked that Saturday was Johnny pulled the bittersweet vines down off the trees, and then I cut the parts that had berries up into pieces the way he showed me, and together we tied the pieces into bunches. When we had three burlap bags full of bunches, and had eaten all our sandwiches and drunk all our milk, Johnny said it was time to head back. "Sides, we don' wanna be hikin' up that road when it's comin' on dark."

I noticed he was getting itchy as we drew close to the Cupeck place. He kept looking toward the orchard fence and muttering about all we were carrying, not paying a bit of attention to what I was talking about.

"S'pose you could get 'cross that ditch?" he asked.

"Easy," I replied.

"Le's cross right here, 'n you climb over the fence, 'n I'll hand you the sacks."

"Why go to all that trouble, Johnny, when we can walk straight up the road?"

"On count I ain't goin' pas' tha' spook house. No way!" He stood there shaking his head.

"What is there to be afraid of?" I asked. He stopped shaking his head and looked at me as if I was not bright. "I mean it, Johnny. There's nothing there but an old empty house. I was going to ask you to help me get inside so we could explore it on the way down here this morning."

"No way is I goin' near tha' spook house full of hants, 'n you bes' not be goin' near neither."

"Johnny, are you sure there are ghosts in the Cupeck house? Have you really seen them?"

"I'se seen 'em."

"What do they look like?"

"Tha's not easy to say."

"I mean, are they like Halloween ghosts in sheets with holes for eyes?"

"Neva seen ghosts' eyes."

"Have any of them ever hurt you?"

"Neva give 'em a chance t'."

We stood there on the side of the ditch, Johnny as if he was putting down roots, me dying to get going and as close to the Cupeck house as possible. The only thing we could see of it from where we were was the leaning chimney. Johnny's gaze was glued to it as if he expected something to pop out of the top any second.

"What do ghosts do, Johnny?"

"Mos' anythin' they wants to do, I spect."

"When you've seen them, what did they do?"

"Mos' times nothin'. They jes is 'n tha's enough."

"Do they fly at you?"

"I don' wait 'roun to find out."

We were getting nowhere. I really wanted Johnny to be serious, but he was just carrying on. If he'd never been hurt by a ghost or even chased by one, I couldn't figure out why he was acting so scared. He was the only ghost expert I knew and he wasn't helping me find out more about them at all.

"What are ghosts?" I'd heard people joking about what they were, but if Johnny had seen them, he would certainly know better than people who were just having fun.

"They's dead folks riz up outta they graves."

"Do they look like dead people? Can you recognize them as people you knew?"

"I tole ya, 'n tole ya, I ain't 'bout to hang 'roun to find out more'n I knows now."

"But, Johnny, how do you know anything if you run every time you see one? How do you even know what you are seeing is a ghost?"

"Oh, I knows right nuff, 'n you knows too effen you gets caught by one."

Now we were getting somewhere. "Have you ever been caught by one, Johnny? Is that why you're so scared of them?"

He didn't answer right away, just scuffled his shoes in the dirt. I wasn't going to let him get away without answering, so I stared at him and nodded my head up and down as if I was saying, have you? have you? When he couldn't stand my stare and my nodding any longer he replied, "I'se almos' caught once, 'n I 'bout died, I'se so scared. Then the hant laughed, 'n I knowed that white thing in the dark ain't no ghost at all, cuz I 'nized the laugh."

"The ghost laughed? That must have meant it was a friendly ghost."

Johnny's voice was angry. "Effen I ain't so scared, I'd a smelled him 'fore he laughed, 'n I'd knowed it was Charley Smith right off."

My heart sank. If ghosts were only people like Charley Smith dressed up, then what was the use of trying to see a ghost? "Damn," I said.

"Tha' don' mean there ain't true hants," Johnny reassured me, probably wondering why I was disappointed. "Jes mean ta onliest time I'se close ta bein' grabbed by one, it warn't one."

I couldn't persuade him to stay on the road, so we climbed the fence and passed the bags over, then took a shortcut across the orchard to the end of the grape arbor in the garden and climbed another fence.

The last question I asked him that day was, what made him

so afraid of the Cupeck house if he hadn't really seen any ghosts around there? He explained to me that ghosts love empty houses where they won't be disturbed, and because the Cupeck house had been empty since anybody could remember, it was obvious lots of ghosts would gather there.

"Take my 'vice," he warned as we trudged up through the grape arbor. "Stay clear a tha' ol' Cupeck place. It's the firstest place hants go after they put in any grave 'roun here."

I was no longer sure Johnny knew what he was talking about, but I knew I was going to get inside that house and really explore the first chance I had.

CHAPTER TWELVE

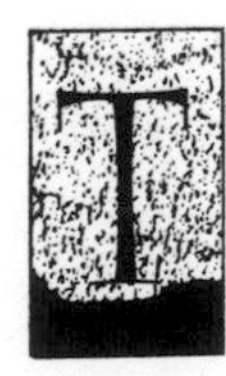

he next day was Sunday, never the most exciting day of the week even when Uncle Will and Aunt Maude had their weekend off and we spent it at the home farm, except that on those Sundays Uncle Will and I could go horseback riding if we wanted to, after we'd gone to church at the Center and had dinner, of course. Church was kind of an iffy thing. It was okay if the kids in the Sunday School class I was put in didn't laugh at me. While I'd thought a lot about God and felt pretty comfortable with Him when He and I were alone, I had not paid much attention to Ezekiel, Nehemiah, Abraham, and all those others, and that's what they studied in Sunday School, so when a question came up about something they'd learned on a Sunday when I wasn't there I looked like a dunce because I "knoweth not the answer," as one jerk said. The Sunday School regulars loved having me goof. In the Bible quiz it was all of them against me, and they always won.

On the Sundays when we stayed at the County Home,

sometimes there were services in the women's sitting room conducted by visiting preachers and sometimes there was only a hymn sing with Blind Theresa playing the pump organ and Pa Fleming reading verses from the Bible. Whatever it was, Aunt Maude made sure my ears and fingernails were clean before I attended. Whether or not there was a preacher, Jimmy North rang the chapel bell, and he'd break my arm if I went anywhere near the bell rope when the time came.

Jimmy had scarlet fever when he was four and they said he never got any older than that in his head, even though in his body he was almost an old man. Jimmy wasn't only selfish about the chapel bell cord, he was also mean about his wagon. He had a four-wheel wagon with sides on it that he used to haul cannisters of milk from the cow barn to the kitchens. Morning and night he made as many trips back and forth as was necessary, and he had a fit if I offered to help pull the wagon or even hold onto the cannisters. If I insisted, he'd push me away and squeal like a mad pig. You could say he was a spoiled brat except I don't think you can be a brat when you're as old as Jimmy was. Everybody else thought he was cute but I thought he needed a hit on the head. If I'd been as bratty as he was about anything, Aunt Maude or Rose or somebody would have given me a tongue lashing at least, and more likely twisted my ear off.

Anyway, the Sunday after the Saturday I went looking for bittersweet with Johnny a fire and brimstone preacher came to the County Home to conduct services and save souls. Rose couldn't stand him. She hated the Sundays when he came because while she couldn't be out where he did his Bible thumping and raving and ranting, she also couldn't get away from the sound of his voice which not only filled the sitting room and her room and the downstairs wards and the upstairs wards but could be heard plainly through the arcade into the lower kitchen, the men's dining rooms, and beyond. In the summertime if the windows were open I bet they heard him way over in Middlebury.

I didn't like him any better than Rose did, but I had to sit in on his raving and shouting because Aunt Maude was worried about my religious education since I didn't get to go to that dumb Sunday School class every Sunday. To tell the truth, I don't think the minister liked me much either. His name was Martin Potts, and he wanted to be called Brother Potts, but that seemed silly for me to do because he must have been almost as old as Gramps, so when I had to call him anything I called him Mr. Potts, and every time I did that he'd correct me in a voice that was sicky sweet and dirty mean all at the same time. "Bruuuther Potts, my boy," he'd say, stretching out the "Bruuuther" for as long as he could hold his breath. He had a fakey smile that only fooled those who wanted to be fooled. I had the feeling he'd pinch me hard enough to draw blood if nobody was around.

"Who's coming to save us this week, that man Potts?" Rose asked as she heard the folding chairs being set up in the sitting room.

"You mean Bruuuther Potts," I said in my deepest voice that made both of us snicker, Rose behind her hand.

"Please, David, tell him or have Julia tell him, or Pa Fleming, or somebody, anybody, tell him I have a highly contagious disease so he must not come near my door. Last time he was here he stood where you're standing and begged me for the fiftieth time to accept him as my route to salvation. No matter how hard I pretend to be asleep, he won't stop. Does he drink, do you think?"

"I don't know. I'll try to get a whiff of his breath today,

though I'll have to do a really deep inhale because his clothes smell so awful."

"It's a combination of old sweat and mothballs, I'm sure. I don't think he washes and probably only takes that dreadful black suit out of the cedar chest when he's saving souls."

"No, Rose, I think he never takes that suit off, not even when he goes to bed. It has patches of green in the seat and on both knees."

"The knees are from praying, I suppose. I don't know what to blame the seat on."

"Anyway, I don't think he's all that close to God, no matter what he says."

"I agree," Rose nodded, pursing her lips, "but why do you say that?"

"I don't know, except I think God likes nicer people than Bruuuther Potts. He's too mealy."

The sitting room was full, with more women than men, but that's because it being the women's sitting room they got there first and took up most of the chairs before the interested men wandered in from their building. Many of the inmates considered the Sunday morning service entertainment. They came and sat no matter who was speaking. Some of them went to sleep before things began and some never woke up until Julia gave them a shake when it was over.

Mary was there in a wheelchair that they pushed down front, so I went down front too to sit next to her.

"Can't you walk, Mary?" I asked her.

"I'm having problems with circulation in my legs so I hobble around worse than ever these days. Julia is afraid I'll fall and break something so she made me come out in the wheelchair."

"I hope you two aren't going to talk throughout the service," Mrs. Ripley snarled from the second row where she filled an entire love seat, her broad behind touching the arms at both ends.

"What's her problem?" Mary spluttered spit in all directions. I shrugged. Church services never altered Mrs. Ripley's disposition.

At the stroke of ten Jimmy North rang the chapel bell and Bruuuther Potts appeared repeating, "Bless you, bless you," as he came down the center aisle toward the portable pulpit that stood in front of a window between two potted palms from Ma Fleming's parlor. Roy helped Julia set up for the Sunday services and he always tried to make it look special with some kind of greenery.

I swear I didn't mean it, I didn't do it on purpose, but on the absolute second Bruuuther Potts reached the front and turned around, raising his arms to once more formally bless us, the multitude, calling us to worship by intoning, "Bruuuthers, Sisters . . .", I let go the most spectacular fart of my life. It wasn't just a single muffled explosion, nor even a series of separate pops, but a loud rolling thunderous rumble that went on and on and on as if I'd eaten nothing but beans beans the musical fruit for a month.

"What was that?" Mary Delancy asked, turning in her chair to peer blindly around the room.

Mrs. Ripley must have gotten the full benefit, because she was closest behind me. "Oh my God," she said in a not prayerful way.

Everybody else was silent, though everybody had heard. They could not have helped but hear—even the most deaf and those already asleep. It was not possible to hope they'd blame somebody else because by the time the fart was finished nobody could have doubted where it was coming from. What was I supposed to do, drop dead, evaporate? It was done, and while I had done it I hadn't meant to do it. Later it would occur to me, and Rose didn't disagree, it might have been God using me to say Bruuuther Potts wasn't high on His list of favorite people either, but in the moments following the thunder all I could think of was how to get out of there.

I glanced up to see Bruuuther Potts glaring down at me over the pulpit, with the sunlight from the window behind him making a glow around his head. For a second I thought maybe Bruuuther Potts was holy after all, but then he smiled his tightest meanest smile and said, without taking his unsmiling eyes off me, "Well, well, well, young man, ha, ha, ha, it's better to have an empty house than a bad tenant."

There was some nervous tittering among the inmates, but mostly there was silence except for old bitch Ripley who leaned forward, causing the love seat to creak, and hissed, "If you have any manners at all you'll leave the room, you nasty boy."

Before I could act on what she said—and I had no intention of leaving now that she suggested it—Mary reached over and took my wrist in a death grip that would have made it impossible for me to get up even if I'd wanted to. "Stay where you are, David, 'Rese needs us to back her up on the hymns."

My fart was the highlight of that morning's service. Bruuther Potts did his usual screaming and shouting, waving a Bible in the air and thumping it with the flat of his hand, trying to hold everybody's attention, but you could tell their minds were wandering. I had asked Aunt Maude about that Bible thumping once because she'd taught me to treat the Good Book as if it were part of God Himself. I couldn't lay anything on top of a Bible, I had to open it carefully and not touch it when my hands were dirty. Yet here was this preacher whose hands looked grimy to me, I could see they were sweaty, and he was pounding and thrashing that Bible around as if it was a rat being killed by a terrier.

He had only one sermon, which was about how much God loved all sinners and how His son Jesus had died to save sinners and because everybody in the room was a sinner wouldn't all those who wanted to be saved for all eternity come forward and accept Jesus as their personal Savior so their sins would be washed away and they could enter the Kingdom of Heaven, which was forbidden to all who did not repent. He said over and over that time was short and delay dangerous, the Day of Judgment was at hand. Because everybody had heard his pleas and warnings a hundred times and most of us had gone forward to be saved at least once, we all just sat there. In the very back row Mr. Brumstead and Chet Foster were snoring up a storm.

When Bruuuther Potts realized he wasn't getting any takers, not even after he'd given us more chances than an auctioneer who keeps say, "Going, going, going," and you wonder if he'll ever get to "gone," he told us to bow our heads and he began his usual endless prayer about everything except the larder full of new jelly.

While my approach to God when I talked to Him was familiar because it was just Him and me, like sharing secrets with a special friend, I never thought of Him as anything other than the All-Powerful. Bruuuther Potts in his roller-coaster prayers spoke to God as if He was just one of the boys. It bothered me that Bruuuther Potts didn't seem to show any respect.

My neck got so stiff from keeping my head bent I was sure I wouldn't be able to look back up again if Bruuuther Potts ever said "Amen." Mary fell asleep, snoring much louder than Mr. Brumstead, but even that didn't slow him down. I guess he could only hear himself.

I thought it must be Wednesday at least when he finished praying. It took him a minute to come back to us on earth from wherever he'd been, but then he asked Blind Theresa to play "Onward Christian Soldiers" so the congregation could sing while the offering basket was passed. He urged us to open our throats in praise, our hearts in thanksgiving, and our pockets in generosity. Theresa pumped and played and we sang with gusto, glad to be on our feet and alive while Bruuuther Potts himself passed among us holding out the velvet-lined basket. I guess he didn't get enough money the first time around because he told us after we finished the last words, "with the cross of Jesus going on before," how much missionaries to heathens in darkest Africa depended upon the support of God-fearing Christians at home, such as everybody in that room—how we had all turned from hell-bent sinners to Christians without going forward and confessing when he asked us to was a mystery to me, but that's what he called us, God-fearing Christians. Maybe it was all those verses of "Onward Christian Soldiers" did it.

"So," he concluded in a hoarse whispery voice, "I'm going to give you another chance to be generous, another opportunity to support those who carry the divine word. Empty your pockets so that your lives may be filled with the Holy Spirit. Shall we try 'Onward Christian Soldiers' one more time, Sister Theresa?"

"I could play something else if you'd prefer," Theresa offered.

" 'Onward Christian Soldiers' will do just fine, and with spirit please." To show us how he wanted it sung he began bellowing, "Onward Christian Soldiers, marching as to war, with the cross of Jesus," and he never stopped singing as he shook the velvet-lined basket under the nose of each person there, staring down at us from above. Those who had sat back down and were asleep got a sharp jab in the shoulder. I guess he didn't worry anybody else with his threatening eyes any more than he worried me because Bruuuther Potts only picked up a couple more nickels and dimes the second time around.

As usual I kept my dime deep and safe in my pants pocket. Dimes were hard to come by and nothing Bruuuther Potts said convinced me to give it to him for what I didn't know. I doubted the dime would get to Africa. If I spent the dime at Harry Woolf's store, I knew Mr. Woolf would do something good with it. I wouldn't have been surprised to see Mr. Woolf casting coins at the feet of beggars if there had been any beggars around. Aunt Maude said he sent baskets of food regularly to poor families who didn't have enough to eat.

From beginning to end I don't think it was Bruuuther Potts's best service, or at least he acted as if he wasn't particularly pleased. He didn't bother to bless anybody as they tottered out, and barely answered the questions of those few who went up front to talk to him as he was jamming his notes back into that poor battered Bible. I took the opportunity during the confusion of everybody leaving to rush over to Rose's door.

"You okay, Rose?" I hissed through the bars.

She was standing at the window looking out. When she turned to look at me, she shook her head, not as if she wasn't all right but as if to say, David what have you done now? "Are you all right?" she asked, making "you" the important word.

"Did you hear what I did?" I was still embarrassed.

"The world heard."

"Did Aunt Maude hear, do you think?"

Rose walked toward me. "I doubt it. But you had better practice control, David."

"How can you control something you don't even know is going to happen?"

"I guess you can't." Rose smiled and covered her mouth with her hand.

Naturally Bruuuther Potts stayed for Sunday dinner and from the way he always ate Uncle Deane and I were convinced he never had a mouthful of anything between the times he came to the County Home to conduct services. When everybody else was all finished and waiting for dessert, he'd still be gulping down one more helping of whatever it was Aunt Maude had cooked that day. I couldn't have been more delighted than when he let out a big belch after finishing his third serving of roast lamb. Everybody pretended they didn't notice. Uncle Deane and I exchanged looks and I wished I knew some smarty phrase like "better an empty house than a bad tenant." I could have told him what Rose had told me about practicing control, but I didn't.

Immediately after dinner, when Aunt Maude said she and Uncle Will were going to drive over to see Hattie Berkemeyer who was sick with the shingles, I said I'd rather stay at home and take a nap. I managed a big yawn. Aunt Maude asked Roy to keep an eye on me. He said he would, but I wasn't worried he'd keep me prisoner.

After they had gone and I was on my own, I lit out for the Cupeck place.

Because it was fall a lot of the weeds in the front yard had died and dried up, and leaves had fallen off the bushes, so I could see through the jungle, but that didn't make it any easier to get through. I had to push stalks aside or step on them to make a path for myself. If I had been taller and heavier it would have been simpler, but I managed, only getting a few scratches when prickers went through my sweater or my pants. I'd worry later about explaining the snags to Aunt Maude.

The front porch steps had totally collapsed and the porch floor didn't look too safe either, so I didn't want to go up on it, which meant I couldn't look into the front windows because they were too high. I wished the windchime would stop tinkling, but the breeze kept it moving.

I had to figure out a way to get inside. The only thing to do was go around back. I had tried the kitchen door one time before and knew that was not going to open, so I'd have to go all the way around. For some reason there wasn't as much underbrush growing in the back, but there was a lot of junk laying around. I took an old wooden bucket and put it upside down under a window for something to stand on, but the bucket didn't raise me high enough to see anything.

Scrummaging around, I found a piece of log that had been used for a chopping block. I rolled it over to the kitchen window, and set the log on end. Then I put the wooden bucket upside down on top of the log where it sort of fit, which was good because the log itself was wobbly and if the bucket wobbled on top of the already wobbly log I'd never be able to stand on it. Balancing as best I could on top of the bucket, I reached up to grab the edge of the windowsill, using it as support to pull myself up the side of the house. After a lot of huffing and standing up very slowly, I could get my head and chest through the window. Sliding along inch by inch on my stomach I fell inside, onto the Cupecks' kitchen floor.

Sitting there while I got my breath I looked around. An old cast-iron wood stove tilted away from one wall because part of the floor was giving way. There wasn't anything else in the kitchen except a sink with a pump, and an old calendar with a picture of a car on it hanging next to the door that was wedged partially open against a high spot in the floor. Through an open door near the sink I could see a pantry. I decided to explore that first.

Except for rat and mice pellets there wasn't much of anything on the pantry shelves. Oh, a few pieces of broken dishes and an enamel dipper with a hole in the bottom, but no treasures. When I looked out through the pantry window, I saw an old bureau up against the wall. If I'd bothered to walk all the way around the house before taking the trouble to roll the log and set the bucket on top, I could have just climbed up on that bureau and in through the pantry window as easy as nothing. That's the way I'd go out, I decided.

There were two more doors in the kitchen, both of them open. One led to the front of the house and the other to the stairs going up. It seemed best to poke around downstairs first. The first room after the kitchen was big, with windows at both ends. There was a boarded-up fireplace, and a stovepipe hole in the wall above the mantle that had been covered over with black tape. Next to the hole somebody had pasted a colored picture of Jesus at the Well, exactly like the one in the Sunday School room at Center Church.

The big room didn't have any furniture, but the two rooms at the front of the house each had parts of beds in them. One had a wire springs leaning against a wall and some old shoes in the corner. The other room had a brass bed and what was left of a mattress that looked as if birds and mice and other animals had been using its stuffing for nests. That's the room the front door was in. I tried to open the door but couldn't. I wouldn't have dared step out onto the rickety porch anyway.

Upstairs is where all the junk was, and it was in one of those windows that the piece of old curtain hung. The Cupecks had built a kind of partition to make two rooms out of the attic, using the chimney that went up through the middle as a dividing line. This was probably where the kids slept. I poked around piles of stuff but didn't find anything very interesting—old books, some building blocks, a rusty dump truck, things like that. If that's all the Cupeck kids had to play with it was sad, but maybe it was only what they didn't want that they left behind when they went wherever they went.

The ceilings slanted up there so I couldn't stand straight along the front or back wall, but I could on each end where the windows were. Downstairs I hadn't noticed wind blowing through the house even though there wasn't a bit of glass left in any window, but upstairs there was a definite breeze from west to east. I wondered why there was only part of a curtain on one side of the east window. What had happened to the other half?

While it was eerie standing up there looking out the window with the curtain moving in the breeze and listening to the windchime tinkling on the front porch below, it was also peaceful. Maybe if ghosts did come to this house it was because of the quiet as much as because it was abandoned. I wished Rose was with me because she frequently said she wanted to be somewhere peaceful with no distractions. The thought passed through my mind that maybe we could fix up this old Cupeck house for Rose. She'd have the quiet she said she wanted, and she'd have more than one room and no bars. But I realized it was a dumb idea. The house was way beyond fixing up, tilting and sagging in several directions at once, with one chimney gone and the other on its way.

If ghosts came to this house or if they were there at that moment, I decided they must be friendly ghosts because nothing made me afraid. Oh, I'd had chills a couple of times, when I went from the kitchen into the middle room and when I went slowly up the stairs from the kitchen and didn't know what I would see when my head got above the upstairs floor, but they weren't terror chills. Nor were the goosebumps or hair pricking on the back of my head bad bumps or bad pricks.

Feeling brave, I decided I'd explore the cellar too. Why not? There was some problem getting the cellar door open because the floor bulged up right there, but I did it. When I looked into the blackness I couldn't see anything. It smelled sour and musty. "Anybody down there," I called, and was startled by the sound of my own voice.

When I got over the nervousness I lay down on my stomach and tried peering over the edge under the main floorboards and through the first step, but it didn't work. I considered going back to the County Home to get Roy, then decided that would take too long and he might not come, so, swallowing hard I started down the stairs, absolutely convinced something was going to reach through the open place and grab my ankles.

When I was on about the third step, I scrunched down and stared into the darkness. Over on the other end of the cellar I could see dim light which must be coming in through the broken hatchway. As I kept staring I could see more, not much but enough to know there wasn't anything down there worth investigating. Some shelves hung from a rafter, and part of an old lawn mower lay on the dirt floor, that was about it. I was surprised rats didn't scurry when they heard me coming, but there wasn't a sound of any sort.

I was unbending to start back up the stairs when I sensed that part of the top step moved. It wasn't as if I'd seen it move, not even out of the corner of my eye, but I had the feeling even so that there had been some kind of movement. Nonsense, I thought, how could a board move, but then something did move, it moved to the left. I watched it move in a steady slithering motion before it stopped. I held my breath and stared. What moved and then stopped wasn't a board, it was shiny black and had scales.

If I didn't do something I knew my heart would jump from my throat right out of my mouth. Because I was looking up the cellar stairs toward the light I couldn't see anything at all when I quickly glanced back down into the blackness. If I went down the stairs I'd have to go all the way across the dirt floor and hope I could crawl out through the broken hatchway, but what might be on the floor that I couldn't see, and suppose I couldn't get out through the hatchway once I got there, I'd have to come all the way back across that cellar again. Once I had tried pretending I was blind so I'd know what it was like for Theresa, walking around with my eyes squeezed shut, but that was different. I knew I could open them any time and see where I was going. Besides, it was never all the way dark with my eyes just closed, not dark the way it was in that cellar.

The only other thing to do was proceed up the stairs and step carefully over the big black shiny scaly thing that was obviously a snake, an enormous snake. While I was rooted on the step, before I could prepare myself to begin the escape process, the snake began to move again, and this time while his body was moving rapidly to the left on the top step his head appeared on the rafter right next to where I was standing. He didn't seem at all surprised to see me there, though he did stop moving and just looked up at me as I looked down at him. He flicked his tongue in my direction, then raised his head off the beam coming closer and closer to me. I drew back, but couldn't back any farther or I'd have fallen off the side of the cellar stairs.

When I retreated as far as I dared the snake moved some

more, part of him still slithering across the top step while the front end kept inching nearer my face. There was nothing to do but accept whatever was going to happen because I was too scared to move. The snake swayed forward and backward, and from side to side, flicking his tongue. I looked into his eyes in the half light. They looked back and I knew he could see deep inside me. We stared unblinking at each other.

He stopped swaying and slowly moved his head forward, no longer flicking his tongue though I could see the tip of it sticking out of his mouth. Just as he was about to touch his nose to mine, he must have suddenly lost interest because he dropped his head back down onto the crossbeam, then let his whole long body slide onto the wooden step where my feet were, slipping over them and on down the stairs, disappearing into the cellar.

I wanted to get out of there. I wanted to run and I wanted to cry or scream or something, but I just stood for what seemed the longest time; then swallowing hard I slowly turned toward the light at the top of the stairs again, and glancing down to make sure there were only steps under my feet, climbed one step at a time back up into the middle room. Using all my strength I pushed the cellar door shut and leaned against it, trying desperately to catch my breath. I was gasping as if I'd run for miles. There were soblike feelings in my chest but they wouldn't come out.

After looking carefully in all directions to make sure nothing was between me and the door, I walked heavily over to and through the kitchen, into the pantry, and with great effort because my body felt as if it weighed a ton, climbed out the pantry window, jumping back onto the ground from the top of the bureau. Still trying to catch my breath I had to stop every few feet and gulp air, but I made my way around the back of the house and along the path I'd broken coming in from the road.

I didn't tell anybody about going into the Cupeck house. Aunt Maude would have given me a tanning and would have shouted at Roy, too. Roy would have been hurt that I'd done something that made him seem careless about me. Rose would have been mad and called me foolish. I didn't want to tell anybody. It was more than being worried about being punished or yelled at. It was something I didn't understand and couldn't explain.

I could picture the snake perfectly as I lay in bed that night, his shiny blackness, the great length and size of him, the round shape of his head, his forked tongue, and his eyes, his greenish all-seeing eyes, and even though remembering and picturing him as I lay in bed gave me a terrible case of the shivers, I realized I wasn't really afraid. That snake could have done whatever he wanted to me and I couldn't have stopped him. But he didn't do anything except look at me, look me in the eye, flick his tongue and look.

CHAPTER THIRTEEN

uring the night the temperature dropped down to almost zero, and the wind was blowing a gale. Aunt Maude had buckets of oatmeal and cream of wheat on the stove for those who wanted something hot in their stomach. She was determined Uncle Will would drive me to school, but he agreed with me that I'd have to get used to the cold sometime and Monday morning was as good a time as any.

"It's too early in the season to have this freezing weather," she complained.

"Maudie, it's only a freak cold snap," Uncle Will said. "A few weeks ago you complained about the heat."

"Winter isn't due for another month."

"You tell that to the weatherman." Uncle Will gave her back a pat.

Wrapped up like a mummy, I walked to school with only my eyes uncovered. By the time I got there I wished I had pilot goggles to keep the wind from stinging so much. Even with a scarf wrapped over my nose I could feel ice crystals forming in my nostrils.

Birds crowded together on the electric and telephone wires, puffed up and looking miserable. I heard a plop and when I turned around there was a bird on the ground, frozen stiff. Then another one fell and another until by the time I turned into the school yard there must have been a dozen dead birds along the side of the road under the wires. I told Mrs. Barrie what I'd seen, and she said a sudden change in the temperature, especially when it dropped as low as it had the past twenty-four hours and caught everybody unaware, was very hard on wild things such as birds and those animals who hibernated but hadn't yet gone underground.

I immediately thought about the black snake in the Cupeck house. With the wind blowing through the windows it was probably colder in the house than outside. Maybe he had a place in the cellar where he was headed when I saw him. I hoped he was safe. It would be terrible if he froze to death.

The minute I got home from school I borrowed a flashlight from Uncle Will's cupboard. Actually, I just took it, but it was borrowing because I would put it back as soon as I was finished with it. Then I ran down the East Road and in the path I'd made through the weeds, around to the old bureau under the pantry window. Using the places where the drawers used to be it was easy to climb up and in through the window. When I got to the cellar door I opened it as quietly as I could, turned on the flashlight, and pointed it down the stairs. There wasn't a thing, not on the top step where the snake had been nor on any of the other steps. I leaned over to shine the light along the rafter, but the snake wasn't there either.

While I wasn't scared, I didn't want to be surprised, so I coughed a couple of times to let him know I was coming in case he hadn't noticed the light, then gingerly stepped down onto the first step and the second and the third, which is as far as I'd gone the day before. I could go farther with the flashlight. I moved the shaft of light all over the place, along the walls, up against the cellar ceiling, around the dirt floor, but I saw no sign of the snake. At least he wasn't dead right there in front of me. I didn't step off the stairs because the cellar floor still looked dangerous to me, but there was no need to. I was satisfied that the snake was somewhere safe.

Aunt Maude was waiting for me when I came rushing up the stairs to our suite.

"Where have you been? Mrs. Fleming wants you to have tea with her. She's been waiting for you in her sitting room."

"Why does she want to have tea with me?"

"Probably because she wants to ask you about school. It's very nice of her. Now quick, run to the bathroom and scrub your hands and face and comb your hair. I'll go down and tell her you are on your way. She made scones in the kitchen this morning while I was trying to get dinner ready. At least she cleaned up her mess when she was finished. Hurry now, she's waiting."

Double doors opened off the staff dining room into a sitting room where Ma Fleming spent most of her days. She had two card tables set up there at all times, one covered with jigsaw puzzle pieces and the other to be used for whatever other project she was working on at the moment, quilt pieces, scrapbooks, photo albums. I was sure it would be the tea table today. I hoped it would be because the chairs in the sitting room were quite comfortable. In her parlor across the front stairs hall all the furniture was upholstered in horsehair, which was not only too slippery to sit on if your feet didn't touch the floor, but also hurt when broken pieces of horsehair pricked through your pants. Besides, she had a Franklin stove in the sitting room that threw a lot of heat, and while the temperature had risen during the day it was still pretty cold outside.

I smoothed my hair one more time with my hand and knocked on the door, giving it a loud sharp rap. I knew if I didn't, Ma Fleming wouldn't be able to hear it.

"Come in," she invited from the other side.

I was right. The other card table was drawn up in front of her big chair and on it were cups, plates, bowls, pitchers, and jars of jam.

"Ah David, welcome, I've been waiting for you," she said in her echo voice, crinkled eyes smiling through her glasses. She must have fixed her hair for the occasion too because the wig's part was right where it should be. "I've pulled up a chair for you, but if you prefer another you're welcome to change."

"No thank you, this one is fine," I said, sitting down.

"I have the pot on the back of the stove. I'll give it a minute over the flames, then we can make the tea. Do you want China tea or Indian?"

"I don't really know," I replied. "Whatever you like."

"I like them both, but why don't we have China this afternoon if that's all right with you?"

I nodded. Aunt Maude was always telling me to speak up, not to nod or shake my head, but with Ma Fleming nods and shakes were easier because though she couldn't hear everything you said, she could see very well.

"How is school going?" she asked as we waited for the water to boil.

"Fine."

"Do you like Mrs. Barrie?"

"Yes."

"She's a very nice person. I've known her since she was born. She's very pretty too, don't you agree?"

I nodded, adding, "Oh yes," because I thought Mrs. Barrie was beautiful.

"We're fortunate to have her in that little school. She could easily have found a teaching job where they would pay her much more, I'm sure."

She fussed with the tea things, putting heaping teaspoons of China tea into the silver pot that had first been warmed with a splash of hot water then emptied into the waste bowl. Satisfied all was ready, she poured boiling water from the kettle into the pot and stirred it around with a spoon. "While that is steeping, would you like a scone? They are fresh, I made them myself this morning." She looked very proud as she took a covered dish from the top of the Franklin stove and brought it to the tea table. Removing a good-sized scone dotted with fat raisins and currants from the dish, she fixed it for me, splitting and buttering it, then putting on the strawberry jam because I said that's the one I liked best. "Would you like cream on it as well, or do you prefer eating it with your fingers?"

"I'll eat half with my fingers, and put cream on the other half."

"You're a man after my own heart, David. I like scones both ways too, and it's better to have some of each rather than choosing one over the other."

While I was eating my second scone, both halves with cream this time, she asked me, as she frequently did, "What do you think you'd like to be when you grow up?"

Because she had asked me the same question many times I decided she didn't remember she had asked me before and so wouldn't remember what my answer was, which meant I could give her different answers depending upon how I felt at the time.

"I think I'd like to be a doctor," I said, licking cream and strawberry jam off my dessert spoon.

"It takes a long time to become a doctor. Are you prepared to go to college all those years and then work in a hospital for many more years before you can begin your own practice?" She turned her head so the hearing aid would pick up my answer.

"How many?" I asked.

"What's that? You mustn't talk with your mouth full, David."

"I said, how many years does it take?" I leaned toward her and raised my voice.

She shook her head. "I'm not sure exactly, but I know you have four years of college and then four years of medical school, and after that I'd have to ask someone. What makes you think you want to be a doctor?"

I knew she was going to ask me that because she always asked me what made me think I wanted to be whatever it was I said I wanted to be, and I never had an answer. Usually I could shrug and move away, but there we were sitting at the tea table staring at each other across the cups and scones and I knew a shrug wouldn't do. Her eyes were as still as the snake's eyes had been. It occurred to me, maybe he wanted to know why I wanted to be something too.

"Do you believe in ghosts?" I asked.

"What's that?" She cupped her ear.

"Do you believe in ghosts?" I was close to shouting.

"I don't believe so, but what does that have to do with you wanting to be a doctor?"

"Nothing." I said.

She forgot to prod me for an answer as she concentrated on pouring another cup of tea, then said with a bright smile, "I hope you've saved room for a special treat." She must have known I had because she didn't wait for me to answer. "Today is my fifty-fourth wedding anniversary. Were you aware of that?"

I shook my head.

"Well it is. Mr. Fleming and I didn't want any fuss made, so except for an especially good dinner your Aunt Maude had for us today, there's to be no mention of it. However, I thought you might enjoy a piece of my wedding cake." She picked up a box which I'd been curious about when I noticed it to one side on the tea table.

"Your wedding cake?"

She nodded, lifting the lid on the box. I could see something inside, wrapped in linen cloth that had turned brown with age.

"Isn't it stale?" I asked. A cake fifty-four years old? Aunt Maude was always urging everybody to clean up whatever was left on platters and plates, "because it won't keep until tomorrow."

"I've kept the cake wrapped for over half a century, and moistened it with brandy from time to time. We only open the box on special occasions, such as today when we're having our tea, and then we have a little piece."

"What's the occasion?" I asked.

"What's what?"

"What is the occasion? You said you only unwrap the cake on special occasions."

"I told you it is my anniversary, but what really makes an

occasion is unwrapping the cake." Her eyes were dancing as she smiled at me and then down at the layers of linen she was unwinding and then up at me again.

"Oh," I said. "Shouldn't Pa be here if it's your anniversary? I'm sure the cake would mean much more to him than to me."

"He never liked it," she replied, "not even on our wedding day."

When there was a pile of linen next to her plate and the cake was all unwrapped, what I saw looked like a black brick and smelled like nothing I'd ever smelled before, a combination of fruity and Blind Dan's breath after he'd had what he called a snort from the pint bottle he carried in his hip pocket.

"Have you ever seen a cake this old?" she asked, and was delighted when I shook my head. "This cake was made the month your Aunt Maude was born. Your grandmother and grandfather were at my wedding, and Maude was born two weeks later. What do you think of that?"

What I thought was, why didn't she invite Aunt Maude to have a piece of it and leave me out, but what I did was shake my head and say, "Wow." I was wondering how far I had to carry politeness.

She picked up a silver carving knife and dipped it in hot water left in the teakettle. "A wet knife cuts cleaner," she explained, as she sliced a thin sliver of a piece off one end of the brick and put the slice on a clean plate where it lay while she wound the yards and yards of stained linen back around the ancient cake and replaced the bundle in its box. "I'll give it a dash of brandy later before I return it to the cellar," she murmured, setting the box to one side.

"Now, David, are you ready?"

"I guess so."

"Isn't this a treat? I knew you'd be excited. I daresay none of your young friends have ever eaten a cake as old as this one." She was carefully cutting the thin slice into two equal pieces.

"Nor none of my old friends," I said, not in a rude tone, but not loud enough so she could hear me.

"Give me your plate. That's a good boy. Now go ahead, take a bite." She was watching me as if I were about to pass or fail an important test, but I could tell from the way her eyes shone that she wanted me to, expected me to, pass with flying colors.

"Why don't we do it together?"

"What?"

"Why don't we each do it, both eat our pieces at the same time?"

"Like a toast, you mean? What a splendid idea." She picked up her piece of cake and I picked up mine. It was sticky. "May you be successful, David, in your chosen career," she held her piece of cake out toward me. "What is it you said you want to be?"

"A teacher," I answered loudly.

"You'll make a wonderful teacher, David, you are so bright. To David the teacher, may you have a long and happy life." She made a dipping gesture with the cake in her right hand and brought it to her mouth with a flourish, then took a tiny nibble out of the edge.

I tried to copy her gesture and also the tiny nibble. Other than it was very strong-tasting and had a gummy texture, the cake wasn't bad. If Ma Fleming had eaten it from time to time—and I took it she had been at it on special occasions since it was made fifty-four years ago, and she seemed to be healthy, except for being deaf and wearing a wig—I decided it wouldn't poison me.

"Now you make a toast," she nodded happily.

I'd never made a toast, but I guessed based on what she had just done it was like a wish for somebody else, so I thought for a minute while she sat there with her piece of wedding cake raised at the ready, and then said, "To Ma Fleming, the Keeper's wife, may you get what you want for Christmas." We both dipped and took another nibble.

"What do you want for Christmas?" I asked Rose, after I finished telling her about my tea with Ma Fleming.

"I want to go home."

"But you haven't got a home to go to. You told me that yourself."

"That doesn't mean I don't want to go there."

"Where?"

"Home."

I could tell we were headed into one of those weird confusing conversations. "Why would ghosts who never lived there haunt the Cupeck house?" I asked.

"What makes you think there are ghosts anywhere near the Cupeck house?" From the way she sighed and paced around her room I knew she wasn't really interested in what I was talking about.

"Johnny Bullock says it's full of ghosts. He says they go there straight from the grave if they've been unhappy."

"Unhappy where? In the grave?"

"I guess so."

"How happy do you think anybody is in a grave?"

I hadn't thought of that. "Probably not very."

"Why this silly conversation, David?"

"Not any sillier than your conversations about wanting to go home when you haven't got a home to go to."

"You're right."

While she kept pacing I swiveled back and forth on the organ stool. "When I get to be a ghost I think the Cupeck house might be a pretty good place to haunt," I said.

"Why not, it's nearby," Rose said.

"There isn't any treasure in the house, not much of anything except old beds and broken dishes."

"You've been there, I take it?" She stopped pacing.

Oh Lord, I hadn't meant to let it out. "I looked through the windows." I had looked through the windows. It wasn't a lie if I didn't tell Rose everything I knew. She said so.

"You hadn't better go inside. Any house abandoned as long as the Cupeck house has been is probably in bad shape. It might fall down if it's rotten." She stopped pacing and looked at me. "You have not gone inside, have you?"

Not telling her I had if she didn't ask was not lying, but if she asked—and she had asked—and I denied it, that would be a lie. When I didn't answer her, she came closer to the bars. "You have been inside, am I right?"

I nodded.

"Was someone with you, or were you alone? Who went in there with you? Johnny Bullock?"

"Rose, Johnny Bullock won't even walk in the road where it goes past the Cupeck house. He's not about to go inside."

"Who was with you, then?"

"Nobody."

"You went in by yourself?"

I nodded.

"Smart, very smart. If you are in there alone and the floor gives way and you fall into some bottomless cistern, nobody will ever know what happened to you."

"I knew you'd be mad," I said sourly.

"I said you were smart, but not smart enough to be outdoors

alone obviously." At least she wasn't clutching me to her bosom, not that she could through the bars, moaning about what would she do if anything happened to her darling boy, the way Aunt Maude was sure to carry on if she found out.

"David, promise me you won't go in there alone again. I don't know why I say alone. You should promise me you won't go in there again, period, alone or with somebody."

"That's hard to promise, Rose." I was thinking of the snake. In the spring I'd have to go back and see if I could find him again. How could I do that if I promised Rose I wouldn't? And why was I not telling Rose about the snake?

She looked at me as if she knew I was hiding something from her. If she asked me a second time to promise we would have an argument, but she didn't. Instead, she changed the subject. "Did you go in looking for ghosts?"

"Sort of."

"And you went alone?"

"Yes."

"That was very brave of you."

I shrugged.

"Did you see any?"

"No."

She came up to the bars and put her hand through, roughing up my hair. "Don't sound so disappointed. Maybe there aren't any ghosts in the Cupeck house. I tell you what, when I find myself in my grave, if I'm unhappy to be there, and who knows how I'll feel when the time comes?"—her voice slowed down as if her mind was wandering; she snapped back to attention—"If I'm unhappy, as ghosts are supposed to be, I'll fly right over to that old house and wait for you. How's that?"

"Rose, I don't think you're being funny for a minute."

"Who's trying to be funny?"

"You are. All this talk about ghosts when you don't even believe in them."

"How do you know?"

"Because you said so."

"I did? I don't remember. You remember, David, I've told you to never deny possibility, and just because you can't see something doesn't mean it isn't there."

I did remember her saying that to me more than once, but I had to stop and think about what she was saying now. "Are you saying, Rose, there might be ghosts even if we can't see them?"

"There might be all kinds of things we can't see. Blind Theresa can't see anything, yet here we are all and she knows we're here. Maybe those of us who do have eyes don't have eyes that see everything there is to see."

That took some more thinking.

"I'm not saying there is or there isn't such a thing as a ghost, David. What I am saying is not being able to see it doesn't prove it doesn't exist."

"Do you believe in ghosts then, Rose?"

"I don't know what I believe. I'm like you, David, not knowing what you think about Heaven and Hell." She started pacing again, pausing at the window every time she passed it. "I can't make up my mind whether I find that distant elm more powerful in summer when it's heavy with leaves, or in winter when it's stark and black astride the ridge, outlined against the sky."

"So you admit it's on a ridge and not at the edge of the earth." I couldn't help tease her about it because she kept saying it was at the edge of an abyss when I knew it was behind Ott Alwardt's barn.

She turned sharply to glare at me from the window. "I admit

nothing." She said each word by itself with a pause between. I had the feeling she wasn't talking to me, perhaps wasn't seeing me even though I was there. She was looking at me as if I were a ghost.

CHAPTER FOURTEEN

ncle Will was right, the freezing cold spell didn't mean winter had settled in. It only lasted a couple of days so there wasn't too much damage, except to birds, and Uncle Will said most of those who died must have been caught in the middle of migration. It didn't do any damage to my ducks, except to turn the muck in the bottom of their pen into solid cement. If it had stayed cold I suppose the mess would not have been so bad, but when the temperature rose again everything thawed and I was in duck shit up over my shoes.

"David, you have to clean out that pen and take it right down to the dry dirt floor," Uncle Deane scolded when I let it go longer than I should have.

"Okay, okay," I muttered. There were times when everybody in the world felt free to tell me what to do and how to do it.

I did clean out the pen and it was a terrible job. First I had to shut the damn ducks in a box, and then I had to shovel what I could and scrape the rest into about a zillion wheelbarrow loads to take down to the cow barn and push up the ramp so I could dump them into the manure spreader. The job took me all morning and I complained every step of the way, though nobody was there to hear me.

When I was finished, had put clean bedding down, washed and refilled their dishes, and turned the screeching ducks loose again, Aunt Maude wouldn't let me into the kitchen or back hall until I took off all my clothes.

"Outside, you mean?"

"Right there on the porch!" She pointed to the exact spot where I was to stand. "Strip down to your underpants and be quick about it."

"It's cold out here. I'll freeze."

"Not if you get at it and stop arguing. You smell to high heaven. I'll not have those clothes in this house."

"What do you want me to do with them?"

"Leave them by the door. I'll have Roy take them to the laundry. We'll have to throw the shoes away. They're ruined. David, you should have worn boots."

"I should have never gotten the damned ducks," I grumbled to myself so she couldn't hear me.

It was embarrassing taking off my clothes where anybody could see me, but nobody came along so I didn't have to explain what I was doing and why. In only my underpants I ran inside and up the stairs. Aunt Maude had started water in the tub so the bathroom was steamy warm when I got there. She had also poured in terrible-smelling bath salts. "I hate that smell. Can't I have fresh water?"

"The water is fresh and the smell of the bath salts will help get rid of the way you smell now. Scrub yourself good, and hurry, dinner is in half an hour." She went to my room and came back with clean clothes she placed on a chair in the bathroom, then went downstairs to finish getting dinner ready.

I wasn't used to bath salts so didn't know they make water almost as slippery as rainwater. Holding the bar of soap as tight as I could, it would slip out of my grasp and plow across the tub underwater like a submarine. Or I could squeeze it pointing up and the soap would shoot into the air, then splash down like a bomb. I was having so much fun I didn't hear Aunt Maude coming until she was almost there. I reached up quickly and hooked the door in the partition between the sink part of the room and the tub where I was.

Aunt Maude rattled the knob. "Why have you latched this door, David? What are you doing in there?"

"Taking a bath."

"You should have finished your bath long ago."

"I'm tired so I'm slower than usual."

"If you aren't out of there in two minutes I'll come in and scrub you myself."

"I'm too old to be scrubbed. I can take a bath by myself."

"Don't you be impertinent, young man. Do as I say and be quick about it." I could hear her sputtering her favorite complaint as she went back down the hall, "That boy is going to be the death of me yet."

The whole family went to Gramps' and Grandma's for Thanksgiving dinner, everybody except Mother of course. She was still in the hospital, but Dad was there and he told me he was planning to take me to visit her next Sunday. "We'll make a day of it," he said, giving me a hug. He and I sat next to each other at dinner.

Grandma insisted the whole family had to sit at the same table even though there were more than thirty people. She said the only time she missed the big house on the farm where all her children were born was on occasions such as Thanksgiving. The house they lived in after they retired was small enough to fit whole into the big house dining room, she said. What Grandma did was connect tables, lining up two in the parlor end to end, then she put wide boards on sawhorses through the double parlor doors to connect with more tables in the sitting room and so on into the dining room. The whole thing with angles and turns was covered with white tablecloths so it looked like a single piece of furniture built by a madman. Those sitting in the parlor could not see those sitting in the dining room, but the whole family was seated together and that's what Grandma wanted.

Before dinner all the cousins—or most of us, some of the older girls helped with dinner—went to the barn to play with Gramps' horses, Prince and Queen. Queen was too frail for us to climb on so we just brushed her, but Prince stood quiet as a hill while we took turns sitting on his back and playing touch tag underneath his belly. While we were at it we also brushed Gramps' Jersey cow, Lily, and tried to brush the pigs but they wouldn't let us near them. Two of my older cousins walked down to the creek, to skip stones they said, but I knew they were going to smoke cigarettes.

When we were all at the dinner table, Gramps said a grace that made us grateful for the good things God had given us but was funny at the same time. After everybody said "Amen," somebody suggested we sing "Praise God from Whom All Blessings Flow," but Aunt Maude reminded us we didn't sing at the table.

Because Grandma's children couldn't agree on turkey or fried chicken, she always had both on Thanksgiving. There'd be the biggest turkey you'd ever seen on the enormous turkey platter plus three or four platters piled high with crusty fried chicken. No matter whether you liked light or dark meat, there was plenty of both for everybody.

Naturally there was gallons of giblet gravy. Most of the livers, hearts, and gizzards went into the gravy, but because I loved them almost more than anything, Grandma always saved out a couple of gizzards for me which she crisped up in the frying pan along with the chicken. After grace, when dishes of squash, onions, dressing, cornbread, and, and, and, began to be passed, I felt Grandma's arm reaching around me from behind. When I looked up she winked, gave me a quick kiss on my head, then slid two beautiful gizzards out of a little pan onto my plate.

"I saw that, Ma, you're spoiling him," Uncle Deane teased from across the table where he was filling his plate.

"You didn't see anything," Grandma said. "Besides, I spoil all of you. Now behave, Deane, and eat your dinner."

I watched her go back to her place at the kitchen end of the section of table where we were sitting. When she looked in my direction, I mouthed a silent thank you and winked at her. Then I picked up my knife and fork ready to eat. One of the gizzards was gone. The other one was there all by itself next to a grease spot. I glanced up at my dad, but he shook his head. I knew he wouldn't eat my gizzard. I looked across the table. Uncle Deane was licking his fingers and gazing at the ceiling.

"Did you take my gizzard, Uncle Deane?"

He acted surprised. "I didn't know little boys had gizzards."

"The gizzard from my plate," I said. He knew what I meant.

He peered down at my plate. "Why, David, your gizzard, or the chicken's gizzard, is right there. I can see it from here."

"But I had two gizzards."

"Maybe you ate the other one."

"I haven't eaten anything yet." Dishes of food were backing up on both sides of me as people waited for Uncle Deane and me to stop talking and pay attention to what was being passed.

"David, are you misbehaving down there?" Aunt Maude could barely see me if she leaned back from where she was sitting at the entrance of the parlor.

"Somebody took my gizzard," I replied, facing in her direction. As I was trying to explain, there was a quick movement across the table. I jerked my head back and saw Uncle Deane with my other gizzard in his hand just about to pop it into his mouth. "Uncle Deane," I shrieked, but too late. The gizzard dropped between his lips and was gone. Uncle Deane chewed it up, covering his mouth while he laughed and everybody looked at me.

"Deane, that isn't funny. If you weren't a grown man I'd make you leave the table. You should be taken to the woodshed and whipped." Grandma's voice was angry.

Uncle Deane told Grandma he was sorry. He said he'd only been having fun with me. I guess most of the others thought it was funny too because they all laughed. Dad put his arm around my shoulders and pretended to reach for salt so nobody would notice he was drying my tears with his napkin.

Aunt Latzy fussed and clucked when I told her about Uncle Deane, though she admitted she was secretly in love with him because he was the handsomest man she'd ever seen. "His perfect white teeth, and dark hair and eyes, and that dimple." She fanned her face with her hanky. "Though men never took much notice of me, I consider myself an excellent judge of them."

"I'm going to see my mother tomorrow," I said to change the subject. I wasn't in a mood to hear anything good said about Uncle Deane.

"How nice. She must be feeling better." Aunt Latzy snorkled when she talked because of her hairlip.

"I guess so. At least she can have visitors."

"Are you going with your daddy?" She didn't notice Harold poking his pink nose out from under the crocheted edge of her top sheet. His long silver whiskers twitched, and soon his head appeared, round red eyes gazing up at Aunt Latzy, then over at me. I put my hand down so he could sniff my fingers.

"Yes. He is coming for me right after breakfast."

A long sigh escaped Aunt Latzy's lips. She picked Harold up and brought him to her cheek for a powdery pat. "I haven't been to a city for years and years. Thirty at least, probably more. Not since I came here. I'd so love one more visit to a nice store before I die."

She reached into her nightstand drawer to bring out a bit of sausage she'd saved from the breakfast tray and fed it to Harold. The white rat took the meat in his two front paws and sitting up on her bosom with his tail wrapped around his bottom examined the sausage carefully, then nibbled it away, tiny bite after tiny bite. When he dropped a piece he quickly picked it up before continuing with his snack.

"I was born in a large city, you know, London, in a lovely old house overlooking a waterway. When I was a little girl I would watch from an upstairs window for boats to come along, and when I spied one I'd run through the garden to the towpath and call out to the people aboard. They'd wave and call back." Aunt Latzy laughed as she remembered. "Sometimes they would shout, 'What is your name, little girl?' 'Lizzie,'

I'd say, as loud and clear as I could, which wasn't very clear at all because of this lip of mine, so knowing they had trouble understanding me, I'd try again, 'Lizzie, Lizzie Acheson.' "

She sighed and patted Harold, who was washing up. "But they never did understand me. One time, one time"—she was beginning to laugh so hard she couldn't speak for a minute—"one time this old man who was driving the mule on the towpath shouted at the people on the boat who kept saying they couldn't hear me, 'She says her name is Liz, Itchy's son. What's the matter, you people deef or something?' " Latzy laughed and wiped her eyes and blew her nose. Obviously, she thought the towman's mistake all those years ago was still funny.

"Liz, Itchy's son," I repeated to see how it felt in my mouth, and that sent both of us into a fit. She was laughing at me and I was laughing at her, both of us tearing and she blowing her nose. Then I overdid it by collapsing across her bed. I only meant to show how weak I was from laughing, but I came within a hair of crushing poor Harold. It scared him so he gave a leap and landed, not easily as a cat would land, but with a loud heavy splat on the polished floor.

"Get that filthy rat before he escapes," Mrs. Ripley rasped from her bed. She'd been making nasty remarks all the while Aunt Latzy and I were getting sillier. She hated for anybody to have a good time. "I loathe and despise rats. Him being white makes no difference. I don't care what his background is, he's a menace."

"Harold," Aunt Latzy cried, sounding like a mother who had lost her child down a well. "David, David, catch him before something terrible happens to him."

Harold was easy to catch. He wasn't moving, not even his whiskers. He lay there, flat on the floor, his legs splayed out. I always did think Harold was stupid, well, not stupid perhaps, it would be stupid for him to run away and leave the soft life he had in Aunt Latzy's bed, but he probably didn't know how special that was, having never known anything else since he arrived as a baby to replace Alcibiades, Aunt Latzy's earlier white rat, when Alcibiades died of old age. It wasn't stupidity that made him easy to catch; Harold was too stunned to make plans to go anywhere. I scooped him up, gave him a brisk rub, and placed him in Aunt Latzy's held-out hands.

"Harold, whatever made you jump off the bed? You've never done that before." She pressed him to her cheek.

"I squashed him when I fell on the bed."

"Oh, you didn't hurt him." Aunt Latzy's voice went farther up her nose when she was excited. "David wouldn't hurt you, Harold, you know that. I think we all need a peppermint, maybe two."

She tucked Harold down between her breasts and reached for the jars. I took two pink. Latzy put a white into her own mouth and held out a pink to Harold, who forgot he was scared and took a big bite out of it.

"I'm going to be sick," old Ripley gagged.

"Oh dear, I hope not, Mrs. Ripley. Shall I send David to fetch Julia?" Aunt Latzy offered.

"I want you to send David to the barn with that horrid rodent is what I want you to do, where if God is watching He will point out the poisonous creature to a starving cat." Mrs. Ripley's fat cheeks bounced and her eyes showed hatred.

"I do feel sorry for you," Aunt Latzy sighed. "You have such an unfortunate attitude toward Harold and toward life. Would a peppermint help?"

"You old fool!" Ripley shouted, then rolled over with her face toward the wall and her back toward us.

Aunt Latzy shrugged and went back to cooing at Harold.

"I'd better be going now," I said. "I don't know if I'll be back from the city before you go to sleep tomorrow night or not, but if I am late I'll come tell you all about it before I go to school Monday morning."

"Do come as soon as you can, dear boy, and tell your mother I send her my love. I knew her when she wasn't much older than you are now." She opened her arms wide. "Now give me some soft soap before you go."

I bent into her embrace, making sure not to crush Harold this time. She kissed me in the neck, blowing through her lips to make a loud blubbery sound. Then it was my turn. Her neck was a sweet-smelling cascade of wrinkled folds so that when I blew her a soft soap kiss all the folds vibrated and made a really big noise.

"You are the best soft soaper ever." Aunt Latzy scrunched up her neck and laughed.

"I am really going to be sick, no doubt about it, right here where I lay." Ripley rolled onto her back and talked to the ceiling.

"See you tomorrow if I can." I gave Harold a pat, and as I went past Mrs. Ripley's bed, I said, "Hope you feel better soon."

She snorted and swiveled her head in my direction as if she'd like to bite me and hope I'd get lockjaw. When I was safely out of her reach and knew she couldn't see me, I stuck out my tongue at the old bitch, then called out cheerfully, "Bye, Aunt Latzy."

"Bye-bye, dear boy."

The sun on the snow was blinding bright so I had to squint as we drove through the countryside on our way to the city to visit my mother next morning. Dad wore sunglasses. On top of the accumulated snow a fresh dusting had fallen that sparkled like acres of diamonds.

Most of the conversation on the way was about what I had been doing in school, though we'd covered a lot of that ground on Thanksgiving Day at Grandma's, then Dad told me what to expect when we got to the hospital. He told me it would be the biggest building I'd ever been in, and because everybody there was seriously ill I must speak very quietly, and I must not ask the nurses a lot of questions because they were busy, things like that.

Even though he'd told me, I couldn't believe what I saw when the hospital came into view. He was right about it being the biggest building ever. It looked like a whole city in itself, stretching out for miles of red brick and blue slate with giant chimneys and thousands of windows and pillars, each one as big as a house. We parked the car, then had to walk for a long way before we entered the building through a door that said "Visitors' Lobby" above it. Dad said something to the nurse in a glass room who nodded and let us go on to the other end of the building where there was an entire wall of nothing but elevator doors.

"Main floor," Dad said to the elevator operator as we got on, but the man didn't answer or act as if he saw us.

When the elevator doors opened again, there was the main floor. It took my breath away. Acres of what Dad told me was marble spread out in all directions, and up from the floor, which was gray marble, went giant pillars of another color marble. They disappeared from sight against a ceiling I could barely see even when I held my head as far back as it would go.

"Please step off so I can close the door," the elevator man said.

There were windows in the walls at different heights and I could see people walking past them that looked no bigger than my bisque soldiers.

"Come along, David." Dad held out his hand.

I took it and hung on, going wherever he led me without looking because I was so busy turning my head first to the left then to the right. Tree-sized plants in green tubs stood around the edges of rugs that looked as big as the hayloft in the County Home barn. Davenports and chairs were filled by people doing nothing except stare into space. Halls wide enough to drive two three-horse teams abreast went out from where we were on the main floor to both sides and toward the back. In the middle was a high circular marble counter with women behind it wearing badges on their stiff white dresses. The women were answering telephones and talking to people on our side of the counter.

When it came our turn, Dad told one of the stiff women his name and my name and said we were here to see my mother, and he gave the woman Mother's name.

"You're early," she said, pulling her upper lip down over her very long teeth. "Visiting hours don't begin until one-thirty. It is only one-fifteen."

"I know," Dad said. "I thought perhaps we could go up to her floor and wait there until one-thirty, and so not lose any visiting time. We've come a long way."

"Visitors aren't allowed above the main floor until one-thirty. There will be an announcement when visiting hours begin."

Dad thanked her, looked down at me, and shrugged. As we were walking toward one of those barn-size rugs, the stiff woman with the long teeth said, "Sir, sir, how old is the child?"

"Nine," said my dad.

"No I'm not. I won't be nine until . . ." I whispered when Dad squeezed my hand so hard it hurt.

"Are you sure?" the woman asked, squinting her eyes in my direction.

"I'm his father," Dad said.

When we found an arm of a leather davenport for me to lean on, Dad told me quietly that children under nine weren't allowed in as visitors, which is why he had said that's how old I was.

"Mrs. Barrie told us in China you are a year old when you're born, so if we were in China I would be nine now," I whispered.

"Then for today, let's pretend we're in China." Dad smiled. This whole place was so strange to me we might as well be in China.

We kept watching a clock in the wall with an hour hand taller than me as it hovered just past the Roman numeral I. When the even bigger minute hand jerked down to the middle of VI, a voice came through a loudspeaker, "Visiting hours have begun. No more than two visitors are allowed each patient at any one time. No smoking is allowed in any patient's room. No one is allowed to sit on, or place their coats or other garments on any patient's bed. Do not tire or excite the patients. Visiting hours end promptly at three-thirty. Thank you."

While the voice droned on, Dad and I and everybody else hurried to the elevators. They didn't open until the voice was finished, then they all opened at once. Because we were standing right in front of one we were the first on, but that meant we had to go way to the back and be crushed against the wall. I couldn't see anything but grown-ups' behinds. I was glad Dad didn't let go of my hand.

When the elevator operator said, "Six," Dad said, "This is

our floor. Excuse us, please. Please, may we get through?" Nobody answered him, and they didn't move either, so Dad and I had to squeeze through as best we could while Dad kept asking, "Please hold the door, operator."

When at last we got off, people were piling off the other elevators too so there was a race to get to another marble counter with another bunch of stiff white-dressed women behind it. We waited in line while everybody said who they had come to see and were checked in and told which corridor to go to. I could tell by the way Dad kept squeezing and unsqueezing my hand he was either nervous or increasingly impatient.

"Are they going to ask my name again?" I whispered.

Dad shook his head. "This makes me so angry, giving up precious visiting time while they go through their routine. There's no reason this part of it couldn't be done before visiting hours begin."

"Next," a woman said who sounded as if we were keeping her from doing something she was dying to do.

Dad gave her the information she asked for and took off down the hall, pulling me along behind him before she'd finished giving him directions. "I know where to go, I've been going the same route every Sunday for the past ten months," he grumbled.

We rushed down a long corridor with wooden benches against the walls. People were sitting on the benches looking at people sitting on other benches across the hall. Nobody was talking. Dad had told me I must not do a lot of talking in the hospital, so I guess all those people sitting there were just following rules. I tried to get a glimpse into the rooms with open doors, but couldn't see much except beds, or people standing talking to whoever was in the bed.

I was gawping when Dad came to a sudden stop. If he hadn't

been holding onto me I would have tripped over him. "Shit to hell, God damn it," he said, sounding as if he was going to cry.

"What's the matter?" I whispered.

"Look." He pointed to a closed door with a sign on it.

"Is that Mother's room?"

"Yes. They must be doing something because we can't go in until they open the door and turn that damn sign around."

A fat man who smelled of garlic and the woman who was with him moved over so Dad and I could sit on the bench next to them and stare at the closed door for what seemed hours.

"Here, you give these to your mother. It will please her." Dad handed me the bag of oranges we had bought at a fruit store on the edge of the city when we were driving in. He held onto the paper cone of flowers.

The hospital must use the same antiseptic that they used at the County Home because I could smell it, but it smelled better at the Home because in the hospital it was mixed with odors of what I think was people not getting to the bathroom on time. I was beginning to feel sick to my stomach, not bad enough to throw up but not happy either. Also my legs were itching. Aunt Maude had made me wear my wool knickers and knee socks. I hated knickers.

"Dad, I have to go to the bathroom," I whispered.

"Not now," Dad said. "The second they open that door we can go in to see Mom and I'm sure she's as anxious as we are. Can't you wait?"

"I guess so."

The door opened and a nurse came out, carrying a bedpan with a towel draped over it. "You may go in," she said without looking at anybody.

Dad jumped up and started across the corridor, but I didn't

want to all of a sudden. "Come on, David," Dad urged.

I got up but felt weak. Walking was difficult because my legs didn't work very well. They weren't asleep or anything, just heavy. My body began to sweat. I wished Dad had taken me to the bathroom before that door opened. I knew he wouldn't do it now. Besides, he'd gone on ahead and was already in the room. I could see him bending over the second bed near the window. Somebody had pulled the shade down so the room was gloomy.

Before I saw her I heard my Mother cry out, "Oh David, David my baby." Then I did see her. I knew it was her because she looked the way I remembered even though lots of times when I tried to picture her in my mind as I was going to sleep at night I couldn't. Her hair was combed but not curled and she didn't have any makeup on so she looked almost blue white. She was crying. "This is my son," she said to the woman in the other bed.

I didn't know what to do. I wanted to run to the bed and throw myself into her arms. I wanted to cry right along with her. At the same time I wanted to drop the bag of oranges and run back down that long corridor. I wondered if there was a stair I could take to get out of the building, or if I'd have to wait for an elevator.

While I was feeling more things all at once than I could handle, and confused over what I wanted to do and should do and could do, I must have kept walking because even though it seemed an endless way from the door to the bed, suddenly there I was next to it, and I wasn't sure I wanted to be there. I knew she was going to reach out and touch me and I was afraid I'd scream if she did.

Ignoring what the woman had said downstairs on the loudspeaker, Dad picked me up, bag of oranges and all, and delivered me into my mother's arms. She covered my face and head with kisses that surprised me because her lips were warm though her face looked as if it would be cold to touch.

"Oh my baby," she kept saying.

I knew she wanted me to kiss her back but I had gone rigid. I'm not supposed to be on the bed, I thought. "I brought you some oranges," I said, but she couldn't hear me because she was sobbing and pressing my face tight against her. At last she let me go so she could look at me. "I brought you some oranges," I repeated.

"Isn't he beautiful?" she asked the woman in the other bed. "I told you he was beautiful."

I inched away from her and slid backwards off the bed, which made my jacket bunch up under my armpits. My shirt pulled out of my pants and my knickers went up into my crotch so far I thought I'd be cut in half.

"You've grown so tall," she said, using her fingers to wipe tears from behind her glasses. "Aunt Maude must be feeding you well." There were dark places under her eyes and her face was thinner than I'd ever seen it. Her glasses were too big for her, and the square-necked nightgown she wore stood out from her chest so I could see deep hollows at the base of her neck. Her body was even whiter than her face. Where her breasts should be there was only flatness. "Sweetheart I don't mean to ignore you." She pulled Dad down to her and they kissed again.

"How are you feeling today?" he asked. His voice was chokey as if he'd been crying too.

"How could I feel? On top of the world with both of you here." She smiled a broad smile at me and suddenly I stopped being rigid. "Does it embarrass you when I say you are beautiful?" she asked in a teasing voice.

I must have turned red because both she and Dad laughed

at me. That seemed to make her want to cry again. Her eyes filled, but this time she held them back and was truly smiling when she looked up at Dad and said, "Thank you for bringing him, thank you for giving him to me." Dad nodded but didn't say anything.

Because I felt like I was watching something I shouldn't be watching, I half turned and said to the woman in the other bed, "Have you been here long?"

They all laughed at that. I don't know why. The woman said she and Mom had both been in the hospital too long, but they'd surprise everybody and get out one day real soon. Then Mom and Dad began to talk. Dad told her about what he was doing at work. I told her what I was doing at school and other things. Mom said Uncle Deane never did know when to stop after I described losing both gizzards on Thanksgiving Day. Then I ate one of the oranges I'd brought Mother, and the same voice downstairs came over the loudspeaker saying visiting hours would be over in five minutes and everybody had to be off the patients' floors by three-thirty sharp.

"I thought we'd go see a movie and get something to eat, then come back for evening visiting hours," Dad said.

"A movie?" I asked too loud because both Mom and Dad went, "Ssssh."

"What movie will you see?" Mother asked.

"I hadn't thought," Dad replied. "Do you have any ideas, David?"

"I don't know what's on."

"If I could go to the movies, I'd see *Jezebel,*" Mom said. "I love Bette Davis. I think it's playing at the Shea."

"We'll find it, then we'll come back tonight and tell you all about it," Dad said, rubbing one of Mom's skinny arms.

"One minute before all visitors are to be off the patient floors," the voice said over the loudspeaker.

In a mad dash, Dad and I kissed Mom again, grabbed our coats, and hurried toward the corridor, turning at the door to wave back and blow more kisses.

"Eat some good spaghetti and meatballs and tell us all about that too," the woman in the other bed called after us.

Which is exactly what we did. We drove around first to make sure *Jezebel* was playing at the Shea, checked when the next feature would start, then sped across the city to a place Dad called a greasy spoon with, he said, "the best spaghetti and meatballs in town." We saw *Jezebel* from way up in the balcony while we munched buttered popcorn and jordan almonds. Mother listened to every word as I described it in detail when we got back to the hospital.

Evening visiting hours went even faster than the afternoon, and the nurses were nastier about getting us all out of there before the clock struck nine. I slept most of the way home.

CHAPTER FIFTEEN

ou went to the movies on a Sunday?" Rose asked me.

"Yes."

"What did your Aunt Maude have to say about that?"

"I didn't tell her. Dad said it would be better not to."

"Your father is a very wise man. Remember what I said about not repeating everything you know? I'm not the only one who's learned that lesson. *Jezebel* sounds like a strange movie for you to see, however, Sunday or not. Why did your father choose that one, do you think?"

"Mother likes Bette Davis. She said that's the one she would go to if she was able. We wanted to see *Jezebel* so we could go back and tell her all about it."

"And did you tell her all about it?"

"Every minute of it. It's a great movie, Rose. Lots of people die and they carry them off to an island and it ends with Bette Davis sitting on the cart of corpses—well, they aren't all corpses yet, but they soon will be—and she's going to the island too even though she isn't sick so Henry Fonda won't die alone. He's the one she loves though he is married to somebody else and lots of other men love her."

"Sounds fascinating."

"It was. She wore a red dress to a dance when all the other women were wearing white and that got her in trouble, and her horse reared but she didn't care."

"Was this after she'd ridden on the cart of corpses?"

"No, before. The cart came at the very end."

"And you had spaghetti and meatballs for supper, you said."

"That was before too, while we were waiting for the movie to begin, at a greasy spoon."

"Was that particular restaurant by choice or did you have to eat at the first place you came to?"

"No, no. We drove way across the city because Dad said the spaghetti at the greasy spoon was the best in town."

Rose went "hmmmm."

"We had popcorn at the movies and a woman asked Dad if I could eat it more quietly please."

"Did you."

"I tried. We sat in almost the top row of the top balcony because that's the only place where we could find seats. Dad said there were thousands of people in the theater. It's called Shea's Palace. I also had a box of jordan almonds."

"Did anybody ask you to eat those more quietly please?"

"I sucked on them mostly, until the coating was gone, and then I chewed the nut inside with my hand over my mouth."

"You're very thoughtful."

In the weeks between the visit to see my mother and Christmas I must have told everybody, except Aunt Maude that is, all about *Jezebel,* describing scenes from the movie over and over again. Rose got so she'd say a Bette Davis line right along with me when I got to the end of one of my favorite parts, but I knew Rose was just giving me a hard time.

Actually, having her do that let me know she was listening. More and more I had the feeling Rose wasn't really in the room on the other side of the bars lots of times when we were talking. It was as if she'd gone somewhere and left her body there and her voice, because she'd answer my questions and sometimes touch me but it was different.

I would have thought more about it but I was too busy thinking about Christmas and about time dragging. Why was it that each day in school went so fast it would be time to go home in what seemed like only minutes after we got there? Marjorie, who sat next to me and was a grade ahead of me, and I were making an Egyptian scene, a pyramid, palm trees, and other stuff, with Louise's help, that we had to have finished before Christmas vacation and probably wouldn't because we had so much else to do. And Mrs. Barrie was reading a great book to us, *The Wonderful Adventures of Nils.* Even Roger liked it, though he snorted a couple of times at the beginning when the kid in the story, Nils, is made tiny because he's been mean to animals, but then when Nils begins riding all over the world on the back of a goose, nobody, not even Roger, made a peep. In fact we all begged Mrs. Barrie to read more when story period was over, and because she liked the book so much too, sometimes she did.

But, even though each day went like the wind, it seemed to take forever for the X marks I was putting on a calendar in my bedroom to cross off the days until Christmas.

"I just don't understand it," I said to Rose.

"I know what you mean, but I don't understand it either," Rose replied. She was being strange, not sitting on a chair next to the door or even looking out the window, but pacing around all the time, so her slippers made their swishing sound every minute we were talking. "Unfortunately, my days go more slowly than the weeks or the months or the years if that is possible."

"It isn't, I don't think. Maybe you should have something to do, Rose. I could bring you materials we're using to build the Egyptian scene, Mrs. Barrie calls it a diorama, and you could make your own diorama right here in your room."

"Why would I want to build an Egyptian scene in my room?"

"Well, to give you something to do first of all, but you'd get so involved you'd forget everything else. Pyramids are neat."

She paused in her swishing to glance down at me. "You do know what a pyramid is?"

"Of course I know what a pyramid is. That's what this whole project is for, to learn about pyramids and pharaohs."

"A pyramid is a tomb."

"Yes."

Again she paused to look down at me. "Why would I want to build a tomb when I'm already in a tomb?"

"Rose, your room isn't anything like a pyramid. A pyramid is enormous, and it has a lot of rooms in it, big enough to store all the things the pharaoh will need in his next life. They take years to build and years more to get all those things in there. Besides, pyramids don't have a flat ceiling, they have a point on top."

She stopped walking and stood by the window looking out, her back to me. I went on for a while telling her all I'd learned about pyramids and why I thought they were so great and why she should get busy and make one.

"I've constructed my own tomb and lain in it for years and years and years. I want to escape the tomb, not build another, certainly not one that comes to a point, though maybe there should be a point to all this." She didn't turn around. She wasn't talking loud enough to be sure I could hear her, though I did. That was the last she said about anything. She didn't even say goodbye when I told her I had to go wash up for supper.

At last the days were crossed out up to December 24th. We only had school in the morning of that day, and there weren't any regular lessons. We sang carols and had a snowball fight and Mrs. Barrie gave each of us a present. Mine was a book, *David the Incorrigible.* Having a book about somebody with my name was amazing. I told Mrs. Barrie I'd read it during vacation. Each of us gave her presents too. She said it had to be something we'd made. I'm terrible at making things. They never come out right. Even the pyramid I tried so hard to do with Marjorie didn't look much like a pyramid when it was finished, so I wrote a story about Mrs. Bullock remembering songs she had learned maybe a hundred years ago, and to prove it I carefully copied down the words to one of those songs at the end of my story. Mrs. Bullock had to sing it about five times before I got it all copied, but she didn't mind. Adeline left the room while we were working on it.

Mrs. Barrie was very pleased with my present, and told me to ask Mrs. Bullock if she could come and see her sometime soon to learn the melody so she could teach the song to us.

Everybody raced out of the school yard expecting to run home, but there was Mrs. Barrie's husband with a steaming team of Belgian horses hitched to a bobsled filled with hay. We all climbed in, including Mrs. Barrie, and Mr. Barrie delivered us home. I was luckiest because I was the only one who lived south of the school, and that meant if Mr. Barrie turned left out of the school yard I'd have the shortest ride and be the first one left off, but instead he turned right and headed for the Center, turning around when the last kids in that direction got out, so I had a complete round trip, the longest ride of anybody.

With only himself and Mrs. Barrie and me in the sled, he gave the horses their head as we raced over the frozen snow making bells on the harnesses jounce and jingle as plumes of frosty breath shot out the Belgians' nostrils. We were sung out because we'd done about a dozen choruses of "Jingle Bells" already, so we rode in silence, the wind biting our cheeks and noses and sparkling snow dazzling our eyes.

Pa Fleming was out on the front porch when we arrived, waving and shouting, "What a glorious sound those bells make." He insisted that Mr. and Mrs. Barrie come in and have dinner with us, even though they both said they had a lot to do yet to get ready for Christmas. Nothing would convince Pa, so they had to accept. Mrs. Barrie got out of the sled and went in the front door with Pa. I rode down to the steer barn with Mr. Barrie where he unhitched the team and turned them into a pair of box stalls.

I was glad Mrs. Barrie would see the Christmas tree in the Keeper's dining room. It touched the ceiling at the end of the room between two tall windows. There were hundreds of ornaments on it and tinsel and ropes of different colors and dozens of candleholders, each with a tiny candle that would be lighted Christmas Eve and again on Christmas morning. For days people had been putting wrapped presents under the tree. I was told I couldn't get near enough to peek at the name tags upon pain of death.

"It must be the most splendid tree in the county," Mrs. Barrie said when I led her into the dining room.

"In the state," Pa Fleming cried. "Maybe in the country."

"On earth," I shouted.

"In the universe," Pa roared.

The Keeper's tree was the biggest but not the only tree at the County Home. There were lots of others. We had a much smaller tree up in our sitting room that Uncle Will and I decorated, and there were trees in the women's sitting room, the men's sitting room, little table trees in all the wards and some of the single rooms, and each one was decorated, some only with popcorn and pinecones because that's the way whoever did that tree wanted it. Mr. Beveridge suggested we should have a contest as to whose tree was the closest to what a Christmas tree was supposed to be. His tree in the bakery was a tiny fir he'd found in the woods and dug up before the ground froze, then put in a pot and kept outside until Christmas week when he brought it in and hung sparkly Christmas cookies all over it. He didn't mind if I ate a cookie off the tree. He said that's what they were for, to be eaten. I knew he had a box of replacements on the bakery shelf.

Rose didn't have a tree. She didn't want one. Nor would she look at the very nice tree in the women's sitting room when she went back and forth to the bathroom. "The less said about Christmas the better," she told Julia. "That's not a very nice attitude," Julia replied, to which Rose said, "This isn't a very nice Christmas." I heard Julia reporting the conversation to Aunt Maude.

Because the only fireplace at the County Home was in Ma Fleming's polite parlor, that's where I hung my stocking. Uncle Will teased me because I borrowed one of his knee-length socks rather than hang one of my own puny things on the mantle. "Greed will get you everywhere," Pa Fleming said.

Christmas Eve meant scalloped oysters, great flat pans of them, made from oysters Pa Fleming had brought in especially for that once a year treat. He talked about them weeks before Christmas, as anxious for the oysters to arrive as I was for Christmas. I don't think a couple of the men liked them very much, so Aunt Maude had lots of other things to eat too, but Pa twitched his white mustache in their direction and said you couldn't have Christmas without oysters. I agreed.

The last thing before I went to bed I sneaked over to Rose's room to wish her a Merry Christmas, telling Aunt Maude I'd forgotten something downstairs. Rose was lying on her bed, not in it but on it. Her room was dark, but I could see in the dim light that shone from the sitting room. Nothing I did made her respond to me in any way. She didn't move a hand or raise her head, nor would she speak. I was frightened as I stood there looking at her, saying over and over again quietly, "Merry Christmas, Rose. Merry Christmas, Rose."

Aunt Maude told me when she tucked me in that I was not to get up before six o'clock, no matter how early I awoke. When I asked if I could go to the barn with the men when they milked at four, she said, no, I was to stay in my bed until six o'clock, then I could come to breakfast in my bathrobe and slippers. I was afraid I'd not sleep a wink, but I did, and when I woke up it was ten minutes to six according to the luminous dial of the loud-ticking Big Ben that sat on my bureau. Those ten minutes were as long as the whole month of December, but at last they were gone. I jumped out of bed into slippers I'd placed right where my feet would land, pulled on my bathrobe as I ran to the bathroom to pee and brush my teeth, then hurried down the stairs, using fingers to comb my hair.

"Merry Christmas, David," Eunice and Aureta said together as I walked into the kitchen. They were piling sausages on platters. Aunt Maude was in the pantry with all waffle irons going. "Merry Christmas, darling," she called out to me.

"Merry Christmas," I said.

"Uncle Will is coming right back from checking on one of the patients," Aunt Maude continued from the pantry, "Then we can go in and see what Santa left in your stocking."

Pa and Ma Fleming, Aunt Maude and Uncle Will, Eunice, Aureta, and Roy watched while I took the things out of Uncle Will's bulging stocking. He would never be able to wear it again it was so stretched out of shape from being filled with three small cars, six lead soldiers, a Big Little book, a new toothbrush, a piggybank, tangerines and nuts and a silver dollar in the toe. I never liked candy canes so there was no danger of spoiling my breakfast by eating the one sticking out of the top of the stocking. Besides, I wouldn't let anything keep me from eating a stack of pecan waffles I knew Aunt Maude was preparing for Christmas breakfast.

During the night somebody had put folding screens around the Christmas tree at the end of the dining room, so while we ate breakfast all I could see was the top branches. Everybody else must have been as anxious as I because while we all had seconds and some people had thirds, nobody wasted time talking. We all concentrated on eating. As soon as the table was cleared, Pa Fleming and Uncle Will went behind the screens to light a fresh set of candles. When everything was ready the screens were taken away and there it was, even more beautiful than it had been the night before. Best of all I could see what the screens had been hiding.

There was a super sled from Mother and Dad propped against some packages, and on the floor in front of the tree a whole miniature farm, a barn, barnyard, chicken coop, house, well, and all kinds of animals, horses, cows, pigs, chickens, sheep, and people. Everybody watched me as I knelt down to inspect it up close and to touch it. Spread out, it covered more space than the top of a card table and around the whole farm was a tiny rail fence. All I could say was "Wow!" but I said that a couple of dozen times.

Though more of the presents under the tree were for me than all the others put together, because everybody gave me something and some people gave me several things, I had a hard time getting excited over anything but the farm. I'd never seen anything like it. Uncle Will had made patterns for the whole thing, from buildings to animals and people, then he and Roy cut out all the pieces with a jig saw and sanded and shaped them. Aunt Maude and Ma Fleming helped with the painting. The cows were black and white Holsteins just like those in the real barn. There was a team of dapple gray Percherons and a single Belgian stallion like Chub. It was all so real, including a family of ducks painted to look like my Muscovies, except they were cleaner. Roy was in the dining room when I first saw the farm, and he both beamed and blushed when people praised him for the work he'd done on it. Pa Fleming called it the eighth wonder of the world.

At Aunt Maude's prodding, I would open a package. Eunice gave me wooly slippers for which I thanked her, but then I'd play with the farm for a while until Aunt Maude told me I should open another present, so I'd undo another and thank whoever for whatever, and we kept at it until the dining room was a mess of wrappings that had to be cleaned up. I argued about having to go get dressed, but did as I was told, and when I came back the mess was gone and so was everybody else. The women were back in the kitchen working on dinner which would be roast beef and Yorkshire pudding because Pa Fleming said you wouldn't know it was Christmas without roast beef and Yorkshire pudding. A whole herd of cattle must have died so everybody at the County Home would know it was Christmas. Mr. Beveridge baked the sides of beef in his bread ovens, proud of the responsibility but complaining because the ovens would have to be scrubbed before he could use them for his precious breads again.

As much as I wanted to just play with the farm, I also wanted to give out the presents I had for others beyond those whose things I'd put under the Keeper's dining room tree. I had a package of cut plug for Charley Smith. He was in his office behind the furnaces, sitting in the leather chair that didn't have much stuffing left, listening to his radio that didn't have a case so you could see all the tubes and other guts and produced so much static I don't know how he understood what he was listening to. He assured me he heard what he wanted to hear. I handed him the cut plug that I'd wrapped myself and he handed me an unwrapped pound box of ribbon candy. If there is any candy I liked less than candy canes it was ribbon candy, but Aunt Maude liked it so I knew the sicky sweet ribbons wouldn't go to waste. I thanked him and said I couldn't hang around to talk because I had other gifts to deliver.

I gave Aunt Latzy talcum powder. It was in a black enameled can that had butterflies painted on it. Harry Woolf told me it was good talcum, but I bought it for the butterflies not the powder. They were all colors, blue, yellow, orange, and each one outlined in gold. Aunt Latzy said it was the prettiest powder can she'd ever seen, and both she and I liked the smell when she shook some powder on the back of her hand. It was different from the talcum she ordered from Harrod's, but she said that didn't matter. She gave me English butter biscuits in a tin shaped like the Old Curiosity Shop, with hollyhocks and other flowers across the front and a chimney that stood up above the top of the roof. We ate a couple of biscuits, and because it was Christmas I broke off a piece of one with a strawberry jam center and gave it to Harold.

All the Bullocks loved chocolates so I combined presents for Adeline, Mrs. Bullock, and Johnny in a Whitman Sampler, not the largest size, but the biggest I could afford. They had known about the farm Uncle Will and Roy were making for me, so Adeline's gift to me was two little rectangular things with cloth wrapped around four sides and the ends left open so you could see cotton stuffed inside.

"Thank you, Adeline," I said. "What are they?"

"They's bales of cotton, stupid."

"Oh." I'd never seen bales of cotton.

" 'Twas my notion," Mrs. Bullock said. "I don' think we grows cotton up heah, but when I was a chile we growed lots where I came from. Seemed like you oughta have some bales a cotton on that new farm of yours."

"Good thought," I said, aware that Adeline was looking at me as if she'd give me a clout if I didn't appreciate her mother's idea.

Mrs. Bullock's own gift to me was to sit on her lap while she sang one of her favorite lullabies. I told her I was afraid I'd break both her legs, but she just laughed and said boys lot's bigger'n me had sat on her lap and not broken those old pins. I cheated some by keeping the tips of my toes on the floor while she rocked me and sang, but she didn't notice so I didn't hurt her feelings.

Johnny gave me a chocolate Santa Claus that he must have bought at Harry Woolf's store because I saw them there when I was doing my Christmas shopping. He thought it was a big joke that he gave me chocolate and I gave him, them, chocolate. "We all knows what the other likes," he grinned. All four of us took a bite of my Santa Claus, small bites because he wasn't very big, and then we took turns choosing a piece from the Whitman Sampler. Mrs. Bullock chose first, saying she had to have a creamy filling. Adeline was supposed to go next, but took so long making up her mind, Johnny told me to take whichever piece I wanted. I took a nut cup, and naturally Adeline glared at me.

"You made up yore mine yet?" Johnny asked her.

"Why all the rush?" Adeline sulked. "Nobody's s'posed to rush on Christmas." She poked piece after piece before she finally selected one that was wrapped in gold foil. We all watched while she unwrapped it and then stared in silence when she put the candy in her mouth without letting any of us see what it was. She chewed a couple of times and then smiled. "I knew if I took my time I'd be better off."

"What is it, Adeline?"

"Well, it's chocolate . . ."

"We knows that," Johnny groaned.

"An' it's creamy juices, an' it's a cherry." She grinned an open grin, showing us the cherry she was holding carefully between her teeth.

"Don' s'pose they's anythin' left for ole Johnny," Johnny laughed and slapped his knee. He found a caramel which is what he said he wanted so everybody was happy.

Blind Theresa had crocheted a wool hat for me and Mary Delancy gave me her "Jesus loves YOU" fan Bruuuther Pitts had handed out last summer. I gave both of them homemade sachets Aunt Maude bought from the Ladies Aid Society.

I carried all the things people had given me back to my room and picked up my two most important presents. For Rose I had a glass fish bowl that had different kinds of woodsy plants growing in it with a piece of glass over the top to keep the plants and the moss damp. Aunt Maude helped me make it. She told me Rose would have to take the glass off part of each day so the plants could breathe. I thought it was beautiful, with red berries growing on one of the little vines.

Roy's present had taken a lot of effort on the part of several people. It was a record of favorite arias sung by Madame Schumann-Heink. The music store in town didn't have it, so they had to order it, and Uncle Will made three special trips to the store before it arrived. I don't know how much the record cost because Uncle Will paid for it. Roy had seen it advertised somewhere and said he was going to send off for it right after Christmas. I hoped he hadn't sent away sooner.

He wasn't in his room when I got there so I stood the record up on the table next to his phonograph, with a Christmas card I had made for him in school signed, "Love, David." If he was in the kitchen when I got back from Rose's room I'd think of an excuse to get him up to his room so I could watch him open his present.

"Merry Christmas, Rose," I said through the bars. She was still lying on top of her bed exactly as she was the night before. "Rose?" I called out to her several times, but she didn't answer. I could see she was breathing. She didn't look as if she'd moved since Christmas Eve. I wondered if she was still wearing her clothes.

"Oh David, I'm so glad to see you." It was Julia. I hadn't heard her coming up behind me and almost dropped the glass bowl garden. As if her appearance wasn't surprise enough, she actually said she was glad to see me.

"You are?"

"Yes. Maybe you can rouse Rose. She won't respond to anything I do." Julia opened Rose's door and motioned for me to follow her in. I'd never been inside Rose's room. It didn't seem right to go in now unless Rose asked me herself, but Rose wasn't talking.

I don't know what I expected when I went through the door, but it wasn't what I saw. The room felt cold. There were no pictures on the walls, and not much furniture—a wardrobe-bureau combination between the sink and the door, the rocking chair by the window, a narrow table with a mirror above it on the window wall, and a straight chair, the one Rose brought over to the door for our discussions. That and a night-stand like those beside every bed in the women's building and the single bed itself on which Rose lay was all there was.

"Rose, David has come to see you, bringing a lovely Christmas present," Julia said in a soft voice. Her smile was a plea as she leaned over Rose. "Come along, David, here where she can see you."

I walked to the edge of the bed. Rose's eyes were open, staring at the ceiling. I'd think she was dead except she blinked from time to time and I could see she was breathing. The only difference from last night is that somebody, Julia I suspect, had pulled a wool blanket up over Rose almost up to her chin.

"Give her your present," Julia whispered, stepping back as she pushed me toward the head of the bed.

"Merry Christmas, Rose," I said again. "I've brought you a dish garden. Aunt Maude did most of the work, but I helped her dig the woods plants after Johnny Bullock showed us where they were. You have to keep the glass cover on most of the time so it will stay moist, but you have to take it off other times so it will breathe."

I looked up at Julia and shook my head. Rose didn't even shift her eyes in my direction. I decided to try again. "It's

Christmas, Rose. Everybody's having roast beef and Yorkshire pudding because Pa Fleming says we wouldn't know it's Christmas if we ate something else." Nothing. "Did you know about the farm Roy and Uncle Will were making for me? And Ma Fleming and Aunt Maude helped paint it and Adeline gave me some bales of cotton for it."

Julia put her hands on my shoulders. I guess she was telling me to keep talking. "Blind Theresa crocheted a hat for me and Aunt Latzy gave me a box shaped like a store filled with butter cookies." I could feel Julia's grip tightening. "Is she all right?" I asked, turning my head so Rose might not hear me.

"Her pulse is fine. I can't get a thermometer in her mouth because she's clenched her teeth, but she doesn't feel hot. In fact I'm more worried about her catching cold. She hasn't been to the bathroom since early last evening as far as I know." Julia sounded deeply worried.

"Maybe we should call Dr. Davis," I suggested.

"I hate to bother him on Christmas. The poor man is on call seven days a week."

"But what if she's in a coma?" I asked. I'd heard about comas recently from Uncle Will when a male patient went into one and died.

"Oh, I don't think she's in a coma, though she might be." Julia was taking Rose's pulse again, holding her wrist and counting while she looked at her nurse's watch, the one with the jerky second hand.

"Are you in a coma, Rose?" I asked while Julia was counting.

"Her heartbeat is elevated a bit, as if she's agitated. Nothing dangerous," Julia paused, "I don't think." She put Rose's arm back under the covers and sighed deeply. "David, it's beyond me. Much as I hate doing it, I'll call Dr. Davis. I'd never forgive myself if she was in a coma and something terrible happened to her."

All business again, Julia told me to put my dish garden gift on Rose's table where she'd see it if she came to and turned her head. "I think it might cheer her up. You run along now. I'll go to the office and call Dr. Davis."

We were at the door but not through it when what sounded like a growl came from the bed. Julia and I turned around and looked back. Rose hadn't changed position in the slightest, but before we could leave the room or return to the bed she said in a strong, cold flat voice, "I am not in a coma, and I will not eat roast beef and Yorkshire pudding for Christmas dinner."

CHAPTER SIXTEEN

now started falling lazy at first the day after Christmas, flakes floating around in the air as if they had no particular place to go and plenty of time to get there. Then about noon it made up its mind and dropped out of the clouds straight to the ground, and fell and fell and fell, until the snow on the level was more than three feet deep and kept piling up. All sounds were muffled inside as well as out. Ma Fleming said it was "still," so still that even playing on the dining-room floor with my farm, I could barely hear what Aunt Maude and Eunice and Aureta were saying in the kitchen.

Uncle Deane plowed out the sidewalks with Daisy hitched to a small plow, but by the time he finished doing the rounds, including paths to the barns, those sidewalks he'd plowed first were filled in again. Aunt Maude made me put on all the clothes I owned, including the new hat Blind Theresa had crocheted for me, when I went to feed my ducks. I used paths as much as I could, but when I got to their barn I had to just push my way through. Fortunately, though the snow was deep it was dry and light, so getting to the ducks wasn't much of a problem. From their barn I pushed my way over to the horse barn but couldn't get the sliding door open so gave up and went back to the house, where I spent most of the morning playing with my farm.

Rose hadn't touched the roast beef on Christmas Day, so after everybody else was fed Mrs. Davies made scrambled eggs for her. Rose said thank you, but according to Julia she didn't eat the eggs either. When I went to see her after I got back from feeding my ducks, she was in the bathroom taking a bath, so I couldn't ask her if she liked my dish garden. It didn't bother me that she hadn't given me anything. There was no way she could go shopping.

Roy loved his record, pretending to be surprised at what it was. "How did you know I wanted Madam Schumann-Heink?"

"You said you were going to send for it right after Christmas, that's how."

"But, David, you didn't need to buy it for me. I'm very pleased you did, however, because now I'll think of you every time I listen to it."

"Roy, you can't think of me when you play it. You've always told me to not think of anything when I listen to music, to just let the music take hold of me and wipe everything else away."

"What I mean is, as I put the record on I'll think, David gave this to me, and I'll appreciate what I'm about to hear even more."

Roy's music was the most important thing in the world to him. When he was listening to it he didn't even look like himself. There were extra lights on inside him or something. He preferred playing records on his regular phonograph, the louder the better, but if he wanted to listen late at night or when he thought he might disturb somebody else, he'd listen through earphones attached to another Victrola. When he did listen that way he was funny to watch because expressions kept going over his face, silly smiles and deep frowns while he moved his head from side to side.

"Don't just listen to it, David," he told me many times. "Feel it. Feel it first in your ears and in your head, then in the tips of your fingers and your arms and up into your chest until it seems as if your heart will explode. Music is for the heart as much as for the head."

I did feel it as he told me to, so that at times I thought I was flying, soaring like a chicken hawk in a hazy August sky, riding the air in great swoops and dives. If the music throbbed, my whole body became involved. Listening to *La Bohème* or *Madame Butterfly,* I'd find myself reaching out, wanting my arms to stretch as far as the sound of the singer's voice. When Roy played *Carmen* I couldn't sit still but had to march around the room, with an imaginary sword over my shoulder, lunging and thrusting, poking at the bull when the music demanded that. In the barn I never walked close to the bars of the bullpen because I was sure the bull could bash me right through those bars if he wanted to, but in Roy's sitting room, listening to his music, I was a brave bullfighter. When Carmen, Mimi, and Cho Cho San and all the others died on the records, I'd clutch my side and collapse to the floor feeling their fleeting final moments.

Roy also let me conduct because he liked to conduct. He said conducting involved him more in what he was hearing. There were times I think he would have preferred I just sit still and feel, because he'd say, "The beat, David, you aren't hearing the beat, listen to the music." That's when I'd get up and move around the room to the music, not really dancing, just moving. The beat must have entered through my feet from the floor because I could keep time much better when I was dancing. I could never get Roy to do that. He said he was too big and too clumsy. He said if he fell over, as I did from time to time, he'd crash through the men's washroom ceiling. I don't know how he could resist. I couldn't. I had to move, to give myself to what I was hearing. Roy said it was all going on inside for him and from the look on his face that must have been so. Too bad he and Adeline didn't get together, but their music was not the same.

We listened to the Schumann-Heink record I gave him, both sides twice through as soon as Roy finished his after-dinner chores. Madame Schumann-Heink wasn't somebody you danced to, and I didn't feel much like conducting either, so I just laid on the floor and listened. "Let her voice wash over you, David," Roy said, and that's what I did.

When he went to put it on for the third go round, I said I'd had enough for now and walked over to see if Rose was feeling any better.

"Where have you been?" she asked me when I peeked through her bars.

"Up listening to Roy's new record, the one I gave him for Christmas."

"I wish I could hear it. One of the things I hate most about winter, and I hate everything about winter, is not being able to hear Roy's music. In the summer when his operas float through the air and in my window, they make me forget where I am."

She was back to pacing. She seldom sat down and talked the way she used to. It was as if she couldn't sit, she could either lie on her bed and be silent or walk around. I talked or she talked, but we didn't talk to each other very much. When she asked me questions I don't think she paid attention to my answers.

"Did you finish your pyramid?" she asked.

"Yes, but it wasn't very good. Marjorie made the palm trees and they looked more like palm trees than my pyramid looked like a pyramid. If I'd just done the outside I think it would have been okay, but Mrs. Barrie wanted me to do part of the inside too, the treasure room and the burial chamber—that's where the mummy goes."

"Will this snow never stop?" Rose murmured from the window, which was so coated with thick, clinging snow she couldn't see through it.

"In the treasure room and in a lot of other rooms they put all the things the pharaoh might need in the next life, which is why it took years and years to build. They did all that before the pharoah died. What do you think of that, Rose?"

"Sounds sensible to me."

"When he died, they put his favorite things in last and sealed the tomb."

"You mean he didn't have to do without them in this life so he'd have them in his next life?" Rose asked, but not as if she was really interested.

"That's right."

I was waiting for her to say something more, but she didn't. The dish garden was sitting on the long table right where I put it the day before. I wondered if she'd seen it.

"What favorite things would you like put in your tomb, Rose?" I hoped she'd mention the dish garden.

She glanced back at me from the window. "What makes you think I'll have a tomb, other than the one I've already got?"

"You know what I mean, Rose."

She sighed and began pacing again. "Yes, I know what you mean."

"Your watch, for instance. You always have your watch pinned on your dress. Now if you were a pharaoh, after you died they'd put your watch in with you."

Rose fingered the small gold watch that hung from a pin shaped like a rose on the front of her dress. It had been given to her by her parents on her eighteenth birthday, she told me. "What will I need with a watch after I die? What need do I have for a watch now?" She unpinned the clasp on the rose and held the watch up in front of her face. The case had designs scratched all over the front, the back was plain and shiny from years of rubbing against Rose's dress. She pressed down on the winding stem and the case front popped open.

"Have I ever shown you what is inscribed on the inside?" she asked, coming over to the door. "It says, in Italian of course because Mama and Papa couldn't read English, 'Per Rosa, con amore.' " She held the watch down so I could look inside the case. I could barely see the cobweb-thin words.

"Is your name Rosa or Rose?"

"Rosa to Mama and Papa," she whispered, "Rose to everybody else." She snapped the case shut and was pinning the rose on her dress again as she turned away, but then she turned back and looked at me, really looked at me for the first time that day.

"Thank you for my lovely Christmas gift, David. I will take very good care of the garden."

"You're welcome. Did you hear what I said about taking the glass off so it can breathe?"

"I heard."

She took her hands down from the front of her dress and the

watch wasn't there, wasn't pinned on again. She opened her hands and looked into them for a long time without saying anything, then came toward the door, stopping before she got to me to look into her hands once more. As if waking up from a dream, she straightened her shoulders and reached out to me. "David, I want to give you a Christmas present. Forgive me for not wrapping it." She held out the watch.

I felt as if I was being clutched by the throat, as if something was holding me, squeezing me too tight. "Rose, you don't want to give me your watch." I didn't want Rose's watch.

"I do want to. It's the only thing I have to give you. Here." She held the watch out toward me, commanding me to take it. "If I could, I'd have engraved on the back of the case, 'For my beautiful David,' but that's impossible."

I backed away from the door. "Rose, if you give me your watch, how will you tell the time?"

"I have no need to tell the time," she replied. "You have need, David. You have a lifetime to keep."

When I didn't step forward, she came to the bars and thrust her arm through, then in an angry voice that sounded like I'd said a swear and she was going to soap my mouth, said, "David, I am giving you my watch and I want you to take it."

As I had done when she soaped out my mouth, even though I didn't want to, I stepped up and put out my hand. Now that I was within reach, she paused for a second, then placed the gold watch and its rose-shaped brooch in the palm of my hand, closing my fingers over it. The pin on the back of the brooch stuck into my thumb, making me wince. When Rose stepped away to move toward the window again, I saw my thumb was bleeding.

"It's a girl's watch," I said, trying not to sniffle, knowing I wasn't crying over a tiny thumb prick.

"Then give it to your girl when you're old enough to have one, a serious girl, one you are going to love always." She was facing the snow-covered window and didn't turn around when I thanked her, though she did say I was welcome.

The gift of the watch caused a real ruckus upstairs in our suite. Aunt Maude acted as if I'd stolen it, knowing I hadn't. Uncle Will said I had to give it back because Rose had given it to me only in the emotion of the day. I told them I didn't want the watch and would like to return it, but knew Rose wouldn't let me. Aunt Maude took the watch and went to talk to Rose. When she came back she told us, looking strangely at Uncle Will, "Rose said, 'I can give David anything and everything I want. Nobody can deny me that right.' " Uncle Will thought Rose would calm down and we could try again in a few days. Aunt Maude suggested she should put the watch in a safe place, but even if I didn't truly want it, Rose had given the watch to me, so I insisted it had to stay with me, go in my bureau drawer and not in Aunt Maude's.

It snowed nonstop for five days. Drifts went over the laundry roof, and on the level with no drifting the grape arbor completely disappeared. Paths between buildings were tunnel-like with walls on either side six and seven feet high, and in the driveway between the women's building and the bakery, it was an actual tunnel through hard-packed snow. Charley Smith had to get up on the chicken house and shovel it off or the roof would have caved in from the weight.

No cars could get to the County Home, nor could we get out, so we were truly snowbound. I thought it was great, and didn't mind at all when the telephone and electric lines went down too. Not hearing Jack Armstrong and Little Orphan Annie for a couple of days was no loss when compared to the adventure of pretending we were all alone in the world. Candles and kerosene lamps were used from dusk on, except in the infirmary and in the cow barn, where generators provided enough power for a few hours of light each day.

Not everybody was as excited as I was about being shut in. Adeline spent most of the time sitting on the floor in the corner of her room sulking. Aunt Latzy, who shouldn't have known the difference because she hadn't been out of bed in years, fussed constantly about getting packages of things she'd ordered from Harrods. It never occured to me before how important mail is to somebody who doesn't go anyplace.

Rose went frantic, muttering to herself about being closed in, not listening to anything I or anybody said. Julia told Aunt Maude she was going to give Rose a sedative if she didn't calm down. When I asked Rose what a sedative was, she didn't answer.

Even Ma Fleming who was never nervous got itchy. I was helping her do a puzzle one afternoon, doing the hard part because the puzzle was facing her and I was working on it upside down, when to relieve the monotony I got up and went over to look out the front window. Drifts had covered the window up to its middle, so I had to stand on a stool to peek over. I was standing there watching wind-whipped clouds of snow scutter across the fields and the hill leading up to the water tower and the cemetery when Ma said, "David, get down from there. You will fall and hurt yourself." She never worried about me hurting myself; at least she never let on if she did. Then she burned an English muffin she was toasting on the coals of the Franklin stove to have with our tea, and I distinctly heard her say, "Damn."

Only Roy remained undisturbed, winding up his phonograph and listening to his records hour after hour, happy to have so much uninterrupted time. He couldn't run the churns without electricity.

I was playing hopscotch on the squares in the Keeper's kitchen linoleum when Aunt Maude screeched at me, "If you don't stop that I'm going to snatch you bald-headed."

"There isn't anything else for me to do," I said.

"Go read that book Mrs. Barrie gave you for Christmas. You haven't picked it up since you brought it home. Or go play with your farm. We're going to have to move it soon when we take down the tree."

"I'll read the book," I said, and went upstairs where I started *David the Incorrigible* and didn't want to stop reading until I reached the end, not to eat, not to do anything. Aunt Maude gave me a hard time because I insisted on reading it by kerosene lamplight. She said I'd go blind, but I took the chance and kept on reading. When I brought it to breakfast with me and tried to read while I was eating, that was too much. She told me she was going to take the book away and not let me have it again until I learned proper manners. "At table is not the place nor time to read," she lectured.

When I finished *David the Incorrigible,* I felt as if I'd lost life. The last page was terrible. I couldn't slow down, yet every word I read was taking me closer to the end. What to do when there weren't any more words to read? I, David, had become the David in the book, doing everything he did, being scared and brave, having all the feelings he had. When I came to the end of *David the Incorrigible* I felt that it was the end of me too.

The only thing to do was go back and start again at the beginning. Second time through I didn't skip a word though I knew what to expect, and I was as excited by all that was happening as I had been the first time. Because I couldn't stand not being involved in the book, when Aunt Maude and Uncle Will went to bed early because "there isn't anything else to do," I used a flashlight under the covers to keep on reading.

When I did go to sleep, I dreamed about David the Incorrigible. Sometimes he was my best buddy and sometimes he was me. What I felt for him was so strong I couldn't express it, not even to myself, and I knew he felt the same way about me. Best of all was that whenever I wanted him, he was there. I could pick up the book and go to those pages about his first night alone in the cabin and spend that terrible night all over again, and return to the cabin as often as I wanted to.

"You'll ruin your eyes, reading constantly," Aunt Maude warned. "Go play with your farm."

I took *David the Incorrigible* with me to the Christmas tree at the end of the dining room, but instead of moving the animals and people around, I laid on my stomach and read.

It was while I was reading there in the wintry half light from the tall windows that I overheard Julia telling Pa Fleming as they stood in the open sitting-room door, "I'm afraid she's losing her mind. She rarely makes real contact with me, and she's letting herself go. You know how proud she has always been of her appearance, but now if I try to bathe her because she isn't interested in bathing herself, she fights me away. Rose has never been physically difficult, but this morning she grabbed my wrist and told me she'd break it if I touched her with the washcloth."

"Julia, I'm amazed. Rose has been obstinate since the beginning, but never mean." Pa Fleming's voice expressed disbelief.

"Exactly," said Julia. "This is a very different Rose."

"Do you think she's becoming dangerous?"

Julia was slow to answer. "Oh, I don't think so."

"We must remember when she did what she did it was in a fit of anger."

"But that was anger built up over years of being brutalized."

"Perhaps," Pa said, sounding worried, "her anger is building again. It can't be easy for an intelligent, spirited woman to spend her life in a small room."

I didn't move because I didn't want them to see or hear me.

"I wonder if just to be safe we should begin actually locking her door." I could tell by the way he sounded, Pa was rubbing his chin and smoothing his mustache.

"I'd hate to do that," Julia said. "It seems so cruel. The bars are bad enough."

"Well, keep me informed of her behavior, Julia, and then we'll figure out what we have to do."

That was the end of the conversation. Julia went into the pantry where every afternoon she fixed herself a plate of cookies to have with tea in her room.

I jumped up, and clutching *David the Incorrigible,* ran as fast as I could without falling as I slid around the corners to Rose's room. She was standing not by the window but looking toward me through the bars in her door. Naturally I thought she saw me as plainly as I saw her, but I guess she didn't because she didn't let on she knew I was there until I whispered, "Rose, what's the matter?"

Startled, she looked down at me. "The matter? The matter is I'm trying to cry. I want to cry, do nothing but cry for hours, to make up for all the years I haven't cried, but I can't." Then she said as if she did see me and knew I was there, "David, I have no tears. Isn't that sad?"

CHAPTER SEVENTEEN

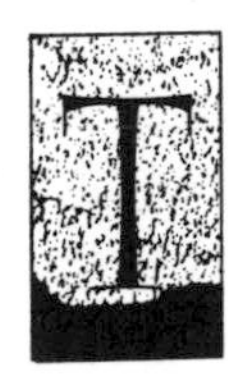

The rest of the winter flew by for me, there was so much to do all the time. Roy let me read *David the Incorrigible* to him and he liked it as much as I did. I wanted to read it to Aunt Latzy, but old bitch Ripley made such a fuss it wasn't worth it. Mary said she couldn't hear a word when I read because I kept my nose in the book, and Adeline fell asleep when I tried out the first chapter on her. That made me mad.

Rose got so she was making sense, but I didn't think she was ready for the adventures of a boy on his own in the mountains, so I told her parts of the story but put off reading it to her until she was well again. Julia told Aunt Maude Rose had turned a corner when she went back to brushing her hair a hundred strokes in the morning and again in the afternoon, and Pa Fleming seemed pleased to report at the supper table one night Rose had asked him to get some special kind of black goods so she could make a new dress. I was excited by that because some of the best talks Rose and I had were when she was sitting on her side of the door sewing and I was on my side talking. Maybe we'd get back to those again.

Charley Smith let me tie my sled to the back of his jitney when we were someplace we were sure Aunt Maude couldn't see us, and then he'd pull me along the Center Road or on the level parts of the East Road. Even with chains on he didn't think he'd get back up the East Road hill. Zooming along the hard-packed snow on my new sled with the chains clanking only inches from my head was an experience I was sure David the Incorrigible would enjoy as much as I did. Charley said he was afraid I'd get asphyxiated from the exhaust, so he rigged up a pipe that took the exhaust from the jitney's tailpipe up over my head where it puffed like a steam engine in the cold air.

Gradually as the snow melted, the tunnel between the women's building and the bakery collapsed, then the walls of the walkways shrank. With power restored Roy could churn every day and all the other routines returned. Overhead belts kept washing machines in the laundry roaring much of the time, as women sat at the rows of mangles pressing mountains of sheets, pillowcases, tablecloths, and napkins.

In the middle of February hogs were butchered and scalded and cut into quarters to go into meat-room coolers. You could hear their squeals no matter where you were on the place. I didn't like it at all, so asked Roy if he'd let me listen to some records on his phonograph while the men were slaughtering. He knew I'd be careful, so said yes, and I turned up Madame Schumann-Heinck as loud as I could. There were times when I wasn't sure which shriek was her and which was some pig being stuck in the barnyard.

The good thing about pig butchering was having fresh livers broiled over coals for dinner. Even people who said they didn't like liver lapped up those pink juicy bits the way Aunt Maude fixed them with thick crisp slabs of bacon and steamy baked potatoes.

Suddenly it felt like spring, Uncle Will called it "false spring." The weather turned warm and the ground turned soft. Aunt Maude made me take my boots off at the back door and leave them on the porch so I wouldn't track in chunks of mud that clung no matter how much I kicked my feet against the steps. Cows began calving in batches, filling the calf pens with first wobbly then curious small black and white copies of themselves. Bull calves went into big pens on the north side of the calf-barn aisle, and heifer calves on the south side, just like men and women at the Keeper's table. The bull calves were given whole milk with the cream still in it, and the heifer calves skimmed milk, because the little males were raised for veal while the females would grow up to be milk cows or sold off early if they didn't satisfy the dairy farmer's eye.

I made the mistake once of watching a veal calf being butchered, and while Uncle Deane assured me it was all right because after being stunned everything happened so quick the calf didn't feel anything, I dreamed for weeks about the calf's leg buckling up against his body when he was hit with the mallet.

I did help catch the baby male pigs when they had to be castrated. There was a lot of squealing but it didn't bother me much, because two seconds after they'd been cut they went back to whatever they'd been doing before. Funny thing about baby pigs, they are so cute to look at, pink and cuddly, but they aren't cuddly at all. When you pick them up, they are tight-packed tubes of hard, solid flesh.

I was explaining to Rose how I'd been helping with the castrating, and how it might seem cruel but was necessary and that everybody was careful not to hurt the little pigs any more than they could help when she interrupted me, not in an angry voice, but questioning.

"Do you think you can tell when another being is feeling pain, David?"

"I think so, at least with pigs. They squeal."

"What if they didn't squeal? Could you tell they hurt if they remained silent?"

I thought about that. Would I know if a pig was hurting if it didn't squeal?

"It is possible to have pain so intense you make no sound at all." She didn't look up from sewing her new black dress.

"Well, then, maybe the pigs aren't feeling any pain at all because they make an awful noise."

"Oh, I'm sure they are." Rose rethreaded her needle and began making tiny stitches around the collar. "Some of us make more noise than others. You remember how Mrs. Ripley screamed night and day when she had that gallbladder attack."

"I could hear her way over in my room."

"Exactly."

"But Aunt Maude, who has had one, says gallbladder attacks are the worst pain there is."

"The worst physical perhaps. There are many kinds of pain. How do you like my new dress?" She stood and held up the dress so I could see it. Except that it was black and most of her dresses were gray, it was exactly like all the others she had made.

"It's very shiny."

"It's bombazine. Mr. Fleming was good to get the material for me as quickly as he did. There's much finishing to do, and I haven't begun covering all the buttons, but I think it will be quite handsome when it's done, don't you?"

"Yes. Why do you make all your dresses alike, Rose?"

"Because the style suits me." She looked up. "This one is going to be a bit different. The pattern is the same, but I'm giving it extra touches. The Keeper managed to get the lovely jet I requested to set off the collar and cuffs. I haven't embroidered in years, but I think I'll remember how."

"It sounds like a party dress."

"It will be my laying-out dress."

"Why are you making it now, then?"

"So it will be ready when needed."

Real spring came early, and we knew it was spring when birdsong woke us each morning, a cardinal whistling from the top of the elm tree in the yard before we could see the crack of dawn, and the bluebirds swooping in the apple orchard where buds were beginning to swell on the twigs. Everybody said they hated English sparrows, but the sparrows didn't seem to care as they chittered and fought and flew in and out of holes they were making in the great stack of bedding straw next to the cow barn.

I rode into town with Charley Smith to get cartons of baby chicks that had come in on the night train and were waiting in the stationmaster's office. Hundreds of tiny balls of fluff peeped nonstop and poked curious little beaks through the airholes. Charley and I lugged them out to the jitney and stacked them up. As Charley was securing them with ropes, before he put blankets over the load to protect them from the wind, I put my eyes as close as I could to an air space trying to see in.

"I love baby chicks," I said.

"Baby chicks is like baby kittens, all cute but the damn things grow up to be hens and cats. Get away from there now so's I can wrap this canvas around."

"I thought you liked chickens, Charley. You spend half your time taking care of them."

"I prefer pigs. Pigs ain't crazy like chickens, like these damn Leghorns especially. God damn White Leghorn ain't got the sense of a earthworm. Makes no difference at all how quiet and gentle I am with 'em, the bastards scream and squawk and end up in a pile in the corner every time I go in to feed 'em. I'd drown these here chicks right this minute if I had my druthers."

"You feel that way about all chickens, Charley, or just Leghorns?" I held down a corner of the tarp while he tightened the rope.

"Leghorns mostly. Can't say as I love any chicken, but I hate Leghorns."

"Why do you have them, then?"

Charley spit out half his chaw. "You ever hear anybody askin' me what kinda chickens we oughta have? Ask me anything for that matter?"

"No."

He snapped his jaw shut and jerked his head. "There you are, then. They don't think I know nothin'. 'Course it's generally agreed White Leghorns give ya the most eggs fer the feed, and you know Pa don't waste a penny. Speakin' a waste, when we gonna eat those Muscovies a yours, or you plannin' to raise a clutch or two? I see the eggs pilin' up in the corner of the cage."

"Uncle Will thinks it would be nice for me to raise some little ones and sell them for spending money."

"Who ya gonna sell 'em to for sweet Jesus' sake?"

"I don't know."

"Any time ya want to eat 'em, let me know. We'll kill the damn things and cook 'em up in the hoghouse kitchen."

"Oh Charley," I said. Just the thought made me sick to my

stomach, not killing the ducks, but cooking them in where Charley cooked all the swill.

"C'mon now, kid, you don't like those useless ducks any better'n I do, so don't 'Oh Charley' me." He gave my shoulder a poke to let me know I should get in the jitney.

"Actually, Charley," I said, when we were bumping over the railroad tracks headed for home, "I don't like Muscovy ducks much better than you like White Leghorn chickens."

Charley let out a hoot and slapped his knee. "That's what I thought. We're both stuck with bastard birds." He let out another hoot and this time slapped my knee. "Here," he reached into his pocket and took out a piece of cut plug, "take a bite outa that. It's good for what ails ya."

"Charley, I don't chew tobacco," I giggled.

He looked at me sort of sober-serious. "There's a hell of a lot you don't do that yer gonna be doin' now that yer gettin' some age on ya, and one thing ya don't wanna miss is chewin' tobacco. Go on, chaw off a chunk. Won't kill ya."

I took the hard brown stuff he was offering me. First I put it up to my nose and smelled. It didn't smell bad, strong and bitter, but not bad.

"You don't inhale it, fer sweet Christ's sake, bite it off and chew it, dummy."

I shrugged. Why not? Once, a long time ago, I found a package of chewing tobacco Uncle Will had hidden in the tack room at the home place and tasted some of that, and while I gagged and spit it out before I really had a chance to chew, it wasn't a horrible experience. Charley's cut plug smelled better to me.

I stuck the bar in my mouth and bit down as hard as I could, but nothing happened.

"Don't gum it, kid. Bite off a piece and chew it like a man."

Charley was losing his patience, I could tell.

With all my strength I snapped my jaw down on the plug and a chunk popped off into my mouth. Suddenly I thought I was going to throw up. Charley took the piece left in my hand and after wiping it off on his pant leg, stuffed it back in his pocket. The longer I held the chunk on my tongue, the sicker I felt. I wondered if brown juices were running out the corners of my mouth the way they did Charley's when he chewed.

"What're ya waitin' for, kid? Chew, God damn it."

I knew if I unclenched my teeth to chew, I'd puke all over everything. The only thing that was keeping my breakfast in my stomach was not opening my mouth so much as a crack. I also knew that if I didn't do something soon, Charley would run the jitney into a tree because he wasn't looking at the road as we chugged along, he was looking at me.

I tried to say, "I'll try," but only made sounds, and then I did try. Expecting an eruption, I opened my mouth far enough to get my teeth separated from the piece of cut plug that my tongue told me was beginning to get slimy. And then, as if my whole future depended upon it, I clamped down again, unclamped and clamped, and on the third clamp my whole mouth collapsed. Not moving my teeth or my lips but swishing my tongue around in what I pictured to be a pool of dark brown juices, I discovered a tooth had fallen out, out of my gum, that is, it was still in my mouth along with the piece of cut plug and all those juices.

That did it. Breakfast gushed out of me, splashing against the inside of the windshield, the dashboard, the seat, Charley, all over everything. Too late I remembered the hole in the floor. Maybe if I'd aimed, I could have sent most of it through that hole.

"Jesus Christ in the woodshed," Charley shouted. "God damn kid. Shit!"

Charley was shaking his hand and arm trying to dislodge what I'd splattered there. The jitney was swerving from side to side on the road. I could hear all those chicks peeping in the back and I don't know why but I began to laugh. More than anything I hated to be covered with guck, whether it was guck from cleaning out the duck pen or guck from vomiting all over myself, yet there I was such a mess that Aunt Maude would make me strip in the road, not even let me on the porch, and she'd want to know what made me throw up and when I told her I'd been chewing tobacco, she'd switch me, but instead of crying or just being disgusted with myself I jounced around on the seat of that out-of-control jitney and laughed as if my mind was gone.

Just when I began to calm down, I noticed something white sliding down the windshield directly in front of me. It was the bloody stump of my tooth caught in all that crap but too heavy to stay stuck, I guess. I watched it with fascination as it descended, but was horrified when it dropped loose from the window and fell straight through the hole in the floor.

"Stop, Charley, stop," I shouted.

"Ya gonna puke again?" Charley yelped as he jammed on the brakes so hard the tires screeched and the jitney turned sideways of the road.

I jumped out and ran back, and there it was, covered with dust, lying in the middle of the road. Bending over, I picked it up, started to wipe the tooth off on my jacket front, then realized that would only make it dirtier. Afraid if I put it in my pocket I'd lose it, I clutched it tight in my fist, opening up only to show the tooth to Charley when I got back in the jitney. When I told him I had to put it under my pillow for the tooth fairy, he said swears I'd never heard before and later had trouble remembering, which is too bad because swears come in handy sometimes.

CHAPTER EIGHTEEN

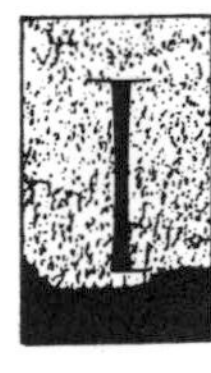

t's finished, David. I've finished my dress." Rose was excited but quiet when she called out to me through her door, as if she was pleased and sorry at the same time. I couldn't remember her making a fuss about finishing a dress before. "I want you to see it full length. Nobody will notice if we open the door a crack for just a minute."

I gasped. Rose never suggested opening her door when we were talking. Sometimes in the summer when we'd sneaked down to the vegetable garden obviously she'd had to open it, but that was part of the game. And she must have opened the door when she went out at night to stand in the moonlight, but the door was never opened just so we could see each other better.

But open it she did. And she showed me her new black bombazine dress with jet embroidery on the collar and cuffs, holding the dress up as far as her arms would reach, moving it about so that light caught and shimmered in its deep rich folds. It was the most beautiful dress I'd ever seen and I said so. Rose was pleased. "Thank you, I think it is the best work I've ever done."

Then I noticed there were no buttons down the front. I'd watched her covering them, button after button, day after day as we talked, enough to go from collar to hem.

"Rose, you forgot the buttons."

"No I didn't." She turned the dress around so I could see the back. That's where the buttons were, down the middle of the back.

"But, Rose, you won't be able to do the buttons when you put on the dress. You told me you changed the pattern to put them down the front after Scheider died because you had nobody to button you up the back. Did you forget?"

She smiled. I hadn't seen a smile on her face in months. "I won't need to reach these buttons. Somebody else will be doing them up for me." I must have appeared confused, which I was, because she said, "I told you, David, this is my laying-out dress."

"Oh," was all I could think to reply.

"And now it's ready. I'm glad you find it as handsome as I do." She was beaming.

"Oh, it is."

She carefully placed the dress on her bed and folded it, putting pieces of tissue paper in the middle, then carried it to her bureau as if it were a birthday cake with lighted candles and laid it in a drawer, covering it with more pieces of tissue paper. "Your Aunt Jessie gave me a lovely sachet for Christmas," she said, "just right, fresh-smelling without being too flowery." She took the sachet from the top of her bureau and placed it in the drawer with the dress. "There," she said, when she closed the drawer, "now we can devote our thoughts to other things. Have the leaves begun to come out yet, David? I think I see a bit of green toward the top of the yard elm, but I can't tell what is happening to the distant elm."

"There aren't real leaves yet, but there are signs. I think those things that drop off trees when the leaves come out will begin falling most any day."

She was at the window. "I wonder if that elm on the horizon is any earlier, being so high, closer to the sun. I wonder if the leaves might be out up there. Maybe I'll walk up and see."

She must have lost her mind. She couldn't walk up to see if the leaves were out. She couldn't walk across the sitting room unless Julia was with her.

"I wonder what else I'll see when I get there, when I look into the abyss."

"You said once you thought your mother and father were there, but I think you were only joking."

She turned to look at me coldly, then returned to the window.

"You also said that elm is at the edge of the earth, that there is nothing beyond but an abyss, but I told you I'd been up there, not at the base of that actual tree I don't mean, but the other side of the tree. Middlebury is over that hill." She had her back to me and wasn't letting on whether or not she was paying any attention to what I had to say. "Actually, there's a lot to see from that ridge. It's the highest spot for miles, Uncle Will says. You'd like the view, Rose. From up there the whole Country Home looks like a toy village, not any bigger than the farm Uncle Will and Roy made for me. From up there the Country Home doesn't look real."

She moved away from the window, stopping to look at herself in the small mirror over her table for a second. Then she snapped out of whatever it was that had hold of her and picked up her hairbrush. Taking the bone hairpins out of her twist as she came toward me, she offered me the brush.

"I heard Mrs. Bullock crying this morning when Johnny left for the summer," she said, as I pulled the brush through her long, thick, gray-black hair.

"Yes, she's very sad. I guess it's because she's so old. She says every time Johnny goes she doesn't think she'll live to see him again."

"None of us knows how long we'll live. She may very well outlive both Johnny and Adeline."

"Why do you say that?"

"No particular reason. Just that she's already survived so much, and she's outlived all her other children—and a number of grandchildren from what I hear. But then, so have I."

"I didn't know you had any children or grandchildren, Rose."

"I don't."

It was like old times, Rose and I talking while I brushed, and her saying things I didn't understand and knew she wouldn't explain if I asked. Occasionally she'd want me to brush harder, and then she'd turn so I could do another side.

"I wonder if Johnny saw any more ghosts while he was here. From what you tell me, he's convinced the Cupeck house is where they all go to roost."

"He didn't say he had. He doesn't believe all ghosts everywhere haunt the Cupeck house, only those from around here. Why do you think any ghosts go to the Cupeck house, Rose?"

"It's as good a place as any, I guess."

"It isn't very interesting, just an old house with not much in it." I wanted to tell her about the snake, but I'd never told anybody. It was as if the snake and I had our own secret club. I think I was almost afraid the snake would get me if I told.

"Ghosts don't need much in the way of furniture."

"Would you go there if you were a ghost?"

Rose shrugged and though she was silent for a while I knew she was going to say something so I waited. "I'm not sure where I'd go if I were going to be a ghost. I think ghosts are supposed to be people who have died unhappy. I'm looking forward to death, to whatever, with some anticipation, so I question whether I'll haunt any place. But, who knows about where or why? I know I wouldn't confine myself to this space again if I could fly anywhere. Why not haunt the Cupeck house?"

She got up from the chair, swooped the brush through her hair a couple of times, then switched it so easily into a knot on her neck that it looked as if the complicated twist was something even I could do.

"David, we had some very tasty pork chops for dinner. I hear Mrs. Davies always has leftovers. Do you suppose you could search around in the pantry and maybe find the platter and filch a couple, one for you and one for me, and bring them back here?"

"What a great idea!" Boy, when Rose got better, she really got better. She hadn't been up to mischief in months. I'd missed doing things she set me to that would get us both in trouble if I was caught. Rose was a darer.

I found the platter of pork chops in no time, and knew where the key to the cupboard was hidden, so that was no problem. I took the two biggest cold chops and ran back to Rose's door. She greeted me with what Aunt Maude would call a naughty grin. We giggled as we ate the chops, their tasty grease covering our chins and fingers. When we were finished I took the bones outside and threw them over the fence into the vegetable garden, hoping they would disappear before the garden was plowed.

"I'm a mess," Rose laughed, actually laughed out loud, when

I came back, as she tried to clean herself with a tiny handkerchief. Rose would never use her sleeve the way I used mine to wipe off the grease.

"What I would like more than anything is a leisurely bath." She said it as if she was talking about what she wanted for her birthday.

"A bath in the middle of the afternoon, Rose?" Taking a bath in the middle of the day was something I'd never heard of. Who would want to?

"I may go across to the bathroom right now, all by myself, and take a bath. I haven't had a bath without someone watching me in so many years I've forgotten what it might be like."

She was sounding like taking a bath that minute would be the very best thing that had ever happened to her.

"Everybody's taking a nap. If you're quick, you might make it without Julia or anybody ever finding out," I said. Suggesting Rose go take a bath by herself was much more daring than sneaking down to the vegetable garden, or to the pantry for cold pork chops.

She stood up straight and stuck her chin in the air. "What can they do if they catch me? Lock me up?"

"Maybe really lock you up, Rose," I said, suddenly worried.

The determined smile that had been on her face vanished in a frown, then that went and she only looked sad. "My dearest David, I am really locked up."

I guess that's when she decided, because she went to her wardrobe and took out a bathrobe, pulled the pins out of her hair, letting it fall down her back again. "Might as well wash my hair while I'm at it."

She came over to the door but didn't open it, reaching through the bars instead to give me a caress on the cheek. "I don't want you blamed for any of this, so you run along now."

I did as I was told. When I got to the arcade steps, I turned around and looked back. She was tiptoeing across the sitting room barefoot, hair hanging loose, bathrobe over her arm. When she turned in my direction, she waved and put her finger to her lips in a sssh signal. I waved in response and nodded with my finger to my lips too. She looked like a little girl as she shrugged her shoulders in a "well here goes" gesture, then disappeared into the bathroom.

Uncle Will, Aunt Maude, and I got up from the supper table that night and went down the road to the home farm. With the light lasting later each day, most evenings were spent there, both of them working outside on the yard or inside the house painting and fixing, scrubbing and papering, constantly improving the place for the time when they'd retire. There was added reason to go early that night, however, because Halla, Uncle Will's prize Thoroughbred mare, was close to foaling, and he was nervous if he was away from her for too many hours at a stretch.

All three of us rushed from the car to the horse barn, but nothing was happening. Halla greeted us with gentle nickers. Uncle Will felt her udder and lifted her tail for an inspection back there. He said he didn't think anything was going to happen that night.

"What's going to happen is rain," Aunt Maude said, "so if we want to get any raking accomplished we'd best be about it."

They were better rakers than I was because I wasn't tall enough to manage the long rake handles. Uncle Will suggested I'd be the biggest help if I'd load the piles of leaves and sticks they raked up into the wheelbarrow, then roll it over to the compost heap and dump it. Not only did I not mind doing that, it was fun. The compost heap was behind the empty henhouse, and behind the compost heap was a fence at the foot of the lane. Primus and Queet watched me through the fence, standing there with their heads down, but Buster and Lindy and Wanda put their heads over the fence, curious about what I was doing. This meant that I took time after each dumping to walk over to the fence and rub a nose or two. Naturally Buster laid back his ears and tried to nip me. He always did that. Aunt Maude said it was because Uncle Will spoiled him by sneaking sugar cubes to him.

"David, don't lallygag or we won't finish before it begins to rain," Aunt Maude complained for about the third time.

I looked up. Purple and gray clouds were in a rolling boil around the sky and off to the west it was black already. It wasn't going to rain, it was going to pour. The next time I got to the compost heap I told the horses I had to hurry so couldn't do any patting. They obviously didn't understand and stood waiting for me, but then there was a terrible clap of thunder that scared the life out of me, followed by lightning which startled the horses so they wheeled around and tore up the lane, manes and tails flying out behind them.

"David, are you all right?" Aunt Maude shrieked as she came around the chicken house looking for me.

We quickly put the tools away and rushed into the house just as the clouds opened and rain poured down. Aunt Maude thought we should be ready to run for the car and get back to the County Home as soon as it let up at all, but Uncle Will said he wanted to stick around for a while longer to make sure Halla didn't panic. He lighted an applewood fire in the fireplace which gave the little back sitting room a pungent smell. We didn't turn on any lamps because of the wild lightning, sitting instead in the flickering light of the flames. Aunt Maude said something about being cozy and warm inside when it was so terrible outside.

"Have we got any marshmallows?" Uncle Will asked.

"In the cupboard next to the stove," Aunt Maude replied.

"I could do with a toasted marshmallow," he said. "Why don't you go get them, David, and I'll bring a bottle of grape juice up from the cellar."

"Bring up a few apples too," Aunt Maude said.

We toasted marshmallows and drank grape juice and ate apples that Uncle Will peeled and sliced for us using his pocket penknife and listened to the storm thrashing and crashing around outside. The wind came up, driving heavy rain against the windows until you'd think they might break. Gusts sent occasional spurts of water down the chimney where it spat and steamed on the coals. Aunt Maude was worried a spark would fly out and land in my eye, so she kept telling me to move back from where I was lying on my stomach staring into the fire. As soon as she started talking about something else, I'd crawl up close again. I wished I'd brought *David the Incorrigible* with me.

About ten o'clock, when the fire was dying down, Aunt Maude said we had to get back whether we wanted to or not because I had school the next day. While she and I cleaned up our mess and banked the ashes, Uncle Will went out for a final check on Halla.

Even though the wind had let up, the rain was still pounding down nonstop. The Ford's windshield wipers went as fast as they could but sheets of water covered the glass. If the Center Road wasn't straight as a string Uncle Will couldn't have driven us back in that storm because nobody could see where we were going.

"Thank goodness the thunder and lightning stopped," Aunt

Maude said, sitting sideways in the front seat so she'd be ready to grab at the wheel if she thought Uncle Will was taking us into the ditch. The way she screamed all the time about the ditch, you'd think going into the ditch was worse than having your throat cut. I'd seen cars in the ditch and nobody was killed.

The County Home was lighted up like Christmas when we drove around the Keeper's building and into the yard, and lots of cars were parked where cars never parked.

"What in the world is going on?" Aunt Maude cried. "Something must have happened."

"Calm down, Maudie," Uncle Will said. "We'll find out soon enough."

The Keeper's kitchen was full of people. Pa and Ma Fleming were there, and Uncle Deane and Julia, Aureta, Eunice, most of the farm workers. "What is it, what has happened?" Aunt Maude was on the verge of tears already, and she didn't know yet what was wrong.

"Rose has disappeared," Pa Fleming said.

"She's taking a bath," I wanted to say, but she wouldn't still be in the bathtub, that was hours ago, and if she was still in the tub somebody would see her there because people went in and out of that bathroom all the time.

"What do you mean, disappeared?" Aunt Maude asked.

"Disappeared, gone." Uncle Deane sounded as if he thought Aunt Maude was dumb to ask what disappeared meant.

"Where would she go? She never leaves her room, or almost never. Have you searched the women's building?" Aunt Maude had just arrived but she was taking charge.

"We've searched everywhere, Maude," Pa Fleming said. "We're here now for a cup of coffee and to decide what to do next."

"Well, then, I'll make us some coffee right away. There are fresh sugar cookies in the crock." Aunt Maude made a move toward the stove.

"I made coffee," Aureta interrupted her.

"You made the coffee?" Aunt Maude asked. "Aureta, your coffee is terrible."

"Even so, I made it." Aureta was defiant in the face of Aunt Maude's disbelief, but only I suspect because she was surrounded by people who would defend her if necessary.

"Sit down, Maude, while we bring you up to date." Pa Fleming's voice forced her into a chair.

When Julia took in Rose's supper tray, Rose was in her bathrobe brushing her hair. Julia thought that was strange because Rose was fussy about being properly dressed, and since her lapse at Christmas time was never anything but "totally together," as Julia put it. When Julia asked Rose if she was feeling ill, Rose said she'd never felt better, and Julia said she acted cheerful as a chipmunk. "I could swear I heard her humming as I left the room after putting her tray down," Julia said.

"And then?" Aunt Maude asked impatiently.

"That's the last anybody saw of her," Julia replied, wiping her red-rimmed eyes with a damp hankie.

When Julia went back for the tray, Rose's door was wide open. Julia's first reaction was anger, then shock because Rose didn't disobey rules, except on infrequent occasions, and she had for years honored the unlocked–locked door arrangement. Pa Fleming told us Julia checked out the bathroom, but Rose wasn't there, nor was she in the women's sitting room. Women clearing supper things in the dining room said they hadn't seen her.

"I was silly enough to think she might be in the vegetable

garden which is what lures her occasionally during the summer, but of course the garden isn't plowed yet. Even so, I ran out and scanned the vegetable garden and went the full length of the grape arbor and back," Julia sniffled.

"Had she eaten her supper?" Aunt Maude asked.

"Every crumb," Mrs. Davis said quietly from the corner where she was standing.

When Julia sounded the alarm, Uncle Deane was the first to search because he's the one who brought her back from the vegetable garden most times. Then others got involved and pretty soon inmates as well as staff were looking in closets and under beds. They concentrated on the women's building first, but then spread out into the men's building and the infirmary and the Keeper's building.

"Did you search the attics?" Aunt Maude wanted to know.

"Of course," somebody said.

"All the attics?"

"All the attics we know about."

"Well," she vowed, standing up, "I'm going to search them again. There are more attics in this place than most of you know exist."

"Maude, we have searched all the attics and the cellars." Pa Fleming made her sit down again. "We have searched all the buildings, including the barns and other outbuildings. She isn't any place we've looked."

"She's at the tree," I said. My voice squeaked because my throat was seared from tears of terror I was swallowing.

"What's that, David?" Pa Fleming asked.

"She's at the tree," I repeated.

"David, you have got to get to bed. You have school tomorrow. Now upstairs with you, quick. I'll come tuck you in shortly," Aunt Maude had forgotten about me until I spoke, but then she remembered and gave me my orders without getting out of her chair.

"We'll let you know the minute we find her," Pa Fleming assured me, putting his hand on my shoulder. "I know how close you and Rose are, but don't you worry, everything is going to be all right."

"She's at the tree," I said again, with greater force this time. "Please, have you looked there?"

"What tree, David?" Pa Fleming was being noticeably patient with me.

"The tree at the edge of the earth. The tree on the ridge. That big elm that blows in the wind. You can see it when you look up south." I was close to shouting.

"He means the tree behind Ott Alwardt's barn," somebody said.

"That's the tree!" They were listening to me. "Have you looked there?"

"Why would Rose go there? She'd have no way to get up there. It's much too far to walk." Pa Fleming was listening but he hadn't heard.

"Especially barefoot and in this weather," Julia added.

"You mean she went without any clothes?" Uncle Will wanted to know, the first time he'd been heard from.

"As far as we know, she is wearing nothing but a nightgown and bathrobe." Julia was the expert witness again.

"God bless her," Uncle Will said. "If she's outside, she'll never make it in this cold rain."

"Please go to the tree," I said, but they'd stopped listening to me. Most of them were sipping coffee and staring at the floor.

"Let me take you upstairs," Ma Fleming said, coming to put her arm around my shoulders. "By the time you wake up in the morning, Rose will be back safe in her room."

"Please," I begged, but they thought I was begging not to go to bed.

All the while Ma Fleming was helping me out of my clothes and into my pajamas I was thinking how I could get over to Roy's sitting room. If I got to Roy, I knew he'd believe me and together we could go find Rose. All we had to do was walk up to the tree. I knew Rose would be somewhere between the County Home and the tree if she hadn't made it all the way.

But how to get to Roy? I couldn't sneak out my window and go across the porch roof. The tin would be slippery. I'd fall off onto the sidewalk and break my neck if I didn't get killed. Besides, there was a storm window over my regular window and no way to get through that. Nor could I sneak down the stairs and through the back hall because somebody would see me from the kitchen. Instead of Ma Fleming letting me go brush my teeth and tuck myself in, she said she'd wait and make sure I was snug before she went back downstairs, which meant we went through the whole bit of being tucked in tight and kissed goodnight and assured that everything was going to be fine by morning and Aunt Maude would be up shortly and on and on and on.

At the click of the latch on the door at the top of the stairs, I struggled out from under the damn tucked-in covers and ran to the hall. Through the window in the stair door I could see Ma Fleming almost at the bottom. I ran down the hall and into the bathroom, pushing with all my might to get the bathroom window open. It hadn't been opened since fall and was so tight I could barely budge it, but then it did give enough so I could push it up, but damn, damn, damn, there was the storm window. I opened the little slat that covered three holes bored for ventilation and put my mouth to them, knowing it wouldn't do any good.

"Roy," I yelled as loud as I could. "Roy. Roy."

I could see Roy sitting there listening to records with his earphones on. I knew he couldn't hear me, but he could see me if he would only look up and out the window in my direction. The bathroom window and Roy's sitting-room window were at right angles to each other, not much farther apart than I was tall. I'd be willing to risk crawling across the tin roof that far if I could only get out the window. I turned the light on and off in the bathroom and jumped up and down, waved a towel, clapped my hands, cupped my fists to my mouth and shouted, "Roy, Roy." He didn't look up.

When I heard people going out onto the porch below and slamming the kitchen door, I decided I'd better hurry back to bed, which I did. But then nobody came up the stairs so I got up again and went into Aunt Maude's room and looked out the south window, staring to see if I could see anything in the dark. I couldn't even see the outline of the tree. All I could see was rain beating against the glass.

I must have fallen asleep there by the window because next morning I half remembered Uncle Will picking me up and putting me back in bed. It was the cardinal whistling that woke me, that and the sun shining so bright it looked brand new.

"Your Uncle Deane found Rose," Aunt Maude told me, without scolding me for running downstairs in my bathrobe before brushing my teeth or combing my hair. She said he found her just after daylight lying in the cow pasture on the south slope. She was unconscious when he found her and she was still unconscious.

"She was going to the tree," I said.

"David," Aunt Maude sank down in a chair and pulled me to her. "I'm afraid we're going to lose Rose. You have to be prepared. She's very sick."

"Does she have new monia?"

"Dr. Davis is on the way and he'll tell us, but she's had a terrible experience, poor thing."

"People always die of new monia, don't they?"

"If they are as sick as poor Rose they do." Aunt Maude dabbed at tears running down my cheeks.

"Not always," Aureta said from the stove where she was stirring fried potatoes.

"Sometimes they surprise us and live for years after a bout of pneumonia," Eunice added as she loaded up the cold cereal tray with boxes of Shredded Wheat, Corn Flakes, and Grape-Nuts.

"Go have your bath and get dressed. If you hurry, you'll be ready to eat with the men." Aunt Maude got up and went back to getting breakfast.

As I sat in the tub, I wondered did Rose enjoy her bath without being watched? I was sure she'd washed her hair because Julia said she was brushing it when Julia took in her supper tray, and I'd already brushed it more than a hundred strokes that day. Apparently nobody had seen her in the bathroom because nobody mentioned it. I thought that was nice. She'd gotten away with it. Well, there were times when we'd gotten away with going down to the vegetable garden too, though most times somebody saw us and just as we'd be cutting into a cucumber or salting a tomato from the salt shaker Rose brought out of her pocket Uncle Deane would walk up to us and say, "Rose, you know you're not supposed to be out here." Sometimes I think he waited until we'd had our fill of whatever it was we'd gone down there to eat before taking her back.

I gulped down as much breakfast as I could and then, grabbing my books, kissed Aunt Maude and ran off as if I was on my way to school. Instead, I turned down the East Road when I got to the corner and hurried in the back driveway. As quietly as possible I went up the sun-room steps and then into the hall of the women's building. I couldn't see anyone from the doorway, so put down my books on a windowsill and tiptoed, which wasn't easy in those damn boots Aunt Maude made me wear even though it was spring, along the stairwell to Rose's room.

Her door was open. Pressing myself as flat as I could against the wall, I kept moving until I could look in. Julia was beside Rose's bed, washing her face very carefully with a steaming cloth. I could see the covers rising and falling so I knew Rose was breathing, but I couldn't see her face. I wished Julia would leave the room so I could sneak in. My wish was granted but it almost meant being discovered because while I was trying to figure out what to do, Julia put the cloth back in the wash basin and was coming straight for me. She must have had her mind on something else however because she didn't see me as I quickly backed around the stairs and waited while she went into the bathroom, then came out and went through the arcade.

I couldn't believe the Rose lying there in bed was the same Rose I'd watched tiptoeing into the bathroom. Her face was an awful color, yellowish-purple, and her lips were blue. Julia or somebody had combed the hair on top of her head and down about to her ears, but the rest of it was a snarled mass on the pillow. Her eyes were closed. For a minute I wondered if there were any eyeballs left because the sockets were sunk so deep.

From the hall I hadn't been able to hear her, but up close she sounded like a file rasping in and out as it scraped away.

"Rose, can you hear me?" I whispered. I guess she couldn't because nothing happened. "Did you try to get to the tree?" I tried again. I took hold of her hand. "Rose, if you can hear me, squeeze my hand." I'd seen Uncle Will do that to an old patient who had had a stroke. Rose didn't squeeze.

"Please, Rose," I began, not knowing what I was going to say next, when Julia came back.

Naturally the first words out of her mouth were, "David, what are you doing? You know you shouldn't be in here."

"I'm never supposed to be anywhere," I screamed. "Where do you all think I should be most of the time? Maybe you think I should be dead, too. If I was dead I wouldn't be in anybody's way." I was starting to cry and I didn't want to cry. At least I didn't want Julia seeing me cry.

She stood there looking as if I'd hit her. Before she could decide what to do about me, I took another look at Rose, then ran out of the room giving Julia a shove as I pushed past her. Shaking with sobs and having no idea what to do next, I stumbled down the hall and out of the building toward the vegetable garden and into the grape arbor. The brilliant sun shone through naked branches but there was nobody sitting on the long benches. There wasn't even an old man taking a stroll. If the arbor had been a room and I had cried out, it would have echoed.

I ran faster, as fast as I could to the very end, crashing against the orchard fence. Heifers seeking early spring shoots among the dried brown winter grasses were startled by what must have seemed an attack against them. With tails in the air they ran to the farthest corner of the orchard before turning around to stare back at me. I clung to the fence as if my life depended on it, because I knew I'd fall to the ground if I let go.

What would I do without Rose? There wasn't a time in my whole life when she wasn't there in her room so I could talk to her. I could tell her anything, everything—I hadn't told her about the snake. Oh God, why hadn't I told her? I didn't want any secrets from Rose. Rose knew more about me than anybody except God maybe, and I couldn't talk to God the way I talked to Rose. I'd tried but there wasn't much response. God couldn't take Rose's place.

"Damn it, Rose, you can't die!" I cried. "You were stupid to go walking around in the rain without any clothes on." I sank to the ground cursing her, wanting her, needing her, hating her for being about to die and wishing I could die too. Through the sounds of my own blubbering I could hear somebody calling my name, but I didn't want to see anybody. I didn't want to see anybody ever again.

CHAPTER NINETEEN

Rose did have pneumonia, but worse, Dr. Davis said, she had the will to die, whatever that meant. He gave her lots of medicine and everybody tried. Julia spent most of her time, nights as well as days, at Rose's bedside, talking to her in a soothing voice, wiping her face with damp flower-scented warm cloths, brushing her hair very gently, rubbing her back. Mrs. Davies and Aunt Maude both made special beef and chicken broths to give her strength. When I told them about Rose wishing she had some veal parma john, Mrs. Davies went to see Mrs. Frescobaldi who lived just north of the Center and learned how to make it. Then she came back and together she and Aunt Maude fixed a wonderful-smelling dish that made Rose smile a little, but she didn't eat more than a couple of forks full.

I reminded Roy that Rose had said she loved to listen to his music in the summer when both their windows were open, so, after getting permission from Pa Fleming and Julia, he and I lugged his phonograph and some records from his room down to the women's sitting room where we set it up just outside Rose's door. Roy gave her a choice of several operas. She nodded when he mentioned *La Traviata* and that's what we played. I cranked and Roy put on and changed the records.

Pa had told us to keep the volume low so as not to bother the others, and we did, but a lot of the others liked the music they heard, coming out of their rooms to sit and listen. Mary Delancy held up her ear trumpet for a minute, then said in a loud voice, "I don't think you know this song, Theresa." Theresa said she didn't and somebody else said, "Sssh." Every rocking chair in the sitting room was in motion as they came under the spell of Verdi.

The music could be heard upstairs too and that was fine with everyone except old bitch Ripley, of course. She kept shouting, "Stop that godawful caterwauling." To her, all music was caterwauling. And, "I'm going to call the sheriff if that racket continues one more minute." Julia told Aunt Maude later that Aunt Latzy finally shut Ripley up by threatening to get out of bed and go over there and gag her, which was pretty funny when you remember Latzy hadn't been out of bed in at least twenty years. Julia also told us Mrs. Bullock kept wishing she could go downstairs so she could hear the music better.

I'm sure Rose liked the music, though she didn't say anything one way or the other. When Roy went in to tell her we had to stop now because he had chores to do, she smiled at him.

Julia said that was about all Rose could do because her fever was so high, and I believed her when she said Rose would break the thermometer if her temperature went up any more. Adeline sulked because she had suggested tying a bag of dried weeds she put together around Rose's neck as a way to break the fever, but nobody paid any attention. Mary was sure a mustard plaster would do it. There was hardly a person who didn't have an idea of how to make Rose better, and each one told Julia his or her cure. Blind Theresa insisted we must all pray a lot and Pa Fleming said that was the best thing to do, especially because it wasn't just the pneumonia but Rose's death wish that had to be overcome.

What made her pneumonia so maddening was after that one night of terrible cold rain when she was out in it, the weather turned warm and the nights as well as the days were balmy. Chances are if Rose had gone walking any other night she wouldn't have gotten sick. I was convinced that if we could keep her alive until spring turned into summer, she'd be all right.

A week less a day following her getting soaked, I was whispering that summer thought to her after supper just before I had to go upstairs and get ready for bed. Nobody else was anywhere around and I hoped I might have a few minutes alone with her to cheer her up. If I did maybe she'd speak again because she wasn't doing any talking at all. I was telling her a few lies but if everything went well maybe they wouldn't be lies. I was telling her I thought Pa Fleming would let her leave her room for walks any time she wanted, when she got well, and that we could stroll in the grape arbor together, and wouldn't have to sneak down for fresh vegetables, and now that Mrs. Davies and Aunt Maude knew how to make veal parma john we could take a picnic basket filled with it to the pine forest. I told her Adeline and I would show her how to do a fertility dance. She opened her eyes and looked at me when I said that, so I nodded vigorously, assuring her a fertility dance was fun to do.

Fortunately I was quiet for a few minutes to give her a rest, or I wouldn't have heard his shuffling step before he got to the door. I don't know what old Scarzi would have done if he'd seen me. He held his black leather hat in his hand, and something else that looked like a couple of sticks, but I couldn't figure them out before I ducked down behind Rose's bed. After a pause when Scarzi must have stood there looking around, it sounded as if he was coming into the room. I slid under the bed and held my breath. His feet came closer and closer, until they were partially under the bed almost up against my face. I could smell his shoes.

Then I heard a guttural voice muttering in Italian. He was talking very low, very gentle, saying words I couldn't understand, but Rose must have known what he was saying because for the first time since she'd been sick, I heard her say something. She was talking Italian too. Her voice was weak but she was speaking. That excited me so much I wanted to shout, but I had sense enough not to. I didn't want Scarzi to discover me.

I don't know how I knew but slowly it came to me that Scarzi was praying and in her small strained voice Rose was praying too. It was then, as I lay there listening to them, that I suddenly realized she wasn't better, she was going. Maybe she'd waited for Scarzi to come and pray with her before she let go, or before she did whatever was necessary to die. My breath stopped. I was strangling as I listened to their soft voices saying words I'd never heard. It was actually happening, and I was aware of it, as sure she was dying as I had been only minutes before that I could cheer her up and keep her alive until summer. Summer? Rose would not be here tomorrow. She would be gone, gone forever.

The soft words stopped. I felt the need to gasp for air but didn't dare. Then there was a sound as if Scarzi might have kissed her on the forehead. His sour-smelling old shoes turned and I watched from my hiding place as he shuffled out of the room, halting briefly at the door to say one more word in Italian before he left.

As soon as I was sure he had gone, I crawled out from under the bed and stood up. Rose didn't look the way she had for days. The scowl was gone from her face and her color was more natural, not that awful yellow-purple it had been. She seemed relaxed. I stared at her, stared at her hard, so hard my eyes hurt, trying to fix her in my mind because if she was gone tomorrow—and I knew she would be—I was afraid I wouldn't be able to remember her.

As closely as I was concentrating on her I didn't notice when her eyes opened, and was startled to see she was looking up at me.

"Are you dying, Rose, really dying?" I whispered.

She nodded yes, and her mouth slipped into an ever so slight smile.

"Have you seen Scheider yet?"

She slowly shook her head no.

"If you don't have to die, Rose, I wish you wouldn't."

She moved her left hand across the blanket cover. The motion made me glance down and I saw that the sticks Scarzi carried into the room was a cross he must have made and placed on Rose's chest. Her hand touched mine, patting me. I tried to smile as I looked into her eyes. They crinkled the tiniest bit as she closed them. Then, with a gentle sigh, she died. The room went from being filled by her to echoing empty. Where had she gone?

"Rose, wait, I forgot to tell you about the snake," I whispered. "It was in the Cupeck house, Rose, a big black snake that almost put its nose against mine." But Rose wasn't there.

I stood with her hand resting on mine, gulping air to keep from drowning.

I lay awake for hours in bed, listening to night sounds, pretending each time Aunt Maude came in to check me that I was asleep, but I must have really gone to sleep eventually because Uncle Will shook me in the morning to say I didn't have to go to school if I didn't want to. I didn't want to.

But I did get up for early staff breakfast. There was little conversation. Though nobody at the Keeper's table was as close to Rose as I had been, except maybe for Julia and she was close to Rose in a different way, they were sad that she died. "You had to respect the old girl," Uncle Deane said. "She had grit." He laughed and blinked his eyes.

Aunt Maude fussed because I didn't eat much. "You have to eat or you'll get sick," she said.

"Maudie, leave him alone. It won't hurt him if he misses a meal or two." Uncle Will never told Aunt Maude what to do, but this time he did, in a nice way. She sniffed a couple of times but left me alone after that.

Chet Foster made Rose's coffin first thing the morning after she died, using what he called prime-grade white pine he kept stored on the second floor of the carpenter shop for just such purposes. Those who died at the County Home and didn't have a family to take them away were buried on the place in coffins Chet Foster made especially for them.

I didn't go into the carpenter shop on a regular basis because both Chet and old Brumstead who hung around in there were grouchy, always asking, "What do you want?" if I so much as stuck my head inside, but the morning Chet was working on Rose's coffin he was close to being friendly.

"There isn't a knot in one of them boards," Chet said, showing me the box he'd about finished, "and each one is straight and true." He had dovetailed the corners for a perfect watertight fit, and rubbed the outside until it was smooth to the touch. If you closed your eyes when you were near the box you'd think you were in the pine forest, that's the way it smelled.

The coffin didn't look very big sitting on the sawhorses when Chet tried the cover that was shaped exactly like the box. I was afraid the coffin would be too small for Rose.

The next time I saw it was in Rose's room. Rose was in it, and the whole room smelled of fresh clean pine. Aunt Maude and Aunt Jessie had helped Julia lay her out. After they bathed and powdered her and dressed her in her best underwear, they put on her brand-new black bombazine laying-out dress with the buttons down the back. Rose was right, somebody else had buttoned them. The jet-embroidered collar and cuffs glittered in the sunlight streaming through the open window. I don't think anybody knew where the crude cross came from, but they had put Scarzi's gift to her in Rose's hands which lay folded on her chest.

Aunt Jessie was putting the finishing touches to Rose's hair. "I didn't know exactly how to do it so it looked natural," she explained. "I tried several ways before deciding to do a twist at the nape of her neck the way she always wore it. I'm afraid I didn't do as good a job as she did, but I tried."

"Nobody will see the twist, and you've got the middle part right," I said. "Why is her hair so black? Her hair was gray."

"That happens sometimes when people die, their hair goes back to its original color. Lizzy Acheson says she hopes hers reverts to glorious red." Aunt Jessie laughed a little laugh, looking at me sideways because I was standing back from the coffin. "Rose looks younger, don't you think, like she must have looked as a bride."

"She looks as if she's going someplace special."

"She is, David. She's going to Heaven."

"Are you sure?"

Aunt Jessie stopped fussing with Rose's hair to look back at me anxiously. She knew I wasn't being smart-aleck. "Of course I'm sure. If you're worried about what she did all those years ago, David, only God knows why she did it, and I haven't a doubt but that He's long since forgiven her." She resumed smoothing Rose's hair. "No, our beautiful Rose is at peace now in the loving arms of Jesus."

If what Rose had told me about Scheider was true, and I knew it was because Rose said it, then I knew why Rose had killed him, and I wasn't nearly as certain as Aunt Jessie where Rose might be headed or where she might be at that very moment. I had no idea how long the trip to Heaven or Hell took, nor how Jesus would feel about her if she did arrive at Heaven's gate. He might not want her in his arms after what she'd done to Scheider, especially when she made me think she was never really sorry. And if Jesus didn't want her in Heaven and she had to go to Hell, what would Scheider do if he was waiting for her down there? I wished somebody could explain it to me.

Rose's funeral was set for the following morning, with a service to be held in the little cemetery on the hill below the water tower. If Rose had any relatives nobody knew who they were, so nobody would be coming to take her away. I was glad of that. She'd be resting on that County Home hillside for all eternity. Not that it mattered much where a body was buried, she'd told me lots of times. Once she said she didn't care if they threw her out on the manure pile in back of the barn.

All the day before the funeral, after she was laid out and ready to be seen, anybody who wanted to could go in and look at her. The door was wide open, no need to pretend anymore that it was locked, and a line of people shuffled through the first few hours, most of them only curious because they'd never seen her close enough to really look at before. I stood over in the corner by the window and watched and listened. "Why, she's quite beautiful, isn't she?" several said, surprised I suppose that she didn't have two heads or horns or something.

Aunt Maude told me it was morbid of me to stand there hour after hour. She kept coming to tell me to get out in the air, to go play. I doubted I'd ever play again. Uncle Will rescued me once again, assuring Aunt Maude it was all right for me to do just what I was doing. The only harm I did was twist the ends off a couple of fronds of the potted palms Ray had brought to Rose's room from Ma Fleming's parlor. I didn't realize I was twisting them until it was too late, but they'd grow back.

When people stopped coming to gawp I moved closer to the coffin and stared down as most of them had done, except I was trying to remember how her voice sounded, trying to remember words she used when she said things to me. I began to worry about Rose's hair in a twist. Aunt Jessie said she wasn't able to do it as nicely as Rose did, not that I could do anything to make it better. You couldn't tell from the front whether it was the way Rose liked it or not, but I was sure Rose must know. I took her brush from the bureau and touched it lightly to each side of the part, smoothing out strands that had no chance to go astray. When Rose didn't sit up and turn around so I could do a good job of brushing the back, I accepted it as one more proof she was truly dead.

Looking down at her, still hoping there'd been a terrible mistake and she might yet open her eyes, was what I was doing when Uncle Deane arrived to put on the coffin lid. He had a handful of screws and a large screwdriver.

"We've got to make this box tight," he said, glancing toward the cover leaning against the wall in the corner. "They'll be here in a minute to carry her out."

"I nodded dumbly. I knew they had to put the cover on, but it would be so pitch dark in there she couldn't see a thing and there wouldn't be any air for her to breathe. On the other hand, if the cover wasn't screwed down as tight as could be dirt would get in when they put the coffin in the hole, and the dirt would soil her new black bombazine dress with the jet collar and cuffs and self-covered buttons down the back.

"Would you help me with it, David?" Uncle Deane asked. "It's about the last thing you can do for her." He could easily put the coffin cover on himself, he didn't need to ask my help, he was being nice. He picked up the cover and stood holding it.

I took one end and helped him lift it over to the coffin, once more inhaling the sweet clean smell of pine. I meant to take a final look at her before I let it down, but I forgot, and also I couldn't see so well. Tears shot from my eyes unexpectedly. Uncle Deane pretended he didn't notice, glancing toward the door as if he thought somebody might be watching us. There wasn't anyone.

"Hold on," he whispered. He reached up onto the top of Rose's wardrobe. "Sssh." He lifted the cut-velvet bag and took Rose's knife from its hiding place, then with another quick glance toward the door, raised the coffin cover and placed the knife in beside Rose, adjusting the folds of her black dress to hide it. "In case she needs it sometime in the future," he said.

"Uncle Deane, wait. Please wait. Don't screw that cover down yet. I've got to get her watch. She may need her watch."

Without stopping to see if he would wait, I ran as fast as I could back through the buildings and up our stairs where I grabbed Rose's watch out of my bureau drawer and leaving the drawer hanging open ran back. He had waited for me. I wound the watch, then set it to the same time Uncle Deane's watch said. He helped me secure the clasp on the back of the gold, rose-shaped brooch, placing it and the watch hanging from it on the front of her dress where she always wore it. This gave me a chance to look at her face once more.

Because there was only one screwdriver we took turns putting the screws in. I couldn't get them as tight as Uncle Deane said was necessary, so he gave each of those I put in an extra turn or two. "Don't want to make it too easy for the worms," he grunted.

When we finished, Uncle Will came in with two of the farm men and they and Uncle Deane lifted the closed coffin and carried it out of the barred room. The women's sitting room was filled with inmates who could not walk up to the cemetery. Some were sitting, others standing, but all were watching us. Mary Delancy croaked, "Good luck, Rose. I'll be following along up the hill soon." Nobody else peeped, though several women waved handkerchiefs as we went down the hall.

Outside, Daisy, the dappled-gray Percheron, was hitched to a flatbed wagon that had been lined with cedar boughs. She had a black tassel on each side of her bridle and a black saddle blanket. Most of the County Home staff were waiting too, and quite a few inmates. Adeline was there in a heavy black coat with a ratty-looking brown fur collar. I hadn't seen the coat before and wondered if she was naked underneath. Charley Smith must have taken a bath and shaved for the funeral because he smelled different and his hair was slicked down tight to his head. He had on parts of three suits—the pants were black, the coat blue, and the vest green. He made a face at me as I came down the steps and I could see the cud of tobacco in his cheek. I hoped he wouldn't spit.

"Are you all right, sweetheart?" Aunt Maude asked, coming over to cuddle me. I squirmed and she stopped when she noticed Uncle Will watching her.

Uncle Deane went around to Daisy's head and rubbing her nose said, "Okay, old girl, nice and steady now." Uncle Will took the other side of Daisy's bridle to help Uncle Deane lead her and we started off, Aunt Maude and Aunt Jessie on either side of me, each holding a hand. We and Julia were in the front row behind the wagon. Behind us everybody else fell into straggly lines.

All the way to the cemetery, through the passage between the women's building and the bakery, past the porch and the pump, around the Keeper's building and across the road and up the hill, following the wagon and the jiggling coffin, I kept swallowing as hard as I could and blinking fast. Aunt Maude was mopping her eyes with the hand that didn't have a firm grip on me. Aunt Jessie was more calm, but didn't let go of me either. I couldn't have wiped my eyes or blown my nose if I needed to.

Pa and Ma Fleming stood by the open grave when we got there. They had driven up in their Buick and brought Blind Theresa and her little field organ. Ma had a wreath made of pine boughs and some of those same berries we'd put in Rose's dish garden. When the wagon came abreast of her and halted, Ma Fleming stepped forward and put the wreath on the coffin.

"Are we going to sing 'Rock of Ages'?" she asked in her hollow deaf voice.

"Of course," Pa replied. Theresa began pumping the little organ and Pa Fleming in a deep, wavery voice started singing, "Rock of ages, cleft for me . . ." It was a hymn most everybody knew so they all joined in. I tried to sing, but it didn't work. My voice was all wispy. I didn't even try when they sang "Amazing Grace."

I was able to say the Twenty-Third Psalm when they got to that, but most of the things people said I didn't hear. Several spoke besides Pa, who read from the Bible as well as saying nice things about Rose, "our dear departed friend."

Then Uncle Deane and Uncle Will and two other men lifted the coffin from the wagon and carried it to the grave on a pair of reins. When they got to the hole the coffin was suspended for a minute, swaying heavily while Pa said something about ashes and dust. After everybody said "Amen," the coffin was slowly lowered into the hole and the reins pulled out.

As the box was going down out of sight something was happening to me, something terrible. I felt as if I was being wrapped in a smothering blanket tighter than I'd ever been tucked in bed. My circulation was cut off. I was beginning to feel numb, the way you feel when your leg goes to sleep. I thought I was going to fall over. From far away I heard Pa Fleming speaking to me. Aunt Maude tapped me on the shoulder.

"Perhaps David would like to throw the first handful of earth." Pa was smiling in my direction. I could tell that he was smiling as I looked up at him even though the sun was directly behind him so his head glowed.

This wasn't my first funeral. I knew about throwing dirt on the coffin. I knew what to do, but I stood there for an eternity dumb and scared. After handfuls of dirt were thrown on Rose's coffin we'd leave and the men would shovel dirt in, filling the grave, rounding it up to take care of sinkage, and that would be that. Rose would be under all that dirt, in the ground six feet down. She was already six feet down but if I stepped forward I could see the box. I could if I tried picture her in her black dress with her watch pinned on the front. And I could see where Uncle Deane had hidden her knife. After the coffin was covered I wouldn't be able to see anything but a mound of dirt, dirt that Rose had never touched. At least her body had touched the coffin, and if I touched the coffin I'd be touching something she was touching. The worst thing I could do was start the process of really burying her, of hiding the coffin so I could never see it again. Not only was that a terrible thought for me, it was finishing Rose. There would be no turning back once it was begun.

I wanted to run, run as fast as I could down the hill and away from all that was going on. I decided to do it, to run rather than agree to what was expected of me, but as I began to turn Aunt Maude's hands gripped my shoulders, propelling me forward toward the pile of dirt and the open grave. Firmly but gently, as if I were a stuffed puppet, she doubled me over so that my rigid arms and hands thrust into the cold damp earth.

The feel of that icy clay made me want to scream, but then I became calm as if Rose was sending me a message through the earth we would use to fill her grave. In a flash everything was clear and I was all right. I stood up to pry Aunt Maude's fingers from my shoulders, then bent double again and gathered fists full of the dirt that no longer felt as cold and frightening. I walked around to the head of the grave, where Pa had stood with the sun shining around his head, and though looking down into it made me dizzy, I forced myself to do it as everybody watched me lean over the open pit as far as I could and say in a loud whisper, "Rose, the Cupeck house. I'll see you at the Cupeck house."

"Will, he's going to fall in," Aunt Maude shrieked.

"No, I'm not," I said, straightening up to my fullest height. I lifted my arms as high as they could reach and brought them down together, saying, "Ashes to ashes and dust to dust," as I threw the first two handfuls of earth onto Rose's coffin.

The thudding sounds they made were followed by a series of thuds as others stepped forward to perform their duty. When everybody had a turn, Pa pronounced the benediction and we turned and marched down the hill behind Daisy and the empty rattling wagon, the Flemings' Buick bringing up the rear of the procession. I didn't bother to look back because I knew Rose wasn't there.

Nor did I feel sad any longer. On the way up I'd struggled to keep from crying. On the way down I had all I could do to keep from singing. I did swing my arms until Aunt Maude caught the one on her side and gave it a yank, hissing that she didn't know what had come over me. The sky was brilliant blue and the sun now directly overhead, almost hot as it shone down on us. I could see swallows darting under the eaves of the barn. It must be noon. My stomach rumbled. I was hungry.

"What's for dinner, Aunt Maude?"

"Roast pork. I hope Aureta has been basting the potatoes the way I told her."

"I do too."

Without thinking I skipped a couple of skips, but Aunt Maude's instant grip reminded me I should not be so cheerful returning from a funeral.

If I hadn't been starving I would have raced right down to the Cupeck house that minute, not that Rose would be there yet, I suspected it took ghosts a little time to get from the grave to the haunt. The minute Aunt Maude went up for her afternoon nap I planned to be off down the East Road to check out the house and refresh my memory so I'd know where everything was when I was ready to go back after dark. I wondered if the big black snake was out of hibernation yet.

CHAPTER TWENTY

unt Maude insisted I had to lie down after dinner even if I didn't sleep. She said I must be exhausted from the "emotional turmoil" of the past few days and it made no difference that I didn't feel tired. "Sometimes you're tired when you don't know it. An afternoon nap will be good for you."

The minute I heard deep breathing and occasional snores from her room, carrying my shoes because I would make less noise in my stocking feet, I crept across the sitting room and down the stairs. While I was putting on my shoes in the kitchen I remembered I wanted to take Uncle Will's flashlight so I could go down in the cellar of the Cupeck house, but nothing was worth waking Aunt Maude for, and I knew if I went back upstairs for the flashlight my goose was cooked.

I don't know why I stupidly climbed over the orchard fence at the end of the arbor and cut through the trees instead of simply going down the East Road. Maybe I thought if anybody saw me headed in that direction I could say I was looking to see how soon the apple buds would burst. The heifers watched me from a distance at first, then when they decided I wasn't going to chase them they began following along behind, getting closer until they were almost bumping into me. Silly animals, they must have thought I was going to feed them. When I climbed over the fence opposite the Cupeck house the heifers lined up, an audience waiting for me to do something.

Getting into the house was easy because I knew how to do it now, but I wondered as I crawled up on the abandoned bureau and in through the pantry window if it would be as easy to do in the dark. It also occurred to me that I might not want to come back after dark alone. I could probably persuade Roy to come with me, but Roy couldn't get in through the window. His weight would smash the bureau before he even got up to the window. I would have to get a door open this afternoon far enough so Roy and I could squeeze through when we came back tonight.

First I walked through the whole house, top to bottom; well, not all of the bottom because I truly didn't feel like walking around down in the cellar unless I could see. I did what I'd done the first time, went down the cellar stairs a ways, then scrunched down so I could peer around. That's what I'd been doing when the snake appeared. There was no sign of him today. Nothing had changed a bit in the rest of the house. Oh, a few leaves had blown in and were piled up in corners, but except for that it was all the way I'd first seen it. If ghosts did come to the Cupeck house they sure didn't disturb anything.

I could not budge the front door. The way the floor had buckled made it impossible. I would have to use an ax or a sledgehammer to get rid of the bulge. The door from the kitchen onto the falling-down back porch was already partially ajar, but it too was wedged up against a heave in the floor. No matter how hard I pulled at the bottom of the door, I wasn't moving it an inch. In a fit of temper I grabbed hold of the door about halfway up and yanked on it with all my might. There was a screeching, tearing sound and the next thing I knew I was flat on my back on the kitchen floor with the door on top of me. I had pulled it away from its hinges.

"Wow," I said aloud after I'd pushed the door to one side and picked myself up. I didn't know I was strong enough to do that. Before I could become too impressed with myself, or begin to think I was anywhere near as good as David the Incorrigible, I saw that the wood was rotten, which is why the screws that held the hinges on came out. Even so, success in getting that door open made me feel as invincible as Jack Armstrong, my second-favorite All American Boy. I couldn't wait to tell Adeline.

After one more complete tour of inspection I decided everything was set for a return visit with Roy after dark when whoever was haunting the Cupeck house would be there, maybe waiting to welcome Rose. I wondered what I'd see. Would Rose be in her black bombazine dress? Or would she be all in white, floating around in the air? Johnny Bullock had been vague about how ghosts look exactly when they appear. The sheet thing had been only Charley Smith.

"You gotta be locked up," Adeline snorted when I got back and told her what I was doing. "They's no hants in the Cupeck house or anyplace else, boy."

"You don't know, Adeline, you just think you know. You think you know everything. Rose told me to never deny possibility." Leave it to Adeline to not be impressed with my report of tearing the door off its hinges. Charley would think it a great feat when I told him.

"I don' know what Rose was talkin' 'bout, possibility, but ghosts jes ain't, tha's all, possibility or not."

"Just because we can't see something doesn't mean it doesn't exist. Rose told me that too."

"Well, then, effen you cain't see nothin' why you botherin' to go look?"

I didn't bother to tell her that I knew I could see Rose. Rose had said if she was going to haunt any place the Cupeck house was all right with her. There wasn't a chance Rose would let me down. She'd be there and be as happy to see me as I was going to be seeing her. I wondered if I could touch her, or would my hand only feel air?

"But, David," Roy said, when I asked him to go to the Cupeck house with me after dark, "Isn't it true that ghosts, if there are ghosts, wander because they died unhappy? And you told me Rose's eyes were smiling when she died. Dr. Davis said she wanted to die. That makes me think she's probably happier now than when she was shut in that room."

"But, Roy," I began.

"David," he pulled me toward him so I was standing between his knees. "Rose hated being locked up and she'd lost all hope of ever being free. The only way she knew to free herself was to die. If she wanted to die, and died smiling, Rose will not be coming back as an unhappy ghost."

Why was everybody determined to argue with me? Why wouldn't anybody believe what I knew? Rose had made a promise. She wouldn't disappoint me. "Are you afraid to go with me, Roy?"

"Afraid of what, David? There's nothing to be afraid of." I

squirmed, but he held me firm between his knees, his hands resting on my shoulders.

"Johnny Bullock is terrified of ghosts. He won't walk in the road when he goes past the Cupeck house because he's afraid they'll reach out and grab him." I was feeling defiant and nasty. I'd been in the Cupeck house over and over and nothing had happened to me. If ghosts were there when I was there, they didn't do anything to hurt me. The snake had startled me, but even he didn't harm me. "You must be scared, too, Roy, or you'd go with me. That's okay, I'll go by myself."

Roy let out a deep sigh. "I'll go with you if you want. Come along, we'll go down there right now before suppertime."

"Roy, you aren't listening," I cried, my fists pounding his legs. "I've been there already today. I just got back from there a little while ago. We have to go at night, after dark. That's the only time you can see ghosts, I think."

"Your Aunt Maude is never going to let you go into the Cupeck house after dark, David. She'd have a fit if she knew you'd been near the place in daylight. That old house is ready to fall down."

"I'm not going to tell her that's where we're going," I said, wondering why Roy was being dumb all of a sudden. "I'll tell her you and I are going for a walk."

"After dark? Where are we supposed to be walking after dark? David, I'll do most anything for you, but I'm not going to lie."

"Damn it, Roy, sometimes little lies are necessary. God doesn't make a fuss when Charley lies." I caved in. "Nobody will help me. What will Rose think if she's there and I never show up?" I was doing my best not to cry, but my voice was shaky.

"We'll think of something," Roy said, rubbing my neck.

We didn't have to think of something. At the supper table Aunt Maude said she and Uncle Will and I were going down to the home place to do a few things. Halla still hadn't foaled, so if she seemed close we'd be late getting back.

"Do I have to go?" I asked.

"I thought you wanted to see Halla's foal the minute it's born." Uncle Will sounded disappointed.

"You don't know it's going to be born tonight," I said.

"No, that's true."

"I'd only be in the way," I said.

Both Aunt Maude and Uncle Will raised their eyebrows at me. Somebody else tittered but I couldn't tell who it was. I persuaded them Roy would take care of me, and when Aunt Maude checked with him after supper he said he would. She told him if they didn't get back until after my bedtime he should bring a book up to their sitting room and read. If Halla went into labor and they were going to be really late, they'd call Pa Fleming.

I hated to disappoint Uncle Will, and I was disappointed myself. I not only wanted to see Halla's foal the minute it was born, I wanted to see it born. I'd seen pigs and calves and lambs, but I'd never seen a mare foaling and I wanted to very much. Maybe she wouldn't have it tonight. Maybe she'd wait until the next night when I'd be there.

Roy and I watched Uncle Will's Ford disappear down the Center Road, then we started for the Cupeck place. We had Roy's flashlight because Uncle Will had taken his. Dusk was deepening but there was no problem seeing. Because Roy had never been in the Cupeck house, I thought it would be better to get there while there was still some light so he wouldn't fall over anything. We could get ourselves settled and be ready for the ghosts when they began to appear after dark.

"What do we expect to see?" Roy asked as we walked down the hill.

"I'm not sure. I wish I knew."

"You've no question that Rose will be there?"

"I know she'll be there, not when we get there probably, but she'll come as soon as it gets dark."

"Try not to be miserable if she doesn't show up."

"I'm not going to be miserable, Roy, you'll see."

Thank goodness I'd opened the door in the afternoon because Roy balked at even going in that way. He was sure the porch floor would collapse. A lot of boards had already fallen in and the rest were rotten. What would he have done if the only way in was by climbing on the bureau and going through the pantry window. I suppose we could have tried bashing through the hatchway and gone through the cellar and up the stairs, but I didn't like that idea. The cellar was the only part of the house that scared me.

Telling him I'd go first didn't reassure him too much because he said I was two hundred pounds lighter than he. Eventually he agreed to try, and walking as if every step was his last, he made it across the groaning porch and through the door. He had to duck when we went through the inside doors, and did bang his head once on a crossbeam in the long room ceiling.

"What do we do now that we're here?" he said in a low voice.

"We wait. I don't think we have to whisper. You want to sit down?"

"I can't see anything to sit on."

"There isn't any furniture. We'll have to sit on the floor."

I sat down cross-legged. Roy stood for quite a while, then said he'd try sitting too, adding with a tight voice that he hoped he could get up again. We just sat there for a few minutes without talking. When a bush outside scratched against the wall of the house, Roy said he hoped there weren't any rats in the house. "I hate rats," he said.

"So do I," I agreed.

"Worse than snakes," he went on, "but I don't think snakes come into houses so there isn't much chance of meeting one of them."

I didn't say anything. As fascinated as I was with the big black snake, I didn't like the idea of him slithering around me in the dark when I couldn't see him. I sincerely hoped he was still in hibernation, or if not would stay in the cellar. I forgot to close the cellar door so got up and pushed it shut.

"There could be bats," Roy was talking almost to himself. "Probably bats would like an empty house like this, but they'd most likely be upstairs, don't you think?"

"Most likely." I hadn't seen any bats.

Then we were silent for a while again. By that time it was really dark. I had been able to make out Roy's shape and doorways to the other rooms until that was impossible. Now the only shapes I could see were the windows. There was no moonlight but it was still lighter outside than in the house.

"Should we be quiet so as not to scare the ghosts away, or talk so they will come to see who's here?" Roy asked.

"I don't know. I've never waited for a ghost before."

We tried the quiet routine. Nothing happened except I could hear blood throbbing steadily in my ears.

It was Roy who broke the silence again. "What do we do if somebody else's ghost shows up?"

"Just be friendly, I guess."

"Has anybody, including Johnny Bullock, actually seen any of the ghosts he says haunt this place?"

"Lot's of people, I suppose, but Johnny is the only one who

has told me about them." I didn't want to be disloyal to Johnny but I liked the idea of keeping a conversation going so I added, "Adeline says Johnny's not the most reliable witness when it comes to ghosts. He calls them hants."

"Mmmmm," Roy said.

Nothing happened for the longest time, except the bush kept scratching against the wall outside. No bats flew through the windows, no rats scurried around. If the snake was there, he didn't make enough noise for us to notice. The only noise other than the bush was wind in the trees.

"How much longer do you think we should wait? We must have been sitting here an hour or more," Roy whispered.

I shrugged, which Roy couldn't see naturally, so he asked his question again, and I answered by saying halfway between a whisper and loud, "Rose? Rose, are you here? Rose, if you're here, we can't see you, make a noise or something to let us know." Nothing happened.

"Perhaps we're expecting too much," Roy said after a couple of minutes. "People might not turn into ghosts just like that. Maybe it takes time." I didn't say anything. "What do you think, David?"

"I don't know. I was sure she'd be here, Roy." I decided to try again. "Rose, please say something or do something if you can hear me." The silence after the sound of our voices was heavy enough to be felt.

"Rose, please be here," I begged.

Roy didn't say anything for quite a while, but then he suggested we'd tried long enough for tonight. "We can come back if you want, another time."

"Can we, Roy? Will you come back with me?"

He told me he would. I helped him get up and he used his flashlight to show us the way out so we wouldn't crash into a wall. Once outside he turned it off and we walked up the East Road in the dark.

We did go back to the Cupeck house. We went back three nights in a row, each time because Aunt Maude and Uncle Will were away. Roy didn't ever lie to Aunt Maude, but he didn't disagree with her either when she thanked him for reading to me every night. By the third night I knew Rose wasn't going to show up. I still didn't know whether or not there were such things as ghosts, for all I knew the Cupeck house was full of them, they just didn't let me see or hear them. But I did know that Rose wasn't with them because she would have touched me or something. She would have known that I was silently begging and sobbing for her to be there.

If she wasn't at the Cupeck house as a ghost, where was she? She couldn't just stop being. I went up to her grave thinking maybe I'd feel her there, maybe I'd been wrong when I looked down on the coffin and decided she wasn't in it. I knew her body was in it, but whatever it was about Rose that was real went the instant she died. I had felt a hand that was Rose's hand resting on mine, but Rose wasn't there. It was whatever had gone that I was desperate to find. What I was looking for was Rose, not Rose's body.

I felt nothing when I stood by her grave staring down. Somebody had put another wreath on top of the dirt, a wreath that was fresh once but was already turning brown and brittle. I thought about the wreath and I thought about the dirt and the other graves in the little cemetery, but I found it impossible to think any of it had anything to do with Rose. Rose was not there.

No window shade ever hung on Rose's door, over the bars where the window should be. After she died, I began thinking about Rose never being in that room without people able to look in at her if they wanted to. Even when she was asleep in her bed, people could glance through the bars and see her lying there. I wondered if that was what she meant about being locked in. Maybe it was people's eyes more than bars or the lock on the door.

There was nobody in bed in that room now. There was nothing on the bed, no bedspread, blankets, sheets, or pillows, only a thin mattress in blue and white ticking. The wardrobe had been cleaned out, as had all the bureau drawers and the top of the table, and all of it scrubbed with extra-strength disinfectant. Everything of hers was gone, the cut-velvet bag, her hairbrush, the dish garden. The room was bare.

I took to standing there for long periods of time, gazing through the bars. Sometimes I stood there for so long I wondered why I didn't drop from exhaustion. I could have brought over the organ stool to sit on, but Rose wasn't there to sit in her chair on the other side. I could have gone into the room, the door was part way open, there was no one to stop me, but there was no reason to go in.

So, I just stood there, not saying anything because there wasn't anybody to say anything to. Nor did I do anything but stare and think, trying to figure things out. Women rocking in the sitting room pretended they didn't see me. I guess they thought my mind had stopped working, at least during those times I stood there looking in. My mind was working all right, but I was more confused than ever about so many things I couldn't count them.

Aunt Maude said she was worried about me. She said I acted depressed and little boys didn't get depressed. I should be happy, she said, in spite of missing Rose. I should think of Rose as free now, in Heaven where she'd be loved forever. But

I couldn't get it out of my mind that Rose had committed murder and murder is supposed to be a deadly sin, and though sins can be forgiven, Rose didn't think she'd done anything to be forgiven for, I was sure. She refused to see priests when they came to the County Home, and she made faces during Bruuuther Potts's revivalist meetings.

Maybe Rose had accepted Jesus all by herself when nobody was around and asked Him to forgive her. She could have, I suppose, but if she had there was no way Aunt Maude would have known it, or Aunt Jessie, and both of them were so sure Rose was with the angels and Jesus. From what Rose had told me about Scheider I was sure he was in Hell, so I prayed Aunt Maude and Aunt Jessie were right about Rose being in Heaven. She had to be someplace. I wondered if she was wearing the black bombazine dress. Rose had worked so hard on that dress, and it was very important to her. I didn't know any more about how you dressed in Heaven than I did about what ghosts wore, and I'd given up on ghosts.

I didn't know much about anything that mattered. If Rose was truly gone and that's the way it was meant to be, why couldn't I let go of her? Why did I feel we were still connected? Why did I know, or thought I knew, that she was somewhere if only I could find her? The one thing I had no question about was that living wasn't as much fun anymore.

CHAPTER TWENTY-ONE

unt Jessie had a thought to cheer me up. She suggested that she, Aunt Maude, and I take a bus trip to Niagara Falls. I'd been to Niagara Falls before so I didn't care one way or the other, but Aunt Maude got all excited. "Won't we have fun, honey, going to Niagara Falls?" she kept saying to me. I'd nod my head, trying to appear enthusiastic.

Early one morning Uncle Will drove us to town to catch the Blue Bus, stopping at the home farm on the way to check Halla and her filly who looked just like her, a deep rich chestnut color with a white diamond in the middle of her forehead. Uncle Will said I could consider the filly my own if I wanted to because he would rather keep her than sell her to the cavalry when she was full grown and trained. I knew he hoped saying that to me would make me more excited than I could be just then.

When we got to Aunt Jessie's house she came out in a heavy tweed suit and black velvet hat, but no coat. "Jessie, you'll freeze," Aunt Maude sputtered. I was dying of heat in my winter coat and the crocheted hat Blind Theresa made for me, and Aunt Maude was bundled up for a trip to the Arctic.

"This wool suit is more than adequate," Aunt Jessie replied. "Good morning, Will. How's my boy?" She got into the back seat and sat down next to me. I noticed she was wearing the amber beads I'd always liked so much. When I was a baby Aunt Jessie had let me gum them, or so she said; I didn't remember.

I hated the smell of the bus. If I was the kind of kid who got carsick, everybody would have been in trouble. Aunt Jessie persuaded Aunt Maude I wouldn't be kidnapped like the Lindbergh baby if I sat all by myself on the front seat opposite the driver while they sat directly behind me. That way I could see both sides of the road. We went through miles of farmland and a lot of little towns before we drove into Niagara Falls where we had to keep stopping and starting because of red lights and traffic. I could hear Aunt Maude asking where all these people were going. She didn't expect an answer.

When we pulled into the terminal, we got off the bus and stood on the sidewalk like three blind mice.

"What now, Jessie?" Aunt Maude's tone suggested Aunt Jessie had gotten us into a mess, it was up to her to get us out.

"Now we walk to the Falls. They aren't far, follow me." Aunt Jessie acted as if she knew how to get there, and I guess she did because Aunt Maude and I had to hurry to keep up with her. Very soon we could hear the roar of falling water. Then up ahead we could see mist rising above the gorge. I hadn't been too enthusiastic about the trip until I saw that mist. As we turned a corner and saw a thicker column of mist swirling high above the whirlpools, I rushed past Aunt Jessie.

"David, take my hand," Aunt Maude cried.

"And Maude, you take mine," Aunt Jessie said.

"Jessie, you are old enough to take care of yourself, but I am responsible for that child and I won't let anything happen to him." She was gaining on me.

I slowed down to let the aunts catch up but wriggled away when Aunt Maude reached for my hand. We walked and walked, stopping at every observation spot to look out over the falls. On Goat Island at a point where there was nothing but a rickety wire fence between us and the precipice was the absolute best place to see the Horseshoe Falls across the gorge, and the nearest you could get to the edge of the American Falls, close enough to stick your hand in if you could reach over the fence. The roar was so great people had to shout to be heard.

Wanting to be part of that erupting torrent was making me too excited to just stand looking through the fence. I climbed up on the first rung of rickety wire and then the second so I could see over the top. I didn't want anything between me and the blue-green water.

"David!" Aunt Maude's shriek was blood-curdling. "You'll fall and be killed."

"Maude, if he's dumb enough to fall over he's not worth saving," Aunt Jessie yelled, grabbing Aunt Maude's arm before she could pull me back.

I was laughing hysterically. This was something. I was sure if I just went up a few more rungs and jumped, I could soar out over the falls and swoop above the gorge like a bird, dive into the mist, down, down and then up just before I touched the seething riverbed. "Oh God, I wish Rose was here," I shouted, then added, "and Roy and Adeline." I could picture Adeline dancing to the rhythm of the roar. Roy would tell me to feel it way out to the tips of my fingers, and I was feeling it. "Rose, Rose, if you think that old elm tree is free, riding the crest of the ridge, what do you think about this water? This water is free, wilder and freer than the wind, Rose," I shouted into the din.

I had never felt as happy as I did that minute. I didn't mind Aunt Maude shrieking at me to stop, I was used to being told not to do things. I jumped backward off the fence and ran to hug Aunt Jessie around the waist. "Thank you for bringing me here." I buried my head in her bosom. Her amber beads felt smooth and forever against my cheek.

Even though it was chilly for a picnic we sat at a table in the park and ate hot dogs and skinny french fries that came in a paper cone. Afterward, Aunt Jessie said, "Now, let's do some shopping."

"Shopping, Jessie? We didn't come to Niagara Falls to shop. If we've seen all there is to see, we can catch the early afternoon bus." Aunt Maude reached into her purse for the Blue Bus schedule.

"We have three hours before the late afternoon bus, Maude, and that's the one we told Will to meet. You sit here if you want, but I'm going shopping. There are sales in all the stores. I read about them in the Sunday paper." Aunt Jessie was being pleasant but firm. "Care to join me, David?"

"Sure."

"We'll pick you up on our way to the bus," Aunt Jessie called out as we started to walk away.

"Jessie, wait." Aunt Maude rushed after us. "You're not leaving me here all by myself for three hours. But why go this way, the stores are in the opposite direction."

"Not the Canadian shops."

"You're going to Canada, Jessie? You have to cross that long bridge! It's too far."

Aunt Jessie turned her head but didn't slow down. "It's foolish to be this close to a foreign country and not pay a visit. Besides, American money buys more in Canada because of the exchange rate."

It was freezing cold when we went out onto the bridge across the gorge. We got a wonderful view of both falls, but we also got strong gusts of wind and all that mist in our faces which wasn't as light as it looked from a distance. I raised the collar on my coat. Aunt Maude shielded her face with her pocketbook. Aunt Jessie paid no attention.

At customs we had to tell uniformed guards why we were entering Canada, how long we planned to stay, and whether we were going to make any major purchases. Aunt Jessie did all the talking, "Just to look around," "Only an hour or two," and, "No."

Then they asked us where we were born, and each of us had to answer. When I told the guard not only the town but the hospital, a guard in another kind of uniform who'd been standing to one side watching us said, "He's okay. I was born in that hospital too."

"You're an American then," Aunt Jessie said. "When did you move to Canada?"

"I didn't. I just dropped in here to see my Canadian buddies. I'm with American customs, and now it's back to work." He grinned at me as he walked past.

We wandered up and down several Niagara Falls, Ontario, streets, poking into shops, though Aunt Jessie, who had suggested going in the first place, tried to keep us moving. I bought a Royal Dalton Mr. Pickwick toby jug. Roy had read *The Pickwick Papers* to me, so I recognized who it was the minute I saw the jug on a shelf. Aunt Maude bought a hand-painted English bone china sugar and creamer set on a matching tray. Aunt Jessie bought an Ainsley cup and saucer to add to her collection.

All the walking we'd done while shopping used up what I'd had for lunch so Aunt Maude gave me money to buy a bunch of bananas in a fruit store. Neither she nor Aunt Jessie cared to have one as we walked along, but I didn't mind looking like a monkey, dropping peels from two bananas as I finished them into bright red trash cans.

Then we came to a fur store, a salon, it was called. I was not looking where I was going so banged into Aunt Jessie's back when she stopped in front of the door. There was a small fancy sign in the window that said: "Annual Spring Sale."

"I think we should go in here and look around," Aunt Jessie said.

"Whatever for?" Aunt Maude asked. "We aren't going to buy anything so there's no point in wasting time." She pulled back her coat sleeve to look at her wristwatch. "I think we should head for the bus station. Where do you suppose we can find a taxicab to take us back over the bridge?"

While Aunt Maude was peering up and down the street for a taxicab, Aunt Jessie opened the door and walked into the fur salon. With my bag of bananas and my boxed toby jug I followed, holding the door for Aunt Maude whose eyes were blazing. A woman with a thick, not Canadian, accent greeted us, asking if we were looking for anything special.

"We're just looking." Aunt Maude was setting her jaw.

I spotted an upholstered bench and went over to sit on it, thinking maybe I'd have one more banana while waiting for the aunts to look.

As fast as it took me to see there was no place to put a banana peel, Aunt Jessie appeared from the back of the shop wearing a fur coat that went almost down to her ankles. It was black and had a big collar. "What do you think?" she asked Aunt Maude. Aunt Maude stared with her mouth open. She couldn't have looked more shocked if Aunt Jessie had appeared in her mended underwear. "Someday, not today, but someday I'm going to have a coat like this." Aunt Jessie was pointing her hands and her feet in different directions in front of a mirror.

"Jessie, put that coat back where it belongs." Aunt Maude had found her voice.

"Relax, Maudie," Aunt Jessie said. "Fur coats are meant to be tried on. Isn't that so, Mademoiselle?" She smiled at the woman with the thick accent.

"Oui Madame," Mademoiselle bowed.

Aunt Maude was in the early stages of a stroke, I could tell. Her face was blotchy, her forehead was damply beaded, and she was breathing funny. If it wasn't a stroke it would be a screaming rage. Whichever, I wished we'd get out of there. I wasn't sure what might happen to us in a foreign country if Aunt Maude went bonkers. They understood her at the County Home.

Aunt Jessie disappeared again. Not realizing what I was doing, I unpeeled a banana and took a bite out of it. That brought me back to my senses. What would I do with the peel? Then I noticed the biggest ashtray I'd ever seen, a great clear blob of glass with swirls of dark blue in it and a ruffle around the edge. Trying to be neat, I rolled up the banana peel and placed it in the center of the glass blob.

"Maude, how much money do you have with you?" I heard Aunt Jessie whisper. The fur coat she had on this time was different, black but not anywhere near as long as the first one, nor did it have a big collar; the collar on this one was rolled something like the collar on Rose's bombazine dress, and the fur was like curly sheep's wool.

"I think I have a hundred and fifty dollars. Why?" Aunt Maude looked confused.

"Maude, this gorgeous caracul coat is marked down to two forty-nine American. It's a third more in Canadian dollars. I have a hundred and some change in my purse. If you loan me what you have, I can buy the coat. It will take me a few months to pay you back, but I will. You know I always do."

Aunt Maude had her pocketbook open and was taking out the folded bills even as she said, "Jessie, you can't take every cent we have to buy a coat." In a swooping gesture Aunt Jessie plucked the bills out of Aunt Maude's hand and disappeared again into the rear of the salon.

"Jessie," Aunt Maude cried in a voice that made me feel sorry for her. I wondered what I'd do if she fainted. There wasn't a sign of a sink in the place so I couldn't get a drink of water for her.

In what must have been record time for a sale, Aunt Jessie returned to us, folding a paper into her pocketbook. "There's no need for a box, Mademoiselle," she was saying over her shoulder. "I'll just wear the coat."

We helped Aunt Maude out into the street. She stumbled dizzily along with Aunt Jessie on one side and me on the other. Aunt Jessie never stopped talking about how she'd always wanted a fur coat but never thought she could afford one until she'd read those ads in the Sunday paper. "Isn't it wonderful that we happened to come to the Falls today, Maude, just when they are having these marvelous sales? That one hundred and fifty you loaned me I'll pay back quickly. I have money for emergencies hidden away at home."

"Where can we get a taxicab to take us to the bus station?" Aunt Maude repeated the question she was asking back when Aunt Jessie walked into the fur salon.

"Maude, did you give me all your money?" Aunt Jessie asked. Aunt Maude nodded. "David, do you have any money left?" I shook my head. "Then," said Aunt Jessie, "I'm afraid, my dears, we'll have to walk, and we'd better get cracking if we're going to get to the terminal before the late bus leaves for home."

She started up the street, leaving Aunt Maude and me staring after her. Then she stopped and turned around. "Perhaps we'd better walk over the lower bridge in case those same customs people are on duty in the upper bridge. Come along, it isn't much farther."

"Jessie!" Aunt Maude let out a strangled cry.

"What, Maude?"

"Are you telling us we not only have no money to pay for a taxicab, but you have no money to pay the duty on that coat?"

"Duty?"

"You have to pay duty on the coat."

"Not if I'm wearing it, dear. Maude, stop fussing and come along."

"Jessie, duty is duty. It doesn't matter whether you're wearing the coat or not. You bought it in Canada and you have to pay duty to get it back into the United States."

"Nobody is going to take this coat away from me, duty or not." Aunt Jessie puffed out her cheeks like I'd seen a grouse do with its feathers when it wants to scare off an enemy.

There followed such an argument about paying duty, how much it might be and what did that matter if we didn't have enough to pay it anyway, and whether or not it was one's moral duty to pay duty, and how they'd fought since they were little girls, and on and on and on, that passers-by paused to listen. I ate another banana and still they fought. "It's the same as stealing," Aunt Maude squealed, bending over almost double.

"It's not stealing, I paid for the coat." Aunt Jessie also bent over in a fighting crouch.

"It's stealing from the government if you try to smuggle it in without paying what you owe them in duty," Aunt Maude cried.

"I am not a smuggler," Aunt Jessie grouse-puffed again. Then they argued about when was a lie not a lie.

The only thing that brought the argument to an end was when both realized we were going to miss the bus if we didn't run for it, and neither wanted to be stuck in a foreign country, no matter how friendly, after dark without a dollar, American or Canadian.

"Who can tell what might happen to us?" Aunt Maude cried, on the verge of real tears.

"Maude, Canadians aren't cannibals," Aunt Jessie snorted.

We didn't run, but we did a trot that winded Aunt Maude so we had to keep stopping while she took a breath or two. Our cheeks were bright red when we came to the customs building. We were inside before we saw that the uniformed guard was the man born in the same hospital as I was, the one visiting his Canadian friends earlier when we'd come across the upper bridge.

"Well, hello again," he said, gesturing that we should come up to the counter and not stand in the doorway. "I know where you were all born, so we don't have to bother with those questions. The only thing left I guess is, do you have anything to declare?"

Not one of us said a word. Nor did we shake our heads. We stood motionless and silent. I had a toby jug but not a penny to pay duty. I already owed Aunt Maude nineteen cents for the bananas. The guard was looking down at me. "What do you have in the packages, son?"

"Bananas," I replied. I didn't think there could be duty on bananas.

"You went all the way to Canada to buy bananas? How many did you buy?"

"Six. I've eaten four."

"So, now you have two bananas in the bag?"

I nodded. I couldn't see Aunt Maude or Aunt Jessie, only him. A bright overhead light shone in my face. Next he'd be asking me about the box. What would he do to me if I had committed a crime, buying a Mr. Pickwick toby jug? After what seemed a month, he said, "Okay, friend, go on through."

Clutching my bag of bananas and the box with the toby jug, I walked through a gate that clicked shut behind me. I guess I was back in the United States, but Aunt Maude and Aunt Jessie were still in Canada.

Aunt Maude had taken out of her package the bone china hand-painted sugar and creamer on a matching tray. The tissue paper rustled in her shaking hands. She held everything up toward the guard as if she was the minister offering communion. "I bought this," she said.

"That's fine, ma'am," he smiled. "You're allowed up to fifty dollars, and I don't think you paid that much, though it's a very pretty set. Go on through."

"Oh thank you, thank you," Aunt Maude said. Aunt Jessie had an "I told you so" look on her face as she watched Aunt Maude push through the swinging gate and come stand next to me in the United States.

"I didn't tell him about Mr. Pickwick," I whispered to Aunt

Maude as she repacked her china, "but I guess it's all right because he didn't cost fifty dollars." I was beginning to relax.

"You look warmer this evening," I heard the customs man say to Aunt Jessie.

"Oh I am." Aunt Jessie smiled her brightest smile. "I purchased this cup and saucer for my collection." She was showing him the Ainsley china. "I paid almost nothing for them. One of the main reasons I come to Canada is because the prices on china are so reasonable."

"Prices on china, you say," the man stressed "china."

"Yes. I have a lovely collection. You must come and see it the next time you are home visiting your family."

"My family is all dead," he said. There was no expression on his face as he gazed at Aunt Jessie. You could imagine all sorts of things but you couldn't tell what he was thinking.

Aunt Jessie stared back at him. She didn't do her grouse puff, nor tilt her head the way she did when Aunt Maude told her she looked like Queen Mary.

"That's a beautiful coat you're wearing," the man said.

"Thank you," Aunt Jessie replied as more color came into her face.

"It must keep you very warm."

"It will . . . it does," Aunt Jessie stammered.

Eye to eye, neither blinked, but it was obvious even to me the customs man was winning a battle. There was a silence so deep I could feel it in my ears until he said quietly, "May you always be at peace, ma'am, whenever you wear it."

Aunt Jessie wilted. I thought she was going to cry. The guard reached across the counter and swung the gate open for her. She didn't move right away, but then took a small step and then another and another, each one with a pause between.

When she was far enough through for the gate to close, she put her hand up to hold it open and turned back. "Mr. Customs Inspector," she began.

"Sorry, ma'am, I've just gone on break. My relief will be here momentarily if you have any questions."

"No. Thank you," Aunt Jessie said in a little voice.

"You're welcome, ma'am." He grinned the same grin he had earlier in the day when I said where I'd been born.

We hurried to the Blue Bus station, arriving just as the driver was about to back away from the platform. We had to go way to the rear where Aunt Jessie and Aunt Maude sat together and I sat across the aisle by myself. As we rolled along through the darkness, I heard Aunt Maude mumble tearfully, "This was the worst day of my life. My own sister, cheating, doing the same as lying. I pray God will forgive you, Jessie, because it's going to be a long time before I do." She blew her nose and then took up the line again, about how miserable and ashamed she was.

I held the banana bag and the boxed toby jug in my lap, asking myself why I hadn't told the man what I had, other than bananas. I thought I knew why I hadn't, because I had no money to pay duty, that was before he said anything about the $50 allowance. Had I lied the way Aunt Maude said Aunt Jessie had lied? I hadn't done anything different than she had done. Did he ask me just about the bag, or did he ask me about the box too? I couldn't remember.

Aunt Maude's voice droned on and on. I knew how Aunt Jessie felt. Once Aunt Maude got to jawing you, she never stopped. When it happened to me I wished she'd switch me or twist my ear and get it over with. When it seemed as if she'd never stop, I heard Aunt Jessie interrupt in a low, firm tone. "Maude, nothing you say can make me feel any worse than I feel already. I'll never be able to wear this beautiful coat without feeling like a criminal."

"I would hope as much." Aunt Maude was using her righteous voice. I think she wanted to say more but she didn't have a chance.

"Enough, Maude." I heard Aunt Maude try to start again, but Aunt Jessie continued, "I said enough, Maude, and I mean enough. You will say no more."

All the rest of the way home the sound of tires singing on the pavement was punctuated by the sound of Aunt Maude's muffled sobs. So much for a trip that was meant to cheer me up.

CHAPTER TWENTY-TWO

I didn't wake up the next morning until almost nine o'clock, and couldn't believe what the dial of Big Ben was telling me. Why hadn't Aunt Maude called me? It was not like her to let me sleep so late even if I wanted to, and I never wanted to. When I got downstairs there was an eerie silence in the kitchen. Roy had already gone to the dairy and left the unread morning paper in his chair. Aureta was putting breakfast dishes away, not humming or even singing softly as she usually did when she was alone. Obviously the Flemings had finished their breakfast because nobody was at the Keeper's table when I looked in through the pantry.

"Can I get something to eat?" I asked.

"Of course, dear, what would you like?" Aureta answered.

"Dear"? Aureta calling me "dear"? Aureta thought I was a pest and never lost a chance to tell me so. I know she's the one who tittered when I said something at the table about being in the way. What was all this "dear" stuff?

"Your Aunt Maude left you a large glass of orange juice in the icebox. I can scramble eggs for you, and we have corn muffins. Would you like me to grill a muffin?" Aureta wasn't much taller than I which is why her clothes looked as if they belonged to her mother, but still she was bending over so our eyes were on the same level. Louise did that in school and I hated it. Older people bending over to be at my eye level made me feel smaller than I was.

"Where is everybody, Aureta?"

"You slept late and missed them all, everybody has gone to work." Without waiting for me to tell her if I wanted a scrambled egg, she took a frying pan off its hook and dropped butter in it, then went to the icebox for eggs.

"Is Aunt Maude in the lower kitchen with Mrs Davies?"

"That's where she is." Aureta broke two eggs into a bowl and attacked them with a fork.

"While you're cooking those eggs I think I'll run down and let her know where I am. I'll be right back, and I would like a grilled muffin if you don't mind fixing it for me."

Usually Aunt Maude and Mrs. Davies did their conferring at the work table that stood in the middle of the lower kitchen, sitting on stools with cups of coffee beside their notepads, but when I walked in that morning the lower kitchen was as silent as the Keeper's kitchen had been, with nobody in sight. Something was going on.

"Aunt Maude? Mrs. Davies?" I called. "Is anybody here?"

"David, I'll be right there." Aunt Maude's voice came from the big larder off the kitchen where barrels of brown and white sugar and flour and shelves of canned goods and other food supplies were kept. She and Mrs. Davies must be taking stock.

"Hi," I said, when I finally spotted them at the far end of one of the long aisles. "Sorry I slept so late. I must have been really tired. If you called me I didn't hear you."

"That's all right, sweetheart, I knew you needed your rest." Aunt Maude was blowing her nose.

"Good morning, David," Mrs. Davies greeted me but patted Aunt Maude's arm.

When I was close enough to notice, I could see Aunt Maude's eyes were red-rimmed. Then I saw her put a soaked handkerchief in her apron pocket and I knew she had been crying. She must have been telling Mrs. Davies about our adventure with the customs inspector and how Aunt Jessie not paying duty on her fur coat made yesterday the worst day in Aunt Maude's life. While I didn't think it was as bad as that, I was sorry Aunt Maude was still upset. It was unusual for somebody other than me to be the cause. I put my arms around her and pressed my head against her. I thought it would make her feel better, but instead it made things worse because she began boohooing and hanging onto me as if I was all that kept her upright.

"Maude, Maude." Mrs. Davies tried to calm her.

"Aunt Maude, what's the matter?" I asked, but my voice was muffled so I know she didn't hear me.

After a near eternity of sobbing and crying, "What am I going to do without my darling boy?" she let me go and blew her nose on the dry handkerchief Mrs. Davies offered. Getting herself under control at last, she wiped her eyes and said, "Forgive me, sweetheart, for carrying on so. Aunt Maude is just an old bawl calf, but I can't help it."

"Maude," Mrs. Davies pleaded when it seemed obvious Aunt Maude was about to beller some more.

"Are you still upset about yesterday?" I asked.

"Yesterday?" Aunt Maude asked, blinking and straightening her dress and apron.

"Aunt Jessie's fur coat." She couldn't have forgotten so soon.

"Jessie's fur coat?" Mrs. Davies asked.

"I never did get to tell you about Jessie's coat," Aunt Maude said to Mrs. Davies, clamping her jaw in the familiar, wait until you hear this, fashion.

"If it's not about the fur coat, why are you crying?" I was going from feeling sorry to beginning to be annoyed. Everybody was acting strange but nobody was telling me why.

"David," Aunt Maude put her shoulders back the way she did when about to perform an unpleasant task. "After you went to bed last night Uncle Will told me your father had called while we were away with the good news that your mother is coming home from the hospital tomorrow."

"Tomorrow?" I asked. "Wow, that is good news, she hates being in the hospital."

"And he has found a very nice woman to be at the house to help her until she is strong enough to be alone," Aunt Maude continued, as she began to slump, "which means there is no reason, he says, why you should not come home too. He is coming for you on Saturday."

"Saturday? Dad is coming for me Saturday, to take me home?"

Aunt Maude nodded and I knew from the way she shuddered that tears were going to flow again any second.

"But I'm home now," I said.

That did it. Aunt Maude would have collapsed onto the floor in a soggy heap if Mrs. Davies hadn't pushed a stool under her. I'm afraid I wasn't much help. Without meaning to ignore Aunt Maude I couldn't think of anything at the time but going to be by myself somewhere. I had to think.

I heard Aureta calling me from the Keeper's kitchen door, telling me my eggs and muffin were getting cold, but I didn't respond. Nor did I say anything when I met Mr. Beveridge on the walk and he told me cinnamon buns would be out of the oven in less than half an hour. Without knowing where I was going, I ended up in the grape arbor. Several men and a couple of old women were sitting on the benches, some of them with their faces tilted toward the sun that was shining through the still bare grapevine branches.

I went down to the end of the arbor where I could be alone. I was truly glad Mother was coming home from the hospital, glad for her. Thinking about her being in the hospital was worse after I'd been to see her and knew what it was like in that enormous brick building with all those stern nurses and unbreakable rules. I was sure she'd be happier in our own house in town. But I didn't think I would be. It was an all-right house, nothing wrong with it, a nice living room and dining room, a dull kitchen, it wasn't anything like the County Home. How could I sleep in my bedroom in that house if I didn't hear the sound of people getting a drink at the pump in the night? In my bed at home all I'd hear would be cars going by in the street. And there was no comforting disinfectant smell in town, nor any earth smells that change with the weather, nor smells of hash cream potatoes baking. I'd smother from a lack of good smells.

I got up from the arbor bench and walked to the orchard fence. The heifers approached to see if I had anything for them to eat. A couple let me touch their cold wet noses and one licked my hand with her big rasping tongue.

"David, cinnamon buns are out of the oven." Mr. Beveridge had walked part way down the arbor to make sure I heard him.

I sat in the hot bakery, fragrant from what was in or fresh out of the big ovens, eating my third cinnamon bun, washing it down with a second cup of Mr. Beveridge's great Dutch cocoa. I looked around the room, at his stuffed birds perched on pieces of branches in the corners under the ceiling. There was no place you could go in the bakery where the hoot owl's eyes wouldn't follow you. Mr. Beveridge had stuffed each one of those birds himself and they looked so real you expected they'd fly down if you offered them a piece of cinnamon bun.

"I hear ye'll be going home soon." Mr. Beveridge had a thick Scots burr, rolling his r's and pronouncing going "gayin."

"Does everybody know?" I asked.

"Bad news travels fast, laddie. We're all going to miss ye."

"How come everybody knew before I did?"

"That I canna answer. Roy told me at breakfast table."

I didn't finish the third cinnamon bun, though I thanked Mr. Beveridge for it and the cocoa.

"Fresh fried cakes in the mornin'," he reminded me as I left the bakery.

Roy was packing crocks of soft cheese in the dairy, bent over the wide tin-covered counters, so intent on his work he didn't hear me come in. I startled him when I walked over and leaned against his leg. He didn't say anything, but put an arm around me and patted me with his enormous ham hand that covered my whole chest.

"Why can't I stay here, Roy, and go to town to see my mother and father? It's no big deal going to town, Charley Smith sometimes does it twice a day."

"Because your mother and father want you at home with them, David. That's a wonderful thing, to be wanted." Roy lifted me onto the tin-covered counter. "Much as we are going to miss you here, your place is at home with your parents."

I nodded. I knew Roy was right, but that didn't make me feel better about leaving. I had a thought. "Roy, my ducks! I can't have ducks in town. I'll have to stay to take care of them.

Everybody said I wanted them so I had to take care of them. It wouldn't be right to go off and expect somebody else to do my chores. Those ducks are my responsibility."

"Have you taken care of them this morning?" Roy asked.

"Not yet, but I'm going to. That's where I was headed when I came in here." It was an out-and-out lie, but things were getting serious. I pushed myself off the counter and smiled at Roy as I hurried out the back door of the dairy, taking a shortcut to the barn and the ducks who I thought until a few minutes ago I'd grown to hate.

They were a mess as usual, but I didn't mind. I brought over the wheelbarrow and the pitchfork, cleaning out every speck of dirty bedding, then put down fresh straw before I washed out their feed dishes and water bucket and filled them all, standing back to watch the ducks instantly make a terrible mess of everything all over again. So, I'd have to clean them up tomorrow, and the next day. That's part of having animals, you have to take care of them. I had decided ducks weren't so bad after all when Charley Smith clumped in.

"Now that yer leavin', I s'pose we'll kill them ducks and eat 'em. If we waited much longer they'd be tough. Muscovies ain't as tender as some other kinds of duck at best."

"Charley, nobody's going to kill these ducks. They are pets."

"Pets, shit," Charley spat. "On a farm there ain't no such a thing as pets. You raise livestock same as vegetables and fruit and grain, to eat, or to sell fer somebody else to eat to get money to buy other necessities. That's life on a farm, kid, and you know it. Everything's a crop to be harvested."

"Well, these ducks aren't a crop." If Charley spoiled my plan to have the ducks as an excuse to stay on at the County Home, I didn't know what I'd do.

"I'll take care a your ducks," Adeline said out of the blue. I hadn't heard her come in.

"Adeline, I don't want anybody to take care of my ducks. I'll take care of them myself. Where did you come from, anyway?"

"I see you from my window when you headin' down here to do chores, so I followed soon's I got dressed." She was even wearing shoes.

"Why'd ya bother puttin' clothes on, girl? Runnin' nekid's what ya do most a the time." Charley leered at her.

"Wipe off that face, Farthead, or I'll put holes in ya." Adeline picked up the pitchfork and made thrusting motions in Charley's direction.

"Why, you nigger bitch." Charley backed away but stooped over as if he was going to lunge for Adeline.

"Charley," I yelled. "Stop it. And you stop it too, Adeline."

Charley straightened up, spat in Adeline's direction, and looked toward me. "I'll be drivin' down to the Center shortly if you wanna go. I'll honk at the kitchen door." He let loose another splat of tobacco juice but missed Adeline by a mile. He could have hit her if he dared.

"You think it's too cold for a fertility dance?" Adeline asked when Charley was gone.

"We've done it when the temperature wasn't much higher than it is today, I guess."

We went to the opening in the pine woods and took off our clothes. The sun was shining but it wasn't warm. Both of us were covered with goosebumps when we started, and though we warmed up as we pounded and jerked and whirled around, neither of us worked up any sweat. I know my heart wasn't in it and I don't think Adeline's was either.

The ground was too damp to lay down when we were dressed again, so we walked over to the pump-house pond and sat on the fallen tree trunk above the dam. I told Adeline I'd been to the Cupeck house half a dozen times, both during the day and after dark, and I'd never seen any sign of a ghost.

"I tole you they ain't no sech thing," Adeline said, but not in a nasty way.

"I wanted there to be ghosts, Adeline, because I thought if there were ghosts maybe Rose would appear. I don't know where she is."

"She's in a grave on the hill. Tha's where we put her and tha's where she's at."

I shook my head. From the sounds of birds in the trees around the pond, spring was really here. They were flitting and chittering, and being noisy and busy in the underbrush. "If that's where she is, Adeline, why can't I feel anything when I go up there and stand by the grave?"

"Cuz they's six feet a dirt 'tween you an' her."

"Adeline, I was with her when she died. She was patting my hand, and she smiled and died. The second she died, the absolute second, that room was empty, yet I could see Rose's body on the bed, I could feel her hand on mine, so why was the room empty? What had gone?"

"She had gone, dummy."

"But where had she gone? That's what I'm trying to figure out, Adeline. If Rose is her body, the body in the grave on the hill, and the body that was still there in the bed, then Rose was not gone, she was in the bed. But she was gone, you just said it, and I was alone. Don't you see? That's why I've been trying to find Rose ever since. And if I go home, if I go to town to live with my mother and dad, I'll never find her because Rose was never there. She won't know where I am."

Adeline shook her head slowly. "I thinks you's losin' yore grip, boy. She is, she ain't. All this talk don' do nobody good. Speakin' of is 'n ain't, I truly don' wanna do it, but I will chore your ducks effen you want me to."

"Thank you, Adeline, but I'll take care of them myself. When I explain everything to Aunt Maude she will see that I have to stay here. Maybe my mother can come here and visit me. That would be nice."

Explaining was more difficult than I thought because every time I tried to explain Aunt Maude broke down and cried, and it always ended with her telling me I had to go to my mother and father who couldn't wait to have me back living with them.

By Friday noon I'd given up. There was no use fighting it any longer. Aunt Maude was packing clothes, all freshly laundered, even clothes that I hadn't worn since they had been washed the last time, and Roy was helping me wrap my farm and soldiers and other toys in newspaper before putting them into boxes. I didn't wrap *David the Incorrigible* because I wanted to carry the book myself. Roy told me he was giving me one of his phonographs and several records so I wouldn't forget how to listen to music. They were in a box in his sitting room which he'd bring down Saturday morning before my dad arrived.

I made a final trip to every spot on the farm Friday afternoon, going up in the hay mow to walk around, climbing up the chute on the inside of the silo to shout a couple of times and hear my echo bouncing around before it died in the ensilage at the bottom. I patted each of the work horses in their stalls, except for Chub who was in a box stall. I patted him through the opening in the top of his door. That morning I was awake before dawn so went down to open the gate letting the cows into the lane from night pasture.

Charley Smith let me gather a whole pail of eggs and didn't swear at me when I made a quick movement with my arm that sent those stupid Leghorns flying to the other end of the hen-house. He knew I'd done it on purpose.

I went down to the Cupeck house and wandered through, even going down to the bottom of the cellar stairs, but there wasn't anything there. The black snake must have been out of hibernation but I didn't see him. Leaves stirred in the corners of rooms, but I knew it was the wind and not a ghost.

Supper Friday night was like a funeral. There was some of the usual teasing, but nobody laughed much. I don't remember what we had to eat, though Aunt Maude said once she had fixed things I especially liked. After supper we drove down to the home farm where I played with Halla's filly until it was time to go back to the County Home. That night I cried myself to sleep.

Saturday morning I had breakfast with Ma and Pa Fleming, and they both talked more than at all our other breakfasts put together. Ma said she was sending me home with a stack of jigsaw puzzles we'd put together over the winter. "You and your mother will enjoy doing them" she said hollowly, nodding and smiling and spreading marmalade on her toast, then dabbing at her nose with her handkerchief. Pa Fleming gave me a brand-new silver dollar that he said I could spend any way I wanted or keep as a good-luck piece, whichever.

After breakfast I went to the women's building to say goodbye to Blind Theresa and Mary Delancy and the Sawyers and Aunt Latzy, who made me soft soap her twice and gave me a jar just like the one on her nightstand filled with pink and white peppermints. Old bitch Ripley snorted when I said goodbye to her, so I stuck out my tongue at her when I got back in the hall. Across the hall Mrs. Bullock gave me a hug and said she hoped I'd remember some of the songs she sang. I told her I'd try. She didn't know where Adeline was, hadn't seen her since breakfast, she said.

Mr. Beveridge gave me a big brown paper bag with two loaves of fresh bread in it, one white and one rye. He said he'd think about me every day. Uncle Deane was fixing machine belts in the laundry so had to give me a hug without letting his hands touch me. "Your Aunt Maude would skin me if I got grease on your clean shirt," he laughed. Chet Foster and old Brumstead were standing in the carpenter shop door when I went past and they both nodded. Neither one asked me what I wanted which was a surprise.

The biggest surprise was when Aunt Maude told me somebody wanted to see me at the kitchen door when we were waiting for Dad to arrive. It was Scarzi. I would have run if Aunt Maude and Mrs. Davies hadn't been right behind me.

"You wanted to see me?" I asked.

He nodded and held out a small round basket with a handle on it.

"For me?" I asked.

Again he nodded. As I stepped toward him to take the basket, I saw it contained the dish garden I'd given Rose for Christmas. The moss and tiny plants were bright green and there were still red berries on the vine.

"How nice of him, David. He has made a basket to fit around your dish garden," Aunt Maude said.

"Rose's dish garden," I corrected her.

She didn't notice. "You must thank him. Mr. Scarzi, that was a very nice thing for you to do."

I took the basket from him, our hands touching on the handle. His was much softer than I would have imagined. "Thank you," I said.

He nodded, touched the front of his cap to Aunt Maude, and walked away, disappearing down the stone steps into the furnace room and the tunnel alcove where he worked.

Dad arrived on the dot of ten o'clock as he said he would. He and Roy and Uncle Will loaded the car with my stuff while Aunt Maude and I and a porch full of other people stood and watched. When everything was in the car, Roy asked if somebody would take our picture together, his and mine, with a box camera he'd hidden behind one of the porch posts.

"I didn't know you had a camera, Roy," I said.

"I didn't have until yesterday. Charley drove me down to Harry Woolf's store to buy a Kodak box and the film."

Aunt Maude posed us facing into the sun at the end of the Keeper's building. Roy took off his cap and made sure his hair was not mussed. I pushed mine back with my fingers, then reached up to take Roy's hand. Aunt Maude snapped the shutter and that was that.

"Time to go," Dad said. "Your mother is very anxious to see you and Mrs. Winters is fixing a good lunch to celebrate."

"Who is Mrs. Winters?"

"She's the woman who will take care of you and your mother."

"Why do we call it 'lunch' at noon in town and 'dinner' at noon in the country?"

Dad laughed. "That's just the way it is, I guess. You'll get used to it."

I'll get used to it, I thought. "Dad, wait one minute, please, I forgot something." Before he could object, I jumped onto the porch and ran through the lower kitchen into the arcade, across the women's sitting room, and up to the partly open barred door. "I'm going home, Rose," I whispered into the empty room. "I don't know where you are, but I hope if you come back you'll find me."

At the car Aunt Maude hugged me so tight I couldn't breathe, and Uncle Will blew his nose a lot. I didn't want to go without saying goodbye to Adeline, but Dad said we couldn't wait any longer and nobody had seen her all morning.

"Bye-bye," everybody shouted and waved as Dad turned the car around. Charley Smith honked the old jitney's horn, oogit, oogit, and bobbed his almost toothless head up and down fast. Roy followed Dad's car around the corner of the Keeper's building and stood there waving as we pulled onto the Center road. Ma and Pa Fleming waved from the front porch as we went past.

"You've been a very good boy during these difficult months," Dad said, patting my knee, "but now it's all over with. You'll be at home where you belong and have friends your own age to play with."

"Dad, there's Adeline." She was standing by the historic marker sign with her finger pulling down the corner of her mouth.

"Wave to her," Dad said.

I turned around in my seat and waved, but Adeline didn't wave back. She just stood there watching us drive away.

As she grew smaller I looked up beyond her and saw it moving gently, freely in the wind at the top of the ridge, the elm tree behind Ott Alwardt's barn. Or was it at the edge of the earth?